THIRST

NO. 5

ALSO BY
CHRISTOPHER PIKE

THE THIRST SERIES
WITCH WORLD
REMEMBER ME
THE SECRET OF KA
UNTIL THE END
BOUND TO YOU

COMING SOON

CHAIN LETTER

THIRST

NO. 5

THE SACRED VEIL

Christopher Pike

Simon Pulse

NEW YORK LONDON TORONTO SYDNEY NEW DELHI

SIMON PULSE

An imprint of Simon & Schuster Children's Publishing Division

1230 Avenue of the Americas, New York, NY 10020

First Simon Pulse paperback edition March 2013

Copyright © 2013 by Christopher Pike

All rights reserved, including the right of reproduction in whole or in part in any form.

SIMON PULSE and colophon are registered trademarks of Simon & Schuster, Inc.

For information about special discounts for bulk purchases, please contact Simon & Schuster Special Sales at 1-866-506-1949 or business@simonandschuster.com.

The Simon & Schuster Speakers Bureau can bring authors to your live event. For more information or to book an event contact the Simon & Schuster Speakers Bureau at 1-866-248-3049 or visit our website at www.simonspeakers.com.

Designed by Mike Rosamilia

The text of this book was set in Adobe Garamond.

Manufactured in the United States of America

10 9 8 7 6 5 4

Library of Congress Control Number 2012952196

ISBN 978-1-4424-6731-6

ISBN 978-1-4424-6732-3 (eBook)

For Liesa, my kind and brilliant editor

PROLOGUE

I exist outside of time, for a time. It's no dream. I'm closer to death than to sleep. Yet I'm experiencing only a memory of my death, of the days I spent separate from my body, lost and confused, after Matt shot me in the heart. At last the truth of what happened during that time has come back to me. I discover that I have attained my final goal, to be with Krishna.

I know because he stands before me.

Yet as I gaze into his unfathomable blue eyes, I realize I exist in another dimension as well. I'm still on earth, in a crummy motel in the middle of a waterless desert. My vision of Krishna is actually a month old. Yet it feels so real—he has always felt that way to me—and it's painful to even consider returning to my endless life.

Have I not done enough for mankind?

Then I think of those close to me—Seymour, Matt, Paula, and John—those I love. And I know the answer to my question is no. The enemy has not been destroyed. My friends still need my help.

My internal decision is potent enough to alter my environment. My vision of Krishna wavers. The sweet perfume of his eternal realm evaporates as the dry air of the physical desert stings my skin.

My heart breaks as I struggle to say good-bye.

Krishna raises his hand. Our fingers touch, and he speaks. "Don't weep, Sita . . ."

But I fail to hear his final words.

My sorrow drowns them out. . . .

ONE

I'm back in the motel room, staring down at Shanti's headless body and a mound of shattered glass. The glass is from the window that broke when I threw her head into the parking lot in a fit of rage.

Rage that was very close to pleasure.

"Om, Shanti, Shanti, Shanti," I say to myself. The repetitive sounds constitute a famous mantra in India. It means "Peace, peace, peace." It is similar to the Christian prayer "Peace be with you." How ironic, I think, that the demon I have fought since I first became aware of the Telar and the IIC should have chosen to possess the body of a young woman with such a sacred name.

Yet I feel no pity for the original Shanti. The demon could not have penetrated her heart without her permission. Only at the end did Shanti reveal how much she enjoyed causing others pain, just like her master.

Well, she is dead now, thank God.

But is the enemy? Have I even scratched his armor? Unfortunately, I haven't a clue. If only Umara were still alive. She was the world's expert when it came to demons. But Matt's mother sacrificed her life so I could destroy her people, the Telar, and the evil forces arrayed behind them. The cynical part of me wonders if her sacrifice was in vain. How does one destroy an evil that doesn't have a physical body?

I hear approaching footsteps and know their source. There's only one other in the miserable motel who has my hearing. Matt must have heard the breaking glass and come to investigate. He knocks lightly and I call to him. He pokes his head inside my door.

"Why is Shanti's head sitting on the hood of our SUV?" he asks.

Matt has on white shorts, no shirt or shoes. His well-muscled body is deeply tanned, his dark hair a mess from jumping up from sleep. But even though I just woke him up, his eyes are highly alert. How his eyes remind me of his father, Yaksha, the first and most powerful of all vampires. Matt is half vampire, half Telar, an immortal coin from his head to his toes.

Looking at him, mostly naked in the room's dim light, I feel heat stir down below. Despite the circumstances, the lust does not surprise me. My attraction to him has been there from the start.

"She was the one. She was the spy," I reply.

Matt steps into the room. "You're sure?"

"She told a few lies, and when I confronted her . . ." I shrug. "She confessed who she was before I killed her."

"What does this mean?" Matt asks. His question appears simple but it is multilayered. Like me, he wants to know if we've finally destroyed the demon. He's also asking if Shanti's death means the computer program that was planted on the Internet by the Cradle—a group of psychic children—is going to stop hunting us.

We have been on the run since we blew up the IIC's headquarters and supposedly killed every member of the Cradle except for one, Ms. Cynthia Brutran's five-year-old daughter, Jolie. The two are asleep three doors away. I can only assume they failed to hear the breaking glass.

"I'm not sure," I say. "But at least with Shanti out of the way what we talk about will no longer be heard by those who are trying to kill us."

Matt's puzzled. "You were close to her. You miss nothing. How was she able to fool you for so long?"

The question stings.

"She played me. It's no excuse, it's just . . ." I pause, searching for the key to her deception. "She made me care for her."

Matt glances out the motel door, at the trickle of blood that runs over the SUV hood from the base of her severed skull. "You weren't alone. You know Seymour loved her. This is going to kill him."

"Let's not tell him until morning."

"Fine."

"I don't want him to see her like this."

Matt nods. "Don't worry, I'll take the body and bury it in the desert. No one will find it."

"Thank you."

Matt reaches down and lifts Shanti's headless torso with one hand. The blood of Yaksha and my daughter, Kalika, flows through my veins, which makes me almost invincible. Yet I know Matt is stronger than me, although I'm not sure of the extent of his power. He's reluctant to show it, even to me, but I don't take offense. In this way we are alike: He has a hard time trusting people. That's why his question continues to sting. I was the first one in the group to meet Shanti, and trust her.

"While I'm taking care of the body, go through her things," Matt says. "You never know what you might find."

"Good idea." I had already planned to do that. "Are you sure you don't want help?"

"It's not necessary. I have a shovel in the trunk."

"What made you bring a shovel?"

"Times like this."

Matt stuffs the torso and head into several large-size garbage bags and walks off into the desert. He doesn't take the SUV; he doesn't need it. I feel a wave of relief as he disappears into the dark. Seymour's a night owl. There's always a chance he's up, watching TV or reading. He could even be writing a new book. He once told me he seldom went a whole day without writing a few pages.

Shanti has a small suitcase in our motel room but a larger one in the back of the SUV. I find it interesting that she went out of her way to leave it in the vehicle. When I first open it, I'm disappointed. It's stuffed with clothes, a few magazines, a pair of boots, running shoes, a watch, and a cell phone—devoid of any stored numbers.

Yet when I have finished emptying the suitcase on her bed, I notice a faint bulge on the interior of the lid, beneath the leather lining. Human eyes would never have noticed it. The area is sewn shut; indeed, it looks as if it has never been exposed since the day the suitcase was constructed. If I were to hide something, I think, and it were important to me, I would put it in exactly the same place.

I tear off the inner lining of the suitcase.

There's a manila envelope inside. I open it with a swipe of my fingernail. Inside are two items: a business card and a photograph. The card lists the name of a lawyer: Michael Larson of Pointe, Wolf, and Larson, 1250 Avenue of the Americas, New York, New York. The card is made of high-quality paper, the printing is impeccable. It smells of money.

Written on the back of the card, with a dull pencil, is another New York phone number.

The photograph is of a middle-aged couple. The woman looks familiar, even though I'm certain I've never met her before. The couple sits smiling on a couch beside an open window that looks out on rolling grassland with a lake in the distance.

They appear to be a typical couple. The man has his arm around his wife. I'm certain they're married. There's an ease between them that only comes from having lived many years together. I see their love for each other in their eyes.

Looking out the window, behind them, I'm pretty sure I see a piece of land that belongs to North Carolina. The type of trees, the color of the lake, the way the green fields slope—I've visited the area before.

On a small end table, to the right of the couch where they sit, is a black-and-white photograph. The picture is handsomely framed but it was taken with a primitive camera. The print is grainy, the focus questionable. I suspect the photograph was snapped in the forties or fifties.

Once more, there's a couple, although these two are younger and they're standing on Ellis Island, near the foot of the Statue of Liberty. They're not alone—a hundred people mill in the background. Most look weary and I can understand why. They have just crossed the Atlantic and arrived in the New World.

But the couple at the forefront of the group don't look exhausted. On the contrary, they're bursting with excitement to be standing on the doorstep of New York City. Studying their faces I can see all the hopes and dreams they have for their future. But I also see their joy is tempered with sorrow. Even if I didn't know them, I'd still see the pain in their eyes.

But I do know them.

Their names are Harrah and Ralph Levine.

I met them during World War II, in Paris, and spent time with them in the most hellish place the modern age has ever known: Auschwitz, the concentration camp where over a million Jews were slaughtered. It was only because of Harrah and Ralph that I survived the camp.

Now I know why the woman on the couch looks familiar.

She's the granddaughter of Harrah and Ralph.

I'm still staring at the photograph when Matt returns. I hand it over, along with the card, and tell him who the people in the pictures are. Matt listens closely and studies them with a penetrating gaze. I don't bother to point out the numeric codes imprinted on Harrah's and Ralph's forearms. Matt misses nothing.

"How did you happen to become friends?" he asks when he hands back the picture.

"We worked together in Paris, with the French Resistance."

"Did you stay in contact after the war?"

"Not exactly." I pause. "We were all sent to Auschwitz."

Matt is stunned. "You're not telling me you were a prisoner?"

"I wasn't a guest."

"Sita, how could the Nazis contain you? I don't understand."

Those days are difficult for me to talk about.

"It's a long story, an unbelievable story. Toward the end of the war, I decided to help the Allies defeat the Nazis. My reasons were complex—I'd just as soon not go into them now. But I never imagined for a moment that I'd be taken prisoner by a bunch of fanatical Germans. The idea was preposterous. But the Nazis—they had weapons I never imagined."

"I'm not following you," Matt says.

I shake my head. "It would take time to explain. And even if I do tell you everything, there's a good chance you'll think I made most of it up."

Matt takes my hand. "Sita, come on. I know you'd never purposely lie to me."

His fingers feel good wrapped around mine.

"There's the rub," I say. "I might lie to you and not know it."

Matt stares at me, waiting for me to explain. My body trembles. I feel a sharp pain inside my head and a dull ache in my heart. Loss, I feel loss.

"Those were dark days, Matt. The darkest of my life. The Nazis did terrible things to me, unspeakable things. It got to the point where I didn't know my own name. I don't know how I escaped. But I do know if it hadn't been for Harrah and Ralph, I wouldn't have survived."

"How exactly did they help you?" Matt asks.

His question is reasonable. How were mere mortals able to

help a five-thousand-year-old vampire? I wish I could answer without sounding like a complete nut.

"The Veil of Veronica. Have you heard of it?" I ask.

"I've heard the stories, or I should say the myths. Isn't it supposed to be a cloth that Christ wiped his face on when he was carrying the cross to Calvary?"

"Harrah called it Golgotha but I suppose the name doesn't matter. It was where the crucifixion was supposed to have taken place. But Christ did not wipe his face on the cloth. It was the other way around. Veronica, the woman in the tales, dipped the cloth in water and wiped his brow. And an image of his face was immediately imprinted on the cloth."

Matt considers. "From what I've read, it was fluids from portions of his face that stained the cloth. From his nose and his cheeks and his brow—the raised parts. The liquid contained just a small amount of blood. It was mostly sweat and lymph fluids. Only a rough outline of a face was created. There wasn't supposed to be a clear picture." He adds, "But I'm no expert on the matter."

"The veil isn't popular like the Shroud of Turin. Still, there are dozens of stories surrounding its history. These days, the Catholic Church avoids talking about it. But during the Middle Ages, for at least two hundred years, they had it on display in the Vatican. I saw it."

"Did it have a face on it?" Matt asks.

"It had a face most people associate with early Christian paintings. The image was remarkably clear. It had three *V*s on the bottom, all in a row. One from his beard, the others from his long, draped hair. I always found the symmetry curious. It didn't fit the style of art that was popular at that time."

"Why did the Vatican hide it away?"

"Some say it got stolen. Others say it was shown to be a fake. A few say it burned in a fire."

Matt frowns. "But somehow, a thousand years after the Vatican lost it, your friends ended up with it."

"Yes," I say.

"How? And please don't tell me it's a long story."

"It is, and I have a feeling I'm going to have to tell it to the others. So I might as well tell it all at once."

"You're stalling. You know Seymour's not religious and Brutran is certainly not a regular churchgoer. They won't have any interest in this veil."

"They will when I explain why I had to kill Shanti."

"You think she was going after it?"

"Why else would she have these pictures?"

"Because they're pictures of people from your past."

"That means nothing. I'm not in these pictures. What's important is that these people saved me."

"Using the veil?"

"Yes. But it's not the way you think. You have to hear the whole story." I pause. "Or as much of it as I can remember."

Matt stares at me, his puzzlement growing. "Sita, you're the same as me. You don't forget anything."

I squeeze his hand and lean over and give him a kiss. He reaches out to hug me in return, but I avoid his embrace by sitting back. All of a sudden I feel dirty, unclean. I fear to infect him. I stare down at the photo again.

"Maybe I'm afraid to remember," I say.

TWO

We have a meeting planned for early in the morning. There's much to discuss—like, how are we to stay alive when everyone is trying to kill us? We get nowhere. As soon as Seymour realizes Shanti is missing, he demands to know why. And when Matt tells him the truth—in more gentle tones than I've ever heard him use before—Seymour bolts for the door.

I let him go, feeling he needs to be alone. But as the minutes go by and the temperature outside rises—our motel has lousy air-conditioning—I decide to go after him. The town where we reside, Baker, is what the term "hole in the wall" was born for. I fear Seymour has gone for a walk in the desert. The opposite of an outdoorsman, he has zero survival skills. I worry he'll get heatstroke.

I have no trouble tracking Seymour. He's left a trail in the sand and I can hear his breathing a mile away. I chase after him; it doesn't take long to catch him.

"Go away," he says as I pull up at his side.

I offer him a bottle of Evian. "Take a drink."

"Leave me alone."

"You're hiking into no-man's-land."

"What do you care?"

I grab his arm, stopping him. It's not as if he has the strength to resist me. "You're the one person who knows how much I care," I say.

The pain in Seymour's face is heartbreaking, and he's not someone who wears his heart on his sleeve. His eyes burn and he would probably weep if he weren't so dehydrated. His love for Shanti was like mine—a beautifully foolish thing.

"Why?" he asks, hanging his head.

I let him go. "Matt told you why."

His head jerks up. "Matt! Matt didn't kill her."

"No, I killed her. But what Matt told you was true. She was the spy who's been tripping us up from the start of this nightmare."

"You don't know that for sure. I know how impulsive you are. I bet you never gave her a chance to explain herself."

"Seymour . . ."

"Okay, maybe she was a spy! But maybe she was forced into the role. Did you stop and think of that before you murdered her?"

"You have to trust me, it wasn't that way."

"Oh really, what way was it?"

I hesitate. "She was possessed."

He looks at me as if I'm crazy. "What the hell are you talking about?"

Turning, I stare out at the desert, seeing the air tremble as it superheats and rises in waves over the bleak landscape. The ground is half dirt, half sand, hot enough to fry an egg. I shake my head.

"When I was at IIC's headquarters, while I was trying to take control of their Cradle, I had all kinds of strange psychic experiences. I shared some of them with you, but the worst ones, the ones where I came face to face with this demon, I didn't talk about. I couldn't. It was so awful, it almost drove me mad."

"You always seemed in control."

"It was an act. At the end, I was losing it."

"How do you know you didn't lose it last night?" he asks.

I reach out and put my hand on his shoulder, half expecting him to shake it off. But he is listening, my old friend, he continues to listen. Yet he wants hard answers, logical reasons, and I doubt if I can give him those.

"I caught her in a lie," I say. "A big lie. Then it was only a question of getting her to admit what she was, which she did."

"*What* she was? What's that supposed to mean?"

"I told you, she was possessed."

"Get off it, Sita. This isn't *The Exorcist*. Shanti was one of the sweetest girls I ever met."

"Yeah, sweet as apple pie. I thought the same thing. So damn sweet." I pause. "Look how we found her, with half her face melted away from acid a jealous boyfriend had thrown at her. How could we help but feel sorry for her?"

Seymour is suddenly confused. "That was true. She didn't lie about that."

"Nothing she said was true! She lied to us from the start. Those facial wounds—they were self-inflicted. She poured the acid on herself."

Seymour shakes his head. "No one could do that to themselves."

"No normal human being could do that. But she did."

"You keep saying these things as if they were facts. You don't know."

"I do, I saw her for what she was. At the end she didn't even try to hide it. She was happy that I knew. Please, Seymour, I swear to you on Krishna's name that she was gloating."

Seymour stands silent for a minute, then takes the bottle of water from my hand and pours it over his head. He stares up at the burning blue sky. I have never sworn to him before. I've never had to. Certainly I have never invoked Krishna's name before.

"I thought when we escaped IIC's headquarters, we were safe," he says miserably.

"So did I."

"I thought you said the Telar were all destroyed."

"I think they are."

Seymour sighs and throws the empty bottle aside. "What a way to wake up," he mutters.

"I'm sorry. Honestly, Seymour, the instant I killed her I thought of you. How much it would hurt you. It was all I could think about."

Now he looks to me for comfort, and I'm amazed at his ability to forgive me, to trust me. "Did she suffer?" he asks quietly.

I think of the fires that await those who fail the test of the Scale, and how poorly Shanti will do when she reaches that judgment. But Seymour's expression is so desperate, I believe a lie is better than the truth. Besides, I couldn't have given Shanti a faster death than ripping off her head.

"It was quick," I say.

We walk back to town. Seymour stops once to cry, but he is all right. I know eventually he will be fine.

THREE

inally, the gang is gathered in Matt's room. His air conditioner actually works. Cynthia Brutran sits at the head of his bed, an open laptop resting on her crossed legs, a pillow at her back. She has changed clothes since the start of our flight. Gone are her jewelry and expensive suits. Her pants look as if they were bought at the local drugstore—I suspect they were—and her top is a deceptive T-shirt with a sketch of Baker looking not only exotic but actually inviting beneath the rays of the setting sun.

Even though we are on the run, the woman—an old foe of mine—looks more relaxed than I have ever seen her. I wonder if the destruction of her company's headquarters has given her a sense of freedom. I would not be surprised. Rather than your normal platoon of crooked tax accountants and boxes of records of phony stock options, the firm had demons in its basements.

Yet I am slow to trust Brutran.

She did try to kill me, a few times.

Her five-year-old daughter, Jolie, sits in a chair in the corner beside the TV, flipping channels between cartoons and the film *Rosemary's Baby*. How appropriate, I think, since Jolie was the product of a breeding program designed to manufacture psychic mutants. The child also looks relaxed, happy even.

Seymour and I sit at the desk. Matt stays on his feet. He likes to pace when we have meetings, but not out of nervousness. I may have been the boss while we were trying to bring down the IIC and Telar, but Matt is our natural leader. The change in roles doesn't make me feel threatened. I'm hoping I'll find it a relief.

"Are we still on the list of the FBI's Ten Most Wanted?" Matt asks Brutran.

She nods. "We didn't fall off during the night. The only difference now is that treason has been added to our list of crimes."

"Terrorism and murder were not enough?" Seymour asks.

"Apparently not to whoever is after us," Brutran replies.

"Do we know who that is yet?" Matt asks.

"Our capture is a priority for every law-enforcement branch of the government," Brutran says. "That hasn't happened since Bin Laden and his minions hit the World Trade Center."

"Won't someone high up the chain of command realize, soon, that these charges have been fabricated?" Seymour asks.

"They haven't been fabricated, not entirely, and that's the key to our dilemma," Brutran says. "We did blow up IIC's headquarters, and because the Pacific Coast Highway is loaded with remote cameras, chances are we were seen leaving the area immediately after the explosion. That building was full of children. Those children were incinerated in the blast. The police and fire departments are still trying to dig what is left of their bodies out of the rubble. That footage is running almost continuously on CNN and a dozen other news stations, and it's creating a national anger, a raging wave. The American people want the perpetrators caught. They want them tried and punished. Imagine the pressure that rage puts on the politicians, on the police, the FBI, the CIA, Homeland Security, the NSA."

"But why have they latched onto us as the guilty parties?" Seymour asks. "So we were in a van leaving the area. Lots of vehicles were leaving the area."

"Good question. It leads me to my second point," Brutran says. "In the midst of this mass hysteria, pictures of us in the van are suddenly sent to every law enforcement agency in the government. A fake history of us is created. I just read an in-house email that is being circulated at the FBI that states that Sita—whom they are calling Alisa Perne—spent five years in Syria in a terrorist camp, where she learned the art of bomb making. All of us are being assigned similar pasts, and this information is being widely circulated by the program the Cradle created and placed on the Internet."

"But this is insane," Seymour protests. "Can't these agencies tell fake information from the real thing?"

"Yes and no," Brutran says. "To understand the no part, you have to understand the fierce competition that exists between the various agencies. The disputes between the police and the FBI are legendary. There have been hundreds if not thousands of TV shows and movies that have talked about that. The local police are working on a case and an FBI agent shows up and all hell breaks loose. That's old news. But when Homeland Security was created, the discord was taken to a new level. Homeland feels they are the boss, that all the other agencies should bow to them. While the CIA has been around for ages, and they feel they are the final authority. My point is that these agencies don't cooperate with each other, not easily. They are loath to share information, and when they do, they seldom trust that the information they're getting from another agency is accurate."

"We have nothing to do with their internal disputes," Seymour says.

"That's true," Brutran says. "But the Cradle's program is clever. It knows how to take advantage of this blind spot. By flooding the various agencies with false information about us, it has created a hysterical wave of paranoia that no single agency—and no single person—can stand up and dispute. Remember Hitler's famous line, 'The bigger the lie, the more people will believe it.' It's only been twenty-four hours since the explosion and already this lie has tremendous momentum."

"What you're describing is all smoke and mirrors," Seymour says.

"Yes. But it's rooted in the hard cold fact that hundreds of kids have been murdered. You keep forgetting that. Someone has to pay for that evil deed, and, once again, the authorities are under tremendous pressure to produce suspects. Imagine how pleased they must be that, seemingly out of nowhere, they are receiving all kinds of intel on us."

"Receiving it from whom?" Seymour demands. "It makes no sense they should believe a torrent of information being fed to them by some wild program."

"You haven't been listening," Brutran says. "The FBI doesn't think this information is coming from a computer program. To them, it appears to be coming from local police. In the same way, Homeland doesn't think it's getting this intel from a foreign source. They probably believe it's coming from the CIA or the NSA. That's why I stressed the problem with these agencies not talking to each other."

"You're saying the left hand doesn't know what the right hand is doing," Matt interjects.

"Exactly," Brutran says.

"But eventually the truth has to come out," Seymour insists.

"Probably," Brutran says. "But that will take time. The

Cradle's program has its tentacles wrapped around every computer in practically every government agency. From what I can tell, even the White House is being fed a stream of false updates. If we're lucky, and the president eventually realizes that his people have been duped, then he will still be left with the fact that these children died and we were seen leaving the area of the crime."

"This is ridiculous," Seymour says. "What are we supposed to do? Sit here and rot and wait until the storm blows over?"

"Funny you should say that," Brutran says. "That was going to be my final piece of advice—"

"We cannot sit here and do nothing," I interrupt.

"Why not?" Brutran asks.

Matt holds up his hand. "We'll get to that in a minute. For now I want to finish discussing this program. Cindy, exactly when did it become active?"

I have never heard Matt call Brutran by her first name before. The woman appears to respond well to his questions, to his command. With me, she has always been a little snide.

"Yesterday morning. The instant we blew up IIC's headquarters and wiped out the Cradle," Brutran says. "That act immediately triggered the program's attack on us."

"So there must be someone left alive who is controlling the program," Matt says.

Brutran shakes her head. "It may be on automatic."

"That's a freaky thought," Seymour says.

Brutran disagrees. "In a way it doesn't matter if there's still a living hand at the helm. The program is awake and it's intelligent. The instant we leave this motel, we'll be exposed and it will begin searching for us again. Think of the resources at its command. It just has to give the word and hundreds of thousands of police and government agents will try to converge on us. Why, I wouldn't be surprised if the program goes so far as to use the military's satellites to hunt us down. With power like that, it won't be long before we're caught."

"What if we continue to live off the grid?" Seymour asks.

"It will help," Brutran says. "But it won't save us."

"I disagree," I say.

"With which part?" Brutran asks.

"The last part. I'm not as fatalistic as you." I say.

"I'm being pragmatic," Brutran relies.

"You're giving up. I believe if we're smart and careful we can avoid being caught. Plus I think it's vital that we discover if there's a living hand behind this program. If there is, we kill it. And then, and only then, do we try to erase the program."

"Why wait?" Seymour asks.

I shrug. "If we manage to erase it, but haven't taken down whoever's behind it, they'll just reload it on the Internet and we'll be back to square one."

Brutran stares at me. "Long before you moved into IIC's headquarters, I assigned our best minds to study this program. They got nowhere and we're talking about some of the keenest computer people of our time. They told me they couldn't get within a light year of figuring out how to disable it."

"Why?" Seymour asks.

Brutran leans toward us as she answers. "Because the intelligence that created the program had an IQ of at least a thousand."

"You're suggesting it's being controlled by subtle beings," Matt says. "Nonphysical beings."

"There's a strong possibility that's true, I can't be sure. However, I do believe it was created by something nonhuman."

"We can't kill it if it ain't alive," Seymour mutters, expressing my lingering fear. "What are our choices?"

"Wait it out," Brutran says. "Wait until the government realizes it's chasing a ghost. Eventually they'll see that the bulk of the data they're being fed is false. Plus they can't keep their agents running all over the country looking for us. There are a thousand other threats they have to worry about every day. If we're patient, they'll get weary of the chase. At the same time they'll probably discover the program on their own. Then it will be their problem to figure out how to pull its plug."

Matt glances at me and I nod. "I wish waiting and doing nothing were an option," he says.

Brutran notices our exchange. "Is there somewhere else we have to be?" she asks.

"Yes," Matt says, and proceeds to describe the photograph I found hidden in Shanti's suitcase. Brutran and Seymour listen closely. Indeed, Jolie lowers the volume on the TV and cocks her head in our direction, and I remind myself to keep an eye on her. Even though she looks innocent, she was part of the Cradle, which specialized in remote assassinations.

When Matt is finished, Seymour turns to me. "Why would the people behind Shanti be interested in a religious artifact?" he asks, and I can't help but notice his use of the word "people." Seymour refuses to accept that Shanti was possessed.

"She may have just been interested in those who are taking care of it," I reply. But I have chosen the wrong person to lie to. Seymour looks as if he wants to snicker.

"Gimme a break. They want the veil," he says.

I shrug. "You might be right."

"You really fought the Nazis during the war?" he asks.

"Didn't you say so in one of those books you wrote about me?"

"I'd have to go back and check. But why bother? I have the real deal sitting beside me. How did you get involved in the war?"

"I was living in France when it was overrun in 1940. I could have gotten out but I loved Paris. I decided to stay and see which way the wind blew. But after a while I got tired of watching the Gestapo's brutality and decided to help out the French Resistance." I shrug. "My involvement blossomed from there."

"We had a record of your work with the Resistance in our

files," Brutran says. "But you seem to have vanished after the Allies invaded on D-day."

Matt has brought up the fact that Harrah and Ralph Levine were friends of mine during the war, and that they possessed the Veil of Veronica, but he has not revealed how rough a time I had in Auschwitz, for which I'm grateful. I'm not in the mood to talk about those days. I wonder if I ever will be.

"It's a long story," I say, repeating what I told Matt.

Seymour reaches out and touches my hand. "We have the time to listen," he says.

Matt notices my discomfort and interrupts. "Not now, Seymour. We have more pressing matters to take care of this morning."

Seymour continues to study me, as do Brutran and Jolie. I feel like I'm sitting under a hard white light. The Nazis used to grill me under such lights, for days at a time.

"Like what?" Seymour says to Matt. "You know as well as I do that Sita's already decided we have to go after these people—or I should say their grandchildren—and see if they still have the veil." He stops and turns back to me. "True?"

"I'll go after them on my own," I say.

"Like we'd let you," Seymour says.

"Do you have Shanti's cell phone with you?" Brutran asks me.

I hand it over. "I've already checked for stored numbers. She had none. Not even a copy of her last call."

Brutran accepts the phone and reaches into her bag and pulls out a small electronic device I don't recognize. "The phone might show no obvious record," she says. "But I should be able to read her SIM card."

Brutran opens the back of the cell as she speaks and removes the battery. She clearly knows her business. Beneath the battery is a small transparent plastic card coated with lines of copper and silicon. Without a pause, Brutran slips the card into her mysterious device and plugs the latter into her laptop. She scans the screen, appearing to flip through numerous files. She frowns.

"Shanti was cautious," she says. "This card has been wiped clean. Even my recovery programs can't find anything, and they're capable of reconstructing files that have been ground with sandpaper."

"The phone might have been new," Seymour says.

"No. Shanti used it to make numerous calls. I can detect that much. But she erased all the numbers before she put it back in her suitcase."

"Hand me the phone, please," I say.

Brutran tosses it to me, not worried that my reflexes won't be up to the task of the catch. The woman knows more about me than I would like. Her comment about my activities during the war did nothing to diminish my suspicions about her. Okay, so she helped me destroy the Cradle—IIC's headquarters, even. The company continues to exist, continues to print money like a paperback press rolling out the latest bestseller. She is staying close to us for a reason, I know, besides protection from those who pursue us. She still has an agenda independent of ours.

"I tell you, it's empty," Brutran says. "It's a dead end."

"Maybe not," I say softly as I close my eyes and let my fingers play over the numbers. My hearing is my most powerful sense, but all my senses are more acute than a human being's. The tips of my fingers, in particular, can detect things mortals couldn't imagine. For example, I can tell if something is poisonous just by touching it. My skin cells react, they immediately send a message to my brain—*Don't eat it!* They can also detect disease with the lightest of brushes. That was how I knew Seymour was infected with HIV the moment I met him. But lucky him, while he slept one night, I put a drop of my blood inside his wrist vein and killed the virus.

Now, though, I feel something unrelated to disease or poison. I can tell which numbers Shanti used most often. Five numbers—1, 2, 5, 7, 8, 9. They're obvious to me from the amount of resistance they offer, which is less than the other numbers on the cell's pad. These five numbers are more worn. Deepening my focus on the digits, I even get a sense of the rhythm Shanti used when she struck the keys, which tells me the order in which she dialed the numbers.

1-212-555-7819.

A New York number.

But not the same number on the lawyer's card.

I gesture for the others to be silent while I dial.

Someone answers immediately, before the first ring is complete, as if they have been waiting to hear from me. It's a voice I've not heard before, yet I recognize it. Not from the vocal cords it's using—those are new—but from the evil I hear behind it.

It sounds like a young woman. Intelligent, resourceful.

But I know it's really Tarana.

Ancient Egyptian for "the Light Bearer."

Lucifer.

My blood turns cold, while my hand that holds the phone drips with sweat from the heat that suddenly seems to radiate from it. The pain in the center of my head, from last night, returns with a vengeance, and I feel I'm going to be sick. Worst of all, I, Sita, last of the vampires, am afraid.

There is no way I can put down the phone.

I know this for a fact.

Not without his—or her—permission.

"Hello, Sita," the voice says. "Calling to make another deal?"

The others stare at me in shock. It is as if they sense my pain, or else they feel exactly what I feel. It's possible the horror is not confined to the phone, nor has anything to do with the words I hear. She speaks so softly I doubt even Matt can pick up her voice.

I swallow thickly. "Go to hell," I whisper.

The voice quietly laughs; it mocks me.

"Yes," she replies. "It's as good a place as any to meet."

The line goes dead and the cell phone drops from my hand onto the floor. The others stare at me, stricken. Matt is the only one capable of speech.

"Who was that?" he asks.

I hesitate. "The enemy."

"What does he want?"

I shake my head, unable to answer. How can I say the words? They would sound foolish, so childish. Yet true, yes, it's obvious what he—or she—wants. To make a deal. For our souls.

No, not exactly. She chose her words carefully.

With me it will be *another* deal.

God help me, I can't remember the first one.

FOUR

As a group we vote to leave the motel. Brutran is the only one who is against the plan. But when we're on the road, heading toward nearby Las Vegas, she mentions that she has a safety deposit box loaded with cash and fake IDs in the City of Sin.

"Why did you hide the dough in Vegas?" Seymour asks.

Brutran continues to work on her laptop. "I have drop boxes all over the world. So do your two friends."

"How do you know the Vegas drop box isn't being watched?" Matt asks. He is driving our SUV, being careful not to speed. I sit up front with him; the others are in the back.

"There's no way the box can be traced to me," Brutran replies.

"Do we need so much cash?" Seymour asks.

"Cash is always handy when you're on the run," Brutran

says. "It will allow us to do things without creating a fuss. Like buy a plane."

"That's a huge purchase," Seymour says, doubtful. "It might draw attention to us."

"Sita?" Brutran says, wanting me to explain.

"Our own plane will be safer than flying commercial," I say. "Once in the air, we can choose to move between small airports, where there are fewer restrictions. Right now, we have no idea how long it will take to find Harrah and Ralph Levine's grandchildren." I pause. "Which reminds me. Brutran, check your databases. Look for phone numbers of any Levines living in Clearglade, North Carolina."

"Why that town?" Brutran asks.

"It's a long shot but the terrain in the picture reminds me of that place. It's a small town, just east of Chapel Hill."

"The couple in question probably have a different last name from Levine," Brutran says as she types rapidly on her computer. "Remember, they're at least two marriages removed from your World War Two friends."

"I haven't forgotten," I say. "But I know that your software, along with your countless IIC files, is sophisticated enough to trace Harrah and Ralph's descendants."

"If we hadn't kept such records, we would never have found you," Brutran says. "We wouldn't be together now."

"I should feel grateful?" I reply, letting a chill enter my tone. Brutran knows that I can kill her in an instant, that she is only alive because we need her. She answers my unspoken thought.

"We're stronger together," she says.

"Find them," I order.

Twenty minutes later, as the mass of hotels comes into view beneath the glare of the afternoon sun, Brutran hands me a slip of paper with a name and address. Mrs. Sarah Goodwin, 134 Tree Leaf Lane, Clearglade, North Carolina. She's confident that's the woman in Shanti's photo.

I try calling Sarah. There's no answer but I get a machine. I don't dare leave a message.

I've been to Las Vegas a few times in the last sixty years but have never stayed long. Gambling doesn't excite me, although I can win as much as I want as long I'm allowed to throw the dice at the craps tables. I haven't been to the city since the turn of the century and it's impressive how much it has grown.

Brutran steers us away from the Strip and the fancy hotels. Her drop box is located in a small private bank downtown— one, she assures us, that is very discreet. She takes Matt and her daughter with her as she enters the building, leaving me alone with Seymour in a run-down parking lot that looks like it was last paved when Las Vegas was born.

"I think she has a thing for him," Seymour observes.

"She's not his type."

"Too old?"

"Are you forgetting that Matt was born in the Middle Ages?"

"Well, he still has his boyish good looks." Seymour pauses. "Are you his type?"

"Do you ask because I resemble Teri?" I ask, referring to Matt's recently deceased girlfriend and a descendant of mine.

"That's one reason," Seymour says, waiting.

"There's no reason to be jealous."

"You slept with him."

"I was in another body. It doesn't count."

"That's such an old excuse," he says.

I smile as I turn and look at him. "You are jealous. How cute."

"Never tell a guy he's cute."

"Are you jealous because you want to have sex with me?"

"What guy wouldn't want to have sex with you?"

My smile wavers. "Matt's not over Teri. I don't know if he'll ever get over her."

Seymour is sympathetic. "She was a wonderful girl."

"The best." I add quietly, "But I know she's in a good place."

He sees how serious I am. "You know because of what happened to you at IIC headquarters?"

"There, and last night, at the motel. After . . ."

"After you dealt with Shanti," he finishes for me.

"Yes."

"Do you remember what happened to you when you died?"

I hesitate. "Everything."

Seymour sucks in a breath and leans forward to where I can feel his breath on my cheek. "Did you see Krishna?" he asks.

I have to close my eyes a moment. Just the thought of Krishna, his bewitching smile, his enchanting voice, the love I felt when he said my name, his dark blue eyes, in whose depths all the stars in all the galaxies shone . . .

"It matters not, Sita. Stay or go, you will always be with me."

There could be no greater longing, and I realize I would live a thousand lives, suffer a thousand horrible deaths, just to see him again.

Of course, in a sense, I already have.

"Yes," I say as my eyes burn. I fight to hide any tears, although I'm happy to confide in Seymour. There's no one I'd rather share secrets with. He nods and smiles at my answer. He knows what Krishna means to me.

"Did he ask about me?" Seymour says.

I chuckle. "Before he invited me into paradise, I had to reassure him that you were doing well."

Seymour catches my eye. "Did he invite you?"

A serious question. "Yes."

"And you said no? How could you say no?"

"Because of you." The words just come out. "Because of what I left behind here on earth."

Seymour understands, he's probably the only one who can.

"You returned because your job isn't finished," he says.

"Yes."

"And because you love me."

"Of course."

"Not because of Matt."

"Don't be ridiculous," I say.

Seymour sits back in his seat, satisfied.

The others return in twenty minutes. Brutran carries a leather bag stuffed with hundred-dollar bills and documents. Matt carries a larger bag—they must have been provided by the bank. I have an eye for counting cash. Brutran has probably withdrawn over three million. I'm not surprised at the amount. But the documents are something of a shock.

She has fake IDs for all of us. Driver's licenses. Passports. Credit cards. The quality is obvious, no authority would look at them twice.

"When did you have these made?" I ask as I study my new identity. My name is Lara Wine and I'm from Napa Valley, California. I'm twenty-two and I have a pilot's license.

"A long time ago," she replies.

"How long ago?" It's hard to imagine she could have foreseen our present situation. It makes me wonder if she used the Cradle as an oracle more often than she let on.

Brutran shrugs. "Let's just say I like to be prepared."

Matt hands his bag of cash back to Seymour and starts the

engine. "I want to get rid of this vehicle," he says. "Let's drive halfway to the airport and flag down a cab."

"We can't close a deal on a plane in one afternoon," Seymour says.

Brutran gestures to her laptop screen. "I've already found a list of twenty-four planes for sale at the local airport. A third of them are being handled by a single broker. We show him the money and he'll get us what we need."

The broker's office is in a building that overlooks the portion of the airport where private planes land. Over Matt's objection, Brutran insists on talking to the broker alone, or with Jolie by her side, which is pretty much the same thing. She seems hesitant to leave us alone with her daughter.

"But we haven't even picked out which plane we want," he says.

The words are hardly out of his mouth when Brutran whips out a sheet of paper listing the planes that are available and where they are parked. The woman is so damn efficient, it's scary.

"Check them out and tell me which one you want," Brutran says.

"Aren't we doing things backwards?" Matt asks.

Brutran smiles. "You may be the next Superman but you don't know a thing about negotiating. I'll talk to the broker half an hour before I'll even begin to discuss our price range, or even what plane we want to buy."

Seymour, Matt, and I begin to search the aircraft parking spaces. It's immediately apparent Matt is focused on purchasing a jet, but only three are available: a Gulfstream IV, a Phenom 100, and a Lear XL. With the cash we carry, the Lear is the only jet we can buy outright. The Gulfstream is almost new and carries a price tag of twenty million, and the Phenom is at least half that much.

"A jet will limit the number of airports we can access," I warn.

"But it will more than double our speed," Matt says. He effortlessly picks the lock of the Gulfstream and climbs into the cockpit. I remember when he rescued me from the Telar in the Swiss Alps, the Apache helicopter he showed up in. The boy likes his toys. I can see already he has his heart set on the Gulfstream.

"Brutran withdrew the cash for a specific purpose," I say. "She doesn't want to have to access any of her private or IIC accounts. She's afraid a bank wire can be traced."

"I never heard her say that," Seymour remarks.

"It doesn't matter, I know the way she thinks," I say. "And in this case she's right. We should focus on the propeller planes. There's a twin-engine Cessna in lot 13B that looks promising."

Matt frowns as he plays with the Gulfstream's controls. "We can work on the broker's brain if we have to," he says.

"I'd rather not screw with the man's mind," I say, thinking of the Denver cop and his wife I recently damaged with my fiery gaze. Matt is instantly alert to my concern. He has my same power. His might even be stronger.

"You only had a problem because you were in Teri's body," he says.

"The broker will have trouble explaining to the Gulfstream's owner why he only got a fraction of the price he was asking," I say.

"The broker doesn't have to call the owner until next week. By then it won't matter."

"Why do we have to buy a jet?" Seymour asks. "Let's rent one."

"No," I say. "Brutran's talking to the broker alone to make sure he understands we don't want a paper trail. That's another reason her cash is important."

Matt climbs out of the Gulfstream and tests the strength of the jet's wings. "North Carolina's on the other side of the country. That's a lot of ground to cover. And I don't just want speed because we're in a hurry."

"You're afraid someone might come after us," I say.

Matt nods. "Yes. This Gulfstream is our best bet right now." He turns toward the broker's building. "I'm going to help Brutran speed up the negotiations."

Without waiting for my approval Matt walks away. Seymour pats me on the back. "How does it feel to not be the boss?" he asks.

I shrug. "Matt's not stupid."

"He ignores your arguments. That's got to bother you a little."

"It will only bother me if it turns out he's wrong."

An hour later we're in the air, two hundred miles east of Las Vegas, flying at twenty thousand feet and a speed of five hundred miles an hour. Matt hasn't told me about the details of his hypnotic session with the broker but has assured me our flight plan has been properly filed and no authority should question us as we cross the country. He has also pointed out that the Gulfstream will allow us to reach our destination without having to stop and refuel.

"That was another reason I insisted on a jet," he says.

The two of us are alone in the pilot's cabin, Matt in the driver's seat, the others in the luxurious rear. The Gulfstream IV is the stuff of celebrity dreams. It has two wide-screen TVs, private sleeping quarters, a bar and kitchen, and probably the most comfortable leather seats that can be found in the air. Before we left Vegas, Brutran made sure it was stocked with plenty of food and drinks.

"You don't have to explain yourself to me," I say.

Matt shakes his head. "I should have let you vote on the matter."

"You know more about planes than I do."

"You know more about the world."

"Are you saying you want me to be the boss?"

"I wouldn't go that far," he replies.

"I don't mind if you're in charge."

He shifts uncomfortably in his seat. "I hope you're not saying that because of what happened to Teri."

I hesitate. "Maybe I am."

"I don't blame you for what happened to her."

I don't respond. We both know he's lying.

"Look, what happened in the Rockies was a confusing time for me," he continues. "First I learn you've injected Teri with your blood. It didn't matter that it was to save her life. I'd long ago sworn that I wouldn't do anything to keep her from having a normal life. And if that meant she died before her time then so be it."

"You're stronger than me," I say.

"Who knows? I wasn't there when you did it. Maybe I would have broken down and done the same thing. Anyway, I no sooner find out what you've done when that damn Cradle blasts my mind. The next thing I know you're dead and Teri's walking around in a daze. I had never seen my father make a vampire before. I had no idea how she was supposed to behave and I sure as hell had no idea that you were in her body."

"That's why you haven't forgiven me. Because I lied to you then."

He goes to protest but stops. "Yes."

"I felt I had to lie. I was afraid you'd kill me."

"I know."

"I had a right to be afraid."

He stares at me. "No, Sita, that's where you're wrong. Sure, you saw my temper, you heard my threats. But I could never have hurt you any more than I could have harmed Teri." He pauses. "You don't believe me."

"It's not that simple. I know I'll never be as important to you as Teri was. I'm not complaining—I couldn't have loved her more than I did. But I think—from now on—that it's important we're honest with each other."

He continues to stare at me. "I am being honest, Sita."

He's a hard one to read. "Fine," I say.

Our flight continues uninterrupted. Matt puts the jet on automatic pilot and leaves me in the forward cabin to keep an eye on things. He goes in the back to talk to Brutran, or at least that's what he says. I could listen in on their conversation, but since he knows that, I doubt he's going to say anything secretive to her.

Matt is gone an hour, and we're approaching the Mississippi River when Seymour knocks on the cabin door and enters. He sits in Matt's chair.

"I assume you know how to fly this thing," he says.

"All jets have the same basic controls. But this plane is so advanced, it can fly itself. At least until we land."

"That's reassuring." He looks troubled.

"What's on your mind, Seymour?"

"When are you going to tell me about this veil?"

"Soon."

"Now feels like a good time."

"I'll do it when we're on the ground and I can get you and Matt alone." I pause. "Something else is bothering you."

"It's about Paula. You haven't called her in a few days. She has no idea what's going on."

"Paula's priority is John. Protecting him. If she was anxious for an update, she would have called me."

"What if we need her advice?" he asks.

"Then I'd call her."

Seymour looks out the window. "You've never reacted that well to what she has to say."

"Well, she can be a bit blunt at times."

"But she's usually right. Let's face it, the woman's a genuine psychic. And her son, John, God only knows what he is."

"What's this about?"

Seymour squirms in his seat. "Matt. He's in the back, playing that computer game John told us to stay away from."

"The one the Cradle installed on the Internet? The one that gave you headaches?"

"Yeah."

"What's the big deal? You said it didn't have any effect on Matt."

"He said that. On the surface, it didn't appear to bother him. But just now, when he flipped open his laptop, I got a creepy feeling, and I didn't even know what he was doing.

Then, when I saw he was playing the game, I reminded him what John had said about it. He told me to mind my own business."

"Sounds like Matt," I say.

"That game's weird. It's so addicting, especially if you play it with headphones. Remember the subliminal messages we found on sections of it?"

I remember. "Is Matt playing with headphones?"

"Yeah. He acts like he can screen out all the garbage—and maybe he can, I don't know. I just know the game gives off a weird vibe if you're in the room with someone who's playing it."

"You've only told me a little about how the game works. Give me more details."

"It starts off simple. Your character is always a visitor to earth, and your goal is to find a hidden spaceship and fly it to the center of the galaxy. You start with only your hands and feet to defend yourself, but you can pick up weapons along the way. You need them because, like most games, you're attacked the further you go. You can form alliances with other characters the game creates, and they can help you in tight situations. But just when you begin to depend on them, you usually discover they're Shadows."

"Shadows?"

"People the game is secretly controlling. They're the most dangerous part of the game. You need Shadows to get past certain areas—you can get killed if you don't agree to work with them—but they'll often stab you in the back at the worst times. Like when you're eating or sleeping."

"You eat and sleep in this game?"

"It's very realistic. You even meet beautiful women that you'd swear are other people out there playing the game with you. And maybe they are real, it's hard to tell. Remember, the game is tied into the Internet. I have no idea how many people are playing it."

"So these characters seem to have a life of their own?" I ask.

"Yeah. That's why it's so upsetting when they betray you."

"Have you been killed in your sleep?"

"I've been murdered sitting on the toilet. But dying isn't the worst thing that can happen. If you die, you just start over. The worst thing is when a Shadow turns you into one of them."

"How does it do that?"

"They get you to trust them."

"Go on."

Seymour hesitates. The question disturbs him more than it should. After, all, he's just talking about a game. I have to wait for his answer.

"That's pretty much it," he says. "I never got close to finding the spaceship and leaving the earth. But Matt told me he's closing in on it."

"Does the game end then?"

"I don't know. There are hints along the way that there are

plenty of worlds out in the galaxy you have to get by before you can reach home."

"Do you have any idea what home is like?"

"The game doesn't say a lot about it, except you get the feeling, when you're playing, that you want to reach it before it's too late."

"Too late for what?"

"I don't know," he says. He practically jumps out of his seat. He rubs his palms against his legs as he looks down at me. "I just thought I should warn you is all."

"Thanks," I say.

He leaves the pilot's cabin in a hurry. Anyone else and I wouldn't be concerned. But I know from experience that Seymour has remarkable radar. If he feels the game is dangerous, he's probably right. Plus anything created by the Cradle can't be too healthy. It's not as if that group was worried about entertaining the teenagers of the world.

I have a secure cell that's been designed by Matt. Paula has a similar device. After a moment's hesitation, I dial her number. Seymour is right, there's a part of me that fears to approach her. Paula knows things about my future I don't know, and her advice is often brutal. It was Paula who warned me to stay away from Teri. Advice I chose to ignore, much to my dismay.

Paula takes her time answering. It makes me wonder if I'm disturbing her meditation. The woman spends a lot of time in silence.

"Hello?" she says. "Sita?"

"I suppose I'm the only one who would call you on this line."

"You or Matt. How are you doing?"

"You read about the explosion in Malibu?"

"It's on TV. They're still carrying out the bodies of the children from the wreckage. They're saying most of them were in some sort of basement."

"I was the one who gave the order to blow up the building."

"That must have been a tough decision."

"That's an understatement. Was it the right one?"

"Why do you ask? You're not someone who looks to others for validation. Or are you looking for something else?"

"I'm not looking for absolution, if that's what you mean," I snap, annoyed at how easily she is able to get to me.

"Good. I have none to offer. What can I do for you?"

"How's John?"

"Great."

"Can I speak to him when we're finished?"

"Not now. Tell me what's on your mind."

I recount how we were able to destroy the Telar and the Cradle. If I'm expecting praise, I don't get it. I move onto Seymour's concerns about the game, going so far as to say that Matt appears addicted to it. She listens silently; the woman has the patience of an Easter Island stone head.

"John warned Seymour and Matt to stay away from the game," Paula says when I'm finished.

"Did he speak to Matt directly?"

"Yes. I was there. Why does Matt keep playing it?"

"What can I say? He's determined to beat it."

"Matt can't beat the game. Nobody can."

"John acts like he can. Your son plays it half the day."

"You know John has his own reasons for doing what he does. I don't even ask him to explain what they are. But I know he sees something in that game that the rest of us should avoid."

"The damn thing's on the Internet. Millions of kids could be playing it for all we know."

"John says the number, worldwide, is over ten million."

"There you go. Are we going to have millions of zombies on our hands soon?"

"You assume it's targeted at all those people. It might be that only a few are susceptible to its influence."

"Would you care to elaborate?" I ask.

"I've never played it. John has said to stay away from it and that's good enough for me." She pauses. "Did we lose Umara?"

"How did you know?"

"I sensed her leaving. A pity."

"She sacrificed her life so I could get to the Telar."

"I'm not surprised. She was a great woman."

"Yeah. We sure could use her now."

The conversation seems to run into a roadblock. Paula lapses into silence. Like Seymour said, she has the gift of prophecy, like Suzama of old. That's the main reason I've called her today, not to talk to her about the game. She's the only one I have told about the Veil of Veronica, back when she was living at Lake Tahoe. I have reached out to her with the hope she'll tell me something that will help me find it.

Yet when I bring it up, she practically cuts me off.

"Sita, stop. I told you that day we were sitting by the lake that the riddle of the veil will be revealed to you when the time is right."

"I know that's what you said back then. But things have changed. The people, or creatures, that we're combating have discovered it exists. I'm afraid they might get to it before I can." I pause. "I need your help, Paula."

"I can't help you."

"Then let me talk to John."

"No. You can't involve him in this."

"Why don't we let him decide."

"I'm sorry, Sita."

"Are you? It must be pretty cool being you. Having a sixth sense that allows you to stand on a tall building and see miles away while the rest of us stumble around in a dark alley."

"You have your own gifts. Be grateful you were able to reclaim your original form and can still use them."

Paula is referring to the time I was trapped in Teri's body. She and her son were present when Umara put me back in my old body. Of course, with John around, it was always hard to know who was doing what. The kid can just sit in a room and make it feel wonderful.

Still, his mother's attitude pushes my buttons.

"Hell, I'm grateful. But you know the only reason I'm back in this body is to help you and your son and the other seven billion souls on this planet. I could be with Krishna right now, but I chose to come back."

"Then be happy with your choice, and finish your task."

"I'll do that just as soon as I figure out what it is."

"One hint, Sita, then I'm going. All right?"

I hesitate. "Okay."

"Since the last world war, everything you've done for mankind has been amazing. Yet it all would have been unnecessary if you hadn't failed at Auschwitz."

Her words hit like a blow to my solar plexus. I have to struggle to respond. "How dare you. I was lucky to get out of that hellhole alive."

"Yes, you were," Paula says, and for the first time there's warmth in her voice. But it's small comfort because a moment later she practically hangs up on me. "Good-bye, Sita."

She is gone. I'm left alone with a dial tone.

"Bitch," I say.

Frankly, I have no idea what she's talking about. What did I do wrong in the concentration camp? Is she judging me because I failed to destroy the place? It makes no sense. I told her enough about my time at Auschwitz for her to know I was in bad shape when I escaped from the camp. But the way she talks it's like she thinks I should have done a lot more to save the prisoners there.

"She's so full of shit," I mutter to myself.

Yet I wonder why I suddenly feel so guilty.

I place another call, this one to Mr. Kram, one of the last surviving Telar and an ex-member of their inner circle. I met him not long before I destroyed what the Telar called the Source, a group of their most ancient leaders. With the help of Brutran's Cradle I was able to wreck the Source's psychic shield—a form of protection that made them virtually invulnerable. But it was Mr. Kram who launched a barrage of missiles at the last stronghold of the Telar and wiped out their physical bodies.

He did so because I offered to spare his daughter, Alia.

Unfortunately, Alia turned on me and I had to kill her.

I spared Mr. Kram instead and held him to a promise to help me destroy his leaders. He did so because he feared me, but also because he hated the Source as much as I did. He had seen what they were capable of.

I have kept Mr. Kram's number just in case.

He seems surprised to hear from me and wants to know why I'm calling. I put my question to him bluntly.

"I want to know why the Telar referred to Yaksha and Umara's son, Matt, as the Abomination," I ask.

Mr. Kram is slow to respond. "May I ask why you need to know this?"

"Personal reasons. Answer me."

"There's the obvious reason. Matt is the product of two powerful bloodlines. He's the only child of a vampire and a Telar. It's no surprise he's as strong as he is. It's as if the two most potent qualities of both races blossomed inside him."

"You say that like it's a good thing. Yet the Telar feared Matt."

"Of course. He killed so many of us. It's no surprise we should fear and even hate him."

"Still, you haven't answered my question."

"Haven't I?"

"The Telar's fear of Matt went far beyond his strength. The name you gave him—the Abomination. It's as if you granted him legendary status, but not in a good way." I stop to let my meaning sink in. "I want to know about the legends surrounding him."

Mr. Kram hesitates. "That's not something we talk about, even among ourselves."

"Fine. But you're going to talk about it now."

"Or else?"

"Or else I will find you and force you to tell me to my face. And that, Mr. Kram, is not something you want to have happen." I pause. "Talk."

Mr. Kram is a long time answering. "The legend of the Abomination existed before Matt was born. It came into existence thousands of years ago when the Source was almost solely focused on attaining the supreme reality. In those days the

Telar's inner circle was in daily contact with celestial beings of almost infinite power and creativity. It was these creatures that warned that if the Telar was not careful, one of their own kind would give birth to a man who was not a man at all. Someone who was never supposed to be born at all. These beings called this no-man the Abomination."

"And when Matt was born to Umara, an ancient Telar, and Yaksha, the first and greatest of all the vampires, the Source assumed that he must be this Abomination."

"Correct. As you know, a vampire cannot reproduce, and yet Yaksha did with Umara. That alone made us think that Matt was a man who was not supposed to be."

"Did you have any other reasons?"

"Not long after Matt's birth the Black Death—what you probably call the bubonic plague—struck Europe and Asia. You were alive during those days. You know that half the world was wiped out."

"The Telar blamed Matt for the plague?"

"I suppose we needed someone to blame."

"What other legends surround the Abomination?"

"The worst one, the strangest one, also came from our contact with celestial beings. They warned that if this man was born who was not a man, then at some point in the future, all mankind's history would be lost."

"Lost? How?"

"The legend is vague on this point. I don't know what

it means. But the legend does say that the Abomination will destroy our history for the love of a witch."

"So you're saying that when the Abomination meets this witch, this catastrophic event will occur?"

"Yes," Mr. Kram replies.

"Does the legend point to a time? When is it supposed to happen?"

"Soon."

"How soon?"

Mr. Kram's voice drops to a whisper. "Any day now."

I force myself to laugh. "Do you honestly believe this nonsense?"

"I'm afraid I do, Sita." He pauses. "Kill him, before it's too late."

"What?" I begin. But Mr. Kram has hung up.

It's just as well, I was about to do likewise. Of all the crazy legends I have ever heard, this one has got to be the strangest. Of course it's pure nonsense, it has to be.

How could Matt personally destroy history?

FIVE

We're attacked a hundred and fifty miles west of Raleigh, where we planned to land. We're so near the city that Matt has already dropped us down to ten thousand feet and begun to decrease our speed. Fortunately, he doesn't overreact in the crisis. He quietly calls me into the pilot's cabin and points to the two objects on our radar screen.

"They're fifty miles behind us and closing fast," he says.

"Can you ID them?" I ask.

"Not specifically but they've got to be military jets. They're traveling faster than the speed of sound. We have to assume they're armed."

"And that they have orders to shoot us down," I add.

He nods grimly. "It's possible they won't bother to try to take us alive. Whoever's after us clearly knows we're hard to handle. We should assume they'll fire on us when they have a clean shot."

"Do you have a plan?"

"I have a few ideas." Matt nods to heavy cloud banks not far in front of us. "Those might give us cover we need to make an escape."

"Are you kidding? The clouds won't block their radar."

"I'm not talking about staying in the plane."

I shake my head and smile. "How did I know you were going to say that? What should we do?"

Matt glances toward the rear of the plane. "We have parachutes for all of us, although I want Cindy and Jolie to jump in tandem. They can bail out when we reach the clouds, along with Seymour. Then you and I can take down the jets."

"How?" I ask.

"They'll want to look us over before they shoot us down to be sure they have the right target. They'll come up on our rear. That will give them an easy shot with their missiles. That's when we should strike. If you can time a jump precisely, you should be able to grab hold of one of their wings."

"I'll need a little luck to pull off a stunt like that."

"Sure. But we all know you were born with more than your fair share. When you catch the wing, keep things simple. Rip the canopy off the pilot's cockpit. Once he's exposed to the howling wind, he'll have no choice but to eject. You let go the second he does."

"How are you going to take down the other jet?"

"I'm going to ram it."

I reach out and touch his arm. "You're not talking about a suicide strike, are you?"

Matt frowns as he studies the approaching dots on the radar screen. "It'll be tight but I should be able to bail out just before the collision."

"You'll be playing tag with a heavily armed jet that has twice your speed and ten times your maneuverability. I doubt their pilot will let you near."

Matt acts confident. "I have a few tricks up my sleeve even Top Gun pilots don't know about. You take care of your end and I'll take care of mine. Now get the others ready."

I stand. "Just one thought. I should be the first one to jump. If I'm able to grab one of the jets, it'll cause a distraction for both pilots and give the others more cover to complete their jumps."

Matt nods. "You're right. But don't jump until you're sure you can catch one of them."

"Understood." I stop and lean over and kiss his cheek. "I'll see you on the ground."

"It's going to work, Sita," he says.

Brutran takes the news calmly when I explain our situation, and so does Jolie, but Seymour is another matter.

"What is it with you?" he complains, not bothering to hide his fear. "You're always having us jump out of something."

"True. But this time you'll be wearing a parachute."

"Great. And I suppose it makes no difference to you that I've never worn a parachute before."

I smile. "A kid can do it. All you have to do is be sure to pull the rip cord when you reach a thousand feet."

"I'll pull it the moment I jump," Seymour says.

"Listen to Sita," Brutran warns. "Your chute will be easy to spot, even with the clouds. You want to get as close to the ground as possible before pulling the cord. A thousand feet is good. That way their pilots will have less chance of calling in your location."

"Exactly," I say. "It will do us no good to escape the jets if they're able to radio their people where we've landed."

Brutran has already taken out a parachute and is fitting it over her shoulders. She puts one on her daughter as well, but—following Matt's advice—she has no intention of allowing Jolie to use the chute. She only wants her daughter suited up so she can buckle onto her and perform what's called a tandem jump. Despite what Hollywood movies would have people believe, it's physically impossible for a human being to hold on to someone else when they pull their rip cord. The jolt is too strong. But Jolie will be safe if she is locked on to her mother.

"You and Matt are glossing over a major problem," Brutran says as she preps her daughter, who looks excited at the prospect of jumping out of the plane. "You're assuming the jets will line up behind us, in classic attack mode. Remember, these guys have been briefed. They'll know you and Matt are to be treated with extreme care. They might fire on us as soon as they come into range, which could be any second. Their missiles can hit us from thirty miles out."

"Matt feels they'll want to eyeball us before firing," I say. "Also, if they fire too early, our radar will alert us, which will give us a good chance of bailing out. Matt doesn't think they'll risk that. That's why he's pretty sure they'll come in close and go for a kill shot."

"Why don't we wait and see if they'll let us surrender?" Seymour asks. "If they do, then you and Matt can overpower them."

"That ain't going to happen," I say.

Seymour looks miserable. He glances out the cabin's windows. "I hate heights," he mutters.

Matt and I have guessed right. Minutes later the twin jets come into view, but they make no effort to contact us by radio, nor do they fly up beside our cockpit and wave us down. Instead, they take up a position behind us, two hundred meters away. I have my parachute on but am still doing a last-minute check on Seymour's equipment. I worry he hasn't fastened all the necessary buckles. He can't stop trembling.

"I wish you were coming with us," he says.

"I'll see you on the ground, don't worry," I say as I finish checking his chute. I stride toward the side door, which is located near the front of the main cabin. The door has a locking mechanism that prevents it from opening in midair, and I have to call out to Matt to override it. Just before I yank it open, I give the others final instructions.

"We've dropped to eight thousand feet, so oxygen isn't going to be a problem. But we're cruising at two hundred miles an hour. The instant I open this door, it's going to feel like a hurricane in here. Grab on to something solid and hold on tight. After I jump, wait half a minute, then follow me out the door. I want to give them time to react to the fact that I'm hanging on to one of their wings. But don't wait any longer than that. They can shoot us down at any moment. Understood?"

"How do we find you once we're down?" Brutran asks.

"Don't worry, I'll find you," I say as I grab the door handle. "Is everyone ready?"

They nod and I rifle open the door, using my strength to jam it so it won't close. The roar from the wind is deafening. Jolie cringes and buries her face in her mother's chest. Brutran looks determined but Seymour is pale as a ghost. Still, I'm confident they'll be able to weather the storm. Leaning over, holding on to the edge of the door, I peek outside.

We're inside the cloud bank. Giant cumulus clouds surrounding us on all sides. Nevertheless, the jets—two F-16s—are clearly visible behind us, their tail engines glowing a fiery red.

I know the planes. The F-16s are equipped with four Sidewinder heat-seeking missiles each. The Sidewinder dates back to the 1950s, but is so reliable it's been repeatedly upgraded instead of replaced. I can't tell by looking at the weapons if they've been armed. However, the missiles are still firmly locked in place, which reassures me that we have time.

The jet on my right—as I face toward the rear of our Gulfstream—already looks like my best bet. It's separated from its companion by only thirty yards, and it's directly behind us. Unfortunately, it keeps bobbing up and down. One moment it's a few feet above us, the next below. I assume the pilot is fighting the turbulence created by our own engines. Whatever, it makes the timing of my leap more difficult. I only have one chance, and if I miss the jet wing, Matt will die.

The F-16 suddenly stabilizes at our height.

Spreading my arms wide, I jump out of the plane.

The fighter jet rushes toward me at insane speed. Even my well-tempered vampiric senses and muscles have to strain to compensate. It's only in the last instant that I'm able to pivot in midair and place my feet behind me, toward the jet. A millisecond later I feel the tips of my toes inside my shoes scrape along the top of the jet wing. Immediately I thrust my arms down and grab. I don't care what I grab, just as long as I make contact and don't let go.

Luck favors me. I catch the front of the jet's wing.

And hang on. God, the wind is a monster. I feel like

Dorothy riding a tornado into the sky. Only I know there's no enchanted land waiting for me at the end of this day. I'll be fortunate to disable the F-16 and escape in one piece.

The pressure on my fingers is immense. I feel as if my grip is actually tearing into the metal. My eyes sting from the impact of ice crystals inside the clouds. It might be summer at sea level but it's cold at this altitude.

I'm above the wing, the missiles are below, the cockpit is to my right and forward. I felt the plane swerve when I grabbed hold of it but the pilot has compensated for the drag of my weight and the impact my dangling body is having on the aerodynamic flow of air around the jet. The guy is good but I can see him glancing anxiously in my direction while talking excitedly into his mask.

I'm every pilot's nightmare—the mythical gremlin who suddenly appears on their wing in the middle of a lightning storm. Yet, except for a few clouds, it is midday over a peaceful green landscape, and I have long blond hair instead of horns.

However, I'm much more dangerous than a gremlin.

The pilot knows that. He's been warned.

He suddenly yanks his jet through a 360-degree spin, almost catching me off guard. I tighten my grip so hard I hear the metal screech. My chest and hips briefly fly off the wing just before they smack back down like an angry fist. He tips the nose up, slams it down, and again my entire body strikes the wing. I'm amazed I'm able to hold on.

Out of the corner of my eye, I see Seymour, Brutran, and Jolie leap from the Gulfstream. Both pilots in both jets are so preoccupied with me I doubt they notice them escaping. My friends quickly vanish into the clouds, their rip cords untouched.

Time, that's my problem right now. I've created a distraction for the others, but both pilots can still fire their missiles any second, and when they do, the Gulfstream will be incinerated. I know what Matt told me, to rip off the cockpit canopy and force the pilot to eject, and let him worry about the other plane. But the more I think about his plan, the less I like it. If I attack my pilot, his partner's going to get pissed and retaliate, and Matt's not going to get a chance to show off his fancy ramming skills. A Sidewinder will strike his right wing and that will be it—game over, his plane will explode.

The only way Matt will survive is if I take down both jets.

I have to get my pilot to eject, normally, without ripping off the canopy. It's the only way to preserve the cockpit's sensitive equipment—equipment I'm going to need if I'm to have a chance at shooting down the other jet. In other words, I need to boost my jet pilot's total confusion into overwhelming panic.

I have an idea. It's crude but it might work.

Crawling forward, I momentarily let go with my right hand and reach down and around the front edge of the wing, grabbing the tip of one of the missiles. It's still locked in place, of course, but not as tightly as before. That can mean only one thing. The missile is now armed and the pilot is preparing to fire.

I pull it free, half expecting it to detonate in my hand.

The pilot looks over at me and even with his mask I can see his eyes widen. They swell so big it's clear he knows he's entered that twilight zone known as the last few seconds of life. To drive home the precariousness of his situation, I point the tip of the missile at him and flash a wide grin.

The pilot immediately ejects.

The jet wobbles violently, and once more I'm almost thrown into the clouds. Tossing the missile aside, I scamper along the edge of the wing and reach for the cockpit. Unfortunately, it's still out of reach.

The hard plastic canopy is still attached but the interior is taking a pounding from the wind. I have to get inside now! Yanking myself forward with both arms, I spin in midair and make one last desperate grab for the rear of the cockpit, catching it with my fingertips.

A moment later I'm inside, sitting on what's left of the pilot's chair, which is not much. Pulling down the canopy, I secure the latch and study the instrument panel. It's coated with a layer of frost but it's still intact. A pair of headphones lies on the floor of the cockpit. I put them on.

The other pilot is trying to raise me. Or, rather, his friend.

"Alpha One, this is Alpha Two. Please respond, over?"

Did the guy not see his buddy eject?

Or is he playing dumb on purpose?

I clear my throat and press the transmit button while simultaneously easing back on the engine so I drift behind the other fighter jet.

"Alpha Two, this is Alpha One," I say. "Are you as stupid as you sound? Over?"

He doesn't answer right away and I take the time to rearm my missiles—they apparently disarmed when I snapped the one loose—and take aim at the rear of Alpha Two's engine. I can see the pilot twisting his head around and can only assume he has major denial issues. He replies in a bitter tone.

"This is Lieutenant Andrew Simmons of the United States Air Force and I'm ordering you to land and surrender immediately."

"Alpha Two," I reply. "Would a crash landing be acceptable?"

He struggles to speak. "Huh?"

"Alpha Two, you have three seconds to eject or else you're going to get ripped apart when I blow up your jet. Over?"

I really wish he'd listen to me but he's a stubborn SOB. He refuses to eject. My first concern is Matt. The other pilot can still shoot him down at any moment. I don't have a choice. I break the connection and fire a single missile.

It strikes the glowing interior of the jet engine in front of me and explodes. The ball of flame is massive and I have to thrust the control stick to the side to avoid it. I feel bad the man had to die for no reason, but what can I do? I creep up alongside the Gulfstream and wave to Matt.

He waves back. With hand signals, he makes it clear we should turn around and fly over the spot where we dropped the others, before bailing out. A smart move—in the short time since they jumped, we've flown at least thirty miles east of their position. Indeed, I can see Chapel Hill and Raleigh fast approaching.

Matt smiles and gives me a big thumbs-up.

I'm surprised how warm his approval makes me feel.

SIX

*M*att and I parachute into a wide green field, not far from the others, and very near a dense forest we were fortunate to miss. I almost forgot how much of North Carolina is wooded. Just the thought of Seymour dangling from a strapping birch or massive maple makes me nervous. It's wonderful to have him by my side on this adventure, and it scares me. He's my best friend but when it comes to fighting he's my child. I find myself constantly worried that I'm going to get him killed.

Like Teri.

We all meet up in the center of the field and I quickly note a dark stain of blood on Brutran's slacks. My nose picks up the odor of freshly burned gunpowder. There's a bulge beneath Brutran's blouse, at the belt line, that wasn't there before.

"Have any of you seen the pilot who ejected?" I ask.

"He's not going to be a problem," Brutran says.

I give her a hard look. "I want you to leave such decisions to either Matt or me," I say.

She shrugs. "I wasn't sure when you'd get here."

Seymour blinks. "Am I missing something?"

There's an uncomfortable silence, until Jolie speaks. "Mommy shot a man in the head," she says, once again excited for all the wrong reasons.

Seymour glares at Brutran. "We're not murderers," he snaps.

Brutran smiles thinly. "Why don't you ask your sweet Sita where the other pilot is."

"That was different," Matt interrupts. "She tried to get him to eject but he refused. She was forced to shoot him down."

"Of course," Brutran says. "She weighed the risks and acted. I did the same thing. I'm not going to apologize. That pilot could have called a squadron of helicopters to this spot. They might still be on their way here. We have to get moving."

Matt points toward a sloping rise. "As I was coming down, I saw a road two miles north of here. We can reach it in a few minutes if you guys will let Sita and me carry you on our backs. I can take you, Cindy, and Jolie."

Jolie claps with pleasure. "Will it be like horseback riding?"

Brutran kneels beside her and wipes the hair from her daughter's big green eyes. "This will be even more fun. Uncle Matt's faster than a horse. But you're going to have to hold on to Mommy real tight while I hold on to Matt. Okay?"

Jolie is raring to go. "I want to hold on to Uncle Matt's hair!"

Seymour looks at me and blushes. "I feel kind of weird treating you like a horse," he says.

"Just don't put a saddle on me," I say.

Our race to the road takes five minutes and could have taken even less time if Matt and I had wanted to push it. Still, our timing is good. A freight truck swings by moments after we reach the asphalt. The driver, a crusty middle-aged man who obviously likes to listen to his country music at full volume, pulls over and offers us a ride. Since I'm the cutest, I speak for the group.

"Where are you heading?" I ask, flashing my all-American smile.

"Miami," he replies with a southern accent, which tells me he's from a small town in Virginia or West Virginia. He's fifty and has a beer gut but there's a strength in his heavily lined red face. The man's spent most of his life on the road, the sun staring through his open window. "Where are you folks going?" he asks.

"Raleigh would be fine. Chapel Hill even better," I say.

"Geez, Chapel Hill's just down the road a ways. I can drop you there if you want."

"Great," I say. "We don't mind riding in the back. You got a spread?"

"You know it, girl. I don't spring for no motel rooms, not

in this economy and with the money I'm making. You can climb in the door on the passenger's side. It's open." He pauses and looks me over. "But if one or two of you want to ride up front, that'd be fine with me."

"I'll take you up on your kind offer," I say, giving the others a look that says I want him all to myself. My reason is simple. If we run into a roadblock, it will be less suspicious if I appear to be alone with the man. Of course, if things go bad, I can always hypnotize the guy and have him tell the authorities what I wish. But I'd rather not fool with his head, especially since he's being so friendly.

We're on the road in minutes, and Mr. James Jackson—"call me Jim, honey"—does me the favor of turning off his radio. Jim hasn't gone to college but reads the paper every day and is up on current events. He quickly begins to talk about politics and what a mess the president has made of the country. However, he's not as right wing as I'd expect, and when he admits he voted Democrat in the last election, I have to laugh.

"Jesus, Jim, you're a home-fried Confederate if I ever met one," I say. "What got into you?"

Jim chuckles and fiddles with a piece of tobacco caught between his yellow teeth with a toothpick. "I thought that'd surprise you, Lara. It shocked my buddies. Some of them haven't spoken to me since. But if you search the history of this part of the country, you'll find that it was the Democratic party—after the war—that stopped them damn Yankees from stealing what was ours to begin with."

The war he refers to is the Civil War, the only war that matters to people of Jim's persuasion. He's technically correct, the Democrats did everything they could to hinder President Grant's Reconstruction. But the modern parties have totally swapped roles since those days, which I happen to know for a fact since I lived in Washington DC after the Civil War.

I tell Jim as much—about the politics—and he studies me with fresh appreciation.

"How did a young thing like you get to be so smart?" he asks.

"By flirting with intelligent men like you."

He blushes. "You're too sassy for your own good, Lara. I love it, but I've got to warn you, it's going to get you into trouble one of these days. The world's a hard place and not all the men are as civilized as old Jim."

"I hear ya. I'll give it some thought."

"That's all I ask. Just watch your back."

We run into a roadblock five minutes later.

The fact that it exists means that Brutran didn't kill the pilot who ejected soon enough. It also confirms that those chasing us have an extraordinary network at their disposal. Only thirty minutes have passed since Matt and I landed in the grass field and already the area is being cordoned off.

I feel a wave of despair, something I seldom experience.

It's as if a huge net has been thrown over all our heads and it's just a matter of time before the powers that be tighten it. We can't pursue the veil with everyone else pursuing us. Somehow, we have to throw the government and its many agencies off our trail.

Even this simple roadblock could cost us.

"Shit," I whisper, and Jim looks over.

The checkpoint is manned by a local sheriff and his deputy. Their vehicles are parked in an open *V* position that barely allows enough room for a car to pass, never mind Jim's truck. The cops probably didn't expect a vehicle of Jim's size to come by, since the road we're on is narrow and isolated. From talking to Jim, I know the only reason he's not on the interstate is because he swung off the road to visit an old friend.

We pull up to the roadblock alone. The sheriff moves toward Jim's door, the deputy toward mine. I give Jim a quick glance, let a note of fear enter my voice.

"Don't tell them about my friends in the back," I say softly.

Jim hesitates. "You folks in trouble?"

I bite my lower lip. "We messed up some but we didn't hurt anyone."

Jim nods. "Don't worry about a thing, honey."

The sheriff peers up at Jim before squinting in my direction. He has a half dozen faxed sheets in his left hand. His right hand stays near his gun.

"License and registration," he says briskly. The sheriff is

near sixty, obese but strong-looking. He is a tough SOB, obviously someone who's used to barking orders and having people jump. Jim hands over his documents without an argument and the sheriff studies them closely.

"Mr. James Jackson," he says. "Who's that traveling with you?"

"My niece," he says.

The sheriff hands back Jim's license and registration. "I need to see her ID."

"I've got my driver's license," I say, handing over the Lara Wine ID Brutran gave me in Las Vegas. I didn't jump out of the sky with nothing in my pack or pockets. I have a fully loaded .40-caliber four-inch short-barrel Glock in my bag, which I drop between my legs and smother out of sight while I dig out my license. Even though Jim sits by my side, I move too fast for him to see the weapon. The cops, of course, even the nerdy deputy staring up at me on my right, don't notice a thing.

I hand my license to Jim, who gives it to the sheriff.

"Lara Wine," the sheriff says as he studies my ID. "How come you two don't have the same last name?" The man's not dumb, he's trying to trick us with the question. But Jim answers smoothly.

"Lara's my niece on my sister's side," Jim says.

"She don't look anything like you."

"My sister thanks the Lord for that every day."

"Ain't you on the job? Why she's traveling with you?"

"She's got a boyfriend in Florida she's missing. I'm heading that way so I offered to give her a ride."

"Do her parents know she's with you?"

"Excuse me, Sheriff," I interrupt. "You're holding my license. You can see I'm twenty-two, legally an adult anywhere in this country. I don't need my parents' approval to travel."

"Is that a fact?" the sheriff asks before looking down at his faxed papers. He rifles through them and I catch a glimpse of several blurred photos. One looks like me, another like Matt, but the quality is extremely poor. It's possible the sheriff doesn't recognize me. Still, he's suspicious and I'm forced to contemplate another round of violence. It doesn't matter how I try to live my life, I think, blood follows me like an extra shadow.

"May I have my license back?" I ask.

The sheriff ignores me, glances toward the rear of the truck. "What you carrying?" he asks Jim.

"Levi blue jeans, the originals, five hundred cartons." Jim pauses. "You want to see my paperwork?"

The sheriff takes a step back and waves his hand. "I want to see what you've got in the back. Open her up."

"No, sir. Not until you give me a legitimate reason why I should."

The sheriff shakes the papers in his hand. "I have a fax here from the Federal Bureau of Investigation that contains a photograph matching the young woman seated beside you. She's said to be in this area, and I want to know if her partners are traveling with her, in the back of your truck. Does that give you a good enough reason to do what I say? Because if it doesn't, we're going to have a problem."

Jim turns to me and his eyes are worried. "Lara?"

I shake my head and pat his arm. "It's not going to be a problem. Sit tight and let me take care of this. Okay?"

His eyes stray downward and he finally catches sight of the Glock wedged between my legs. "What are you doing?" he says in a tight voice.

"Trust me, it'll be fine," I reply as I throw open the door on my side of the truck and smash the face of the deputy, who has enough sense to land on his back in the thick grass that lines the road. An instant later I have my gun in my hand and point it at the sheriff. I fire a single shot that takes off the tip of his left ear. The sheriff drops his papers and staggers back a step, going for his gun.

"Not so fast!" I snap in a voice Jim has yet to hear. My ruthless tone, the sheer power of my order, makes it impossible for the sheriff not to obey. He freezes with his hand on his revolver's handle, blood flowing freely from the side of his face. I continue. "Now Sheriff, listen closely. Your partner's unconscious, he's out for the count, and you've just been given a vivid demonstration of my shooting ability. That's right, I nicked your ear on purpose, when I could have put a bullet in your forehead. The only reason you're still alive is because I'm letting you live. Understand?"

The man looks startled but far from ready to surrender.

"Go to hell," he says.

"Been there done that," I reply before I shoot off the tip of his right ear. This time the sheriff staggers back several steps and turns as white as the fax papers in his hands. Blood drips from both sides of his head. Yet he has the nerve to reach for his gun. "I'll blow off your hand!" I shout.

He freezes. "What do you want?" he demands.

"Remove your gun from your holster and throw it in the grass. Move slow, Sheriff, like you're in a dream, and you may live to see tomorrow."

"Lara," Jim gasps. A pity for him the tip of my gun is only two feet from where he's sitting.

"It's all right, Jim. No one has to die here. Isn't that right, Sheriff?"

He has his gun in hand, pointed toward the ground, but he's reluctant to give it up. "You're not going to get away with this," he says.

"Throw it in the grass. You have two seconds. One . . ."

The sheriff tosses his revolver into the tall grass.

"Stand perfectly still. Don't move an inch," I say as I climb down from my seat and circle the front of the truck. I move faster than is humanly possible, but both the sheriff and Jim are so shaken they don't notice. In a moment I'm standing three feet in front of the sheriff, my Glock pointed at his head.

I'm not surprised Matt hasn't rushed to my aid. He can hear and understand everything that's going on and knows I have the situation under control. He also knows it would be a mistake to reveal that the others are with me.

The sheriff stares at me with scorn. "Put a gun in your hand and you think you're hot shit," he swears. "You'll get life for this."

"That would be a very long sentence. Longer than you can imagine." I pause. "Do you have a video feed on the front of your vehicles?"

His chest swells in defiance. "Everything you're doing right now is being taped. In fact, bitch, it's being watched live back at headquarters."

His first remark is true. His cars are equipped with cameras. Also, he's probably right to call me a bitch. He's going to need plastic surgery to reconstruct his ears. But his last comment is false. He's all alone with his unconscious deputy.

I allow a degree of my persuasive power to enter my voice.

"Listen closely. Jim picked me up as he was driving down the road," I say. "He thought I was an ordinary hitchhiker but I've kept him hostage since I climbed in his truck. He's innocent and has nothing to do with me. Remember that."

"Bullshit," the sheriff mutters, but I can tell he believes me, which means I'm finished with him. In a blinding move, I strike him on the sweet spot on his jaw with the short barrel of my Glock. He's out before he hits the ground.

"Sweet Jesus," Jim whispers behind me. "Who are you?"

Putting my gun away, I turn and look up at Jim. "It's not what you think. We're not terrorists or anything evil. It's true the government is after us, and you might even find us on the FBI's list of wanted criminals. But all that's going to get cleared up in the next few days. You'll see, we'll vanish from the list and you'll realize we were innocent after all." I pause. "Are you okay, Jim?"

He's turned his own distinct shade of gray, I'm afraid. I suppose my shooting would make any man feel less tall. "I believe you," he mumbles. "I don't know why but I do."

"Because I'm telling you the truth and you're not easily fooled. You've been a good friend and a big help. If you're too freaked out and want to leave us here, I'll understand, no hard feelings. Drive on down to Miami and deliver those jeans. All I ask is that you don't talk to the cops about us for the rest of the day."

Jim considers before shaking his head. "I'll take you to where you need to go," he says.

"Are you sure? I can't guarantee we won't get stopped again."

Jim forces a smile. "If we do, Lara, I'm not worried about who's going to come out on top. Climb in."

"Thank you. Give me a minute."

Moving fast, I locate the cop's cameras and tapes and destroy the lot. Then I drag the police into the grass so they cannot be found off the bat. I put a hand on their bloody heads and suggest they stay unconscious for the next six hours. It doesn't matter that they're not awake to hear me. They'll obey me, and we'll be long gone before they can report to anyone, high or low, what Lara Wine did to them.

SEVEN

Ninety minutes later we sit in a restaurant in Chapel Hill, only five miles west of Clearglade and 134 Tree Leaf Lane—the address Brutran plucked from her database for Mrs. Sarah Goodwin, the granddaughter of Harrah and Ralph Levine.

Outside, it's dark; the night feels early for all of us. Traveling from the West Coast to the East has pushed us through three time zones. Brutran, Jolie, and Seymour are tired and hungry, or they were hungry. Seymour has just devoured four pieces of fried chicken and mashed potatoes. Brutran and her daughter have shared a piece of swordfish and a bowl of rice. Even Matt and I have fed. Matt ate a hamburger and fries while I shared some of Seymour's chicken.

Jim dropped us off in Chapel Hill an hour ago. We're holed up in the restaurant as much to think as to eat. None of us can be sure we've thrown them off the scent. I've stretched out my hearing as far as possible. The best I can tell, no one is talking about us in the immediate area. But I fear the eyes in the sky, the network of earth-orbital satellites, more than the agents on the ground. For all we know their mechanical vision has followed us from the roadblock. A pity I can't see what their cameras see.

"The question remains," Brutran says as we discuss our next move, "should we risk approaching the Goodwin house when we know our foe knows we're in the area?"

"I think we've lost them for the time being," Matt says.

"Your reasoning?" Brutran asks.

Matt shrugs. "We've hardly moved in an hour. They should have come after us by now."

"There's just as much chance they're waiting for us to move," Brutran says. "So they can learn our destination, what we're looking for."

"We're going to have to pay the Goodwins a visit at some point," Seymour says. "How long do you want to wait?"

"At least overnight," Brutran says, glancing at me. "Sita?"

I set down my cell. I've just called the Goodwins' number again without any luck. "I'd agree to wait if I knew they were at home. The last thing I want to do is show our hand. But the fact they're not answering worries me."

"I don't take stray calls," Seymour says. "Not unless the person leaves a message. The Goodwins are probably no different."

"I can't leave a message," I say. "Too risky."

"No one knows where we're heading," Seymour says.

"Maybe," I say.

Matt looks at me across the table. "You're concerned about the person who gave Shanti the photograph."

"Yes," I say.

Brutran's radar is alert. "Are you worried the photograph was a plant to bring you here?"

"It's a possibility," I say. "But whether it was a plant or we were fortunate to find the picture, it still means that whoever's after us knows about the veil."

"Are you sure?" Seymour says.

"Let's assume it was a plant," I say. "And that whoever is after us wanted to draw me to this part of the country. They would only have used the photo if they knew about my past."

"They?" Brutran says.

"We've never settled on a good name for what we're running from," I reply, feeling no desire to bring up Tarana. Simply speaking his name aloud disturbs me in ways I can't explain.

"I think I speak for all of us when I say our chasing this veil would make more sense if *we* knew about your past," Seymour says.

"I've promised to tell you about it and I will. Later."

"We can talk all night," Matt says. "We have to make a decision. I think we all agree there's a good chance the house is being watched. For that reason, I'd prefer if only Sita and I visit it. If we're attacked, we should be able to escape, but only if we're alone."

Brutran considers. "When are you planning on going?"

"Now." Matt stands and stretches, before pointing out the window. "There's a motel down the block. It looks like the kind of place that would be happy to take cash. Check in and we'll catch up with you later."

Seymour shakes his head. "I don't think we should split up."

"Matt's right, the house could be a powder keg," I say. "It's too dangerous."

"It's more dangerous if we don't have one of you nearby to protect us," Seymour says.

Jolie pats Seymour's arm and says sweetly, "I'll protect you."

Seymour smiles. "How will you protect me, Jolie?"

"I can make people die with my mind," she says simply.

Seymour loses his smile and turns on Brutran. "You should never have shot that soldier in front of her," he says.

Brutran shakes her head. "I should have shot him earlier."

Seymour appeals to me and Matt. "I don't know if I'm going to feel very safe at that motel," he says.

"I'm sorry," I say. "But ask yourself, how safe are the Goodwins right now?"

Before knocking on the door, I know we have the right house. The scenery is identical to what can be seen in Shanti's photograph. The residence is surrounded by maples and birch and there's a small lake two hundred yards from the back porch. The trees do not crowd the home, however, and there's plenty of room to walk around the gardens. It's a lovely property, and I'd even go so far as to say it's peaceful, except all the lights are out and the front door lies wide open.

Plus I smell blood.

Matt gives me a look.

He doesn't have to say it. We're too late.

The car we're driving comes from the motel where we deposited the others. We plan to return it well before morning, no harm done. Because it's obvious the Goodwins have already been attacked, we don't bother to hide our approach but park at the end of their long driveway and walk to the door. The smell of blood thickens, and it's not a sweet smell, not even to me, a vampire. Blood spilled in violence never smells fresh. We hear the sound of labored breathing and draw our handguns.

Matt leads the way. It's dark, but that's no obstacle for either of us. I see the couch from the photograph, where the happy couple was sitting, the wide windows that look out on the grass and trees. Yet the place is a mess, it has been ransacked: the sofa cushions gutted with a sharp blade, all the drawers thrown open, even the backs of the wall paintings torn off.

Whoever came was looking for something.

The home is a two-story but already we know there is no one upstairs. The gasping breaths come from a hallway near the back door, the sounds of two dying men. Matt gives me a questioning look and I nod. He turns on the living room light and we go to see what has become of Mr. Goodwin.

I recognize him from Shanti's photograph.

But who is the other man?

Mr. Goodwin lies on his back in a pool of blood, his head propped up by the screen door. His face is battered, swollen around the eyes and mouth, and the stab wounds to his gut are deep. The one on the right side will be fatal. It goes through the liver and it is still leaking. His features would be black from the bruising if he weren't so white from blood loss. Matt feels the man's pulse and shakes his head.

"I don't know if we can revive him," he says.

"We have to try." I pause. "I don't hear or smell Sarah in the area."

"She's not here. They must have taken her." Matt gestures to the other man, who has a single massive bruise on his left temple but no other apparent injuries. He is thirty, dark-haired, extremely handsome, and has on gray slacks and a smartly tailored black sports coat that speaks of money. Matt leans over him and checks his vitals. He even goes so far as to remove the man's right shoe and pinch his Achilles tendon.

"He's out cold," Matt says, gently feeling the guy's head. "He has a skull fracture. Any idea who he is?"

"No," I say. "But let me concentrate on Mr. Goodwin. He's not going to last much longer."

Matt pulls out his cell. "Should I call for an ambulance?"

I shake my head. "It's too late for doctors. But I might be able to reach him."

Placing my left hand on his forehead and my right over his fading heart, I lean forward and whisper in the man's ear, putting all the power of my voice into my words. Yet I don't try to overwhelm his will with blunt persuasion. There's a pleading tone in my voice and in my own heart.

"Mr. Goodwin," I say. "My name is Sita. You don't know me but I'm an old friend of your family. I'm here to help. I know you're out, you can't hear me, not consciously, but you can feel me. My hand is on your head, my fingers are next to your heart. Let my energy flow from my body into your body. Feel my heartbeat. Feel my breath."

I lean over farther and breathe through his closed lips.

His chest rises and falls.

A sigh escapes his swollen mouth and his eyes open.

He blinks. "Sita," he whispers.

I nod. "You've heard my name before."

He coughs weakly. "Long ago. How . . ." He doesn't finish and his eyes close. I shake him gently.

"Mr. Goodwin, tell me your first name."

His eyes reopen. "Roger."

"Roger. Try to stay awake. We need your help to find your wife."

Pain fills his face. "Sarah. They took her."

"Who took her? Describe them."

"A man and a woman. Cruel. They beat us. They wouldn't stop."

"Did they question you?" He doesn't respond. I shake him harder. "Did they come for the veil?"

Roger Goodwin's eyes suddenly come into focus, and it's like he's seeing me for the first time. "Who are you?" he demands, blood spilling over his lips. He's bleeding internally, of course, he's been stabbed a half dozen times. Nevertheless, Matt gestures to his cell phone, silently insisting he should call for an ambulance. I shake my head.

"I told you, my name is Sita," I say.

A note of suspicion enters his voice. "You're blond, blue-eyed. Are you German?"

He's really asking if I'm Aryan and in fact I am. I'm an original, a product of the race that conquered India thousands of years ago. I look like a poster child for Hitler's perfect race— one of the reason the Nazis trusted me at the start of the war.

"I'm not German. I'm a friend. My family knew your wife's family. They knew Harrah and Ralph Levine. They were with them in Auschwitz. That's how I know about the veil." I pause. "I'm a friend and this is my friend Matt. We can help save your wife."

He gropes feebly with his hands, searching for something he's lost. The move is reflex, nothing more. "My wife, they took my wife. Sarah."

"You said a man and a woman took her. Did they take the veil as well?"

Again, he freezes at the mention of the veil. It's obviously something the two kept secret. "Your family was in the camp?" he asks warily.

"Yes. My grandparents were in Poland during the war. Harrah and Ralph told them about the veil, and together they escaped from Auschwitz."

"What were their names?"

"I'm named after my grandmother. Her name was Sita. Roger, I know you've heard the name before."

He nods weakly. "From Sarah's grandmother. Harrah."

"Then you know you can trust me. You have to trust me and my friend. We're the only ones who can get your wife back. You have to tell us what you know. Did the people who kidnapped Sarah take the veil?"

An unlooked-for strength enters his voice and his face hardens. "No. They tortured us, but Sarah wouldn't tell them where it was."

"Do you know where it is?" I ask, and it's difficult to keep the desperation out of my voice. Of course, I'm relieved to hear it hasn't fallen into enemy hands, at least not yet, but I fear what they will do to Sarah to get her to talk. Roger Goodwin sighs, the sound as sad as his approaching death. The man knows he's finished.

"Sarah never told me where she kept it," he says. "She said only women could know."

Harrah had told me something similar.

Only women could possess the veil.

It was a rule in the Veil of Veronica tradition.

"Can you describe the man and woman who took your wife?" I ask.

"The woman, she looked like you, a little older. Blond, beautiful, but with cold eyes."

"What did the man look like?" And I half expect him to describe the man lying only ten feet away.

But Roger Goodwin's face twists into horror at the question. "He was the Beast. I swear it was him." He stops and frowns. "But he was young."

For a moment I don't understand the reference.

Yet his choice of words sends a chill through my body.

At Auschwitz the Jews called Himmler the Beast.

Roger Goodwin's spasm of strength is fading. His eyes fall shut as more blood leaks from his mouth. I don't have to hold his pulse to hear his heart skip in his chest. Physically prodding him to talk will no longer work. Once more I lean over and whisper in his ear.

"Roger. There's another man lying here. He's unconscious, we don't know if he'll wake up. Who is he?"

Mr. Goodwin's voice is faint. "A man came. He came to help us. He burst through the door. But they struck him down."

"Do you know who this man is?"

"Never saw him before. But he fought . . . he fought for us."

"Roger. You're dying, but Sarah is still alive. You've got to tell us something we can use to save her."

The words come out in a fading gasp. "They took her into the sky."

"Into the sky? I don't understand."

"In a vim . . . A vim . . ."

"Vim." His last word, and it means nothing to me.

His breath rattles in his chest and his heart stops.

I stretch him out so he can rest more comfortably on the floor. A useless gesture but I want to do something for him. A brave man, it's sad he had to die brokenhearted. The way he said Sarah's name, it was obvious he loved her very much.

Matt puts his hand on my shoulder. "Did he tell you anything we can use?" he asks.

"Not really."

"Sarah must be strong to hold out under such torture."

Standing, I shake my head. "A mortal can only hold out so long. She'll break eventually." Frustrated, I pound the wall, and my fist goes right through it. "Damn it! We should have gotten here earlier."

Matt gestures to the dispersal of the blood on the floor, how some of it has dried. "This happened two or three hours ago. Even if we'd come straight here, we would have been too late."

I brush the plaster from my fist, my anger still raw. "True. But we could have gotten more out of Roger."

"What's done is done. What do we do now? Do you want to try to wake the other man?"

"Not yet. I need a moment." Linking my mind with Mr. Goodwin's has drained me. The man is dead but I still feel his pain, his anguish.

"I understand," Matt says.

We survey the mess the assailants have made of the house. The man and woman did a thorough job, and we can tell by the force they used that they might have the strength of a vampire or a Telar. However, we both agree that we should be able to see things that they missed.

Yet the land behind the house draws me. Roger was clearly heading that way when he fell. It must be the direction they took Sarah.

"Search the house for anything unusual," I say. "I'm going to check outside."

"Why?" Matt asks.

"I want to know what he was trying to tell us when he died."

The backyard is a field of grass, sprinkled with trees, that leads to the lake. The first twenty yards are carefully trimmed, then the growth turns wild and the footprints are easy to spot in the matted green blades. There is a combination of three sets of footprints, followed by only two, which makes me think that Sarah stumbled and was swept off her feet and carried away.

But to where?

The footprints suddenly dead-end at the edge of a clearing. At the center of the meadow is a three-foot scorch mark. Here the grass has not simply been burned—it's been incinerated into a fine black powder. Yet the footprints stop thirty feet from the mark, and the grass around it appears untouched.

I kneel to examine the powder, but something keeps me from touching it. What's left of the grass—and the underlying earth for that matter—is giving off a sickly glow. Humans couldn't see the faint radiance but I can and know what it signifies.

The burned powder is radioactive.

"They took her into the sky," I say to myself.

Matt calls from the house. He has found something, I can tell by his tone. I'm tempted to take a sample of the powder but doubt the Goodwins have a lead-lined container in their kitchen or garage. I can tolerate tremendous heat, your standard house fire for example, but radiation and I do not get along, especially in high doses. For me to be able see the glow emanating from the scorched circle means it is hot enough to drive a Geiger counter wild.

Inside, Matt shows me a handwritten diary.

The book is small; it could fit in my back pocket.

"It was hidden in the bedroom wall, in a wooden panel," he says. "They plastered over the spot. Recently, too, the only reason I was able to spot it was because the plaster was still damp."

I study the book. The feel of the paper, the smell of the ink, the style of the binding—all these details tell me the book is extremely old. Indeed, it reminds me of handwritten books I owned in in France during the seventeenth century.

But the text is not in French. At first I assume I'm looking at three alternating languages: Latin, Greek, and Aramaic. But there appear to be twice as many Aramaic letters. Then I realize that the author also used an ancient Hebrew script that at first glance can be mistaken for Aramaic.

I can read and write the four languages, of course, I've lived with them. But I can't read a line of the book. It's in code, a complex code, that someone spent a long time developing.

I'm older than Matt and know more about old languages. I explain to him my thoughts on the book, but he surprises me by pointing out a fact I've missed.

"Whoever wrote this was copying it from another book," he says. "Note the style of the script. The guy wrote without pausing to think."

"You're right. But why do you assume it was a man?"

"Few women were taught to read or write that long ago."

"True. But women were always the custodians of the tradition of the Veil of Veronica."

"How do you know the book is related to the veil?"

I skip to a line near the back of the book. It stands alone

and it's the only line that's not in code, although it was still written in the four separate languages. It says simply, *The Story of Veronica.*

I translate it for Matt. He stands thoughtful.

"You have to break the code," he says.

"I will." I tell him what I discovered out back. His puzzlement deepens.

"Are you saying something landed there?" he asks.

"There's no sign a craft set down on the grass."

"But the radiation. Who walks around with radioactive materials?"

"Dangerous people. Crazy people. I don't know."

The mystery man on the floor begins to stir. Matt and I turn in time to see him open his eyes. He groans in pain and we move to his side. I kneel near his head and take his hand.

"Try not to move," I say. "You have a serious concussion."

He stares up at me. His eyes are a warm brown, deep set, and even though he is groggy, I sense a deep intelligence in them. "It's you," he says.

I'm immediately suspicious. "You know me?"

"Sita," he whispers.

"Who are you?"

"Mr. Grey."

"Why are you here?"

"I was waiting, watching."

"The Goodwins?"

His eyes fall shut. "I was waiting for you."

He's unconscious. I glance at Matt. "Well?" I say.

"He must be from the government. They must have figured out our destination."

"How? We had the photograph, they didn't."

"It doesn't matter. Brutran could have given away the Goodwins with all her poking around online." Matt pauses. "We should kill him. Or leave him here to die."

"Roger Goodwin said he fought to save them." I consider. "As far as we know, the government agencies are not calling me Sita."

"What are you saying? That we take him with us?"

Reaching over, I cradle Grey in my arms and stand. "Chances are he'll wake up again. We can question him more at the motel. We can decide there."

Matt doesn't share my point of view. "You're exposing the others to unnecessary risk."

"I know but it's not like we have a lot of leads. We have to take a few risks."

On the way back to our car we spot another trail in the grass. The footprints match Grey's shoes and lead to the spot where he was spying on the Goodwin home, a cluster of bushes not far from the road. I put Grey in the backseat of our car before hiking to the spot with Matt. There we find a black bag filled with electronic equipment that could have been purchased at Radio Shack. Yet the components are arranged in ways I don't understand.

"I don't think he was carrying a gun," I say.

Matt nods as he studies the bag's contents. "This doesn't look like spy equipment."

"Still think he's government?"

"I don't know what to think," Matt says.

We return to the motel where we left Seymour, Brutran, and Jolie. Matt goes to check on the others while I lay Mr. Grey on my bed and carefully feel around the bruise on his head. The tips of my fingers are sensitive—I don't need an X-ray to pick up the hairline fracture. The man would probably be better off in a hospital but I'm reluctant to part with him.

Why would he fight so hard to protect the Goodwins?

Matt enters my room, Seymour at his back.

"Brutran is resting," Matt says. "She told me to tell you she'd talk to us in the morning. Jolie is sound asleep. They're both exhausted."

"How come you're not sleeping?" I ask Seymour.

"Like I could with you two out prowling around." He pauses. "Matt told me what happened at the house. Pretty creepy."

"It was sad," I say.

Seymour comes close, points to the man on my bed. "Should we be making new friends?" he asks.

"He tried to protect the Goodwins. He's hurt. I didn't want to leave him there."

"You could have called 911."

"Did Matt tell you he called me Sita?" I ask.

It's clear from Seymour's expression that Matt left out that particular detail. "I'm not suggesting you kill the guy," Seymour says.

I nod. "Go rest, both of you. Let's talk in the morning."

Seymour is tired and doesn't argue. But Matt is reluctant to leave. He hovers by the door.

"I hated to leave Mr. Goodwin lying there," he says.

"I've already placed an anonymous call to the police. They'll take care of the body." I pause. "You're worried about something else."

"You know I have faith in you, Sita."

"Just say it."

Matt hesitates. "There's no reason to think the veil's going to help us with the Cradle's program."

"Tarana wanted Shanti to find it. That's good enough for me."

"You assume he's behind the program."

"Yes."

Matt is doubtful. "You were under a lot of pressure at IIC's headquarters. You can't be sure everything you saw or felt was real."

"It was real enough that your mother sacrificed her life to help destroy it."

The reference to Umara stings Matt and I regret having brought her up. "My mother believed in a lot of things my father never did."

"Umara believed in Krishna. So did your father."

"So?"

"So they trusted each other with what matters."

Matt goes to snap but stops. He doesn't take his eyes off me. They're beautiful eyes, but when he's annoyed, when he's outright angry, they burn. He speaks in a low voice.

"Do you honestly feel Krishna sent you back to save the earth?"

"It was my choice to return." I meet his glare. "I came back for you and Seymour. I don't know about the rest of the world."

"Did you really see Krishna?"

"Yes. When I died. I mean, when I was dead, before I entered Teri's body."

"What was it like?"

Suddenly there's a lump in my throat. "There are no words."

"Then why did you return?"

"I told you."

Matt turns and opens the door, although he stops before leaving. "Since everyone got up this morning, we've been going nonstop. I didn't want to pressure you about this, but Seymour and Brutran need to know why we're chasing this veil."

"You said that already."

"I'm saying something else. It would help if you told them what happened during the war."

"It would help you."

Matt nods. "You brought it up but never explained what the Nazis did to you. And how the veil saved you. You should share what you know."

"Even with Brutran?"

Matt shrugs. "For better or worse, she's part of our team. And she is awfully competent."

"I think you like her. Her and her daughter."

"Jolie's a doll. But I haven't forgotten who Brutran is."

"For all we know it was Brutran who gave the order to take over your body when we were stuck in the mountains. It was that decision that led to Teri's death."

Matt hates the fact I have brought up what happened that morning. When he lost all control and accidentally shot me in the chest with a Telar laser. Once again—the guy does have a temper—his face darkens.

"Fine," he says. "Tell me and Seymour the story. Leave Brutran out of it. But please give us all the facts. Remember, you're the one who keeps harping on how few leads we have."

"I doubt a record of my days in Auschwitz will help us locate Sarah Goodwin."

"You think? Even when her husband said the man who attacked them looked like Himmler?"

"I didn't know you understood the reference."

"You weren't the only one who helped defeat the Nazis." Matt turns and steps through the door, talking over his shoulder. "I'm in the next room. Shout if you need me. I won't be sleeping."

"Stay away from the game. Okay?"

Matt nods but I can tell he's not listening. He leaves.

I'm upset, and I seldom get upset. It was his damn question. Why did I choose to return? I feel as if I could weep, and wipe at tears that are not there. Then I realize my hands are trembling. They never tremble.

What's wrong with me?

It's pretty obvious.

I can't stop thinking about what it felt like to stand at the threshold of Krishna's realm. The joy, the utter contentment, the relief . . .

Why did I turn my back on paradise?

Do I really know? Did I lie to Matt?

I push the questions away. I'm here on earth now, that's what's real. I have a job to do. I have to decide whether Mr. Grey is for us or against us.

Like with Roger Goodwin, I try my best to link with Mr. Grey's mind. Closing my eyes, taking a few deep breaths, I allow the now-familiar dome of magnetism to surround my head. It has become so strong that I feel I can almost reach out and touch it.

Instead, I will it to expand and encompass the sleeping man's body. Since my dark days working with the Cradle, I've discovered my telepathic abilities have greatly increased to where I can directly read other people's thoughts, not simply sense their emotional states. Yet as I reach for Grey's mind,

I encounter a curious barrier. It's not like the psychic shield someone like Brutran has deliberately cultivated over years of practice, which relies upon intense concentration to be maintained. This wall appears intrinsic to the man's mind. It's blocking me even though he's unconscious. Also, I don't feel as if there's anyone there. It's a puzzle; it's almost as if Mr. Grey were a corpse.

"Who are you?" I wonder aloud.

His breathing concerns me. It's shallow and irregular. Plus his pulse is thin and ragged. It's possible the blow to his head is causing his brain to swell, which could lead to death if not treated. Still, I hesitate to take him to a hospital. I can't forget the way he looked at me when he opened his eyes, the way he said my name. It was like he was happy to see me.

I decide to do something I almost never do.

Pricking my thumb with the nail on my index finger, I allow three drops of my blood to drip onto his egg-sized bruise. When I struck at Ray's father long ago, and crushed his skull, he begged me to save him from dying. I told him the truth, that I couldn't save him, I couldn't heal, I could only kill.

But since then three significant events have changed who I am. First, my maker, Yaksha, gave me all his blood just before he died, which greatly enhanced every one of my abilities, while adding a few new ones. Second was the infusion of my daughter's blood before she left this world. Kalika was a terrifying being, but she was also a goddess, and when her essence entered me, a part of me opened up to worlds unseen. Finally, when Umara put my soul back in my body, she used a vial of Krishna's blood to complete the process, and after that I no longer had to believe in a spiritual realm, I sensed it in my heart.

As my blood drips onto Mr. Grey's ugly bruise, the swollen tissue immediately absorbs the red fluid as if it were hungry, and a sigh seems to go through the length of his body. Placing my hand on his wrist, I feel for his pulse and sit back and wait.

The transformation comes quick. Within minutes the bruise has shrunk in size and his breathing has deepened and gained strength. His pulse has improved as well. His heart steadies at sixty beats a minute.

"Mr. Grey," I say softly. "Time to open your eyes."

His long brown lashes blink as he looks up at me and smiles. "You didn't kill me, Sita. I'm glad."

"How do you feel?"

He tries to sit up and falls back down. "Weak. Dizzy."

"Do you know who I am?"

"You're the Last Vampire."

"Who told you that?"

"My superiors. They told me about you and Matt. His father was Yaksha, greatest of all the vampires, and his mother was Umara, one of the ancient Telar."

"Impressive. Who are your superiors?"

"That's going to be a problem. I can lie to you or I can

admit that I can't tell you." He pauses. "I'd rather do the latter."

"Are you working for the government?"

"I have nothing to do with the manhunt that's chasing you."

"Then how do you know about the manhunt?"

"My superiors told me about it."

"Is that going to be your answer to every difficult question?"

"To a lot of them."

"Why were you watching the Goodwins?"

"I was there to protect them. And I was hoping you would show up so we could meet."

"What made you think I would show up?"

He hesitates. "The veil."

"How do you know about the veil?"

"It's famous, in certain circles." He pauses. "Will you please not kill me if I tell you that my superiors belong to those circles?"

I sigh. "You're not giving me a lot to work with. My friends don't trust you. Come morning, if all I can tell them is your superiors sent you, they're going to want me to get rid of you. And I mean get rid of you in a permanent sort of way." I pause. "Give me something."

Mr. Grey considers. "Tell Matt and Seymour and Brutran that I can help you guys find the veil."

"You know where it is?"

"I know the next best thing. I know how to call off the manhunt."

"How are you going to do that?"

He winces in pain and closes his eyes. He continues in a quiet voice. "There's a bag I had with me, when I was outside the Goodwins' house. It should still be there. It's near the road, in a bunch of—"

"We found it, we have it."

He's surprised, which is in itself a surprise. Not much seems to startle Mr. Grey. Opening his eyes, he tries again to sit up. "Give it to me. I can help you."

"Tomorrow," I say, pushing him gently down. "The two who attacked the Goodwins cracked your skull. You have a serious concussion. You have to lie still."

He feels his scalp wound. "It was worse earlier. Did you . . . ?"

"Yes. I gave you a few drops of my blood."

He suddenly smiles. "Does that mean we're going steady?"

"You're weird. Has anyone ever told you that?"

"My superiors." His eyes close and his breathing deepens, sleep forcing itself on his beaten body. "Sita," he whispers.

I lean close. "Yes, Mr. Grey?"

"I'm happy to be here . . . with you."

He blacks out and I'm left alone with my thoughts. Rising from the bed, I huddle in a chair in the corner of the room, determined to stay awake to keep an eye on Mr. Grey. I'm not a neurologist but I know enough about head injuries to be concerned. Even with an infusion of my blood there's an excellent chance his concussion could drag him into a coma from which he might never awaken. It's critical I monitor his heartbeat and breathing. I'm exhausted but long ago I learned how to rest without sleeping.

I sit quietly, eyes closed, and think of Krishna's eyes.

Unfortunately, the memories of the Nazis and the war intrude on my meditation. Dark thoughts that would keep any man or woman awake until dawn. The nightmare of Auschwitz: the trainloads of refugees; the screams in the gas showers; the mountains of corpses; the ovens; the stink of burning flesh. It was more than seventy years ago and it still feels like yesterday.

No, I think. I won't sleep tonight.

EIGHT

I have only ten days left, I think miserably. Ten days to rescue Anton Petit, a key leader in the French Resistance, from the Nazis' Gestapo. Ten days to finish mapping the minefields on and off the coast of France. The pressure on me is immense. Yet, ironically, even the leaders of the British and American forces don't realize how much they are depending on me.

Only a mid-level officer on General Eisenhower's staff named Lieutenant Frank Darling knows who I am and *what* I am. It's Frank who's told me that in ten days the massed might of the Allies will attempt to storm Normandy's beaches. Of course, it could be nine days, or eleven or twelve, depending on the weather.

Anton, a dear friend, is key because he's the only member of the French Resistance who has complete knowledge of their plans to disrupt the Nazis prior to and immediately following the invasion. Just his luck that he was captured six hours ago while quietly sipping coffee at a café outside the most famous museum on earth, the Louvre. Anton's casual behavior—I should call it foolhardiness—was typical of him. With the fate of his nation hanging in balance, he screamed at me that he absolutely could not miss his morning coffee and cheese sandwich, before vanishing out the door.

I love Anton, I truly do, but a part of me worries I will kill him when I rescue him. Like many French men he can be terribly stubborn.

Ah, but he's wonderful in bed.

I must keep him alive, I remind myself, even as I stare across the dark cobblestone street at the unimposing three-story building where he is being held captive. I'm in the southwest corner of Paris, on the fringe of the city, studying what used to be an elementary school. What's interesting about the structure is how few of the local population know it's a Gestapo stronghold. A secret entrance, which opens two blocks away, is the reason it has gone overlooked. But the fact it even has such an opening makes me think it was used by French intelligence before the country was overrun.

Whatever, the gray brick wall around the building is tall and I happen to know that its hidden front and back yards are choked with layers of barbed wire. Up top, on the roof, what looks at first glance to be a simple ornamental tower is really a machine-gun nest manned by three Germans. The men are clever and manage to keep themselves, and their .30-caliber weapon, out of sight.

But I know they're there. And I know they'll probably have to die if I'm to enter the building. Yet I'm reluctant to kill them. Eventually their bodies will be found, which will create a fuss, and besides, I've been listening to them while I've been studying the building, and all they seem to care about is their girlfriends back home. Plus they hate Hitler. Every time his name comes up one of them is obliged to fart. They're Nazi soldiers, true, but they're not Gestapo, the secret-police arm of Hitler's insane war machine. I can only assume they're on loan to the Gestapo from some idle division.

Of course, if they were Gestapo, I'd enjoy killing them. I'd probably even drink their blood. It's been a while since I've fed.

I know Anton is being held in the elementary school because Ralph and Harrah Levine, roommates of mine and close friends, saw him being dragged into the building. Yet, despite my supernatural hearing, I can't hear Anton inside. For that matter, I can't hear anybody being tortured, which leads me to believe the building has several deeply buried basements. I shudder to think what's going on in them. Anton used to tell me he didn't fear death, but pain was another matter. Brave men do not necessarily hold up under torture any better than cowards.

I need to get Anton out. Now.

To see the precise extent of the barbed wire, how far it stretches beyond the wall, I'll have to leap to the top of the brick barrier. Chances are I can take a second leap and reach a door of some kind, but there will probably be outside guards, and if I have to stop and deal with them—for even a few seconds—the three men on top will become aware of my presence and open fire. Their bullets don't worry me so much as how I'll be forced to retaliate. Once again, they seem like good old boys, I don't want to send them home to their girls in body bags.

My thoughts turn to the secret entrance two blocks away and I fade back into the night, momentarily leaving the old school alone. A friend in the Resistance told me about the hidden entryway but didn't explain exactly where it was. I'll have to scan every building I run into in a two-block radius, look for signs of a mysterious gate. Anton had said the entrance was accessible by car.

The time is two in the morning and this portion of Paris has a strict curfew. I've searched less than three blocks when I bump into two German soldiers. They're smoking and sharing a bottle of wine on a park bench when I appear, but quickly jump to attention and demand to see my papers. They're impressed by my good looks. One calls me *Fräulein*, the other *Mademoiselle*. Naturally, I speak perfect German and French, and I'm tempted to flirt in their native tongue, but then I'll have more explaining to do. There's no good reason for a blond and blue-eyed Fräulein to be wandering the streets of Paris in the daytime, never mind at night.

They smile as I hand over my Alys Perne passport. The taller of the two men takes it. The short one continues to smile but puts his hand on his handgun. German soldiers can be friendly, especially to a pretty girl, but they are well trained. They may like what they see but they are already suspicious.

"You are out late, Fräulein," the tall one says in decent French.

"I was with a friend. You may know him—General Hans Straffer?"

They both stiffen at the name, exchange a hurried look. "Did the general drop you in this neighborhood?" the tall one asks.

"Yes." I nod down the road. "My apartment is not far. I told him I wanted to stretch before sleeping so he let me out a few blocks away." I pause. "Is there a problem, officers?"

They're not officers but they don't mind the title. Still, they are alert and hastily speak in German to each other, assuming I can't understand what they're saying. The tall one prefers to let me go but the short man wants to call General Straffer to verify my story. His opinion holds sway and the tall one asks if I will accompany them to a nearby "office."

"It was General Straffer's assistant who dropped me here," I say. "I'm afraid the general is asleep now." I add with a wink. "After the night we shared, he must be sleeping very deeply. It would be a mistake to wake him, don't you think?"

The short one wants to know the name of Straffer's assistant. The tall one translates for him.

"Lieutenant Jakob Baum," I say. "You must know the lieutenant. He has that striking mustache and commanding voice. He reminds me of the Führer."

Hitler is not necessarily a favorite of front-line German soldiers, but I have a feeling the short man might respond favorably to the reference. Also, I'm sizing Lieutenant Baum up the same way Straffer's staff has, which I hope will give both men confidence that I'm telling the truth.

Unfortunately, the short man still wants to make a call. He insists I come with them to their nearby office. Office, I think. Christ, there could be a dozen men inside the place, if not a hundred. I have to end this here, in the street, one way or the other. I back up a step, as the short one reaches to take my arm, and let the power of my will enter my voice. I speak in fluent German.

"I am not some whore you can order about in the night," I say. "I am not just a friend of General Straffer, I am his lover. And yes, I know what you are thinking, that he is married and will leave me the moment he leaves Paris, but it is not so. He has given me his word we are to be married come July in Berlin, and he is a man of his word. And he has pledged to protect me from any harm, come what may. Now both of you, stop and think how he will react when I tell him how shabbily you have treated me this night." I pause. "I won't be surprised if you are shot come morning."

My words have a deep impact on the tall man and he immediately starts blubbering his apologies. However, the squat fellow seems immune to the wiles of my voice, which happens now and then. If anything, his suspicions soar and he pulls out his handgun and points it at my head. He speaks to me in barking German, a language that often seems designed for temper tantrums.

"Do not think you can frighten us with your empty threats," he says. "You are in violation of curfew. Your reason for wandering the streets at this time is laughable. If General Straffer really cared for you, he would have made sure you were escorted to your door. I can only assume you are a liar and a secret enemy of the Nazi party. Now turn and walk into that building across the street or else I will shoot you where you stand."

I smile. "Shoot me."

The tall man shakes. "Herr Faber, please put down your gun. I have heard talk Straffer is seeing a blond beauty. This must be her. Her papers are in order. If we upset her—"

"Halt den Mund!" the short one screams. Shut up! "I don't care if she has bewitched the general. There's something strange about her. Her eyes, they are not normal. I don't trust her. We must check out her story."

I nod as the short one speaks. He's highly perceptive. Few humans can tell I'm not human; I'm impressed to meet one who can. However, his unique insight has made it unlikely he will live to see the dawn.

"Shoot," I repeat.

The tall man is a mass of nerves. He is close to tears and I feel sorry for him. In two minutes, the lazy night has transformed into a life-and-death situation. He drops his cigarette and accidentally knocks over their bottle of wine, which he left resting on the bench. The sound of the breaking glass echoes in the night like the sound of snapping nerves. The short one is close to pulling the trigger.

"Fräulein," he warns me as he cocks his weapon.

I take a step closer. The muzzle is inches from my head.

"Shoot," I say again.

The short man grins bitterly. I realize something else about him right then. He should have been Gestapo. He is a true Nazi, a sociopath. Orders aside, he wants to kill me because he enjoys killing.

"*Hündin,*" he says, calling me a bitch.

The man squeezes the trigger.

I instantly reach up and turn his aim on his partner.

The roar of the shot, in the silent night, is deafening. The bullet hits the tall man in the chest and ruptures his heart. He's dead before he hits the ground. The short one stares in shock at the grip I have on his wrist, the pressure I'm applying. The shock changes to desperation as I slowly twist his aim toward his temple.

"*Arschloch,*" I whisper, calling him an asshole, an instant before I slide my hand over his finger and pull the trigger. The bullet cracks open his skull and a glut of dark blood erupts from his mouth. I leap back to avoid being sprayed.

I run away, fast. There's no point in trying to hide the bodies. The streets don't flood with cars searching for me, not that I expect them. Even during the day there are few vehicles on the road. The Nazis have taken away most French driver's licenses. The hometown crowd is reduced to riding mostly bicycles. Only the Germans are allowed to drive freely, and those who have cars are almost always Gestapo.

Yet I'm several blocks distant from my dastardly deed, when I see three black cars suddenly plunge into the street from behind a garage door. The cars appear at a steep angle, as if rising from the deep, and I realize, by sheer accident, that I have discovered the secret entrance to the Gestapo headquarters.

I wait for the posse of cars to vanish and rush beneath the garage door a second before it closes. I expect to confront a handful of guards but find no one. The doorway must be controlled from a distance. I'm alone in a black tunnel that stretches for far longer than the two blocks Anton's friend described. However, I'm certain I'm on the right track.

The dark is an old friend and the tunnel is poorly lit. Running silently along the right wall, I eventually come to a claustrophobic underground cavern jammed with a dozen cars, three tanks, and ten jeeps loaded with high-caliber machine guns. I'm staring at riot control center, and yet, like at the entrance, the area is unguarded. I don't have to stretch my imagination far to realize why.

The Nazis are an arrogant bunch. In their wildest imagination, they can't conceive that a group of Frenchmen might storm their stronghold. I can't wait to share my discovery with Anton's comrades and prove how wrong they are.

Still, Anton remains my priority and I'm relieved, finally, to hear the faint cries of screaming men. The sound is far from pleasant but it tells me my goal is near. Clearly the Gestapo prefer to do their dirty work far underground. I pray they have not reached the point of torture with Anton. He's only been in custody since this morning, and it's generally the Gestapo way to first use gentle persuasion to achieve their goals, never mind that they almost always execute their prisoners when they're done with them.

A single door stands at the far end of the cavern—an unremarkable barrier. Not only is the door made of ordinary wood, it's not even locked. Again, I'm reminded how arrogant the Nazis are. I enter without making a sound.

The screams are suddenly no longer so faint. I find myself standing in a stark hallway with gray metal for walls, and a ceiling so high the mazes of rooms on my left and right are not nearly tall enough to reach it. I take a moment to understand. The individual rooms do not have ceilings, but are exposed to whoever is watching from beyond the metal-plated ceiling.

A wave of uncertainty strikes me. Even if I identify the compartment where Anton is being held, if I burst in and try to remove him by force I'll alert the whole compound. True, so far I have not run into anyone but I know the "eye in the sky" never sleeps. Right now, high above, there are probably several people on duty. It's possible they're watching me. I have to move fast.

To my left, around the corner of the hallway where I stand, I hear an unexpected sound. A female German telling her superior she has to use the restroom. Whoever she is speaking to chuckles and tells her she is going for a smoke, which she knows is forbidden.

I assume that smoking is taboo because of the poor ventilation. The air I breathe stinks of sweat, blood, and pain. Also, it's probable that if the whole Nazi gang smoked while on duty, the stink would reach the streets and alert the French men and woman who innocently stroll past the old elementary school. German culture is a mass of rules—they're a rigid species—but most exist for a reason.

I want the woman, I want her uniform. If I can get to her before the spies above spot me, I should be able to move around freely, if only for a few minutes. Hurrying to the corner, letting my nose be my guide, I pick up a faint smell of urine and feces coming from a nondescript door. Of course the Germans wouldn't have a separate restroom for the ladies. For all I know, the woman I heard is the only female in the compound. I hope that's not the case—it would make my disguise that much less effective.

I try the door, gently, but it's locked. The woman must have wanted privacy. I snap the lock, also gently; it makes a dull, grinding noise. I'm inside in an instant and am grateful to see the restroom, at least, has a ceiling. Three urinals stand on my right, three stalls are on my left. The woman is in the last stall, against the wall, sitting on a toilet with her long skirt intact.

Her boss knows her well; she has come to smoke.

Nazis love to wear black, to instill dread into their enemies, although they occasionally dress their attire up with red and white, like the Nazi flag. However, when they're stationed in occupied territories, the Gestapo usually have on gray-green SS uniforms. Their choice of colors is shrewd. The SS and Gestapo are equally hated, and their uniforms make them impossible to mistake for civilians.

The woman sings softly as she smokes, a French song about a lost lover. I recognize it from the radio and am surprised how pretty her voice is. It's possible at home she's a professional performer. Not that I care. She's not going to leave the restroom alive.

I come at her like a spider dropping from the sky, using the adjoining stall to climb up and over into her cubicle. Her cigarette falls from her dry lips and she tries to cry out, but my palm closes over her mouth as I crouch by her side, my own lips inches from her bulging eyes. I speak in whispered German.

"Please, Fräulein, do not to be afraid. I know I have taken you by surprise and I know it is hard to comprehend my strength. My grip feels like a vise, does it not? Don't worry, you are not imagining it. I'm stronger than a dozen men put together. I was born that way, and I can break your neck in an instant if you refuse to cooperate. Do you understand?"

The woman nods frantically. Fortunately, she's about my size—her uniform should fit. Her hair is short, dark, her eyes brown and teary. Veins pop through the whites. One bursts from the intensity of my stare. Let her feel my fire, I think.

She's a Gestapo officer, in her mid-twenties. On the collar of her coat she wears the rank of lieutenant, which leads me to believe she's witnessed her fair share of torturous interrogations and probably conducted a few. Even though there's terror in her eyes, there's also a deep coldness.

For me, the true mark of the Nazi secret police is their extraordinary lack of empathy. I have met many cruel people in my five thousand years, but I have never met an entire organization that is so consistently evil.

"This morning the Gestapo took a friend of mine into custody," I say. "He was sitting in a café near the Louvre when he was arrested. I suspect he was eating a cheese sandwich on a roll and drinking coffee. This man is a good friend. His name is Anton Petit. Have you heard of him?"

She hesitates, then shakes her head. She is lying.

I smile. "I know he's here. Let me describe him to you. He's tall and thin but strong. He walks like a puppet, like he might fall at any second, but he's fast in a pinch. His hair is black, like his eyes. He's handsome, if you saw him you wouldn't forget." I stop and tighten my grip. Another vein in the whites of her eyes pops and the red spreads over her anxious gaze. I add, "Nod if you intend to tell me where you're holding him."

She struggles to breathe through her nose. The passageway appears slightly clogged; nevertheless, she is hyperventilating and might pass out if she doesn't stop. I pinch her nose shut and speak in her ear.

"I need to know what you know. I'll kill you if you don't talk."

She struggles in my arms for a few seconds, then stops. Her eyes stare at me, pleading. She blinks rapidly as if trying to say yes. I release her nose.

"Good," I say. "Now I'm going to take my hand off your mouth. But I warn you, if you cry out you'll die. Be very certain of this. Don't forget how strong I am. How easy it will be for me to shatter every bone in your neck. Do you understand?"

The woman nods and I remove my hand. She is a mass of nerves. Hanging her head, she immediately breaks into a fit of coughing, and I pat her back helpfully, encouraging her to take deep breaths. It takes her two minutes before she's ready to speak. By then her lit cigarette has filled the stall with smoke and I crush it with my boot.

"Who are you?" she gasps.

"My name is unimportant. My friend Anton is. Tell me, now, is he on this floor? And don't lie to me. I'm as sensitive as I am strong."

Her eyes turn up, as if searching for help, then wander in the direction of the restroom door. Quickly, too fast for her to see, I pinch the flesh of her chin, bringing a smear of blood. I shush her when she goes to cry out.

"Start talking," I say.

She swallows thickly. "If I tell you what you want to know, will you promise to let me live?"

"How many dying Frenchmen have you made that promise to?"

She shakes her head. "I don't do such things. I work in an office with a typewriter. I keep records, I do what I'm told. I never wanted to join the party."

"Why did you?" I ask.

"The war came, I wasn't given a choice. It was either join or become an outcast."

"You didn't have to join the Gestapo to serve your homeland. I live here in Paris, I have seen many of your kind. Yet few are women. You're young for an officer. And officers don't spend their time in an office typing. You must be good at what you do, a bright young woman like you. You must know everything that goes on here." I pause. "Last chance. Tell me what I want to know or die."

She goes to speak, then glances at my hands, the sleek beautiful hands that have no right to be so strong. Her fear seems to crystallize; it appears to give her clarity. Suddenly she understands how close she is to death.

"He is here," she says. "Room six-H."

"I saw a number of rooms coming here. None were labeled. Where is room six-H?"

She stammers. "When I said he's here, I meant he's in the building, one floor up. There are stairs at either end of the hallway. Both lead to his floor. The rooms are clearly marked." She adds, "I can take you there if you wish."

Finally, she's telling the truth.

"Does six-H have an open ceiling like the rooms outside?"

"No, only scum . . . I mean, the Jews are interrogated down here. People we consider important, they are taken upstairs."

"What condition is Anton in?" I ask.

She shrugs. "He's okay. We've only begun his interrogation."

"We? I thought you didn't do such things."

She pales. There's so little blood left in her face I cannot see a juicy spot to bite. Naturally, I wish I had time to drink her blood. I'm thirsty and, besides, I enjoy seeing a Gestapo witch up close as she bleeds to death.

"I wasn't talking about myself," she pleads. "I like the French. I don't want to be here. I'm just obeying orders."

"I've heard that line before. Tell me, what is your name?"

She hesitates. "Rika Schnell."

I lean close. "Do you believe in God, Rika?"

She trembles. "No. Why?"

"I understand your doubts. I think I met him once, long ago, and I still find it hard to believe he exists. But I like to think he does and that he forgives me for what I'm about to do next." I pause. "Close your eyes, Rika, and be still. You won't feel a thing."

She cringes, tears spring from her eyes. "No! Please!"

Her cries, she's too loud. I cannot let her continue.

Reaching out with both hands, one palm beneath her chin, the other on top of her skull, I jerk her head up and around, through a violent half circle. As I promised, every bone in her neck breaks.

Progress, I tell myself. Now I have a uniform and a room number. After changing into Rika's clothes at breakneck speed, I prop up her body in the stall and head for the door, listening closely before stepping into the hallway. I have no intention of trying to pass myself off as Lieutenant Rika Schnell but I'm confident I can appear to be the new girl in town.

There's no one in the hallway. I head back the way I came, searching for the promised stairs, passing two occupied rooms. In the first a German male is grilling a French woman. In the next a man is being pounded with a heavy fist. If not for my fear of being seen from above, I'd put a permanent end to both interrogations. It's hard to walk by and do nothing, but I have to stay focused on Anton.

Ten days until Operation Overlord. Lieutenant Frank Darling—my friend and partner on Eisenhower's staff—has said that's what the Allies are calling the main invasion. Specifically, Frank said, the attack on the Normandy coast is code-named Operation Neptune. I prefer the latter title, probably because I used to live in Rome when the original Neptune was worshipped.

Rome. The thought of the city reminds me of Harrah. My friend and roommate is obsessed with the city. We're close, along with her husband, Ralph, and I have entrusted them with the truth of what I am, and how old I am.

Since I confided in them, Harrah has begged me to tell her stories about ancient Rome. A strict Jew who often behaves like a Catholic—she reads the New Testament as often as the Old—she's also asked me to tell her everything I know about Galilee. But since I never visited the region when Christ was alive—I never heard of him until many years later—I'm unable to satisfy her curiosity.

I reach the stairs and have to force myself to take them one at a time. At the top is another door, but this one leads to a crowded hallway. At least this floor has a reasonable ceiling. My earlier fears were unwarranted—there are numerous female Gestapo. Odd, I think, how I have never seen any on the streets.

I nod to the men who pause to admire me, but keep walking. I see a row of doors marked 1B, 2B, 3B—no *H*s. I must have entered the floor through the wrong door. Yet of the rooms I do pass, prisoners are being beaten and questioned in every one, and to the busy Gestapo, prowling the halls, this all seems quite natural. Inside, my blood boils and so does my hunger for German blood.

Two minutes later I find the corridor for the *H* rooms. Unfortunately, before I reach the sixth door on my left, I'm stopped by a Gestapo major. He's young, his face so stamped with artifice he could be made of wax. Addressing me as Fräulein—not Lieutenant—he steps directly in my path, giving me no choice but to stop. His eyes remind me of gray marbles; they blatantly scan my curves before fixing on my face. Yet when he speaks I sense a keen mind and caution myself not to hurry with this one. His German is clear and precise.

"Your name, please," he says.

I give a warm smile. "Lieutenant Hida Blunt, sir. Thank you for stopping for me. I fear I'm lost. I only just arrived at this facility."

He returns my smile, his lips shining with a thin coat of skin oil. He has just washed and shaved—I smell the soap. He's probably just come on duty. Despite his age, thirty at most, I sense his aura of command, and suspect he is the man in charge.

"Did your commanding officer not show you around?" he asks.

I gesture to his major strip, acting impressed. "I was told by Rika Schnell you are the man in charge."

A brisk nod; he's flattered. "And you wish for your own personal tour?" he asks.

I chuckle softly. "Only when my commander is not on duty and has time."

He checks out my body again, nodding to himself. "At eight in the morning I will breakfast in my office. Feel free to join me."

"Is there a name, at breakfast, that the major prefers to be called?" I ask, letting him know that I know why he wants to meet in private.

He stiffens and I fear I might have gone too far. But his voice betrays no suspicion. He gestures to the people down the hall.

"While I walk these halls you will call me Major Klein. But come breakfast time you may call me Karl."

"Understood, Major Klein."

He waves a hand. "Dismissed."

"Thank you, sir." Stepping around him, I walk directly past 6H and around the corner, feeling his eyes on me the whole time. There I pause, waiting for the sound of his footsteps. He takes a moment before he continues on, a bad sign; he must be thinking, debating. Finally, though, his boot steps are lost among the others.

I return to room 6H and stand near the door. Anton is

inside, I hear his suffering in the ragged rhythm of his breathing. A faint groan escapes my lips and I grimace. His torture is already underway, the Gestapo must be in a hurry. Perhaps other prisoners have pointed the finger at him, told the Nazis of Anton's importance. It would not require a traitor. The Resistance is made up of brave men and women, but contrary to popular belief, every person has their breaking point.

Something Krishna once said comes back to me.

"Pain is pain, death's dearest friend. The reason no man lives without fear."

How true, I think. And how sad that the reverse—"There's no death without life, no pain without birth."—is also true. It does not matter to me that my creator, Yaksha, a demon by birth, said the latter. To me he was agreeing with Krishna. After more than five thousand years a part of me still fears to suffer.

How much better it is to seek revenge.

I knock and step through the door before hearing an answer.

A Gestapo man, his coat off, his shirtsleeves rolled up, stands over Anton, who is chained to a chair that's bolted to the floor. My lover has been stripped naked. Blisters cover his chest, the result of cigarettes extinguished in his flesh. Red welts connect the hideous dots. I need only glance at the car battery on a nearby desk to know their source. An old Nazi favorite—sprinkle the prisoner with water and shock him until he answers, or else faints, whatever comes first. Never mind the blood smeared over Anton's body from a broken nose and twenty missing nails. His tormentor has been most thorough; he has not left a finger or toe untouched.

The Gestapo sees my rank and leaps to attention. "Lieutenant!"

I look down at Anton, who stares up and winces. He's afraid he's hallucinating. He cannot believe I have come to his rescue, although he, too, knows who I am. In a moment of weakness I told him my secret to keep him faithful. Usually, I'm extraordinarily casual when it comes to sex. But something about Anton makes me jealous of other women. When it comes to love, obviously, the years have taught me nothing.

"What have you learned from the prisoner?" I snap.

The Gestapo grins, his dark mustache dripping sweat. He's no Hitler, he's too big and strong, but he gives off the same stink.

"A great deal. He's been most cooperative." He pauses. "But I was told to report my findings to Captain Blanch."

"I'm here on behalf of the captain. Answer my question."

The man gestures to Anton as if he were an object. "We may have struck gold, if what he says is true. As you know, we have learned from other sources that he's important to the Resistance. He may even be one of their leaders. None of this is a surprise. What matters are his connections." He pauses. "I'm convinced he's in direct contact with the British."

"You haven't had him long. What makes you so sure?"

The Nazi's smile widens. "A place he mumbles when he passes out. A name. A date."

"Please, you try my patience. Make your point."

The man stiffens, a flicker of anger passing over his eyes. He hides it quickly. It's clear he wants credit for what he has leached out of Anton.

"Pas de Calais. Operation Overlord. June eighth."

I shake my head as if I'm not impressed, but inside I'm relieved. It's true Anton has revealed the code name; however, he might have done so on purpose. A little truth takes the bitterness from the lies. Despite all he has suffered, Anton has told them exactly what the British would want the Nazis to hear—the wrong location of the invasion. He's also blurted out a false date, although the insanely unpredictable Channel weather might make it correct. No matter, Anton has planted an important false seed.

"Well?" the Nazi says when I don't answer.

"Nothing," I reply, before lashing out with my right hand and striking his left temple. He falls hard to the floor, where he lies unmoving, but he's still alive. Anton blinks as if he's finally waking up.

"Kill him," he says softly in French.

Kissing the top of his head, I kneel beside Anton. I break his wrist and ankle shackles. "No, he lives. We want him to carry your message to his superiors," I say.

Anton's hands are suddenly free and he grabs my hand. "If

you kill me and manage to get out of here alive, the message will carry more weight. That will prove to them that what I knew was dangerous."

"The hell with that. You have done enough for God and country."

Anton frowns. "Please, Sita, that's a British saying. Haven't I been tortured enough?"

Leaning forward, I kiss his lips, tasting his blood. Half his teeth are loose. Most will fall out in the next few days or weeks, if he should get out of here alive.

"You deserve everything they did to you for going to that same café day after day. You must be insane."

A man screams next door and Anton gestures in my direction. "Look who's talking. You might be old but you can still be killed. You should have let me be. There's no way you can get out of here alive, not with me dragging you down."

"Then you had better get to your feet," I say, pulling him up. But he's weaker than I feared and I have to hold him steady. "Quick, take this towel, clean up as best you can. You have to change into the Nazi's uniform."

Anton scowls at the unconscious Gestapo. "It will never work. He's twice my size."

I grab Anton by his chin and gaze into his eyes. "We leave here together or we don't leave here at all. I mean it. Pull yourself together."

He nods but sways in my arms. He gestures for me to let

him sit back down and I let him slip through my arms. He groans in pain as his bare ass hits the seat. At least he takes the towel and begins to wipe his bloody skin.

"I need a minute," he says.

I fear to linger but he's right, he needs time. His ribs are swelling a ghastly blue where he's been repeatedly punched. He might have internal bleeding. Kneeling beside the fallen Gestapo, I begin to undress the man.

"I'll have this uniform off in a minute," I say, my tone encouraging. "Then, while you're dressing, I'll scout out this floor, maybe the floors above. We're pretty far underground."

"You don't know the way out?" he mumbles.

"I don't want to go out the way I came in. The last thing anyone will expect is for us to escape through the front door."

Anton dabs at his bloody nose. "Where are we anyway?"

"Beneath an elementary school at Vigne and Arago."

Anton sighs. "That is where I went to grade school."

Two minutes later I leave Anton and creep back into the hallway and head for a nearby flight of stairs. I go up eight flights before I taste fresh air and know I'm at street level. Fortunately, the stairway is not occupied. The Germans appear to stick to their designated floors while on duty.

A surprise greets me when I return to 6H. Anton is fully dressed and leaning against the wall. He has found a fresh towel and is wiping at his hair.

"Am I leaking?" he asks.

"A little." I take the towel and remove the blood from his ears. I give him another kiss. "If we're stopped, let me do the talking."

He's offended. "My German is as good as yours."

"Not to another German."

"Bastards." He takes a breath and kicks the unconscious man on the floor. "I'll remember this one," he says.

"Let's go." Taking him by the arm I pull him toward the door. Before opening it, I listen for passing boots. It's always boots with the Nazis, never shoes. There's a rare lull outside and I hurry Anton into the hallway, and from there into the stairway.

Anton can stand, he can walk, but he can't climb. Three steps from the bottom and he collapses in my arms. He's still awake but his legs aren't working. I don't have time for a pep talk. Throwing him over my shoulder, I begin the long climb to ground level.

The pressure is intense. Rika's dead body in the rest-room . . . the unconscious Gestapo in room 6H . . . the combination of the two has set a clock ticking inside my head. Anton is right—it's foolish of me to try to rescue him.

Before the advent of modern weapons it wouldn't have mattered. I could storm any fortress without fear. Swords, spears, arrows—none of them could harm me. But bullets fired into my head or heart, grenade shrapnel sprayed in my face, bazooka shells exploding in my back—all these new toys can end my life. And the reality is, I'm not used to having to worry about dying. I'm not used to fear. It's a novel sensation but that does not make it a pleasant one.

"You make an excellent mule," Anton says as we wind up the stairs.

"You calling me a jackass?"

"I'm trying to tell you that I love you."

"That's sweet. Now, we're almost to ground level. Tell me you can stand."

"I can stand," he says.

Once again I smell the fresh air, even hear the birds chirping outside. I have been inside longer than I planned—it must be near dawn. Propping Anton against a wall, I peer out the first-floor door and search for the main entrance. I see it only fifty feet away, but between us and freedom are eight armed guards. Unfortunately, they are spread out, and I estimate I can only take out five or six before the remaining two or three will start shooting.

I quietly close the door and explain the situation to Anton.

"We're screwed," he says.

"Shh! You just told me how great your German is."

"I lied."

"Stay upright, please, act normal," I say, straightening his collar and coat. "I outrank anyone in our path. If they stop and question us, no matter what I say, just keep walking toward the door. All we have to do is get to the street and we'll be safe."

"What if someone sounds the alarm?"

"No one is going to sound the alarm," I say.

Synchronicity sure can be a bitch.

The alarm suddenly goes off.

On the other side of the door, I hear the guards leap to attention and cock their rifles. The front door slams shut and a thick steel bolt is thrown. Throughout the building the alarm brays like a wounded animal. Below us I hear a stampede of boots—more guards preparing to shoot. What the hell, the guards are only half our problem. Every Gestapo officer in the building has a sidearm.

Anton looks at me and shrugs. "I'm not going to tell you I told you so," he says.

"Shut up."

"Do you have a backup plan?"

"Quiet! I'm thinking!" Obviously Anton's interrogator or Rika has been found. Yet the Nazis do not appear to know where we are. People are running left and right but they lack direction. Also, the Gestapo have not sent anyone to reinforce the main entrance. That seems to be a blunder on their part until I remember the three soldiers, and their machine gun, on the roof of the building. Clearly the Germans have faith no one is going to get past them.

However, I see the boys on top as a possible boon.

I grab Anton and throw him back over my shoulder.

"Hey!" he cries as we continue up the stairs. "You're going the wrong way."

"We have friends upstairs. Maybe," I say, taking five steps at a time.

"Why maybe? Are they on our side or not?"

"They're not Gestapo," I say.

Anton is quick. "Interesting."

We run into a single guard on our way to the roof. I knock him out with a stiff blow to the face and take his sidearm and rifle. We pass through an attic loaded with small arms and ammunition. Before we exit into the fresh air, I set Anton down. He insists I give him the rifle.

"I don't have your hands and feet," he says.

"Don't shoot them."

"What if they shoot at us?"

"Shh." I crouch beside the door, open it a crack, peer outside. The three young men have prepped their machine guns and are peering down at the wired yard and brick wall that surround the school. Yet they don't appear to give a damn about the alarm that shakes the rest of the building. They continue to talk about their girls back home.

Anton gives me a look and shrugs. It's up to me, he's saying.

I push the door open and in a single leap I'm standing behind the nearest soldier with my gun pressed to the back of his skull. Bent over the machine gun, the other two have to turn and look up to see me. Their eyes swell in fear and one reaches for his sidearm.

"Easy, boys," I say in German. "No one has to get hurt here. My friend and I—this is my lover, Anton—just want to get out of here alive. But we need your help."

They take time to digest my words. The guy with my gun to his head trembles, and I pat him on the back and tell him to relax. But I do not take the gun away. His buddies stare at me as if I'm some kind of supernatural creature, which is actually pretty perceptive on their part. The one with his finger on the machine gun, which is pointed toward the gate, finally speaks.

"Are you the reason the alarm has sounded?" he asks.

"Yes," I say.

"Are you German?" he asks.

"I'm neither French nor German. But to be honest, I am working with the Allies."

He shakes his head. "Then we can't let you go."

"Why not?" I smile. "I've been listening to you boys talk for some time. I know all you care about is getting home alive to your girls. I know you despise Hitler and all he stands for. Why not let us escape?"

"We'll be punished. Executed," he says.

"Not if you play it right. Off to your left is the facility entrance. It's manned with guards. Off to your right is the gate. It's locked, bolted with a thick board. You have a clear shot at both sites. You can choose your fate."

"I don't understand," the guy says. Although, previously, he was the one who talked the least of the three, it's clear he's their leader. He's a cool customer, he talks as if we're having lunch at a café.

"You can see my friend has been tortured. He's not in good shape. But I'm in incredible shape. I'm probably the greatest athlete you've ever met. In the next two minutes, I'm going to creep down the slope of this roof and leap into the yard. My friend will be on my back. What I need you to do is—when we land—open fire on the entrance. You don't have to kill anyone, just spray the porch with a hundred rounds or so. That will drive back the guards. Then turn your machine gun on the gate. Cut the board to pieces. That way we can run out into the street and escape."

"You have someone waiting for you?" the soldier asks.

"Yes," I lie.

He shakes his head. "It's three floors to the yard. The jump could kill you."

"I've done it before carrying a lot more weight. Please, it's a simple plan and I promise you won't get in trouble. You can always tell your superiors that you saw us rushing toward the entrance before we turned and ran toward the gate. No one will contradict your story because no one will see what really happens. Once you open fire on the entrance, they will all hit the floor and huddle in the corners." I pause. "Do what I say and both of us will win."

"What if we refuse?"

I smile casually and cock my pistol. "I will shoot the three of you in the head. Now. And make no mistake, you will be dead before you can get off a shot. Remember how easily I snuck up on you. I'm faster than I look."

Their leader considers before he looks to his partners, who nod enthusiastically. Still, he is troubled. "I can give you my word we will do what you ask," he says. "But once you leap into the yard, you're at our mercy. We can mow you down in seconds."

"You won't do that," I say.

"Why not?"

"Because you're a man of your word. And I have news for you. The Allies will invade very soon, and Paris will fall in a matter of weeks. The entire Nazi army will be overrun, from the east and west. My friend here, Anton, is a man of great influence. He can help you once the war is over. He may even be able to keep you from being executed."

"That is hard to believe," the German soldier says.

"I won't forget you," Anton says. "Give me your names."

"Think of it as insurance," I say.

After a moment of hesitation, the young men tell us their names and ranks. They are being truthful, and I am hopeful they will keep their end of the bargain. Of course, I can hypnotize all three so they have no choice in the matter, but I prefer their cooperation be genuine. As a sign of good faith, I holster my pistol.

"There," I say. "You can shoot me now if you want. You'll

be a hero to the Gestapo, they might even recommend you for a promotion."

The leader snickers. "Those filthy bastards. Their praise is the last thing we want." The alarm continues to bray. The man peers into the yard. "You had better go. If they don't find you inside, they'll search the streets."

"Thank you." I pat the other two on the back and lean over and kiss their leader on the cheek. "Don't let this war kill you. Stay alive," I tell him.

"You too," he says with feeling.

Anton climbs onto my back. He's reluctant to leave behind his rifle but I insist. Really, what good will it do us? I need both his arms free so he can maintain his grip. Quietly, we begin to move down the steep slope of the roof. The stone tiles, with their swabs of old cement, provide plenty of footholds. Behind us, I hear the boys talking to one another in excited whispers, obviously impressed with my strength and balance. When I reach the edge of the roof, I turn back and give them a sign.

Their leader opens fire on the main entrance. The high-caliber bullets explode on the bricks, around the wooden door, like a circle of fireworks. Through the windows, I can see the interior guards diving for cover. The jump is nothing to me. I leap off the building and land like a cat from a tree.

Anton groans in pain but is full of praise. "How come you never show me such tricks when we make love?" he asks sweetly.

"You would not survive," I say, watching as our partners swivel the turret toward the gate and again open fire. The leader has sharp aim. The board that holds the gate closed splinters under the hail of bullets. Five seconds and it cracks and falls to the ground. Of course I could have broken it myself, but this way, with the constant hail of fire, the interior guards keep their heads down. Also, the open gate is one less obstacle to slow us down.

The machine gun falls silent. The deal is done.

I run into the street and around the corner of the wall. Again, Anton groans in pain but I don't slow down until we're a mile from the compound, which takes me less than a minute to cover. There I let Anton rest in a dark alleyway. I feel his ribs, find several broken, and listen for any sounds of internal bleeding. His spleen and liver are both swollen but I don't hear any squirting veins. I'm confident he'll survive and share the good news with him.

"I may live but I won't be happy," he complains.

I chuckle. "Why not?"

He shakes his head. "Do you know what a woman like you does to a man's ego? I should be the one rescuing you. Instead, you shame me. I'll never be able to get it up around you ever again."

"No problem. General Straffer can keep me satisfied."

Anton scowls. "Tell me the truth, seriously, Sita, are you sleeping with that pig?"

"No, Anton, I swear it," I lie, draping him in my arms and lips. "He uses me as an ornament, nothing else. All he wants is young boys."

"To each his own," Anton replies, believing me because it's easier to do so. I feel no guilt about my lies or being unfaithful. My love for Anton is not affected by who else I spread my legs for, and besides, the Resistance needs the information only the general can provide.

I let Anton recover for another ten minutes before I hoist him on my back and take off at a faster clip. This time I move so quickly I'm not visible to anyone patrolling the streets. They feel a brush of air, perhaps sense the heat of my breath, nothing more. My goal is a small apartment not far from Pont Royal and the Seine River, the home of Harrah and Ralph Levine.

Later, I stand holding Anton upright and knock softly on their door. By this time light has begun to glow in the east, and the birds are singing as the stars fade. Wars come and go, but Mother Nature couldn't care less about mankind's foolishness.

Harrah is quick to answer, her lovable face bursting into relief at the sight of both of us. She is still dressed in her day clothes. She has been up all night, bless her heart, waiting.

"Sita!" she cries. "You did it!"

"Why does she get all the credit?" Anton complains.

"Come, come, inside." Harrah gestures as I help Anton over the meager threshold. We are fortunate Harrah is, like her husband, a doctor and has a secret store of medicine and surgical equipment in the spare bedroom, where I often stay. Ralph, a highly trained surgeon, comes out of the bathroom in a robe, his eyes sleepy. But he brightens when he sees Anton and helps me stretch him out on my bed. Ralph's eyes are a warm gray, the same color as his hair, which sticks off the sides of his head like the wings of a bird. Before the war, he often wore a *kippa* just to cover his bald spot. Now, when he goes out, along with his wife, he's forced to wear the Star of David on his arm.

Ralph knows of my diagnostic abilities and looks to me before examining Anton. I tell him what I know and he frowns as he pokes his patient's nose and mouth.

"Your smile is never going to be the same," Ralph tells him.

"Give me morphine, let me worry about it tomorrow," Anton pleads. Ralph looks to me for my opinion.

I nod. "They beat him a long time. Let him rest. I'll stay with him."

Ralph reaches for a small vial and a fresh syringe. "Good, I'll sleep easier knowing you're near. But watch his breathing, wake me if it gets too slow."

I stand. "I promise. I'll be back in a few minutes."

In the kitchen I find Harrah making tea. We sit together at the small table and sip the hot chamomile. She offers me honey, which I love, and sweet shortbread cookies. She made them herself—she loves to bake. I wonder where she got the sugar but don't ask. Probably a grateful patient.

Prior to the war, they lived only four blocks away, but it

was in a lush flat that overlooked the Seine. But the Germans took their place, they took their doctor's office and its surgical room. Now they work out of a small neighborhood clinic during the day, while treating men and women at night who fight for the Resistance. They seldom get any rest.

Harrah's brown hair, which was long and curly before the war, has now been cut short and has streaks of gray. Short hair is best, she told me. It makes her less conspicuous to the Gestapo. Not that anything helps with that star on her sleeve, I think.

It's a thought I keep to myself. Despite our bond, there is much I don't share with them. Naturally, they have both heard the stories of the camps in the east, the whispered rumors, where Jews go and never return. Yet, for such a pragmatic couple, they don't want to talk about it. "No, it can't be," they tell me. "The Germans are not animals."

God, how I wish I could ram the facts Straffer tells me down their throats. Tales of terror that haunt even the general. If I could frighten them enough, they might take me up on my offer to relocate them to Spain. But they don't want to hear. They say they will never leave Paris, not while they are still needed.

What can I do? I'm strong, but long ago I learned the one person I can't protect a person from is themselves.

"Tell me how you got him out," Harrah asks, excited. She loves to hear about my exploits against the Nazis. I try to give her a brief rundown but she insists I share every detail. Her face glowing, she claps when I get to the part about the three young men stuffed in their machine-gun nest.

"How did you know they wouldn't shoot you in the back?" she asks.

"They had good hearts. I could see it."

She nods. "I told you they are not all bad."

I stop with my cup to my lips. She is talking to herself again, I know. "They trusted me, even though I threatened them," I say. "But the Gestapo, the SS, they live in constant fear of their leaders. It drives them mad."

"More reason to be grateful for Operation Overlord." Like most French, Harrah has more faith in the Americans than the British, perhaps because the English have already come and gone. I find the attitude unfair but amusing. However, it pains me that she refuses to face the dark side of the invasion.

"Invading the coast will cost the Allies a lot of men," I say. "But they know there's no going back. I've told you I've met Eisenhower and Patton. Incredible leaders. Even if Rommel pulls all his tanks to the west, he won't be able to keep their armies pinned down. They hit the flatlands ten miles from the coast and they'll be in Paris in days."

"Good," Harrah says.

"In the long run. But when the Allies begin to storm toward Paris, the Germans will step up the pace of their Final Solution. They will begin to round up—"

"Please, Sita, you know I hate that term. It's just something Straffer told you to impress you. I've never heard another German say the same two words in the same sentence." She pauses. "It doesn't exist."

I speak carefully. "Do the Jews they've rounded up still exist?"

Harrah stands and goes to the sink, where she pours out her tea before reaching for the pot to fill a fresh cup. She won't look at me. Staring east, out the window at the growing light, she speaks in a hurt tone.

"Help is finally coming, it's a good thing. I have faith."

"So do I," I say quietly.

She glances my way. "We have Anton back. It's been a good night. We should be celebrating."

I stand and cross the room and hug her tightly. She is so many things to me: a friend, a counselor, most of all, perhaps, an inspiration. I admire her faith and don't think it's a coincidence that such a precious gift has been passed down to her.

I try to tell her these things and she lets me talk a few minutes before she puts a finger to my lips. "This isn't like you, Sita. One moment you're warning me and the next it's as if you're asking for advice."

I stare at her. At times like this I swear I see *my* mother in her face, although I have only the faintest memory of the woman. "I've been having bad dreams," I say.

"You? You hardly sleep."

"I have them. Then, when I awaken, I feel something coming. An evil—I can't explain it."

Suddenly she is worried about me, when it should be the reverse. "How can I help?"

My eyes are also drawn to the window, to the glow that warms the horizon. "Ralph has given Anton a shot of morphine. I should stay with him, watch his breathing. But I was wondering . . . can I hold it?"

She doesn't hesitate. "Of course."

I hold up a hand. "You don't have to say yes. If there are rules against me—"

She clasps my hand. "You sat with Krishna. How could there be any rule against you holding it?"

I nod, grateful, although I feel like hanging my head in shame. She would never say but I have put her on the spot. "Thank you," I reply.

Harrah fetches the worn leather bag from the closet of her bedroom and hands it to me. With two quick kisses, she retires to sleep beside her husband. I finish my tea before entering my room. It comforts me to watch the sun rise.

Inside the bedroom Anton snores on his back. The window is open and I fix the blankets so he won't catch cold. But I don't lie down beside him. Not tonight, I think.

The brown bag opens with a long zipper. Inside, the veil is carefully wrapped in layers of white silk. The veil itself is made of the same material. The threads are coarse, by modern standards, and the color has yellowed with age. Nevertheless, it's impossible for me to imagine any other two thousand-year-old cloth that could have survived the centuries. Long ago, the veil should have disintegrated into dust and vanished from the face of the earth.

The face of . . .

The words . . . naturally the words come to me. For I cannot look at the stained outline of the face on the veil without feeling as if someone dear to me is looking back. Yet the face is not that of Krishna. When we met, he had no trace of a beard, and if there was sorrow in his expression, then it was lost in the joy that always seemed to swim below the surface in his presence.

Still, this face, the one the legends say belongs to Christ, seems familiar to me. I don't know why. I never met the man. I have stared at the veil before, with Harrah, trying to fathom its mysterious effect on me. But it's always left me more confused than ever.

Now, though, as I study it beneath the orange rays of the fresh sun, I see things I missed before. There's tremendous sorrow in the image, as if the man really was burdened with the weight of so many others' sins. Yet there is joy, yes, happiness, despite the obvious suffering. It's in his eyes. They are enchanting. I see a fullness that is somehow empty, or a love perfectly balanced by the freedom of dispassion.

I see more, I realize, but not the complete truth.

The veil is still a paradox to me.

Perhaps it will always be that way.

I don't care. I press it to my heart and feel fatigue overwhelm me. Sitting upright in the chair will not prevent the inevitable. Soon I'll pass out, and I know I will dream. But tonight, or this morning, the nightmare will not touch me. The darkness won't come. I hold the veil in my fingers and yet it is I who feel safe in his hands.

NINE

*I*n the morning the others awaken before Mr. Grey, who continues to sleep deeply. We meet for breakfast at a different restaurant from the night before, but stay near the motel.

At some point during the night I must have dozed, but the sleep was not restful. Memories of the Nazis haunt me. Our pursuit of the veil has stirred them up, no surprise, and I suspect they won't stop until we find it.

Still, my fatigue does not inhibit my hunger. Matt has bacon and eggs and coffee. Brutran and Jolie share a tall stack of pancakes. Seymour has yogurt and toast, and I eat a bowl of fruit and a blueberry muffin. We all steal pieces of Matt's bacon, the smell is hard to resist. I end up asking our waitress for a side order, which I split with Seymour.

The main topics are, of course, Mrs. Sarah Goodwin and

Mr. Grey. I give the gang a full account of what Matt and I saw at the house. Seymour and Brutran are immediately suspicious of Mr. Grey.

"It sounds like he fed you a story," Seymour says. "He's outside their house, spying on them so he can protect them. Then, when they're attacked, he rushes inside without a weapon and is immediately smacked on the head and loses consciousness. That's pretty convenient."

"He never said he wasn't armed," I reply. "He might have had a gun and lost it in the fight."

"If he had a gun he should have used it," Brutran says. "He should have been able to take the Goodwins' assailants by surprise. If it was me, I would have killed them both."

"That goes without saying," Seymour mutters.

"We don't know if he surprised them," I say. "For all we know, they might have been waiting for him. They might have tortured the Goodwins after."

"You sound like you're protecting the guy," Matt says.

"You were there. With his dying breath, Roger Goodwin told us how hard Mr. Grey fought to save them. That counts for something."

"Goodwin was barely alive when you found him," Brutran says.

"He knew what he was saying," I reply.

Brutran is unconvinced. "For all we know this could be a setup. The people who are after us could have planted Mr. Grey there."

"If they did, they left him in lousy shape," I say. "If I hadn't treated him, he'd be dead by now."

"So they made it look convincing," Brutran says. "The bottom line remains the same. The guy refuses to explain why he was there and who he's working for. When someone is hiding something, there's always a reason, and it's seldom innocent." She pauses. "Was it wise to leave him alone?"

"He has a cracked skull. He's not going anywhere," I say.

"He just has to lift the phone, Sita," Brutran says.

I have yet to tell them about Mr. Grey's offer to stop the manhunt. The guy said so many strange things, I don't want to stack the deck any more against him. Except for me, no one at the table trusts him. And I'm going purely by instinct. Logically, the others are right, nothing he's told us adds up.

"Let's leave Mr. Grey aside for the moment and focus on Sarah," I say. "We have to find her and fast. If they tortured her last night in her own home, think what they'll do to her in their space."

"But where do we look?" Seymour says. "What leads do we have?"

"We have the business card Shanti had hidden beside the Goodwins' photograph," Matt says. "The card belongs to Michael Larson. He works for Pointe, Wolf, & Larson. That's a New York City law firm. The card has another number scribbled on the back. Could be his cell number. Brutran has researched the firm. It's small but prestigious. It represents celebrities and rich people."

"Does the place have a specialty?" Seymour asks.

"It's an all-purpose firm," Brutran says. "It has defense lawyers, investment lawyers, tax lawyers. From what I've been able to discover, Larson seems to be what we in the business world call a closer. He brings in new clients and fixes their problems when they arise. He's best known for putting powerful people together."

"Has the IIC used his firm in the past?" Seymour asks.

"No. But I've heard about them through the grapevine."

"What have you heard?" I ask.

Brutran shrugs. "That they're top-notch."

"Is the firm rich?" Matt asks.

"They're doing extremely well," Brutran says, her eyes flickering to her laptop. She's never without an Internet connection.

"What is it?" I ask.

"This is pure speculation, but you all know that at IIC we mastered the art of hiding assets. From what I'm picking up on Larson's law firm, I'm confident they're hiding the bulk of their money."

"How can you tell?" Seymour asks.

"I would need a day to answer that question. Trust me."

"Anything else unusual about them?" I ask.

Brutran continues to study her laptop. "They're funneling

a lot of their assets through Swiss banks. And they . . . this is very odd."

"What?" Matt says.

"Well, we were talking about their client list. The famous and the rich. I just hacked into another one of their files. They're doing a lot of work with the Pentagon."

"What kind of work?" Matt asks.

"I don't know, it's odd. They can't be fulfilling defense contracts. Yet, they have an extensive list of Pentagon contacts. A few are generals and admirals. From what I can see, they talk almost every day."

"Does the firm bill the Pentagon?" Matt asks.

Brutran frowns. "Not exactly. If I didn't know better, I'd swear they were handling their money."

"The House and the Senate handle the Pentagon's money," Matt says.

"That's what they taught us in high school," Brutran says.

"This gets more interesting all the time," Seymour says.

"We need to talk to this Michael Larson," I say. "Today, in person."

"Sounds like a plan," Brutran says. "Except for the small problem of the manhunt. We're fortunate they haven't zeroed in on us here. I can only assume that's because we've stopped moving. But we board a plane or a train and we'll be spotted."

I stand. "Maybe not. I have to check on something."

Matt jumps up. "What?"

I turn toward the door. "Finish your breakfast. I'll call you in a few minutes."

I return to my motel room and find Mr. Grey propped up in bed and working on my laptop. He has plugged it into the metal box we found near the Goodwins' house. He smiles when he sees me.

"No breakfast?" he says. "I was hoping you would bring something."

I step near the bed so I can see what he's working on. The screen is half filled with binary code, the rest with assembler language, a computer code that most operating systems are written in. He would have to know a lot about computers to understand the language.

"I can bring you whatever you like," I say. "After you tell me what you're doing."

"I'm disabling the program that's pestering you," he says.

"You know about that. Your superiors told you about that."

"I told you last night I could call off the manhunt on you guys. At least for a while."

I sit beside him. "Are you having any luck?"

"I've already managed to remove your names from the FBI's Ten Most Wanted. I've also disrupted the flow of e-mails about you and your friends between the FBI, the CIA, the NSA, the Pentagon, Homeland, and the White House."

"Does this mean we're free to move about?"

"For the time being. These agencies haven't stopped talking

to each other. But the leaders in each agency are probably beginning to question the original orders to hunt you down. That's the good news. The bad news is that the program's sophisticated. It knows it's been attacked and it's adapting to meet the attack. I can't say for sure how long your freedom of movement will last."

"Estimate," I say.

"Two days. But I might be able to extend that time. I have to wait and see how the program reacts. But I can tell you already it's annoyed."

"The program has emotions?"

Mr. Grey chuckles. His color is better, his energy, but I can tell he needs more time in bed. His cracked cranial bones are not going to knit together in less than a day. However, we probably have no choice; we're going to have to take him with us.

"It behaves like it does," he says.

"What is your opinion of the person or people who created it?"

He stares at me. "You want to know if they're human."

"Yes."

"I've never met anyone who wasn't. Except you."

"But?"

He sighs. "I've also never encountered this style of programming. When I said it's sophisticated I was understating the facts. The mind that created this computer code is beyond normal human intelligence."

"Yet you are able to disrupt it. You must be pretty smart."

Mr. Grey bows his head. "I appreciate the compliment."

"Actually, it was more of a question. But you know that, because you're so smart." I pause. "My friends are restless. They want me to get rid of you."

"They won't feel that way once you've shown them how helpful I can be."

"On the contrary, your computer wizardry will just make them more suspicious. I'm trying to help you here, Mr. Grey." I pause. "What's your first name?"

He hesitates. "Mr. Grey is fine. Go on."

"See. That's just another example of how peculiar you are. You appear out of nowhere. You almost get yourself killed try-ing to defend people you don't know. You know Matt and I are not human. You pick up my laptop and defeat a program the best minds in the world have not been able to scratch—in less than an hour. And you don't even have a first name!"

"You look beautiful when you're mad."

I stand and pace. "I'm not mad, not at you. I'm frustrated. There's a difference."

"In either case it's nice to have you on my side."

I stop and shake my fists at him. "How do you know I'm on your side?"

He shrugs. "I'd be dead if you weren't."

I sit and take his hand. "You might die even with me in your corner. I'm strong, but I can't hold back Matt once he makes up his mind. Please, you have to start talking. Who are you? Where are you from?"

"I can't tell you."

"Why not?"

"It's against the rules."

"Whose rules?"

"The rules set down by my superiors."

"Who are your superiors?"

"I can't tell you."

"Besides being a genius, do you have any supernatural powers?"

"No."

"How do you know so much about our situation?"

"I only know what my superiors have told me." He adds, "And what I have researched."

"Are you here to help us?"

"Yes." He pauses. "And myself. And others."

"Who are these others?"

"Just other people. Everyone."

"Everyone in the world?"

"Yes."

"Who is the priority? You or us?"

He squeezes my hand. "You are my priority, Sita."

He is telling the truth. Indeed, he's going to great lengths not to lie. Unfortunately, his truth is so full of holes it will never fly with the others.

I really am worried about Matt. I can feel the gears grinding inside whenever we talk about Mr. Grey. When in doubt, Matt prefers to reduce the variables in any given situation to a minimum. It's his way of playing it safe. Something his father taught him. Yaksha used to think along similar lines.

I squeeze Mr. Grey's hand and stand. "We need to fly to New York right now. Is it safe for us to take a commercial flight?"

"Probably. But a private plane would be safer."

"Can you travel?"

"Sure."

"No, this is a serious question. Have you been out of bed yet?"

"I got up to use the bathroom and picked up your laptop."

"Did you feel dizzy? Tell me the truth."

"I did have to hold on to the walls for support."

I shake my head. "Then you should remain here. You need to heal."

He sits. "No, I can't stay here. I mean, my reason for coming is to be with you, to help you. I know my physical condition is delicate. But all you have to do is get me on a plane. I can sleep there, I can rest and recover."

"We don't know what we're going to run into in New York. It could be dangerous."

"I accept that. When I was chosen for this mission, I accepted that I could . . ." Realizing his mistake, he doesn't finish.

"Why do you call this a mission?"

He shakes his head, he doesn't speak.

I sigh. "You were going to say that you accepted that you might die."

"Yes."

"I don't want you to die, Mr. Grey."

He brightens. "Really?"

"I don't know why but I like you. You remind me of Seymour."

"I was told about him. I can't wait to meet him."

"Don't be in such a hurry. He's one of the people who wants to get rid of you. In fact, except for me and Jolie, everyone wants to get rid of you. You don't have a lot of support in this mission of yours."

"You're enough." He struggles to get out of bed. "I should get dressed. Where are my clothes?"

I gently push him back down. "Your clothes are covered in blood. I'll get you some new ones right now. It won't take me long. And I'll explain to the others that you've given us some breathing room. Are you absolutely sure Brutran will be able to verify what you've done?"

"She'll be able to verify the effect of what I've done. But not how I did it."

"When we're on the road, can you explain to her how you did it?"

"No."

"Because your superiors won't let you?"

"No. Because she wouldn't understand what I did."

I'm forced to laugh. "You know, if you didn't have such a serious concussion and hadn't been covered in blood when I found you, I'd swear you were a robot."

He smiles. "Careful, Sita. You're getting warm."

TEN

To put it mildly, Brutran doesn't believe in Mr. Grey's incredible accomplishment. Even when she checks the FBI Ten Most Wanted list and finds our names removed, she remains unconvinced. She's of the opinion the Cradle's program has erased us from their files in an attempt to bring us out in the open.

Yet the deeper Brutran digs, the more puzzled she grows. She admits she can't locate any chatter about us in the various intelligence agencies. She also says her bank accounts—her personal accounts and those connected to IIC—have been released.

"It makes no sense the program would give us access to our money," she says.

"Then you believe him?" I ask.

Brutran glances at Mr. Grey napping on my bed. He

was asleep when we returned to the room and our talking hasn't awakened him—another sign of how severe his injuries are.

"I wouldn't go that far," Brutran says. "How did he work this miracle?"

"He says it's too complicated for us to understand."

"He gives an answer like that and you trust the guy?"

"'Trust' is a relative term. I trust he means well and that he can help us. That doesn't mean I'm not suspicious that he may be a pawn for people who do not mean us well." I pause. "Rent a private jet. I want it fueled and ready for liftoff from the Raleigh airport in one hour."

"Are we going top-of-the-line again?" Brutran asks, turning back to her laptop.

"Leave that up to Matt," I say.

Ninety minutes later we're in the air, in another Gulfstream IV. Matt likes what he likes, there's no arguing with him. He also considers himself our team leader. This time, when he demands to know what happened in the war, he refuses to take no for an answer. He orders Seymour to the cockpit and locks the three of us inside.

If Brutran is upset about being left out, she doesn't complain. To my surprise, she ends up taking a liking to Mr. Grey. It might be his amazing intellect. Brutran grills him about computers, hardware and software, and whatever he says keeps her enthralled. I can only assume he's able to show off and still not give away any trade secrets—info his elusive "superiors" deem confidential.

At the same time Mr. Grey bonds with Jolie. Except when Seymour plays with her—chess or checkers or any number of board games—the child has been relatively quiet since we blew up IIC's headquarters. At first I assumed it was the trauma of losing her old playmates, but now I'm not so sure. Jolie remains a mystery to me.

"The Veil of Veronica," Matt says when the three of us are seated in the cockpit. "Talk."

"How long until New York?" I ask.

"Ninety minutes," Matt says.

"I can't tell my story that fast. You need to hear some background first." I pause. "Is that acceptable?"

Seymour shrugs. "As long as you're not stalling."

"I want to get this off my chest. It's been bothering me."

"I know. Last night you were talking in your sleep," Matt says. "I heard you through the wall."

I'm insulted. "I don't talk in my sleep."

"How would you know?" Seymour asks.

"I wasn't sleeping. I was watching Mr. Grey."

Matt snorts. "You were sound asleep for over two hours, and several times during that period you whispered the names Anton and Himmler."

I'm dumbfounded. "So I *was* having a nightmare."

"See this as therapy," Seymour says, patting my leg.

I tell them the first part of my tale, how I worked for the Resistance, how I broke Anton out of the Gestapo prison, and how that intense night ended with me wrapped in the mysterious comfort of the veil. By the time I finish, Matt has begun our descent and the New York City skyline is visible up ahead.

Matt is not satisfied with what I've revealed. He wants to know more and I promise I'll give it to him when we have another stretch of time alone. On the other hand, Seymour is like a kid salivating over the start of a great book or movie. He relishes every detail I provided.

"So the face on the veil looks like our idea of how Christ looks?" he asks.

"Basically, although the veil might have inspired the look. The Vatican had the veil for approximately two centuries during the Middle Ages. Many of the paintings of Christ that were created during that period copied the veil."

Seymour leans forward. "Do you think it's genuine?"

I hesitate. "Yes."

"Because of how it made you feel when you gazed at it? Held it?"

Seymour always cuts to the heart of the matter. "That morning in Ralph and Harrah's flat, when she left me alone with it, I felt a special energy radiating from it."

"Was there another time that it helped you?" Matt asks.

I nod. "I'll talk about that later, when we have time."

To spare Mr. Grey a long car ride, we land at LaGuardia

instead of JFK. The airport is close to Manhattan and we're checked into the Marriott in Times Square within forty minutes of touchdown.

I can't stop worrying about Sarah Goodwin. But if I'm honest with myself, I'm just as concerned about the veil. It seems insane to equate a human life with an artifact but such is the spell it's cast over me. Yet I have not thought about the veil in years. Something has stirred a sleeping desire for it inside me.

Mr. Grey lies down as soon as we reach our three-bedroom suite. He insists he accompany us to our showdown with Michael Larson but it's a feeble offer. He knows he's in no shape for what might turn out to be a nasty confrontation. In reality, I prefer Matt and I go alone. Protecting the others is always a balancing act.

"I didn't fly here to babysit," Seymour complains.

"Yes, you did," Brutran says. "You have to stay and watch Jolie." She turns to me. "Larson's a high-priced lawyer in the business world. That's a world I know better than you or Matt. I should go with you."

I shrug. "If you can help us kidnap him without creating a scene, it's fine with me."

"Is kidnapping necessary?" she asks.

"We can't interrogate him in his office," Matt says.

"Use force and you'll alert our enemy that we're in the city," Brutran says. She has a point, and I would agree with her if I didn't feel so rushed.

"Every minute we leave Sarah in their hands decreases our chances of saving her life," I say.

"And recovering the veil," Seymour adds, reading my mind.

Brutran appears to reconsider. "Their security is probably multilayered. There could be shooting. Maybe I should stay here with my daughter."

It's the first time I've seen Brutran act fearful. Does she know more about the law firm than she lets on? Probably—she never shows all her cards.

"If we manage a clean snatch, we'll bring him back here," Matt says.

"Get his computer," Brutran says, glancing at Mr. Grey. "Our new friend can hack into it in minutes."

"Glad to be of service," Mr. Grey says, yawning, ready for another nap.

Matt and I walk to Rockefeller Center—it's only a few blocks. The day is hot and humid, the streets crowded. Once there we stop at a neighboring store and upgrade our clothes. Matt buys a pair of gray slacks, a black Armani sport coat. He forgoes the tie. I pick out a white pantsuit and a red blouse that goes beautifully with the tailored jacket. Matt says I look hot, and I have to admit he can still get my heart pounding. I don't know why I don't just sleep with him and get it over with.

Of course, I've had sex with him before, just not in this body. And that's the problem, I doubt a casual romp will help me get over anything. It's as if the memories I collected while living in Teri's body have never left. I recall a thousand precious moments they shared. Worse, I feel the longing she always felt for him. Teri saw him as far above her, often imagined herself to be a desolate moon circling a warm planet. She only felt full when she was near him.

"You look very handsome," I say, fixing his collar. He stops me, his hands touching mine.

"You're nervous," he says.

"I'm not nervous."

"Do you have a plan?"

"I assumed you had one," I say.

He releases my hand. "Does it bother you I've taken control?"

"Someone had to."

"You didn't answer my question."

"Just don't kill Mr. Grey without asking my permission."

"Why are you so taken by the guy?"

"He's a mystery. What girl can resist a mystery?"

"He's a liar. Someone sent him to us to get something from us."

"He's useful. Until he proves otherwise, I want him alive."

"Fair enough." We resume our walk toward the law firm. "Who are we pretending to be?" he asks.

"Let's be a couple of rich Germans looking to invest in cutting-edge technology. Whatever he brings up, we steer the conversation toward the defense industry. I want to see how he reacts when we bring up the Pentagon and weapons contracts."

"Why German?" Matt asks.

"Just a hunch. How's your accent?"

"Better than Anton's." Matt pauses. "You loved him, didn't you?"

"Yes."

"May I ask what became of him?"

"He's part of my story. I'll tell you later." I pause. "Did I really say his name in my sleep?"

"Yes."

"Why were you listening so closely?"

"I was awake, I hear everything. Like you."

"You were playing that bloody game. Why do you keep at it?"

"Why are you so afraid of it?"

"John told us to stay away from it. I trust his instincts."

"You're no different from me. You listen to his advice when it suits you. Besides, he's never said what's so dangerous about it."

"You and Seymour examined it. You warned me that it's loaded with subliminal images and voice messages. It gave Seymour a headache. The Cradle programmed the damn thing."

"You fear it's brainwashing the youth of the world?"

"I do. It's addictive. I just have to look at you to see how much."

Matt shakes his head. "Its subliminal tricks don't work once you're aware of them. They wouldn't affect me anyway." He pauses. "You have nothing to worry about."

"At least tell me why you keep playing it."

"I want to win."

"Win what?"

He speaks seriously. "The Cradle put the game out there for a reason. I need to find out why."

"The Cradle wrote what they channeled. They had no will of their own."

"Same difference. Whoever was behind them had a reason for putting it on the Internet." Matt pauses. "Maybe it was to lead us all straight to hell."

"I never said Tarana is *the* devil."

"But you think he is *a* devil?"

"Yes."

"Are you sure he's the one we're fighting?"

I hesitate. "It's something evil."

The entrance to Pointe, Wolf, & Larson is located on the fifty-second floor of the GE Building. They appear to rent out three floors. Their lobby has wonderfully comfortable chairs and sofas. We act as a married couple: Mr. and Mrs. Straffer. It pleases me to use the general's name. When the receptionist says she can find no record of our appointment with Michael Larson, we tell her in our thick accents that we have flown all the way from Hamburg to see him. I put a spark in my gaze and she quickly fumbles for the phone and demands that Mr. Larson meet us in the lobby. He appears within a minute.

I study his reaction. He does not recognize us.

"How can I help you folks?" he asks after shaking the hands of "Lara" and "Karl." Michael Larson is big, six-four, forty, with the body of a jock gone soft. His shoulders are broad; he still has a full head of black hair, but he's developed a stoop and needs at least a hundred morning crunches to combat the caloric tire growing beneath his belt. His smile is automatic, joyless. He gives off the stress of someone with too many responsibilities. The bags under his eyes say he's not sleeping well.

But does he have nightmares?

Or is he just a typical overworked New York lawyer?

"We would prefer to talk about money matters in the privacy of your office," Matt says.

"Of course. Please," Larson says, gesturing us deeper into the maze of the firm. It appears larger than Brutran let on. We follow our host to a corner office with a view of Central Park. The man is not just a partner, he has his name on the firm's front door. Forty seems young to have risen so high. Matt appears to read my mind and points that out to Larson. But Matt makes it a compliment. He can be charming when he wishes.

"I work hard," Larson admits. "Probably too many hours, if you were to ask my ex-wife and daughter."

"How old is your daughter?" I ask.

"Nicole will be five next week."

"Wish her happy birthday for me," I say.

"Thank you."

"It must be hard not seeing Nicole after work every day," I say.

Larson nods, glancing at a picture of his daughter on his desk. Her eyes shine; she looks like a happy child. "It's been an adjustment. But it's a cutthroat business. There's no middle ground, not if I'm to give my clients a hundred percent."

"How would you describe your business?" Matt asks. "Or should I say, your expertise?"

Larson pauses, his antennae rising. I find his paranoia interesting. "You must know something about my background to fly so far to meet," he says.

Matt shrugs. "We are rich. We heard you can make us richer."

"What sort of money are we talking about?"

"A billion euros. Maybe two," Matt says. "Maybe more if we like the results. Where would you start if we agreed to invest with your firm?"

Larson flashes his usual smile. "That would be entirely up to you. But with such a sum we could play in a number of courts. It's all a question of risk versus reward. You know that. How exotic do you wish to get?"

"Cutting-edge weapon systems," I jump in. The words make Larson blink. I have hit a nerve.

"Pardon me?" he says quickly.

"We have heard through the grapevine that your firm has close ties to the Pentagon," Matt says. "That you can predict who is going to receive the next major contracts."

Larson loses his smile. He studies us both. "Who told you this?"

"Friends," Matt says casually. "Don't be alarmed. We understand the relationships are very private. But they are the reason we're here. Today, this afternoon, we are willing to write you a large check if you could just enlighten us a little on what you do with the Pentagon."

Larson stands. We have only arrived but we have already crossed the line. The man is visibly upset. His words gush from his mouth.

"I'm sorry you have come so far for no reason. The information you have been fed is false. I know of no one at this firm who is working with the Pentagon. And to imply that we have influence over who is awarded specific defense contracts is not only outrageous, it's . . . a dangerous accusation. Now, please, I have clients I have to attend to. If you would be so kind as to leave. It's possible we can talk at another time. This afternoon is just too busy for me."

Matt and I exchange a look and get to our feet.

"Heard enough?" he asks me.

"Enough to know he's a keeper," I say.

Moving fast—not so fast that Larson cannot follow him

but faster than any human being can move—Matt circles the desk and clamps the lawyer's arms behind his back with one hand. With his other hand Matt presses a .40-caliber Glock in Larson's back. I reach down and pick up the lawyer's laptop. It sits square in the center of his desk and I have a feeling it's loaded with all kinds of goodies.

"Please listen, Mr. Larson," Matt says in a persuasive tone. "The three of us are going to walk out of here together. You will lead the way. I won't touch you, but I will have this gun you feel right now against your spine pointed at your back. If you make even the slightest move to alert your security, I'll shoot you."

"Our guards will stop you," he gasps.

"They might if you warn them. But then you will be dead and their help will not help you," Matt says.

"Cooperate and you'll be okay," I say. "I promise."

"But why are you doing this? What do you want?"

"We will explain everything after we leave here," Matt says. "Do we have an understanding?"

Larson breathes rapidly. "Yes, yes. I'll go with you."

We leave his office. I walk beside Mr. Larson, Matt stays directly behind us. If the firm is equipped with cameras, I can't see or hear them. Yet Brutran told us they would have heavy security. It makes me wonder. Also, Mr. Larson isn't as tense as he should be when he tells the receptionist he's taking us to lunch. He's accepted that he's a hostage rather quickly, which tells me he thinks he's going to be rescued. Soon.

Out in the street, we hail a taxi, put Mr. Larson in the front seat. Matt looks to me. "Where do you want to go?" he asks.

There's no way I'm taking him to where the others are staying. Even though I've frisked Larson and found no tracking device, he continues to act like he's being followed.

"Let's get a room at the Hilton," I say.

It's a short ride; the taxi lets us out a few minutes later. Matt gives him a generous tip. He keeps Larson outside while I go in and get us a room. I actually get three adjoining rooms on the top floor. We lead the lawyer to the center one and force him to sit in a chair in the middle of the suite. Larson is fearful but confident. It's obvious he's waiting for help.

"How much time do we have?" I ask as I sit on the bed in front of him. Matt paces behind Larson.

"I don't understand," Larson says.

"We want to know when to expect your friends," I say.

He shakes his head. "I didn't alert anyone, I swear it."

"No lies," Matt says, pulling a switchblade from his pocket, releasing the steel razor, and yanking Larson's right arm into the air. He practically pulls the limb from its socket. Holding the blade tight to Larson's thumb, drawing a steady drip of blood, he speaks in a no-nonsense tone. "Tell us what we want to know or you'll never be able to lift up Nicole again."

"Who are you people?" he cries, finally getting a glimpse of how strong Matt is.

"Friends of Shanti Garuda," I say.

Larson goes to deny knowing her but his eyes stray to his bleeding thumb and the blade Matt has pressed against it. He's in pain, he struggles to breathe. Matt has lifted him several inches off his chair. I lean forward.

"But before I ask about Shanti, tell us how long before your buddies arrive?" I ask.

He trembles. "Not long. Ten, fifteen minutes."

"How are they tracking you?"

"A microchip. It's implanted in my arm. It can't be removed."

"Want to bet?" Matt says, waving the knife in front of Larson's eyes.

"They already know where I am," he pleads. "They're assembling their team. If you want to live you should leave now."

"Don't worry about us," I say. "Now tell me about your relationship with Shanti?"

"I hardly knew her. My boss ordered me to help her with whatever she needed, no questions asked. She'd call, usually to get information on people. That's not my expertise. I'd pass the task on to private eyes. Then I'd get back to her with what they found out."

"How long did this go on?" I ask.

"Two years."

"Did you ever meet her in person?"

"No."

"Who did she ask about?"

"Plenty of people. I don't know their names offhand."

"Did she ever ask about Roger and Sarah Goodwin?" I ask.

"A few days ago. She wanted to know where they lived, who their parents were, their grandparents. The information was important to her. She told me she needed to know fast."

"Did you get her the information?" I ask.

"Partly. Two days ago I discovered where they live. Somewhere in North Carolina. I gave her the address."

"Did she ask about a veil?"

Larson trembles. "She did. She wanted to know if they had it. She said it was some kind of artifact. I told her I couldn't find anything about it."

"Did she give the veil a name?"

"She just said it was very old and it belonged to the Goodwin family. No, wait, she said at first it belonged to the Levine family."

"Did she tell you why she wanted it?"

"I didn't ask. I mean, who would want a veil?"

"How did she treat you on the phone?"

"What do you mean?"

"Was she rude? Polite? Professional?"

Larson hesitates. "She was cold. She made me feel, I don't know, dirty. I hated getting her calls."

"Do you know why your boss had your firm work for her?"

"He said it was because of the money. But . . . I don't know."

"What made you doubt him?" I ask.

"Hey, I'm cooperating," Larson complains to Matt. "Let go of my arm. I'm not going anywhere."

Matt glances at me and I nod. Matt takes a step back but keeps his knife handy. "Answer," I say.

"He told me once that she was connected to the big deals we had with the Pentagon. It was weird but he acted like she was more important than any general I spoke to." Larson shakes his head. "She sounded like a young girl."

"A cold young girl," I say.

Larson nods. "Yeah. It sounds like you know her."

"I did. She's no longer with us." I let the information sink in before continuing. "How does your law firm help the Pentagon?"

"We arrange financing for black projects."

"Projects the House and Senate know nothing about?"

"Projects the president knows nothing about."

Larson sounds as if he's boasting. Everyone likes to be in on the skinny. "What type of projects are these?" I ask.

He holds out his hands as if he's afraid Matt's going to react to his answer. "The details were all hush-hush. I was never told anything directly. Just heard hints when the partners had a few too many after work. A lot of it sounded like science fiction. They said the air force is building aircraft that can take off from a runway and fly right into orbit." He stops. "They said the whole shuttle program, all of NASA, was just a front to what was really going on."

"Did you believe them?" Matt interrupts. Nothing has gotten a reaction out of him until this. He practically breathes down Larson's neck. By this time the lawyer is terrified of him.

"It was hard to believe," Larson says. "But the money they're spending out there, it's crazy. It would fund a mission to Mars."

"Where is 'out there'?" Matt demands.

"Somewhere in Nevada. I'm not sure where."

"What kind of aircraft are we—" Matt begins.

"Quiet!" I interrupt, listening to what's going on down the hall. The elevator has halted on our floor. It's being held open. Ten very silent and well-trained men are exiting it. One guy is in charge. He leads them in our direction, slowly, cautiously. I hear automatic rifles bump against clips of ammo, concussion grenades, Kevlar vests. I *smell* the weapons. They're worse than a SWAT team, more like a small army.

Matt hears them as well. He hurries to the window, throws it open, pokes his head out, searching up and down. "The roof is near," he tells me.

"Good." I pick up Larson's laptop and speak to the lawyer. "I have excellent hearing, Michael. I've been listening to the men who are outside. They have orders to shoot to kill, and whoever's behind them has told them that you're a hundred percent expendable. This is no joke. They are not going to give us a chance to surrender. They are going to hit this room with everything they've got and pick up the pieces of bloody flesh afterwards. Your only chance to live is to come with us."

It is all too much for Larson. "Where are you going?" he mumbles.

"Up to the roof," I say. "After that we improvise. This is your one chance. Do you want to come with us?"

"How are you going to get on the roof?"

"Sita. We have to go," Matt says, already climbing onto the edge of the open window. I kneel beside Larson.

"I don't have time to explain," I say. "But you've cooperated with us. I don't think you're a bad man. I don't think you even know what you're involved in. For that reason, I promise I will protect you, but I can only do so if you let me. You have to come with me now."

He shakes his head. "I can't. My daughter, I can't . . ."

I stand over him. "You'll never see Nicole again if you don't come with us."

He's too frightened, and I pity him. He starts to cry but makes no effort to follow. Unfortunately, Matt is right, we're out of time. I pat Larson on the back and tell him I'm sorry. Throwing off my freshly bought coat, I run to the window.

Matt has already leapt for the roof. He hangs on the edge of it for a second and then swings his body upward. A moment later he is standing up and looking down at me. I toss him Larson's laptop and he catches it with one hand.

"Hurry, Sita," he says.

Heights do not frighten me, of course. And this move is nothing compared to leaping out of one jet and grabbing onto another. Still, I'm careful to balance on the ledge before I spring upward. I fly past the roof and Matt catches me on the way down. For a moment he holds me in his arms and I swear he's going to kiss me. But the moment passes.

We hurry to the door of a maintenance shed, past a row of giant air-sucking fans that feed the hotel's ventilation system, and I reach for the knob. Matt stops me.

"Wait," he says.

Seconds later there's a loud blast and the glass from the window we just exited explodes outward. A barrage of machine-gun fire follows. I was right, we were never going to be given a chance to surrender. Which means the people behind the security team that's chasing us knows we can't be taken alive.

"Larson's dead," I say.

"You gave him a chance," Matt says.

"Not really."

"He wasn't as innocent as he acted."

"His daughter won't care about that." I sigh. "Let's get out of here."

Our escape is uneventful. We take the stairs down five floors and catch the elevator to the ground level. The explosion and spray of glass have attracted New York's Finest. A herd of cops has gathered outside the Hilton. They do not appear to be looking for us. Holding hands, behaving like newlyweds on our honeymoon, Matt and I walk into the street and catch a taxi back to the Marriott.

I sit alone with Mr. Grey in his bedroom. He is propped up in bed and has eaten for the first time—half a chicken sandwich—but his color is not good. I try to persuade him to go to a hospital.

"I'll take you myself," I say.

He smiles but shakes his head. "It's a kind offer but I'm not going to leave you."

"What if I agree to stay with you?" I ask.

"Then I'd know you were lying. You have to find Sarah Goodwin. You don't have time to sit around a hospital and wait until I get better. Besides, I'm pretty sure you're going to need my help to locate her."

"Did you get anything out of Larson's computer?" I ask. Mr. Grey has barely had a chance to study the lawyer's files, while he was eating, but I know the man works fast. He's already hooked the laptop up to his metal box.

"I got a shock. I haven't been able to access his files. Not yet."

"You'll break in, I have confidence in you."

"You don't understand, Sita. It should have taken me seconds to hack through his firewall. But I can tell already it's going to be a difficult task. Whoever set up his software is as clever as the people who wrote the code for the Internet program that's been causing you guys so much grief."

"You're saying there's a connection?"

"Yes."

"Larson admitted to doing plenty of work for the Pentagon."

"The Pentagon—at least the Pentagon the world knows— does not have the wherewithal to create such software."

"But you do?"

"Yes."

"Excuse me, Mr. Grey, but is it possible that your superiors are in cahoots with the people Larson and his firm are working with?"

"Put that idea out of your head. It's utterly impossible."

"But you can't tell me why?"

"I'm sorry." He sets aside his food tray and turns back to Larson's laptop. "He spoke of a complex in Nevada?"

"Yes." I pause. "Area Fifty-One is in Nevada. You must have heard of it?"

"Sure. It's where the government is supposed to do much of their top-secret research. However, if that was the place Larson was referring to, why didn't he call it that?"

"I wondered that myself. It was like he didn't know the name of the place. But it's odd that he should have such sophisticated software on his computer."

"Not really. I suspect he had no idea what kind of operating system was protecting his files. You said he is a lawyer. Did he act like a lawyer?"

"Yes. He was quick to talk once Matt threatened him. I

don't think he lied to us. And I don't think he had any deep loyalties to his firm." I pause. "I'm almost positive he's dead."

Mr. Grey glances at me. "You tried to save him."

"Not hard enough. We were rushed, and he was convinced the people coming to get us would save him." I shrug. "But they blew up the room."

"Meaning they knew you guys would be hard to take alive. That tells us something."

"Us? Feeling like one of the team, are we?"

He looks hurt. "I thought you'd already accepted me."

"I have. The others still don't trust you."

"Another reason I can't go to the hospital. I have to stay and prove my worth."

I reach over and put my palm on his forehead. "You have a fever."

"I might have picked up a bug."

"Bullshit. I'm worried you've bruised your brain. There could be internal swelling. That's nothing to fool with."

"If that was the case I wouldn't be up and walking around."

"For your information you can hardly walk. Plus I gave you a few drops of my blood. It might be masking your symptoms. You have to go to the hospital." I stand. "I'm not going to take no for an answer anymore. I'm calling for an ambulance."

He reaches out and grabs my hand. "Don't, Sita, please. I can't leave you. I can't explain but I need you to trust me. I have to stay with you."

"What if you die?"

"Then it was meant to be."

I go to snap at him, impatient, but there is something in his voice that makes me stop. He does not say the old phrase in a casual way. He means it, or rather, he knows that's the case. I sit back down, still holding on to his hand.

"Will you ever tell me who you are?" I ask.

"You'll figure it out."

"You're an alien. You've been sent to earth to screw with our minds."

He lays his head back on the pillows. "I wish there were supernatural beings like that. Who would come to earth and make everything all better."

"With three hundred billion stars in the Milky Way, there must be someone out there who is curious about us. Perhaps someone billions of years more evolved than us."

"So advanced they would seem like gods to us?" he says.

"Yes."

He stares at me a long time. "You're thinking of Krishna."

I hesitate. "I think about him a lot. But no, I was thinking about something else. A weird dream I had once."

"A dream?"

"Yeah, a dream. Why do you act so surprised?"

"Seymour wrote about it in his story about your life. Those people you met in the desert. The ones who sent you back in time, to the Middle Ages. To an earlier version of yourself."

I don't know why but my face is suddenly flush with blood as if I'm embarrassed. It's worse, actually, I feel as if he is talking openly about a deeply buried sin of mine.

"What Seymour wrote in his book never really happened," I say. "He was picking up my thoughts, it's true, but certain events got distorted in the process. I never went back in time."

"How can you be sure?"

"Now you're being silly." I let go of his hand and step to the window. Thirty stories below us Times Square bustles with crowds looking for a place to eat lunch. It's one forty-five in the afternoon. I add, "If you did happen to read that part of Seymour's story, then you know I died at the end. So you can see what I mean by distortion."

"I'm not saying he got everything a hundred percent accurate. But the idea that you were able to go into the past, your past, and correct a mistake was fascinating. Something must have inspired it."

"I just told you, it was a dream."

"How did he latch onto your dream?"

"I don't know, how did he write about me at all? We're close, it's a mystery. Let's leave it at that, all right?"

"You brought it up. I assumed you wanted to talk about it." He pauses. "I'm sorry if I upset you."

I turn back to him. "The only thing that upsets me right now is your fever. It's getting worse. At the hospital they can do a procedure where they drill a tiny hole in your skull. It sounds gruesome but it's a relatively simple operation. If your brain is bruised and swelling, then it gives the buildup of fluid a way out. It acts as an escape valve. They do it and I bet that your fever goes away in thirty minutes."

"You're not used to taking no for an answer, are you?"

"No."

He sighs. "We don't have time."

I stride back to the bed. "I know that. But we have nowhere to go right now. So the hospital can't hurt."

"We don't know *exactly* where to go. But there's a good chance this Nevada facility is crucial. Why don't we head that way while I try to break into Larson's computer?"

"Sarah Goodwin was abducted on the East Coast. I'm not willing to leave this part of the country until I'm convinced she's elsewhere." I pause. "How long do you think it's going to take you to hack into that thing?"

Mr. Grey considers. "If I haven't broken through the firewall in four hours, I'm not going to break in."

I pick up his food tray and step toward the door. "I'll let you work. If you suddenly feel like you're dying, give a holler."

"Wait, Sita?"

I stop at the door. "Yes?"

"When you and Matt were gone, I overheard Seymour and Brutran talking about a small book you recovered at the Goodwins' house. I got the impression it's about the Veil of Veronica."

"That's right. But I haven't been able to read it. It's in code."

"Would you like me to take a look at it?"

"Sure. But I can't distract you from Larson's computer. You know finding Sarah has to be our top priority."

"What if there's something in the book that helps us locate her?"

"It's centuries old. I hardly think it can help us—"

He interrupts. "We don't know what can help. Leave me the book." He pauses. "As long as you trust me with it."

"I trust you more than you know." Pulling the book from my back pocket, I hand it over. Once more I step toward the door. "If you should translate it, don't show it to anyone except me. But if for any reason I'm not here, keep it to yourself."

"Are you planning a small trip?"

I open the door. "Work," I say.

In the main living space that connects our suites, I hand the half-finished glass of milk Mr. Grey was drinking to Brutran. I'm careful to only touch the top rim and the bottom, and I set it down on a table beside her.

"What's this?" she asks. Jolie lies on the sofa beside her, reading a book. I can hear Seymour napping in his room and Matt is playing that damn game in the other.

"This glass has Mr. Grey's fingerprints all over it. Do whatever it is you have to do but get it dusted. You should have no trouble getting a clear specimen. Then contact whoever it is who handles your dirty work at the FBI and run the finger-print through their database."

"You want Mr. Grey's real name and address," Brutran says.

"I want it fast."

Brutran carefully lifts the glass and stands. "There's a store near here where I can buy what I need. Can you watch Jolie?"

"It will be my pleasure." I take Brutran's place on the sofa and watch as she empties the milk into the sink, then collects her bag. I add, "Talk to me when you return."

"You're not working with Matt?" she asks.

I give her a look. I don't have to say anything.

ELEVEN

*T*hree hours later I land at Logan International Airport in Boston. I took our Gulfstream IV. I enjoyed the time alone in the air. In my pocket is a paper that contains a faxed photograph of a driver's license that belongs to Joel Grey of 14742 Barney Drive, Lawrence, Massachusetts. Birth date November 12, 1975.

The picture is black-and-white, but there's no mistaking that it's our mysterious Mr. Grey—who, damn my romantic nature, suddenly feels a lot less special somehow. The guy is married to Kathleen Grey, and Brutran's FBI contact says he has two children: a son and a daughter, ten-year-old Hal and six-month-old Sally.

The FBI contact said Kathleen Grey filed a missing-person report two months ago. It concerned her husband.

Two months ago. That was when my world suddenly

turned upside down. When the Telar sent an assassin to my country home in Missouri to dispose of me. The same day Lisa showed up at my door with her boyfriend and told me about Brutran's IIC. Since then my life has been a living hell.

Sounds like I haven't been alone.

I have the Greys' phone number but don't call ahead. After renting a car at the airport, I drive straight to the Grey residence. I don't know what kind of career Kathleen has but I'm hoping with such a young child she'll be at home. Who knows, maybe anxiously waiting by the phone for word on her missing husband.

The residence is a modest three-bedroom redbrick affair that looks like it was built before homes cost more than a year's salary. It sits at the end of a cozy cul-de-sac but the lawn needs cutting and the windows are dusty and I can't help but figure it's because the man of the house has been gone longer than expected. Knocking at the door, I pray Mr. Grey didn't tell his wife he was going around the block to get a carton of milk or diapers for the baby just before he disappeared.

Kathleen Grey answers with Sally Grey in her hands. She peeks through the curtains before opening the door. I suppose I look harmless enough. Go figure, I've killed more people than anyone alive, except perhaps whoever happens to be currently occupying the White House.

"Kathleen Grey? I'm Special Agent Lara Wine," I say, flashing an FBI badge Brutran was thoughtful enough to pick up for me while she was busy tracking down Mr. Grey's fingerprints. "Have I caught you at a bad time?" I ask.

She pales at my question, and with her sunny hair and tan complexion the lack of color is a stretch. My unexpected appearance frightens her. She assumes I bring bad news. However, the woman isn't weak. She's not the type to turn heads but I can see the strength in her face and the intelligence behind her hazel eyes.

"Is this about Joel?" she asks anxiously.

"Please, relax, I'm not a bearer of bad news. I should have called ahead, I'm sorry. But I thought maybe we should talk in person. May I come in?"

"Do you know Agent David Waters?" she asks. Smart girl. She's testing me; there is no such agent.

"I haven't heard of him. Does he work out of the downtown office?"

"Excuse me, I probably got his name wrong." She opens the door. "Come in. Please forgive the mess. I was just about to give my daughter a bath."

We sit across from each other in the living room. Sally bounces on her mother's knee and stares at me with eyes so big and green she looks like she was born with the luck of the Irish. Boston should be a perfect place for her to grow up.

I dive right in. "May I ask a few questions about Joel before I bring you up to date?" I say.

Kathleen is puzzled. "Questions? I told the police and the FBI everything I know."

"I'm sure you did. But to be frank, I'm not familiar with all the ins and outs of your husband's case. My link to Mr. Grey is via another case. I'll explain in a minute. But first, give me a quick rundown on when and where Joel disappeared?"

"You want me to start at the beginning?"

"If it would not be too much trouble."

"It happened two months ago. He left one morning to go to work but he never arrived. They called to ask where he was and I told them I had no idea. But I knew he hadn't been in an accident. He stopped at the bank and withdrew ten thousand dollars before he disappeared."

"Was ten thousand all of your savings?"

"It was less than five percent. Joel would never have left us destitute. He's a very loving father and husband."

"But you haven't heard from him since?"

"Not a word."

"Did the police find his car?"

"You should read his file. They found it at Logan Airport, the keys in the glove compartment."

"Before he disappeared, did he give any sign of being troubled?"

She hesitates. "No."

"Any indication at all?" I persist.

"Well, Joel has always loved astronomy. Since he was a kid, he'd spend months grinding mirrors for homemade telescopes. There are eight of them in our garage. The two big ones—he loved nothing more than to load them in our SUV with my son and drive out to the country where the city lights don't block out the stars. Sometimes he'd stay out all night. Hal, that's our boy, he'd end up sleeping in the SUV."

"Did he suddenly give up this hobby before he vanished?"

"On the contrary. Instead of once a month, he began to go out three times a week. Only he stopped taking Hal. It was strange. How can you stare at the sky so much? I used to ask him that but he'd change the subject. It got so I thought he was seeing another woman. So I followed him one night."

"And?"

She shrugs. "He drove out of town to a secluded spot near Destiny and set up his telescopes. He spent the whole time staring through the lens at the sky." She pauses. "But I did notice one thing that was odd."

"What?"

"He never took any pictures. That's Joel's great love—to do time-lapse photography. But he never even set up his camera equipment."

"What does your husband do for a living?" I ask.

"He works as a systems analyst for General Electric."

"He oversees a team of computer programmers?"

"That's right. He's good at his job."

"Mrs. Grey, how good is he? What I'm asking is—do his fellow employees consider him a genius?"

"He's not like that. He's a competent programmer himself but his greatest skill is managing a team. Getting everyone to work together. You can ask anyone at GE, they all love him." She stops to wipe away a tear. "He's real lovable."

"Is this your husband?" Taking out my cell phone, I show her a photograph I secretly took of Joel while we were flying from Raleigh to New York City. Mrs. Grey's eyes go wide.

"That's him! But he's so skinny. And pale. Where did you get this picture? He looks like he's on a plane."

"It was taken by a partner of mine who's investigating a corrupt law firm. I can't give you as much detail as I would like. It's a high-level case. We're working on the assumption these people are forcing your husband to work with them."

"Doing what?" she demands, getting emotional.

"We're not sure. But it would seem to have something to do with computers. That's why I asked if he had any unusual talents." I pause. "But you say he doesn't."

"Except for being a major daydreamer, he's a normal guy. But look, you can't leave me hanging like this. Tell me who these people are. When this picture was taken. And . . . is Joel all right!"

"As far as we can tell, he's perfectly fine."

"But if your partner got close enough to Joel to take his picture, how come he didn't rescue him?"

"At the time, my partner didn't know that your husband

was a missing person. You see, he's working undercover with these people. It's a top-secret project. Your local FBI office doesn't even know we've spotted Joel."

Mrs. Grey frowns. "Why not?"

"My partner and I bumped into him by accident. Our focus lies with the people who've abducted him. But I'm here for two reasons. First, to reassure you that your husband is alive and well. Second, to get an idea of his background so I can better understand how he's helping this group."

And if that isn't the understatement of the year, I don't know what is. Mrs. Grey acts confused. She should be in my shoes. I don't know what I expected to discover when Brutran located Mr. Grey's address, but I sure as hell didn't expect to find that our resident magician is a totally normal guy.

"When can you rescue him?" Mrs. Grey snaps.

"We have to do so carefully. I think it will be soon."

"That's not good enough. Get him out today. You obviously know where he is." She stops. "Where is he?"

"I'm afraid that information is confidential."

"Why?"

"Because my superiors say so. Look, I'm on your side. I didn't have to come here today. My partner told me not to. The best thing we—"

"And I'm supposed to be grateful?" she interrupts.

I lower my gaze. I hate lying to her. "I'm sorry, honestly I am. But the best thing you can do to help Joel right now is to tell me anything else unusual that happened with him before he disappeared."

She's angry; she doesn't want to help me. But it's clear my question troubles her. "He told me he was having weird dreams," she says finally.

"Dreams about what?"

"He never said. But they'd wake him at night. He got up a lot."

"Were they nightmares? Did he act scared?"

Mrs. Grey wipes away another tear and strokes her daughter's head. "I don't know how he felt. He'd just sit by the window and stare out at the sky."

I leave them. But outside, before getting in my car, I run into ten-year-old Hal Grey. He appears to be returning from a friend's house. Except for having a thick head of black hair and the glow of youth, he's the spitting image of his father. He doesn't act afraid of me. I introduce myself as an FBI agent in search of his father, and we talk out in the street.

"Your mom told me how much you enjoyed going out to the country with your dad. Did you like looking at the stars through the telescopes?"

Hal shrugs. "It was all right. My dad liked it. Taking pictures was more fun. He used to let me load the film and set the timer."

"The timer?"

"The starlight takes time to leave a mark on negatives.

That's why you need a motor to drive the telescopes. So they stay pointed at the same star."

"It sounds like he taught you a rare skill. He must be very proud of you."

Hal shrugs again. "I suppose."

"You're not sure?"

Anger flashes in the boy's eyes. "Well, he left, didn't he? He couldn't have cared that much about us."

"Hal, do you know why he left?"

The boy hesitates. "No."

"Do you think it had something to do with his trips to the country?"

"Sure. I mean, he knew it was dangerous to stare too long at certain stars. He warned me about it." The boy stops to think. "But he broke his own rules. One night, it was like his eyeball got glued to the lens. I shook him and cried for him to stop but he kept right on looking. I finally got so tired I went to sleep in the car."

"Did he apologize to you in the morning?"

"Sort of. But he told me I couldn't come with him anymore. That made me mad."

"Hal, was he was trying to protect you from certain stars?"

"I just told you he was. Didn't you hear me?"

"I heard you, I'm just not sure I understood you. Why was it dangerous to stare at certain stars for too long? What would happen?"

Hal looks away from me, down the street, and his eyes take on a dreamy gaze. "My dad said certain stars could take you to strange places, far away, and it could be hard to get back. He knew what he was talking about. One night I stared at Sirius too long. That's the brightest star in the sky. It's pretty, blue-white, but after a while it grabbed me and wouldn't let go."

"What did you feel when it got ahold of you?"

Hal turns back to me. "Like I was in outer space, and happy, real happy. I didn't want to come back but my dad forced me to."

"That's very interesting," I say.

When I return to the hotel, I find a meeting starting in Mr. Grey's room. He continues to lie propped up in bed and if anything he looks worse than when I left. But he has broken into Larson's laptop and wants to share with us what he's found.

"His computer was a disappointment," he says. "He has notes on his conversations with Shanti but they're not particularly interesting. Basically she had him tracking down info on various people, and moving money around for other people, who we can assume she was working with. The names mean nothing to me but you can read the file if you want and see if you recognize anyone." Mr. Grey stops to take a drink of water. I have not seen him drink anything else. He continues, "Fortunately, I was able to use Larson's laptop to break into the rest of the firm's system."

"How did you do that?" Brutran asks.

"I'll explain the technical aspects later. Right now I can confirm that the Pentagon is definitely building aircraft that can fly faster and higher than anything the public knows about. The research and development, as well as the construction, are taking place at a complex facility located on Nellis Air Force Base. That's near Groom Lake in southern Nevada. The Pentagon's code name for the facility is 'the Can.'"

"Isn't Area Fifty-One located at Nellis?" Seymour asks. "The place UFO researchers are always talking about?"

"Yeah," I say, thinking. "It's curious how the Pentagon often calls Area Fifty-One 'the Box.' Now you say they have a Can."

"*The* Can," Mr. Grey says. "The same files mention Area Fifty-One. It's clear it's a different spot. The Can is closer to the lake, for one thing."

"Can we break into the Can?" Seymour asks.

"From what I found on the law firm's files, the public can't get within thirty miles of the place. Nellis is one of the most secure spots on the earth. Even a vampire would have trouble getting inside."

"Tell us more about the aircraft they're building," Matt says. The others don't notice but a fire has ignited deep in his eyes. For him, this is what he's been waiting for. I wonder why.

"There are several designs," Mr. Grey says. "One looks like the stealth bomber. Another resembles the shuttle, although it definitely takes off on a runway, not atop a stack of rockets. What appears to be the most advanced design is saucer-shaped."

"That might explain ten million UFO sightings," Seymour says. He's jazzed to hear the news. He loves anything sci-fi. He's going to want to go to Nevada as much as Matt.

"Do the files explain how their propulsion system works?" Matt asks.

"Not directly," Mr. Grey says. "And I would have been surprised if the law firm had such top-secret files. But I can say the craft are definitely not burning jet or rocket fuel. However, and you might find this strange, the law firm has recently routed in excess of five hundred million dollars to buy as much mercury as is available on the open market—'without raising any suspicions.' The last line is a quote from a file belonging to the boss of Larson's firm—Urs Pointe."

The mention of mercury gives me a chill.

It reminds me of my time in Auschwitz.

Why? I don't know, or I can't remember.

"Is that German?" Seymour asks, giving me a look. He knows the information has startled me.

"German or Swiss," Matt replies quickly, obviously wanting to stay on topic. He paces at the bottom of Mr. Grey's bed. "Do the files say how they're using the mercury?"

"I'm pretty sure it's a crucial part of the propulsion system. It says so in the man's notes."

Seymour shakes his head. "Mercury isn't that expensive. Why would they need so much?"

"Maybe they're building a lot of ships," Mr. Grey says.

"We're calling them ships now?" Brutran says.

Mr. Grey smiles. "Actually, the Pentagon already has a nickname for them. They call them Fastwalkers."

"Do you know the maximum speed of these Fastwalkers?" Matt asks.

"I know what you're asking," Mr. Grey says. "You want to know if the Fastwalkers can travel faster than the speed of light. The answer is no, although I don't know exactly how fast they go. But it's clear from the files that none of the ships have left the solar system."

"Makes sense," Seymour says. "The nearest star, Alpha Centauri, is four-point-three light years away. Even if these Fastwalkers could get close to light speed, who would want to take more than four years to make one trip?"

"It would depend on what was at the end of the trip," Matt says.

"Have the Fastwalkers explored all the planets in our solar system?" Brutran asks.

Mr. Grey nods. "They're out there poking around."

"Does NASA know about the ships?" Brutran asks.

"It looks like they've never heard of them," Mr. Grey says.

"NASA. 'Need Another Shuttle, Asshole,'" Seymour says,

before everyone turns and stares at him. He shrugs. "Just a joke I read online."

"It's fascinating the government has gone to so much trouble to keep NASA propped up when it's nothing but a front," Brutran says.

"You find it fascinating," Seymour says. "I think it's disgusting."

"It helps keep the Fastwalker program secret," Brutran says.

"Why is it secret?" I complain. "Why is the American government so paranoid about admitting they have such fast ships?"

"Think, Sita, Seymour," Brutran says. "How nervous this technology would make the Russians and the Chinese, never mind every Arab nation on earth. If I were in charge of the program, I'd keep it under wraps."

"Is there anything else you can tell us about this program?" Matt asks.

Mr. Grey considers. "There's a theme that runs through all the notes and conversations I've studied. It's clear there's immense pressure on the scientists in charge of the Fastwalker program to break the speed-of-light barrier."

"Why?" Matt asks.

"I don't know," Mr. Grey says.

Seymour glances at me before asking Mr. Grey, "Do you know the names of these scientists?"

"They're not listed in the law firm's files."

"Why do you ask?" Matt says to Seymour.

"After World War Two, NASA got most of its rocket scientists from Germany. Hell, the head of the Apollo Program was Wernher von Braun. They were all Nazis that NASA cleaned up and turned into American heroes." Seymour adds, "Sort of like rewriting history."

"I don't see how any of this is relevant," Brutran says.

Seymour goes to reply but stops. He sees the look in my eyes, that I'll take off his head if he talks. Of course he was about to say it might tie into Sita's war story. Somehow.

Matt speaks to me. "You remember what Roger Goodwin said before he died. He told us, 'They took her into the sky.' There's a good chance he was talking about one of these Fastwalkers."

"That's a leap," I mutter.

Matt is annoyed. "It's a lead—the only damn lead we have to find Sarah. You're the one who keeps talking about the passing minutes. We're accomplishing nothing sitting around this hotel. We have to go to Nevada. Let's take ten minutes to pack, drive to the airport, and fly straight to Las Vegas. We'll be there in six hours."

He's right, I think. The lead is tenuous at best but it's all we have. I don't know why I feel so reluctant to follow it. Matt misses nothing. He can read the feeling in my face. He expects an argument.

"All right," I say. "Pack."

Matt nods, grateful, and the gang leaves. I'm left alone with Mr. Grey. Sitting on the bed, I reach over and put my palm on his forehead. He's hotter than this afternoon. His eyes are bloodshot and his pulse is skipping.

"We're stopping at the hospital before we go to the airport," I say.

He sighs. "We've had this argument already."

"And we'll have it again until you agree to listen. You're hurt. You need help I can't give you."

He hears the fresh layer of concern in my voice.

"Where did you go this afternoon?" he asks.

"Boston."

He lays his head back and closes his eyes. "Shit."

I touch his arm—his sleeve is rolled up—feel how clammy his skin is. It's the fever, a definite sign his brain is swelling.

"Don't you want to go home?" I ask.

His eyes stay shut. "It's hard to explain. A part of me does. A bigger part of me wants to stay with you. That's what I've been saying all along. I *need* you, Sita. For me, you're the magic key that can open the door. And I think you need me."

"Where does this door lead?" I ask.

"My superiors won't allow me to answer that question."

"To hell with your superiors."

He opens his weary eyes. "The door leads to hope."

"For who?"

"All of mankind."

"Why am I the key?"

"I just told you. You have magic."

"You speak in riddles, my friend."

He smiles faintly and touches my hand. "I'm happy to hear you call me that."

"Why do you care what I call you?"

He clasps my fingers. "Don't you know?"

I lean over and kiss his forehead. "Love is a beautiful thing. You might even feel it for me. But you've got to love Kathleen, Hal, and Sally a whole lot more." I pause. "They miss you. They want you to come home."

He closes his eyes and sinks deeper into the pillows. "Today, my place is with you. Tomorrow, we'll see, maybe I can go back to Boston."

I let go of his hand and stand. "They'll never see you again if you die."

"None of that will matter if I don't help you through tomorrow." He pauses. "I've figured out the code the author of *The Story of Veronica* used. I've begun to translate it. You'll be able to read it soon."

I'm forced to chuckle. "You're evil. You hold out a carrot so I'll have to keep you around. You know how much I want to read that book."

He smiles, although he appears close to passing out.

"So I get to go to Nevada with you?" he asks.

I kiss his cheek and move toward the door. "Sleep. Don't worry about a thing. I'll carry you to the car."

TWELVE

*M*ozart's *Don Giovanni* has just reached the intermission, and General Hans Straffer and I are in the opera's foyer, drinking wine with an excited German and French crowd, when I spot Major Karl Klein. I had no idea the major was attending—I've never seen him at the opera before. The sight of him makes me wish I had listened to Anton and declined General Straffer's invitation. If Major Klein spots me, I may be in serious trouble.

Yet I accepted Straffer's offer to enjoy Mozart's genius for the sake of Anton and the French Resistance. The Normandy invasion is scheduled for two days hence. Any final secrets I extract from my date will be invaluable to all of France, and to the Allies. Straffer is personal friends with General Rommel, Hitler's most brilliant military mind. Straffer can tell me the man's latest thoughts, his schedule, even.

But at the sight of Major Klein, I have to fight the urge to bolt. I need to return home with General Straffer, screw his brains out, and get him to talk before he sleeps. Generally, the man likes to smoke a Cuban cigar and discuss the meaning of life after sex. Actually, I have grown to enjoy the ritual. Straffer is a shrewd general as well as a deep thinker. I never think of him as a Nazi. Privately, in bed, the man has confessed that the finest teachers he had in school were Jewish. Plus he despises Hitler. He can't say his name without betraying disgust. In secret, of course; in front of his men he's completely loyal to the Führer.

"What do you think of the young man who plays Don Giovanni?" Straffer asks in German as he refills my glass. He is dressed in a long tail tuxedo and looks wonderful despite the fact he has a broad, squat face and frown lines so deep one would swear they were genetic. Straffer's strength is his commanding presence. Women find him hard to resist, French and German, and before he met me he was known to bed a fresh treat each week. But the fool, he's fallen in love with me and doesn't know it, and all he cares about is having me by his side.

There's a Mrs. Straffer at home, however, and he has four children. Two are young men, Karl and Len, fighting the Russians on the eastern front. The general often talks about them. The wife, though, never a word.

"I love him, such a natural baritone," I reply in German, knowing the general enjoys my near-perfect accent. I distort it slightly in his presence so as not to appear a superwoman. "He was born to play Giovanni. The way he flirted with Donna Anna the moment they met. Such a scoundrel. Then he kills her father!"

"That girl's a rare soprano. I wonder if she'd enjoy singing in Berlin."

I poke the general in the chest. "Is singing all you would have her do in Berlin?" I ask.

Straffer laughs and drains his wine. "Alys! Give me some credit. She can't be sixteen years old."

I lean near so he can't see my roaming eyes and fix his collar, all the while searching for Major Klein. I must keep track of him. I can't let him sneak up on us. Yet . . . I've lost him in the crowd, and I chide myself. I don't often lose people. He's a squirrel, that bastard. I hope he has returned to his seat. The intermission is almost over.

I yawn as I lean into Straffer.

"Tired, Alys?" he asks.

"A little. It was a grueling day."

He frowns. "Why do you work at that clinic? There are others who can do your job."

"I enjoy the work. It helps me to help people." I put a hand to my mouth to stifle another yawn. "Oh, forgive me, I think I drank too much wine. I'd better sit down."

"If you're exhausted, we don't have to stay for the second half."

"No! I couldn't do that to you. You've been looking forward to the opera all week."

He grips my hands and stares at me with great tenderness. "It's you I've been looking forward to. Come, we both know how the story ends. We miss nothing by leaving now. And we'll have more time to ourselves."

"Thank you, Hans," I say as I kiss his cheek. I play it smooth, we head for the door. Good. I didn't like the odds of accidentally running into Major Klein.

However, I feel I'm being watched as we exit the foyer. As an ancient predator, I'm sensitive to being hunted. Yet it is still remarkable how clearly I feel this pair of eyes focused on the back of my head. I can't put a name to the gaze. I only know that the mind behind it is black.

General Straffer's house used to belong to a famous jeweler—a shrewd but witty Jew named Arthur Gold, ha!— who had the good sense to flee to New York with a suitcase of diamonds before the Germans swept around the Maginot Line and conquered France. Straffer keeps only one maid, who doubles as a cook. His private life is relatively austere.

Except when it comes to sex.

We make love for an hour before he lights our cigars and pours two brandies. He likes that I can hold my liquor. He likes everything about me.

General Straffer is a great admirer of General Patton. To prod Straffer to talk about the Allies—and consequently how the Germans plan to deal with the Allies—I usually only have to bring up Patton. Straffer goes on from there. Tonight is no different.

"It's silly that Eisenhower is trying to convince the press that Patton is not going to lead the invasion of the continent," Straffer says as we lounge on his balcony in warm robes. He enjoys the fresh air but the sky is cloudy. A storm approaches— a storm that might delay the invasion.

"He struck his own men," I say. "The Allies take that seriously. Patton may have swept through Sicily but I've seen the American press. I read a copy of the *New York Times* that is only a week old. They are calling for Patton to be court-martialed."

Straffer snorts and waves his cigar. "He hit the cowards because they wouldn't fight. If they had been my men I would have had them shot. No, Eisenhower has ordered Patton to hobnob around London to deceive us. To make it look like Patton is not preparing his army to invade. But the two are old friends. Eisenhower would not court-martial his most brilliant general just because Patton lost his temper. The idea is so ridiculous I don't know why they expect us to fall for it."

Straffer is wrong, not about the impending invasion but about Patton's role in it. Patton is not slated to lead any army. The American press has indeed been roasting Patton for striking two men who were cringing behind lines with the seriously wounded. I know because I spoke to Patton personally. He was fuming over the incident. He swore he had just been trying to help the men find their guts to fight. He could not believe that he had been demoted. It's no wonder the Germans think it is all a scam.

"The press does not speak for the ordinary American," I say, acting like I agree with Straffer. "The public expects more great things from Patton."

Straffer nods sadly. "His victories will mean our defeat." He stops to drink his brandy. "If only the Führer would listen to Rommel's demand for the mines."

"But the last time we talked, you said fifty million mines were being placed behind the beaches."

Hitler does not believe for a second that the Allies will try to storm the beaches of Normandy. He is convinced the attack will come via a strong natural harbor. Pas de Calais—the spot Anton fed to the Gestapo under torture—is the closest harbor to England. On the surface it appears the logical place to strike but Eisenhower rejected it for that very reason.

Reading Eisenhower's mind, General Rommel rejected it as well. He is obsessed with fortifying the beaches of Normandy. But it sounds like he is getting a lot less help than I thought. This is important news.

Straffer groans at my remark. "Fifty million? Rommel hasn't been able to convince Hitler to place a fraction of that number. If the Americans and British take the beaches, there will be nothing to stop them from setting up a beachhead."

I chuckle. "My favorite general exaggerates. Rommel has

an eye on Calais and Normandy. And he has control of the panzers. There's no way the Americans will be able to rush tanks over the beaches in the first wave of the attacks. Rommel will chew them up."

Straffer eyes me critically. "You make it sound like you might welcome such an outcome. Don't you want to be rescued from us bloodthirsty Nazis?"

I smile and blow smoke in his face. "I've never lied to you about where my loyalty lies. I hope Patton kicks Rommel's ass. I'm merely stating a fact. Hitler's in Berlin, or else in his hideout in the Alps. Rommel is here and he's in control. There's no way the Americans can bring in their tanks until they establish a beachhead. Rommel's not going to give them that chance." I take a swallow of brandy. "I'm not worried. The Americans will just have to find another way to invade. Greece, perhaps."

Straffer is a long time answering. He stares out at the night. We are sheltered on the porch but a light drizzle has begun to fall. The general shivers but it does not appear to be from the cold.

"Control of the panzers has been taken from Rommel," he says.

I chuckle. "You're teasing. That's worse than the Americans saying they're going to court-martial their best general."

"It is true. Hitler no longer trusts Rommel. He's losing his mind—he trusts no one. If an attack comes, Rommel won't be able to make a move without Hitler's consent."

"If an attack comes, Rommel will be given all the support he needs."

Straffer stares at me. "You know, I have been given an order to destroy this city if the Allies ever try to enter it. Level the Eiffel Tower, the Louvre—every important structure."

I gasp. I am honestly shocked. "You've never told me that."

"It's true. The explosives can be placed in hours. Less."

"Would you do it?"

"I have been ordered to do it." He stops and turns back to the skyline. "But no, it would be madness. To me, Paris is the most beautiful city in the world. I'd never allow my name to go down in history as the one who ruined it."

I study Straffer. His mood is pensive, unusual after such good sex. "You're upset. You're trying to tell me something else. You're saying . . . you know the Allies are going to win."

"Of course they are going to win! The die was cast the day Japan attacked Pearl Harbor and dragged America into the war. What a fool's errand that was. We could never match America's industrial capacity. We make a hundred airplanes a day. They make two thousand. We've never stood a chance."

"We've had this argument before. Something else is upsetting you."

He shrugs. "It's nothing."

"Tell me."

"Rommel's gone. He's gone home to see his wife."

"You're joking. Now? He would never leave at a time like this,"

"He has. Tonight at the opera I spoke to Speidel, his chief of staff. He told me Rommel's already left."

"But why?"

Straffer sighs. "Our finest meteorologists assure us that the English Channel will be impassable for the next few days. They say the Allies would be insane to launch an attack. Their ships would sink before they reached the French coast."

"Sounds reasonable," I say. "Why so gloomy?"

"Because it is reasonable! But Eisenhower is a gambler—he knows when to take a calculated risk. Every storm has its peaks and valleys. He will look for a lull in the weather. Then he will attack, I'm sure of it. And he will attack where we least expect. He will hit Normandy."

I nod. "He will do the last thing the Germans expect."

"Worse. He will do it when we least expect." Straffer stares at the burning tip of his cigar as if it represents the forces under his command. He is definitely convinced of his beliefs. He expects everything he has worked for to go up in smoke.

I, on the other hand, can hardly contain my excitement. If the Allies know Rommel is no longer in France, that essentially no one who can even argue with Hitler is in control, they will not postpone the attack no matter how bad the weather.

I must get the information to my contact in the Allies. But I fear to use the Resistance to get it to them. Not because

I don't trust Anton. He would never betray his people. Unfortunately, the Resistance is not as tight as he believes. There are spies close to him. I know because Straffer often knows things he shouldn't know. Although I've tried to warn Anton of the leaks, he sees my fears as paranoia, rooted in my lack of faith in the French. He's very proud and doesn't take criticism well.

There's no choice. I have to go to London tonight.

But I can't take a plane, even a small boat. Despite the fact that the Germans are not expecting an attack in the next week, the coast is too closely guarded.

I'll have to swim across the English Channel.

Straffer has gotten his worst fears off his chest. Even if he suspects me of being a spy—which I think he sometimes does—he believes there is nothing I could do with the information he has supplied. For one thing, he knows no one would believe it.

I stand and lead him back to bed. I kiss him as if I'm ready for a final round but he pats my naked bottom and wishes me sweet dreams. He's asleep in minutes.

I'm out of his house moments later.

The best way to get to the coast is a question mark. Lieutenant Jakob Baum is Straffer's personal assistant and often drives me home at night. The advantage of using Jakob is he'll be able to get me through the many roadblocks that lie between Paris and Normandy. Hypnotizing him to obey me will not be a problem. But once he's deep in a trance, he might have trouble driving, never mind answering questions from the soldiers who are going to want to know what we're doing out so late.

Yet I can see no other alternative.

Jakob—I call him that when we're alone—has a flat near Straffer's house. I knock on his door and find him up, listening to music on the radio. He's happy to see me; the odd hour does not surprise him. He assumes I've come for a ride. He invites me in and slips on his boots before I can say a word. It's while he's sitting that I take the opportunity to gaze deep into his eyes.

Even though Jakob has a threatening demeanor, he's a child at heart, which makes him susceptible to the wild fire in my eyes and silky softness of my voice. We're on the road shortly, and if I have to occasionally grab the steering wheel to keep us from ending up in a ditch, it's all right with me.

We go through a half dozen roadblocks with no difficulty. I make sure that Jakob keeps his answers short and brisk. And, after all, Jakob is an officer and German soldiers hate to question authority. I'm hopeful I'll be able to send him home without incident.

I do not get my wish. Two hundred yards from Omaha Beach, so close to the sea that the noise of the crashing waves sounds like thunder, we encounter a roadblock staffed with a dozen soldiers. One of who happens to be a captain checking up on his men. It's this captain that has to give the final okay to let us pass. He sticks his head in the driver's window while another soldier shines a flashlight over his shoulder. The light is blinding, although Jakob stares into it without blinking—not the least suspicious move on his part. It's not his fault. I have him so dazed he could stare at the sun for an hour straight.

"What business do you have out here?" the captain demands. He's as young as Jakob's twenty-two years but hard as a rocket shell. Jakob gives his standard answer.

"My name is Lieutenant Jakob Baum, General Straffer's chief aide. We are on an important mission for the general. Please let us pass."

"What is your important mission?" the captain demands.

"It is top secret and time sensitive. You must let us pass."

"Who is this woman you have with you? She looks like a girl."

"I am Alys Perne," I speak sharply in rough German. I cannot pass myself off as German, because the papers I carry say I'm French. "I am no girl. Check the lieutenant's papers. You have no reason to stop him."

"I'm more interested in you than him. Get out of the car."

"Why?"

"I said get out of the car!"

I lean over and whisper in Jakob's ear. "If I don't return, drive to your flat and forget all about tonight. You never saw me tonight. Repeat."

"I never saw you tonight," he mumbles.

I get out of the car and stroll around it to confront the

captain. I'd hypnotize him as well but he's surrounded by too many of his men. A few are suspicious. They stand with their rifles held ready. The captain, he has the cruel face of a street punk, demands to see my papers. I hand them over and he studies them in the lightly falling rain, obviously not caring that he's ruining what he must assume is my sole form of identification.

This one I don't like.

This one I would like to kill.

"What is a French bitch like you doing here?" he asks.

I shrug. "Lieutenant Baum told you. I'm here on behalf of General Hans Straffer. I'm sure you know the general. He's a personal friend of mine, and I doubt he'll be happy to hear how you've treated me." I pause. "Bastard."

The men laugh and the captain flashes a cold smile. "You are not here on top-secret business. The Third Reich doesn't use French bitches except for one thing. Now, tell me what you are up to or I'll shoot you where you stand."

A half dozen men point their rifles at my head and heart.

I catch the captain's eyes. The fire in my gaze is like a volcano about to erupt. He winces as I speak. "I'll tell you what you want to know but we must speak in private," I say softly.

"God!" he gasps. He raises his hand as if I've shone a bright light in his eyes. I know he feels head pressure. I can only hope he will obey. He waves me toward a well-lit shack—it appears to be a hastily constructed office—twenty yards off the road.

The captain's men act uneasy but he stops them with a sharp retort when one questions what he's doing. "I'll speak to her in private," he says.

Unfortunately, there are three men in the office, all lieutenants. They sit around a table drinking coffee and studying maps of the local area. The maps show where thousands of mines have been set, as well as mark where every machine gun and mortar nest, plus heavy gun placements, is hidden. The Americans would die to hold such charts.

The captain orders me to take a seat.

"No," I say. "I have to go."

He is amused. "And where do you think you're going?"

"London," I say as I leap up and smash the overhead light with my fist. Simultaneously I kick the captain in the face, sending the whole of his nasal cavity into his brain, and with the other foot I kick the nearest seated lieutenant in the back of his head, breaking his upper neck. Landing on top of the table, I kill the final two men with my feet. The entire operation takes less than a second and I make little noise. Outside, the soldiers by the road notice nothing amiss. After collecting the maps into a tight roll, I find a perfectly sized waterproof container to put them in.

I exit out the back door and run to the Omaha Beach cliffs. Straffer might feel the beaches are not well protected but I'm not so sure. There are a half dozen pillboxes—concrete structures, all lined with narrow windows that peer toward the restless water.

The machine-gun barrels are not visible but it will take only minutes to mount and load them. The Americans who land at this beach will face an inferno of bullets.

They will face something else if they're not careful. The tide is out, and I see that large, jagged mines have been placed all along the edge of the water. In other words, if the American transport vessels come in at high tide—which I assume they will so the men will have less beach to cover before they attack the machine-gun nests—the ships will strike the mines before they can even deposit their men on the sand.

There are countless mines. They can be avoided if visible, but it will be a suicide run if they're not. Just another detail I have to get to the Allies.

I pin my hair back in a ponytail, kick off my boots, and hide my black leather coat in the sand. The tube holding the maps I pin to my back beneath my belt. The night is black as ink and I doubt any snipers will see me. Still, I sprint over the sand as fast as I can before diving into the crashing waves.

The English coast is twenty miles away.

The water is cold and I do not like the cold. I will have to generate my own heat. My arms and legs move like a machine, and I plow through the water faster than a man can run, turning my head to take a breath every two minutes. Nothing can spot me, I know. But if perchance a pair of eyes aboard a low-flying plane or a passing ship should catch a glimpse of my white-water wake, they would assume I'm a creature of the sea.

Three miles from the French coast I begin to have second thoughts about the schedule of the invasion. The swells have grown to ridiculous size. I plow between mountains of water twenty-five feet high. They crash over me and slow my progress. However, I'm tireless, they can't stop me.

But what will they do to the invasion force? The bulk of the men will be stuffed into landing craft like sardines in a can and driven from a British port across the Channel. I have seen the craft, the Allies have thousands. Most are small, cramped, with metal sides that reach only six feet above the surface. If Eisenhower fails to time the attack perfectly and doesn't hit a lull in the stormy weather, a quarter of a million men will drown.

What makes the situation more precarious is how swiftly the Channel's mood can change. Boarding at dock, the soldiers leaving Britain might be looking at calm water. Half an hour later they could be staring at tidal waves. What a roll of the dice the whole plan is. A part of me wishes the Allies would stop and regroup and invade through the Mediterranean.

Yet the more time that goes by, the more Jews are rounded up and sent east. Damn Harrah and Ralph! If only the fools would listen to me about the Nazis' Final Solution. While they continue to pray that the two words mean nothing, their entire race is being exterminated. When I return, I swear, I'm going to drag them across the border into Spain. I don't care what kind of fight they put up. I'll drug them if I have to and carry them on my back.

The sun rises as I crawl onto the beach beneath the white cliffs of Dover. Not so tireless after all, I am exhausted. A soldier in a jeep rushes toward me over the hard sand, sending forth a spray of foam. He jumps from his vehicle with his rifle in hand, but seeing my face he lowers it.

"Who are you?" he asks in amazement.

I slowly climb to my feet, shivering, my flesh like ice. Still, I'm able to adopt a flawless British accent. "My name is Alys Perne. I have vital information. I must see Lieutenant Frank Darling immediately. He's a member of Eisenhower's personal staff." I take a shaky step forward. "Please drive me to London."

He helps me into his jeep. "Did you just come from France?"

"Yes," I say.

He takes a blanket from the backseat and wraps it around me. I lay the sealed maps between my knees. He jumps behind the wheel and revs the engine. We race over the sand.

"Did your boat sink?" he asks.

"It was a plane. It crashed in the sea a mile out."

He hoots. "Lady, you must be one hell of a swimmer!"

"You have no idea," I say.

We reach Darling's flat in an hour. He greets me warmly and thanks the soldier for his help. Frank—he's not big on titles—gives me a change of clothes that belong to his girlfriend: trousers and a heavy woolen sweater. He fixes scrambled eggs, toast, and tea. The dry clothes and hot food do wonders for my condition. We eat together for half an hour before he asks his first question.

"Don't tell me you swam here," he says.

"All right."

"Jesus, Alys, even you can't risk weather like this. You're lucky you didn't drown."

"It's worse than you know in the middle of the Channel. Pray there's a break in the weather in two days."

"We can postpone if we have to," Frank says, picking up our plates, clearing the table. I continue to drink his tea, although I would prefer coffee. Well, actually, I need some blood. I don't need to feed as often as I did when I was young but after a major exertion my craving for blood—especially human blood—soars. I'd prefer not to feed on any Allies, but when I get back to France I'll have a regular feast with a couple of Gestapo. Might even look Major Klein up and drain him dry.

The man saw me at his headquarters, where I had no right to be. He must know I helped Anton escape. One word from Klein to Straffer could be disastrous.

"We can't postpone," I say, before explaining how Rommel is away on holiday and no acting general has control of the panzers. Frank listens with growing amazement.

"Do you know how long he'll be gone?" he asks.

"A few days was all I was told. You're not going to get a better shot at the Nazis without their leader."

"But you say the waves will sink us."

"It's a risk. You'll need your best spotter pilots and lots of luck to make it across the water. And you've got another problem. You've got to hit the beaches at low tide."

"That's crazy. That will give our men three times the beach to cover. The German machine guns will cream them."

"They won't even get off their landing craft unless the tide is out." I explain about the mines I spotted. "The only way to avoid them is for the ships to hit the shore when the mines are exposed."

"You're a fountain of cheery news."

I pick up my waterproof tube and remove the charts, spreading them over Frank's breakfast table. He studies them with glowing eyes. "Forget what I just said. You're an angel from heaven," he whispers.

"Or a blood-sucking succubi from hell. It all depends on your point of view." I explain how fresh the intel on the maps is. Frank shakes his head in wonder.

"These charts could be the difference between victory and defeat."

"Then I've earned my pay for the week. I have to get back. Can you get me a hotshot pilot to dump me somewhere near Paris?"

"Never heard you ask for a ride before."

"Never swam through waves that big before. As long as I have a parachute, the pilot can drop me as high up as he wants."

"You should wait until dark."

"I have business that can't wait."

Frank stands and folds up the charts. He seems preoccupied.

"What's wrong?" I ask.

"Oh, nothing. Except you've just hit us with three major strategic changes. Rommel's gone so we're not allowed to postpone. We have to land at low tide so we can keep from getting blown up. And these charts—they'll probably alter the direction of every planned thrust off the beaches." He pauses. "The high command is not going to accept all this coming from me."

"Eisenhower trusts you."

"Not enough to rewrite a two-year-old invasion plan."

"What are you saying?"

"They'll need to hear it straight from your lips."

"They? They don't even know me." I pause. "That is still true, isn't it?"

Frank meets my eyes. "I told you I'd take your secret to my grave and I will."

"Thank you."

He sits back down beside me. "But there is someone who might have already guessed your secret, with no help from me. And if you can convince him your intel is a hundred percent, it will change everything."

"Who are you talking about?"

"Patton."

"How can Patton know what I am?"

"I honestly don't know. But he's questioned me about you. He's asked *very* strange questions. You need to talk to him. No one has as much influence over Eisenhower as Patton."

"But if he's suspicious of me?" I say, letting the question hang.

"He's not suspicious. He just wants to know."

"What?"

"The truth."

"I can't tell him I'm a vampire. I won't."

Frank shakes his head. "That's not the kind of truth he's looking for."

Frank drives me to a flat, two blocks down from the famous 10 Downing Street, where Winston Churchill, the British prime minister, lives. Patton's apartment is well guarded but relatively small, far from glamorous.

I have been to the flat once before. It's where I was first introduced to Eisenhower and Patton. At that meeting, Eisenhower only stayed for a short time, but Patton kept me late into the night, telling me stories about his battles in Africa and Sicily. I found him absolutely delightful—one of the few living legends who actually lived up to his colorful reputation. At first I assumed he was flirting with me, but as the hour grew late and he began to question me about my history, I realized something was troubling him. Yet it was like Frank said at his flat—Patton was not suspicious that I was a spy.

He just sensed something unusual about me.

Frank and I catch him at breakfast and he asks us to join him. Frank is quick to excuse himself, although he leaves the charts behind after a brief explanation. Perhaps he feel they back up my story.

Patton quickly unfolds the charts. It takes him less than a minute to realize the gold mine they represent. He pounds the table and sends his bacon and sausage flying.

"Goddamn, these are perfect!" he cries. Last time he hesitated to swear in front of me, but once I assured him how crude I was, he lost all inhibition. As he squeezes my hand, his blunt but handsome face breaks into a ferocious grin. Even though he has yet to leave his flat, he's already dressed in uniform, three gold stars decorating his collar. He adds, "Those Nazi bastards aren't going to know what hit them!"

I smile. "Lieutenant Darling failed to mention how recent they are. I stole them from the Germans only a few hours ago."

Patton sits back and studies me with his penetrating gaze. Before the striking incident with the two GIs, the press portrayed him as the greatest strategic genius since Napoleon. Well, I knew Napoleon personally, and many other famous generals, and I know planning a major battle is not Patton's greatest strength. He's clever, sure, knows when to think outside the box, but it's the force of his personality that makes him great. His men trust him. He knows how to lead them into battle. He joins them in battle. He is the only general I know who is not afraid to fight at the front line.

Plus a weird aura surrounds the man. The stories are true. He has had German shells land at his feet and fail to explode. Bombs dropped on his office from a mile up have vaporized the building and failed to give him a scratch. The guy simply can't be killed, and his men believe in that magic, and when they march forward to fight, they feel a little of it will rub off on them. He is without question the most fearless human being I have ever met.

"How did you accomplish this miracle?" he asks, taking out a cigar and offering me one as well. I take it and he lights it with a wooden match struck off the back of his boot. I find it interesting how Straffer and Patton enjoy Cubans so much. I know the two would be friends if they ever met. The truth is, Patton admires the Germans.

"Slept with the Nazi who was put in charge of them," I say simply.

Patton loves it, slaps the table again. "Does he know they're missing?"

"I don't think so, sir. He's dead."

He nods his approval. "So you're a regular black widow, I'm not surprised. Tell me, Alys, what are the other gems Lieutenant Darling said you brought for us?"

I explain how Rommel has left France to visit with his

family, and the problem surrounding the mined beaches. Since Patton won't be leading the invasion force—according to Frank's latest intel—I'm not surprised Patton is glad Rommel will be missing. It's a dream of Patton's to face Rommel in battle himself.

But the mine issue troubles him. "Ike and I have discussed this issue with Churchill," Patton says, referring to Eisenhower by his nickname. "We had hoped the Nazis were too preoccupied with Calais to waste resources on Normandy."

"Calais remains their focus. But I stood on Omaha Beach yesterday. The pillboxes and heavy gun placements cannot be underestimated. The more air cover the men have, the better."

Patton snorts. "Air cover is the first thing to fail in bad weather. Our men will have to depend on their legs and their rifles. That's why your news about the mines is bad. Just the thought of hitting the beaches at low tide could destroy morale."

"They have no choice," I say firmly.

He notes my tone, returns to studying me. "And you wouldn't say it unless it was true?"

"Yes, sir."

He shrugs. "Everything you've told us so far has checked out. There isn't a man in the command center who isn't mystified with the intel you've provided." Patton pauses and leans close. "But some wonder if you've been so right so far so you can be so wrong when it really counts."

"They think I'm a plant."

"They worry. It's their job to worry."

I lean toward Patton. "But you trust me. You trust me as much as you trust your wife, Beatrice. And I know no one's more important to you in the whole world. Why?"

Patton sits back and smiles. "You're shrewd, have I ever told you that?"

"Several times. Last time I was here."

"Well, it's true. You know too much, I shouldn't trust you. The fact you were able to steal these charts—it would take a miracle. How am I going to convince Ike they're genuine?"

"Ike grew up in your shadow. Now he's your boss. But he knows you'd never lie to him." I pause. "You haven't answered my question, sir."

"Which one is that, Alys?"

"The way you look at me. It's odd."

"You're a very beautiful woman."

"Don't play with me, General. You want something from me, besides intelligence. What is it?"

He picks up a small red bound book from beside his plate. He flips through the pages. "The last time we met you told me you had studied the Bhagavad Gita. But I don't recall how the topic came up."

"Your belief in reincarnation is known by your men, sir."

"That's right, that's right. Most were raised strict Christians. They think you die and go to either heaven or hell. But

Krishna had a different take on the matter. And I'm pretty sure he was right."

"Because you remember past lives," I say. "You recall fighting with Hannibal against the Roman legions."

Patton frowns. "I told you that."

"You were very drunk at the time, sir."

"No, Alys, not so drunk. I remember your reaction when I brought up the Gita. Your eyes lit up. The scripture means as much to you as it does to me. Don't deny it."

God, he is perceptive. I remain silent.

"What is your favorite quote?" he asks.

"Pardon?"

"From the Gita. What line means the most to you?"

I straighten. "'All who are born die, oh Arjuna. All who die are reborn. The wise do not grieve over the inevitable.'"

Patton nods. "That line is with me every time I go into battle. I feel it strengthens my *kavach*." He pauses. "Do you know the word?"

The question is a test. He is searching for something.

"It's Sanskrit for 'armor.' It specifically refers to protection against danger. In battle, a person with powerful *kavach* is supposed to be difficult to kill."

Like him. Patton has *kavach*. Curious that he asks about it.

"How old are you, Alys?" he asks.

"Why do you ask?"

"You look so young. Yet you're able to seduce German

generals, and travel back and forth between Paris and London with complete ease. Not to mention that you're a Sanskrit scholar."

"I wouldn't call me a scholar."

"Damn it!" he yells, slamming the book shut. "Who are you?"

"I don't understand your question, sir."

"Why not? You know everything else."

"Honestly, General, I'm not sure—"

"I've seen you before," Patton blurts out. "In a past life, I saw you."

Finally, I see what haunts him. The revelation startles me. It knocks the wind out of me. I take a moment to settle my pounding heart.

"Who were you?" And now I am the one who is asking.

He gazes at me. "I've only told Bee this, no one else. Of course no one else would believe me." He stops and lowers his voice. "But you will. You were there."

"When did we meet? Where?"

"You were at Charleston, with the Yankees, before Lee fled with his army. That was the beginning of the end of the war."

"You're talking about the Civil War." I pause. "You were General Grant."

He's thoughtful. "My men nicknamed me the Butcher. In this life they call me Old Blood and Guts. Interesting how the names don't change that much." He stops. "You called yourself

Lara then. You tried to pass yourself off as a socialite from New York City but I never believed it. You told me to be generous to Lee when he surrendered. I took your advice."

"I was hoping to spare the South decades of Yankee revenge."

"It was a nice sentiment. Too bad it didn't work." He stares at me. "You haven't aged a day since then."

"It's easy to see you as General Grant. You fight the same. Above all else you believe in concentrating your forces. You sacrifice however many men it takes to end a battle as fast as possible." I stop. "But how can you be sure?"

"Am I right about our meeting?"

"How can you be sure?" I repeat.

He hesitates. "I'm not delusional. I put it to the test. I had my wife, Bee, buy his autobiography. I had never read it myself. I asked her to study it, and ask me questions about what Grant said or did when I least expected. I didn't want my mind getting in the way of what my heart knew. I wanted my answers to be spontaneous. I got one question right, then another. She asked me stuff off and on for two weeks before it happened."

"What?"

"The entire life came back to me. Like I had just lived it." He stops and takes my hand. "Alys, I only spent ten minutes with you in that life. But I remember the red dress you wore, the gold necklace, how you kept your hair long and loose like it is now. The thing you told me before you left was, 'General, Lee is tired of fighting. He wants the war to end. If you give an honorable way out for him and his men, he'll take it.'"

I feel shell-shocked. "Those were my exact words."

"Then you believe me."

I remember back to my time with Grant. It was brief, like Patton said, but I could see he was a quiet man, humble, not prone to boast. He led by example, he did not shout or scream at his troops. Personalitywise, he had almost nothing in common with Patton.

Yet as I gaze at the twinkle in Patton's seemingly ferocious gaze, and recall the warmth I felt when Grant hugged me good-bye, I know they are the same soul. Because we're talking about souls, not personalities—that's the answer to the contradiction.

One changes, the other is eternal.

Patton has come to me for a favor but he cannot know how much he has done for me. He has confirmed the truth of reincarnation, one of the core teachings of Krishna. He has restored my faith.

My faith in what?

It doesn't matter. It feels good to have it back.

Patton sees my eyes are damp and reaches for a napkin and brushes it across my cheek. He stares at me in wonder.

"How have you lived all these years?" he asks.

I want to give him something in return for what he has

given me. Yet I don't want to lie. "I'm alive because of Krishna," I say. "I knew him, I sat with him, he was real. That's why I love the Gita."

Patton is astounded. "Five thousand years ago?"

"Yes."

"I believe you, Alys."

"Call me Sita. And yes, I, too, believe you. You were Grant."

He lets go of my hands and crushes out his cigar. "Why did Krishna grant you such a long life?" he asks.

"I don't know. To you, immortality might seem a great gift. But it has not always been easy. When I look at my life, there has been far more pain than joy. Sometimes I fear the grace he gave me has become a curse."

Patton shakes his head. "Don't ever think that. You helped America at a critical point in its history. Today, you help us again. You might even be the key that allows us to win this war. You are blessed, you must be."

I smile sadly. "If only that were true. You've seen only my good side. Alas, there's a darkness in me you can't imagine. It destroys all those who get close to me."

"Nonsense. You've never harmed me."

I stand and lean over and kiss his forehead. "Because you've always had the good sense to take my advice and run. Please, don't forget what you once knew. Let me go now."

He stands and hugs me. "I'll look for you in Paris, Sita."

"Don't look too hard," I say, and know I'll never see him again, that he'll die in Europe. I don't know where the intuition comes from but know it's true.

Despite my high contacts with the Americans and the British, I cannot find a pilot willing to fly me back across the Channel until after the sun sets. I hear excuses why no one is available but know the true reasons. Swooping over Paris is risky enough at night—the Germans have ringed the city with antiaircraft fire—and besides, the invasion is scheduled for morning.

I imagine there are not many pilots who want to risk getting killed on the day *before* the most dangerous day of the war. For a time I consider another long swim but the chill of my night's exertion has hardly left my bones.

Finally, though, Lieutenant Frank Darling pairs me up with Private Jimmy McHarah, a twenty-year-old Irish kid from Boston who talks my head off all the way across the Channel but has the guts to drop me midway between Paris and Versailles. I bail out at an altitude of ten thousand feet but don't open my parachute until I'm six hundred feet from the ground. Just my luck, I land in an icy brook. By the time I reach shore I'm as wet as if I had swum back to the Continent.

The run back to the city warms my blood. I visit Anton first, who is manically busy at one of the four French Resistance headquarters. He has not fully recovered from the torture he suffered at the Gestapo facility but is happy enough to see me that he tries dragging me into a back bedroom. I beg off.

"It's happening. They're coming in the morning," I say.

He nods. "We received word there's a good chance."

"You don't understand. I just came from London. Come hell or high water, they are coming." I quickly explain about Rommel's absence and the need to hit the beaches at low tide. Anton listens carefully but acts insulted when I'm finished.

"How come I'm only hearing about this now?"

"You damn well know why. It's the same reason you must keep what I've told you private. You've got a spy in your inner circle."

"Sita, don't be childish. My men are all loyal."

I laugh. "I could not act childish if I wanted. But I warn you, what I tell you is true. Your position here is compromised. You have to give each of your leaders their assignments individually, in private."

"What assignments?"

I take out a list Frank has given me in a waterproof bag. "These are updated sites the Allies need bombed. Hit as many as possible before dawn. Whatever's left, wait until tomorrow night, then destroy the rest."

Anton studies the targets with a skeptical eye. "Half of these are not critical," he quips.

"Better minds than ours say they are. Please, Anton, this is no time for your ego to ruin your judgment. Too many people are counting on you."

"I know my own country." But he stuffs the list in his pocket and I know he will do what he can. He puts his arms on my shoulders and gazes at me. "I missed you last night. I kept waiting."

"I was swimming with the fishes."

"And before that? Were you with him?"

"Don't be jealous. We needed the intel. And the General couldn't have satisfied a prostitute."

Anton appears reassured. "The Nazi pig could not get it up, eh? What do you expect. God has cursed their dicks in payment for their sins." He pauses. "Hungry?"

"Starving." For blood, not food. "But I can't stay." He grabs my arm as I turn for the door, his face filled with hurt.

"Sita, tonight's our night. You and I, together, we can hit half a dozen of the targets on the Allies' list. You must stay."

I hesitate. "I have to check on Harrah and Ralph."

"I saw them this afternoon at the clinic. They're fine."

"Then I'll be back later." I feel the falsehood in my words as I speak them. I don't wish to lie to him. At the same time, I don't know how to explain how the feeling of being watched that came over me as I left the opera the previous night has never totally left. It's as if somehow I was marked in that instant. Just as the Jews are marked with the Star of David to make real the goal of the Final Solution.

I leave Anton, sneaking out the back of his headquarters. Lack of blood has weakened me but I'm too impatient to stop and feed. I race to Straffer's house, so fast a hurricane could not keep pace. Dread creeps over me when I reach his front porch. His door is unlocked and he never fails to lock his door. Indeed, I locked it when I left him twenty hours ago.

A single step inside and I smell the blood.

It comes from the second floor, from his bedroom.

My climb up the stairs is slow and painful.

I find him facedown at the foot of his bed, a pool of blood soaking the wood floor near his head. He is naked, he was not given a chance to dress, and I can tell by the odor of the blood that he died not long after I left the house.

From the angle of his body, I know he was forced to kneel, before his executioner coolly blew out his brains. Somehow, I sense the mood of the assassin, and know he was smiling when he murdered my friend.

"Oh, Hans," I whisper as I pull the sheet off the bed and cover him, "You didn't know what you were getting into when you met me. I should have warned you." I remember what I told Patton. "I should have told you to run the other way."

Leaning over, kissing his head, I vow to make sure his family is safe when the war is finished. That is, if his sons survive the battles to come.

I rush to the Levines' flat.

Their door lies wide open.

"No," I moan before I step inside. There is no odor of blood, nor is there any sign of Harrah and Ralph. The apartment has been turned upside down. The contents of every drawer have been spilled on the floor, and the cushions on the sofa and mattresses on the beds have been knifed open. The air stinks of a unique sweat I associate with fear. I search for the tiniest sign that Harrah might have left behind for me to find but there is nothing.

The Veil of Veronica is gone.

At my back, at the door, a voice speaks in German, startling me. Yet no one takes me by surprise. How come I didn't hear the bastard coming up the outside stairs?

"They're on a train to Auschwitz," Major Klein says. "You've heard the name? Good. So you know what it means, Alys." He pauses and grins and the falseness of his face appalls me. It's as if flesh-colored wax flows around plastic red lips. "Or should I call you Sita?"

"It was you. You murdered General Straffer," I reply in German.

He holds a small metal box in his hands that has three dials on top: one red, one white, one black. Nazi colors. On the bottom is a speaker.

Odd, but he's left his sidearm holstered. It's as if he treats the box as his weapon of choice. It's clear he doesn't fear me. He keeps the fingers of his right hand on the black dial, shrugs in response to my statement.

"What is the death of a traitorous officer to the Third Reich?"

I take a long step toward him. At least I know who will slake my thirst. I will drain him slowly, I think.

"General Straffer loved Germany," I say.

Klein isn't intimidated by my approach. Shaking his head, he feigns sorrow. "I fear he loved you more. That's the only way to explain his acts. That's how my report to the Führer will read."

I snicker. "As if you have your own personal pipeline to Hitler."

He loses his smile. "Careful, Sita. You risk a great deal by insulting me. Truly, you have no idea."

"How do you know my name?"

"Your name. Your origin. Your nature. The Gestapo knows all there is to know about our lovely Aryan." It's his turn to move closer and his gray eyes expand as he nears. For a moment I'm racked with dizziness. I fight to shake it off. It's as if a strange lust has taken hold of his gaze and is being projected in my direction. I feel as if worms crawl over my skin. He adds in a sinister tone, "Look at your blond hair and blue eyes. You're a perfect specimen, a true original. The forerunner of the superbeings the Führer has promised will arise."

"Your Führer's a damn lunatic," I whisper, shooting out an arm to steady myself. I suddenly recognize the source of my dizziness. It comes from the metal box he holds. He has twisted the black dial, and on the far edge of hearing I detect a shrill note permeating the flat. The tone seems to bleed out of the walls; it grates on my nerves. I doubt any human could hear it. I don't understand how a simple speaker can be projecting such a strange sound.

"Feeling a little weak?" Klein asks as he steps directly in front of me. I feel his acidic breath on my face, notice a faint odor of sulfur, both smells reeking of unseen flames. Raising my free arm, I try to strike him, but my arm falls down uselessly at my side. My grip on the nearby wall begins to slide.

"What are you doing to me?" I gasp.

"A little payment for your insults." His grin returns as he raises the metal box before my eyes and twists the black dial again. The shrill note suddenly jumps in volume and I feel as if a molten blade has been thrust through my chest, with the heat boiling into my blood and rising to my brain. I literally feel as if my head will explode. The pain, the pain—I could never have imagined such pain. Breathing, seeing, living—all feel impossible in the face of such agony. I pray to black out, I pray to die, and I have never prayed so hard in my life.

"Please!" I cry.

Major Klein throws his head back and laughs. He turns the dial a third time and the torture seems to squeeze my very soul out of the top of my head and deposit me in a forsaken realm of phantoms and nightmares. I lose consciousness but it brings no relief. Far off I hear Major Klein exult.

"Now it begins," he says.

THIRTEEN

*I*t's while we cross over the Midwest, at an altitude of twenty-five thousand feet, that I tell Seymour and Matt the second chapter of my World War II tale. Seymour is frustrated when I stop. He insists I plow through to the end. But digging up such foul memories is taxing, and it doesn't help that I have a good idea what comes next. It's not like the story has a happy ending.

"It sounds like Major Klein used Telar technology on you," Matt says after I explain how I was taken captive in Harrah and Ralph's flat. "But it's hard to imagine they would have given the Nazis such knowledge."

"The box didn't come from the Telar," I say.

"Are you sure?" Seymour asks. "Klein's metal box sounds a lot like that Pulse device the Telar used on you in Arosa, Switzerland. Both induced rising waves of pain."

I hold up a hand. "The boxes only sound similar. The Telar's device had electrodes that attached directly to my brain. The Nazis' box used sound that only a vampire could hear to induce pain and unconsciousness. Trust me, the German scientists had their own brand of toys."

"Are we talking about the same scientists who joined NASA after the war?" Seymour asks.

"There was no NASA right after the war," Matt says.

"Right," Seymour says sarcastically. "America didn't even have a space program until they recruited a few dozen Nazis."

Matt brushes aside the remark. "Let's not get carried away with conspiracy theories. Most NASA employees—then and now—are good people who want nothing more than to explore the solar system."

"Sounds reasonable. Except we just found out that NASA's nothing but a front for this country's real space program." Seymour stops to snort. "If that's not a conspiracy, I don't know what is."

"I was referring to the NASA-Nazi connection," Matt says. "Why make a big deal out of it?"

Seymour studies me. "If only our dear Sita would answer all our questions, then maybe we'd know if the connection is genuine."

"I promised to tell you everything I remember," I say. "But you've got to give me time."

"Not too much time," Matt says as he stands and stretches from his position in the pilot's chair. "I'd like to take a break. Sita, can you take over? I've put us on autopilot. I doubt there will be a lot for you to do."

I take his seat. "No problem."

Matt heads for the door to the main cabin. "Come get me when it's time to start our descent. This jet's landing gear has a few quirks—I want to be the one to put us down. And try not to run into any Fastwalkers."

"Take a nap," I suggest. "Once we're on the ground, we don't know when we'll have another chance to rest."

"I'm fine," Matt replies, meaning he's going to do what he wants to do and to hell with my advice. I know he's going to play the game. He's like a heroin addict anxious for his next fix. He can't stay away from the thing.

Matt leaves Seymour and me alone in the cockpit.

"I don't understand you," Seymour says.

"You wrote my biographies. You understand me better than anyone."

"Then why are you so reluctant to finish your war story? You keep taunting us about the big revelation to come, but you never tell us what it is."

"Like I explained, you need to know the backstory first."

"So now we've got the backstory. Now you've run out of excuses. Admit it, Sita, you're stalling."

"I'm not stalling. I'm . . . trying to organize my thoughts."

Seymour is concerned. "Are you saying you can't remember what happened?"

"Don't look so surprised. It was a long time ago."

"Bullshit! Seventy years or seven hundred means nothing to you. Or have you forgotten that you have perfect recall?"

"You're beginning to sound like Matt." I turn and look away, out the window, at the endless cornfields of Iowa swooping far below. The state is mostly farmland. It's amazing how dark it is after sunset. I add, "And like Paula."

Seymour is instantly alert. "What did Paula say the last time you two spoke?"

"Nothing important."

"Sita."

"She told me that all the good I have done for mankind since World War Two was of little value."

"That makes no sense."

"Then she told me that if I hadn't screwed up during the war, all the good deeds I have done since those days wouldn't have been necessary."

"You know I rarely disagree with Paula. But everything you've told us so far about your war days tells me you were as heroic as ever."

"Heroic? What about the fact that I left Harrah and Ralph alone for Major Klein to grab? What about my befriending General Hans Straffer just long enough to get his brains blown out?"

"You didn't know Major Klein was stalking you."

"I suspected it. I should have taken precautions."

Seymour shakes his head. "Paula wasn't referring to what you did in Paris and London. She was talking about what happened at Auschwitz."

"How do you know? I haven't said a word about Auschwitz."

"That's my point. You've done everything you can to avoid the topic. Admit it—whatever they did to you in that camp so messed with your mind that you can't remember half of what went on."

"You're exaggerating."

Seymour stares at me and waits. I stare back. The dark cornfields and dried-out scarecrows stare up at us as we soar over them through the moonlit sky.

"All right, there are a few points I'm having trouble remembering," I say.

Seymour nods like he's suspected all along. "Tell me what happened after Major Klein zapped you with that high-pitched noise."

"I remember the train ride to the camp. How I was chained inside an isolated railcar with ankle and leg cuffs made of a strange alloy I couldn't break. I remember arriving at the camp. The tall smokestacks pumping burnt flesh into the air night and day. Hordes of children screaming at the tracks when they were torn away from their parents. The hood that was tied over my head. The underground dungeon I was led to, where I was cuffed to a metal pole and tortured for ages by Major Klein. With a strange woman always hovering in the background with eyes like a cobra. The SS guards were terrified of her. They never looked her straight in the face or addressed her as anything except Frau Cia." I stop. "You can see, I remember a lot."

"Except how it ended," Seymour says.

I want to protest, to lie, but he has me cornered.

"Not how it ended," I agree.

He sighs. "Can you remember another time you can't remember?"

"Is that a trick question?"

"I wish it were. You know we have a telepathic bond. It's what allowed me to write about your life before I met you. But that bond began to fail me when I reached what I called the sixth chapter of your tale. I didn't know what to write next. Suddenly the images were scattered in my head. I tried to stay with the flow of what was coming to me out of the ether—like I had from the start of your story—but I knew a lot of what I was typing was nonsense."

"It wasn't all nonsense."

"It wasn't gospel, either. I wrote that you changed me into a vampire. That we got attacked by a weird alien chick with a ray gun. That you killed her and fled into the desert, where you confronted more evil aliens. As if all that weren't wild enough, the next thing I wrote about was your rendezvous with a space-ship in the desert. On board the ship were some kind of aliens or angels. I was never sure who they were, but I think there were two of them. Anyway, they flew you up into outer space and explained that once they achieved light speed, the ship would be free of time and space. Not only that, they said you'd be able to send your mind back in time to an earlier version of yourself. That was why they took you into space in the first place. They said you had to go back a thousand years and fix a mistake you made when you accidentally gave your blood to an evil creature. A man from the Middle Ages that the peasants and nobles of Sicily believed to be a necromancer."

"Landulf of Capua," I whisper. The name is as painful to say aloud as Tarana's.

"Yes, Landulf. Who first appeared to be the lord of an evil castle on the southern tip of Sicily, but who later turned out to be your seemingly innocent traveling companion, Dante. The leprous eunuch."

"You're not telling me anything I don't know."

"Are you sure? I've tried talking to you about this time before and you've always changed the subject. Is it because you can't remember those days?"

"I remember them when you talk about them," I say.

"When we're together they're clearer?"

"Yes."

"But when you're alone they're more foggy?"

"Actually, when I'm alone, I never think about that time at all."

"Just like you never think about what happened in Auschwitz."

"What are you getting at?" I say.

"What happened with Landulf and what went on in the concentration camp are the only two periods in your life you have trouble remembering. That can't be a coincidence."

I go to protest but stop. He's right.

Seymour continues. "In my version of your life story it's like your guardian angels or whatever sent you back to the eleventh century to fix a mistake. Now Paula is saying you have to go back to Auschwitz and fix another mistake."

"Paula never said anything about me going back in time."

"Probably because we don't have a time machine. Look, I phrased it that way to make a point. These two periods in time are linked, not just in your head but in history. According to experts on that period, Landulf drew most of his power from a Christian talisman called the Spear of Longinus. The spear that pierced Christ's side while he was dying on the cross. A spear that, by chance, still has Christ's blood on it. Now, jump forward a thousand years and what do you happen to come across but the Veil of Veronica, a second Christian talisman that has Christ's blood on it." He pauses. "Now tell me that's a coincidence."

"What you say is fascinating. But I still don't see how the two time periods are related."

"They're related through *you*. Through your inability to remember clearly what happened during both periods. And through Christ's blood."

"I don't know. You're speculating."

Seymour shakes his head. "If you need cold hard facts, let me give you a big one. Landulf of Capua—what was his wife's name?"

"I hardly remember his wife. But I know he cut out her heart . . ." I suddenly stop. "God. It was Lady Cia."

"Which just happens to be the name of the woman who helped torture you at Auschwitz," Seymour says.

The link hits me like a body blow. "I never thought of that."

Seymour stands and pats me on the back. "We have to figure out a way to punch through your mental block. I have an idea that might work, but I want to talk to Matt about it before I discuss it with you."

"Why tell him first?"

"The less you know about what it is, the better it might work. I'm talking about keeping you innocent, free of any preconceived ideas. Trust me on this, Sita."

"There's no one I trust more," I say.

My words please him. He smiles as he opens the door to the main cabin. "I'm glad. For a while there I thought you were more in love with Mr. Grey."

"I care about him. He's trying to help us."

"But you still have no idea where he came from?"

I hesitate. "Not really."

"That's not a small thing to keep hidden. But if you trust him, I do too." Seymour stops halfway through the door. "Can I get you anything from the kitchen?"

"A quart of warm Gestapo blood."

"You still hate them, don't you?"

"Never to forgive, never to forget. That's what the Jews who escaped Auschwitz swore to each other." I shake my head. "Never mind me, I think a part of my brain has become unhinged in time. I need a dose of reality. I need food. Get me a cup of coffee and a roast beef sandwich."

"It's on its way," Seymour says.

By the time we land in Las Vegas it's evening and Mr. Grey is slipping in and out of consciousness. I put my foot down. I tell the others I'm taking him to the hospital.

"We can't get near Nellis Air Force Base without his computer skills," I say just before we climb out of the plane. Mr. Grey continues to doze in a rear seat, snoring softly.

"What about Sarah Goodwin?" Matt asks.

"She's going to have to hang on," I say. "Please, Matt, take the gang into town and check into a hotel. Give me a call and let me know where you are. It's better if I go alone with Mr. Grey to the hospital."

"Why?" Brutran wants to know.

"Because I say so," I reply.

Brutran shakes her head. "The others deserve to know."

"Know what?" Seymour asks.

I give Brutran a hard look. She's betraying me and I know why. She figures Matt's the one with the power in our group and she wants to show that she's on his side. It's an old tactic with her—always align yourself with the one who's going to win. How little she knows of my temper.

"The FBI is looking for Mr. Joel Grey of Boston, Massachusetts," Brutran says. "They have a missing-person file on him. According to their records, he disappeared two months ago, leaving behind a wife and two children."

"And you were going to tell us this when?" Matt says to me.

"This evening," I say.

"Right," Matt mutters.

"I would have told you during the flight but you were busy playing that stupid game," I say.

Seymour holds up his hands. "Hold on you guys, this isn't worth a fight. Tell us who he is. Does he work for some super-brain-shrink-tank?"

"He works for General Electric as a systems analyst," I say. "He has no special skills."

"That's impossible," Seymour says.

"I talked to his wife," I say.

"In Boston. So that's where you went," Matt says.

"I don't report to you," I say.

Seymour steps between us. "Come on, you're too old to be having a lovers' quarrel. I want to know more about Mr. Grey. You must have found out something unusual about him?"

I have not forgotten his strange obsession with the sky but see no point in bringing it up. Certainly, his fascination with astronomy doesn't explain his incredible computer skills.

"He's a totally normal man," I say, turning toward Mr. Grey, who has begun to slide off the side of his seat. He's out cold, which might be a plus. He can't complain about me taking him to the hospital. I add, "I'm going now. I'll catch up with you guys later."

I put Mr. Grey in the backseat of a taxi, slip in beside him, and take out my laptop. A quick scan of the Internet shows that the Sunrise Hospital and Medical Center specializes in neurology and neurosurgery. They're a nationally ranked hospital, which is reassuring. I tell the driver to take us there.

"Hang on," I whisper in his ear as he breathes softly beside me. It's impossible not to think of his wife, Kathleen. By now she must have called the Boston FBI office, although I told her it would be a waste of time. I'm sure they told her I was a fake. But I'm not sure she would believe them. After all, I told her I'd get her husband back to her within a few days.

Sunrise lives up to its excellent reputation. I'm in the emergency ward less than ten minutes when Mr. Grey is wheeled away on a gurney. I explain to the doctor on duty how my brother suffered a blow to the head two days ago and has been running a fever. The doctor immediately orders an MRI and CAT scan. I sit down to wait.

A neurosurgeon, Dr. William Tower, appears an hour later. A tall thin man with large beautiful hands, he greets me warmly and takes me aside to speak to in private.

"Your brother's in serious condition," he says. "Whatever hit him damaged his left temporal lobe. That's a region of the cerebral cortex that's involved with auditory perception. It's important when it comes to speech and vision, and it contains the hippocampus, which is key to forming long-term memories."

"Are you saying his injury might have affected his memory?"

"There's a good chance. Has he been having trouble remembering things?"

"I think so, yes."

"I'm not surprised. He has a significant contusion on the lobe. To put it in layman's terms, the injury's burst a vein and he's bleeding in that area. Plus he has overall swelling of the brain."

"Will a decompressive craniotomy fix that?" I ask.

"You know something about neurosurgery?"

"I considered being a doctor at one time."

He nods. "The craniotomy will take care of the immediate swelling. But the bleeding lobe will require more invasive surgery. It must be done now."

"Do it," I say.

"Your brother has regained consciousness. He won't let us operate until he speaks to you."

"That's fine, I'll talk to him. But even if he resists, Doctor, you are to do the surgery. My brother isn't clear in his mind. Legally, I'm responsible for him now."

Dr. Tower hesitates. "I'll need you to sign certain papers stating that fact."

"No problem. And Doctor, I'm very rich, I want him to have the best care. Whatever it takes, fix Joel."

"We'll take care of him," the doctor promises.

Dr. Tower leaves to prepare for the surgery. A nurse leads me to a brightly lit room where Mr. Grey lies on a bed with an IV in his arm and an assortment of wires attached to his head, which in turn are hooked up to a device that appears to be taking a steady EEG, or electroencephalograph, of his brain. I know something about EEG printouts, and his looks odd, even for someone with a bleeding temporal lobe. His brain looks like it's stuck in overdrive.

I sit by his side and take his hand. His color is ashen, his skin hot. He smiles weakly. "I should have known better than to black out on you," he says.

"You can help us save the world once you're better."

"That's why I'm here, Sita. You have to let me help you."

"You're serious? You're here to save the world?"

"Yes."

"That's something new. Do you mind telling me how?"

"I told you. By helping you. You're the key."

"Great. Unfortunately, you're not telling me what I'm the key to."

"The future of this planet."

"Which Mr. Grey is talking now? The one with the genius IQ or the one with brain damage?"

"We're one and the same. Listen, I'll agree to have the surgery on one condition. The moment it's over, you get me out of here. You take me with you to your next destination."

"They're about to cut your head open. After the surgery I'm pretty sure you'll be heavily sedated. You'll need to rest if you're to recover."

"And you need to take me with you or everything you love and cherish will be lost."

I recoil at the power in his words. There's no question that he's telling the truth. He believes what he says, which is not, of course, the same as saying his statement is accurate. It's been the same since I met Mr. Grey. Despite all evidence to the contrary, I trust the guy.

"You need to tell me why," I say.

"I'm sorry but I can't."

"You don't even know what our next destination is."

"I do."

"What?"

"It's not Nellis Air Force Base."

I stand. "Then why did you let us fly all the way out here?"

"One road leads to another. You'll find your way. It's your destiny to find it. But this time I must be with you."

I freeze. "This time?"

He lies back and closes his eyes. "You thought I was asleep in the taxi but I wasn't. I know you brought your laptop. Look up the file labeled 'Veronica.' I translated the first part of the book. You'll find it interesting."

"What about the rest of it?"

"I'll translate it when you break me out of here." He stops, his voice dropping to a whisper. "Tonight . . . deal?"

"I want to wait and see how the surgery goes."

He begins to doze. "The end of the book is important. The image on the veil, it's not . . ."

I sit back down, lean close. "It's not what?"

Should I be asking, *It's not who?*

But he can't answer. He's out cold.

I retreat to the waiting room. Dr. Tower stops by with a woman carrying a stack of papers they want me to sign. He says the surgery will last approximately four hours. The time is eight fifteen. He suggests I get something to eat, rest at my hotel, come back at midnight. I agree but after he leaves, and after I sign the papers, I decide to stay in the hospital while I read *The Story of Veronica*.

FOURTEEN

ONE

I heard talk of a man some people called the Master. The way they spoke of him, it was like they saw him as more than human. When I heard he would be visiting our town, I longed to see him.

It was hard to get free. My parents refused to let me go anywhere without my brother, and he had to work the week the Master was nearby. But somehow I talked Thomas into taking the afternoon off. My brother was always very kind to me.

When we reached the place where the Master was to speak, we learned he had already given his talk. We were disappointed but a follower of his directed us to a house where the Master was staying. The man was friendly and said the Master would be happy to meet with us.

The house belonged to a rich merchant. Thomas was reluctant to knock on the door. "Veronica, we can't enter such a beautiful home dressed like this. Let's leave and come back when he's giving another public lecture."

"We don't know if he's giving another lecture," I said. "Besides, Uncle will never give you the time off."

Thomas frowned as he stared at his dusty sandals. "Why would such a great man want to talk to someone like us?"

I took Thomas by the hand. "You heard what his follower said. His Master treats everyone as an equal. Even girls."

We knocked on the door and the merchant himself answered, which surprised us. We assumed a servant would be attending the door. He acted happy to see us and invited us inside.

"The Master is in the back by the fountain," he said. "You will know him when you see him."

"Does he wear a crown?" Thomas asked.

The merchant laughed. "No. He's a simple man. Go, talk to him, you'll see."

I recognized the Master the moment I saw him. The merchant was right. The backyard was crowded with people but the Master stood out in a special way.

I wasn't sure why, but when I looked at him I found it hard to look away.

He was tall with a fine face and nicely trimmed beard. Yet that is not what drew me to him. If it had been dark I was sure he would have glowed. A strange thought to have, I admit. The man was not bright like the sun. Yet I felt as if he had a light hidden inside, a radiance I sensed rather than saw with my eyes. I felt I had to get near him.

But Thomas grabbed my arm and held me back. "He's eating, Veronica, can't you see? We can't disturb him."

"The merchant told us to talk to him. I don't think he'll mind."

Thomas hesitated. "Let me speak to him first."

I shook off my brother's hand. "Why you? Because you're a boy?"

"I'm eighteen now, a man, and you're supposed to obey me."

I couldn't help but laugh. Kissing my brother on the cheek, I said, "Never."

We approached the Master cautiously. When we were a few feet away, he raised his head and smiled at me, and my heart pounded in my chest. The warmth in his gaze—it's impossible to say how kind it was.

"Hello," he said. "Who are you?"

"My name is Veronica, and this is my brother, Thomas. Are we disturbing your lunch?"

"I have had plenty to eat." The Master was sitting on the edge of the fountain. He put his plate aside and bid us take a seat at his feet. "Come, rest. You must have come a long way. Are you hungry?"

"We ate on the road," Thomas said.

"It was a long walk," I added, sitting beside my brother. "We're sorry we got here late. We missed your talk."

The Master waved his hand. "The talk is not important. You are here now. What can I do for you?"

I nudged Thomas to ask a question but he seemed content just to stare at the man. At least my brother was no longer nervous, I thought.

"Why do people call you Master?" I asked.

"I wish they wouldn't. The moment a person is given a title he's set apart from everyone else. As a child, growing up, I was called Emmanuel. If you like, you can call me by that name."

"All the rabbis in our synagogue insist on high-sounding titles," I said. "It annoys me."

"Why does it annoy you, Veronica?"

I liked the way he said my name.

"I think it's because women are not allowed to become rabbis. That doesn't feel right to me."

"Veronica," Thomas said. "Watch your tongue. That's blasphemy."

The Master laughed. "No, Thomas, what your sister says is wise. All people, whether they are rich or poor, white or dark, male or female, Jewish or Roman, are all the same. No one should be seen as higher or lower."

"Are you saying that is what God thinks?" I asked.

The Master considered. "I can't say what God thinks. I doubt any man or woman can."

"But people say you are close to God," I said, feeling disappointed. "They say he is inside you."

"Veronica, if God made all of us, then he must be inside all of us. I am no different from you."

"But you are. I feel different just sitting beside you."

"What do you feel?" he asked.

I had to think before answering. "Happy. I feel happy."

"Happy is good. Where do you think that happiness comes from?"

"You! It has to come from you. I didn't feel it until I got here."

"That may seem to be true but it is not. Happiness is already inside you. It is just when you come here, and we sit together, it is easier for you to feel. But now that you have felt it, you will no longer need me to find it."

"How do you make it come?" I asked.

The Master glanced up at the sun before answering. "You've been to candle shops. You've seen all the perfectly formed candles hanging on the walls. And you know that any one candle, once it's lit, can be used to light all the other candles in the shop. In the same way, the happiness you feel right now is like the light of a freshly lit candle. It will stay with you, and grow brighter, until one day soon you can give that same happiness to others."

"How?" I asked.

"There is no how. Happiness is alive—it jumps from one person to another."

"But how did you get . . . well, happy before the rest of us?" I asked.

The Master put his hand in the fountain and splashed a few drops of water in my face. "Veronica! You ask so many questions. It doesn't matter what I say. You will never be satisfied."

I could tell he was teasing me. I smiled as I wiped away the water. "I want to know. What was so special about you that God gave you this light or happiness before he gave it to anyone else?"

The Master did not answer right away and I worried I had offended him. He put his hand back in the fountain and cupped the water in his palm, taking a sip.

"You don't have to answer if you don't want to," I said.

He spoke in a softer voice. "When I was young, I used to sit a long time by myself and wonder what God was really like. The question haunted me. Night and day, I used to dwell on it. When I asked the rabbis what he was like, they said the usual things: 'he is all powerful; he is all wise; he is all merciful.' But none of their answers satisfied me. I felt as if they were describing a glorious person they had read about in some old book. Not God."

"But the scriptures say these things about God," Thomas interrupted.

"Shh," I snapped at my brother.

The Master nodded. "I know the scriptures, I have read them. But the answers they give, they made me crave a deeper truth. I don't know why I felt this way. But I became certain that the only way to find it was to sit quietly alone, to just be by myself. So every morning and every evening, before and after work, I hiked into the desert and sat and watched my mind."

I raised my hand. "May I ask a question?"

"If you must, Veronica."

I laughed. He was teasing me again.

"What do you mean when you say you watched your mind?"

"That's a good question. Since I was sitting alone, usually with my eyes closed, there was nothing to see or do but watch my mind. I watched how busy it was, all the thoughts I had, and believe me, my thoughts were no different from the ones you're having right now. They were not wise, or profound, or powerful. They were nothing like the way God has been described to me. For a long time I often asked myself, 'Why do I keep sitting like this? I'm not getting anywhere.'"

"Why did you keep sitting like that?" I asked.

"Because I didn't have a choice. I felt compelled to do it. One day, I hoped, an answer would come to me. I can't say I knew for certain it would come, but in a strange way I had faith that it would. Then, one night, it was very late, an answer of sorts did appear. Or perhaps I should say I noticed something I had never noticed before, although it was obvious. I noticed that my thoughts kept coming and going. Kept changing shape and form and content. But who I was—the person who was watching the thoughts—he appeared to remain the same."

"I don't understand," Thomas and I said at the same moment. We both laughed, and the Master laughed with us. Even though he had asked us to call him Emmanuel, it was hard to think of him using that name.

"I'm sorry, it's my fault for explaining it so poorly," the Master said. "Let's try again. When I was sitting alone with my eyes closed, I noticed a part of me was unconnected to my thoughts. That part of me watched the thoughts. But it was not the same as my thoughts because even though they kept changing, it never changed. It was then I realized that that part was the real me, and that it was always there, deep inside, watching."

"What did you do next?" I asked.

"I began to pay more attention to this watcher. I found if I watched the silent part of my mind, rather than the active part, I felt more at peace. It was an amazing discovery. What was even more exciting was that the deeper I went into this watcher, the happier I became. It seemed there was no end to my joy. It was like I had started on a road, by accident, that kept leading to more and more beautiful scenery. Until one day I reached the end of the road. That happened when all my thoughts dropped away and my mind became perfectly silent. At that moment the scenery transformed into a magnificent kingdom."

"A kingdom?" I asked. "What did you see in this kingdom?"

"Nothing."

"Nothing? Then what made it so magnificent?"

"It was unlike any outer kingdom. There were no great castles, no tall trees, no towering mountains. But there was joy, there was light, there was love. I no longer felt those things, I had become them. Truly, I was joy, I was light, I was love. And I knew that this was who God really was."

I sat in awe. "Was that when you knew you were one with God?"

"That was when I realized we are all one with God." He suddenly stopped and glanced at the people who were standing behind us, waiting to speak to him. "That's enough for one day, Veronica, Thomas. Practice what I have taught you and come back soon. I'll be here for the rest of the week."

"Practice what?" I gasped.

The Master smiled. "Why, watching the watcher."

We stood and brushed off our clothes. We both bowed to the Master. "Thank you for taking the time to talk to us," my brother said.

"It was a pleasure to meet you, Thomas."

"I'm not sure if we'll be able to see you again," I said. "May I ask one more question?"

"You know all you need to know right now." The Master plucked a floating flower from the fountain and gave it to me. "Enjoy your walk home," he said.

I accepted the flower and bowed my head. I remember how painful it was to leave him, but Thomas said we had to hurry.

TWO

Three days later I went to see the Master again. I had to go in the evening, after helping my mother all day in the kitchen, and once more I missed the Master's afternoon talk. He was still staying at the merchant's house, though, and he was alone in the backyard when I entered, sitting in the corner with his eyes closed.

I went to leave but he called out without opening his eyes.

"Stay, Veronica," he said.

I sat on my knees in front of him. I had brought a loaf of bread as an offering but felt foolish holding it in my hands, although I had wrapped it in clean cloth. I kept thinking there was nothing I could give him that he needed.

At last he opened his eyes. He reached for the bread. "May I?" he asked. "I've had nothing to eat this evening."

I quickly handed over the loaf. "Can I get you some wine? You must be thirsty."

"This is fine." He picked off small pieces of bread

and chewed them slowly. "Did you practice what I taught you the other day?"

I frowned. "Yes. But I had so many thoughts. I tried watching them but I couldn't."

"Don't try. The watcher is already inside, already watching. There is nothing for you to do. Now close your eyes."

"Pardon?"

"Close your eyes."

I closed them. My legs were tired from walking. It was nice to sit so close to the Master, to rest in his serene company.

"Open your eyes," he said after maybe thirty seconds.

I opened my eyes.

"Look around. What do you see?" he asked.

"I see the fountain, the water. The walls of the merchant's house. The flowers and the bushes. And you, I see you."

"Who sees all these things?"

"I don't understand. I see them."

"Who are you?"

"Veronica."

"You are not Veronica. Close your eyes."

"Why?"

"Do as I say."

I closed my eyes.

"Now, keeping your eyes closed, do you notice you have thoughts?"

"Yes. I'm thinking about you."

"What you're thinking about doesn't matter. Do the thoughts come and go?"

"Yes."

"You notice the thoughts coming and going?"

"Yes."

"Good. Now continue to sit easily and let the thoughts come and go. Do not go looking for the watcher. The watcher is already present, it is already there, you do not have to create it. Now keep your eyes closed."

I did as I was told. We sat together for two or three minutes.

"Open your eyes," he said.

I opened my eyes.

"What do you see?" he asked.

"The same things I saw the last time you asked."

"Who sees them?"

"Me."

"Who are you?"

"Veronica . . . I don't know what you want me to say."

"Don't worry. This time when you close your

eyes, don't try to watch your thoughts. They will come and go as they always do. Just be aware that there is something that watches them. But don't try to find this watcher. Do not think about finding it. Thinking about the watcher is another thought, it is not the watcher. The watcher is already inside you, already separate from your thoughts." He paused. "Now close your eyes."

This time we sat together for many minutes, and I must admit I started to get restless, maybe even a little annoyed. I didn't understand how I was supposed to watch for the watcher without actually watching for it.

Then I decided to listen to his advice about not trying at all and I felt a little better. The peace of his company returned, and yet, it was somehow different. I no longer felt the peace as coming from him. It was coming from inside me. I didn't know if the peace was the watcher or not and I didn't care. Like he said, my thoughts kept coming and going and I let them. They didn't matter. I felt myself sinking deeper into the peace.

Finally, as if from miles away, he told me to open my eyes. It was hard to do as he asked. I felt so deep. But finally I managed to open them.

"How do you feel?" he asked.

"Good," I whispered.

"Look around you, what do you see?"

"I see the same things I saw before. Only . . ." I could not find the words to say what I meant.

"Only there is a change," the Master said.

"Yes."

"What has changed?"

"Me. No, I mean, I am the same but . . ." Again, I didn't know what to say.

"You are the same but you are also different," the Master said.

"Yes."

"So who are you?"

"The person who has the thoughts."

"Who is that?"

"The watcher."

"Very good." The Master returned to picking at my bread. He seemed hungry.

"Thank you," I said, realizing how peaceful I felt. It was stronger than the other day, and I had a feeling I would be able to find it whenever I needed it.

The Master simply nodded. "How is Thomas?"

"He's fine. He told me to say hello for him."

"Say hello for me. Now it's getting late, you should go. Come again in two days."

I stood. "I don't think I can get away again."

"Come late if you have to," he said.

I bowed and left.

THREE

Two days later I suspected the Master had seen my future. I was not able to slip away from my family until they were asleep. As a result, I didn't get to the merchant's house until late. I feared the place would be dark but found the home well lit. It seemed lots of people knew the Master would not be returning to the area for a long time and were anxious to spend a final evening with him.

I don't know why the Master agreed to meet with me alone. I didn't feel like I was special and deserved his attention. We spoke in a bedroom on the top floor. I had never been in such a lovely room. The Master sat on the floor on a rug and motioned for me to sit beside him. He offered me a glass of water, which I finished in one gulp. The night was warm and I was thirsty.

"How is your meditation?" he asked.

"Meditation? Is that what you call it?"

"Yes."

"It works better when I don't try." I added with a smile, "It works better with you around."

"In time it will go by itself. You will just have to start and let go. It will be like diving off a tree branch into a cool lake. You just take the right angle and let go. Gravity does the rest."

"What is that word, 'gravity'?"

"It's a word from another time. It's the force that keeps you from floating off the ground."

I laughed. "You're teasing me. There is no such thing."

He spoke in a serious voice. "This world is not the only world. Each star you see in the sky is like the sun, only so far away you see it as a tiny point of light. Around many of these stars circle worlds like this one."

I shook my head at such a wild idea. "It's hard to imagine."

"One day deep inside your heart you'll see millions of stars and know that what I tell you is true."

"Maybe you can see stars inside. I don't know about me."

My doubts caused him to smile. "What I am, you will become. It is only a question of time."

"The rabbis tell us to pray each day. But this . . . meditation. How is it different from prayer?"

"I'll answer your question with a question. Let's say that one day you are walking down the road and you happen to meet God. He's in a human body and you can talk to him. But he's busy and can't stay with you long. What would you do? Would you let him speak? Or would you do most of the talking?"

"I would let him speak," I said.

"Why?"

"God is wise. He knows so much more than me. It would be a waste of time to try and tell him something."

The Master nodded. "Life is like that short visit on the road. Prayer is for those who wish to talk to God. Meditation is for those who only want to listen to him."

"That's a beautiful story."

"It's called a parable. A story that teaches an important lesson."

"Can I tell it to Thomas?"

"You will repeat it to many people in this life. When you teach them to meditate."

I was surprised. "I have your permission to teach other people?"

"Meditate a few years. When you feel the time is right, then you may begin to teach."

"What if I say the wrong thing?"

"As your meditation deepens, the right words will come to you." He stopped. "Why the sudden long face?"

I hesitated. "It's nothing you can help me with."

"Tell me and we'll see."

"When you talk about the wonderful things I might see and do in the future, I have trouble believing it will happen. I'm not even sure I'll get to meditate. My father has already chosen the man I am to marry. His name is James. He's a good man, he works hard. My father says I have no choice in the matter, that I must obey him and marry James. He says James will take care of me and the children I'll probably have."

"Do you love James?"

"I hardly know him. We have only spoken twice. But I know he's very religious, very strict. He'll expect me to obey him and keep my mouth shut. I doubt he'll let me meditate."

"It sounds like a problem."

"Oh, Master, it's horrible! I don't know what to do!"

"Say you could do anything you liked. What would you do?"

"Anything?"

"Anything at all. Say there was nothing to stop you."

"Well, I love to paint. My father is a stonemason, and sometimes he lets me paint pictures on the walls he builds. But I would love to paint real pictures that people can hang in their homes. And . . ." I stopped.

"Go on."

"What I was going to say next is impossible."

"Tell me and we'll see how impossible it is."

"My brother, Thomas, makes the most wonderful sculptures. He's so good he's been invited by a local businessman to travel to Rome." I stopped and hung my head. "I want to go with him."

"And paint in Rome?"

I looked up. "That's my dream. To be a great artist in the greatest city in the world."

"Then do it. Follow your dream."

I shook my head. "You don't understand, my father would never let me go. I'm a girl, I'm only sixteen years old, I have no rights."

"You and Thomas are close, aren't you?"

"Yes."

"He knows you want to go with him?"

"Yes. He's like you. He says I should come with him."

"Then go, Veronica. Go to Rome."

"Disobey my father? I can't. I mean, even if I tried, he'd stop me and beat me."

"How did you come here tonight?"

"I walked."

"Did you tell your father? Your mother?"

"I just told Thomas. He helped me climb out our window."

"That's how you'll go to Rome. You'll climb out the same window. Only when you leave for Rome, Thomas will go with you. It's simple."

I stared at the Master in shock. "You want me to break every rule I have ever been taught?"

"Why not? They're silly rules." He stopped and spoke in a serious voice. "You'll never be truly happy unless you follow your heart. The joy you find in the world, the joy you find in meditation, both come from being courageous."

I trembled. "I feel what you say is true. But I'm afraid."

"I was afraid when I started to teach."

"Really? You? I don't believe it."

"It's true. I knew what I had to teach would anger a lot of people. This is a primitive world, Veronica. Angry people do crazy things."

"Are you saying you could be killed?"

"We may both die at the hands of others. It may be soon, it may not be for many years. It doesn't matter. What matters is what we do today—that we do what we feel is right." He stopped. "Wherever you go, Veronica, I'll be with you. Remember—you were born in this world to be a candle. To light up many hearts."

His words stirred deep feelings inside me. But I had so many doubts, so many questions. When I went to speak, though, he motioned for me to be silent. He was through speaking. He was telling me I already knew what I needed to know.

I bowed to him and left.

I have just finished what Mr. Grey has translated of Veronica's story when Seymour calls. He says they're at the Mirage, top floor. Brutran has reserved a separate room for each of us. Mine is 1178. I can pick up my key at the front desk. He also says he's figured out a way to punch through my memory block, if I'm interested.

I have time before Mr. Grey gets out of surgery. I decide to see what my old friend has come up with. During the taxi ride to the hotel, however, the small book haunts me. The Master did not sound anything like the historical Christ. I doubt the story was even about Jesus.

Yet all the tales surrounding the veil tie it to a young woman named Veronica, and the present-day custodian of the artifact, Sarah Goodwin, valued the book so much she went to the trouble to hide it in her bedroom wall. Clearly Sarah believes the story is genuine, and that the Master the young woman spoke to was the same man I saw in the veil.

It is all very confusing.

Still, I enjoyed Veronica, her spunky attitude, and several of the Master's lines touched me deeply. I find it interesting that the Master taught Veronica the ancient Vedic form of meditation known as *Vichara*—a Sanskrit term that means "meditation on the Self." That is the Self with a capital *S*—the Supreme Self, or the Brahman.

A close reading of the Bhagavad Gita shows that Krishna taught a similar practice. Ironically, Krishna said in the Gita that the technique was difficult for the average person to master, that the constant repetition of his name was an easier path to realization. Having lived in India, I know the majority of yogis consider *Vichara* a waste of time unless one has been blessed by God. Of course, Veronica, in her own innocent way, made it clear she felt blessed by her Master.

On a lighter note, Veronica's Master was definitely ahead of his time. Equal rights for men and women? Follow your dreams? If he was indeed Jesus Christ then it was no wonder they crucified him. Also, his remarks about gravity and the true nature of the stars—it is like the man was not just enlightened, he came from an advanced civilization.

The book raises more questions than it answers.

It is frustrating not knowing how it ends.

I go to Matt's room first. I don't need supernatural hearing to know he's playing the game on the other side of the door. I knock and he calls for me to come in.

Matt sits on the center of a king-size bed in a hotel robe. He has recently showered; his long dark hair is still wet. He doesn't bother to look up as I enter. I let the door close at my back.

"How's Mr. Grey?" he asks.

"So-so. He's in surgery. His temporal lobe's bleeding and his brain has swelled. He'll be lucky to make a full recovery."

"Is he in good hands?"

I come over and sit on the bed. "I think so. The surgeon's name is Dr. Tower. He has an excellent reputation. I liked him. He's optimistic."

"Good," Matt says.

"Are you still mad?"

"I'm not mad."

"Liar."

Matt shrugs. "Honestly, Sita, I couldn't care less what happened today. My problems with you are much older."

I groan. "Please, Matt, let's not rewind the Teri tape. We've talked it to death, and the truth is we were both responsible for her death. We both made mistakes. I should never have contacted her. You should never have contacted her. I should never have changed her into a vampire when she was dying. And you should never have killed me for making her a vampire."

"I wasn't myself when I shot you," Matt says.

"I wasn't myself when I slept with you."

"Now who's the liar? You knew exactly who you were. You just happened to be in Teri's body."

"I didn't hear any complaints from you while we were screwing."

Matt shocks me by raising his arm to strike me. He takes it a step further, swinging his fist toward my face. His speed is blinding—I'm not given a chance to duck. All I can do is brace for the blow. I know his strength. I'll be lucky if he doesn't break my jaw and send half my teeth clattering across the floor.

But at the last instant he stops himself. His fist makes contact with my cheek but that's it. Drawing in a deep breath, he withdraws his hand and sits back down on the bed. He moved so fast I didn't even realize that he had stood.

"Sorry," he mutters. He picks up his laptop and—it's hard to believe—returns to playing the game.

"I've never seen you hit a woman before," I say.

"You've seen me kill a few."

"Those were Telar females. They don't count."

He nods, but it's clear he's hardly listening.

"What's gotten into you?" I demand.

"Nothing."

"Are you sure? Or is it possible that what John said is true? That the game is dangerous."

"It's not dangerous."

"I disagree. It's pushed you over the edge."

Matt stops playing and stares off into the distance for several seconds, before finally closing his laptop and looking at me.

"I'm not angry with you about Teri. Not tonight," he says.

"Well, that's a relief." When he doesn't respond, I add, "Pray tell what I've done to upset you this time."

His response staggers me. The casual way he says it.

"Do you know how close my mother came to killing you?"

I stand from the bed. "That's a lie! Umara showed me nothing but love and support."

"That was after you met her. But before that, when my father was still alive, she often talked about killing you."

"Bullshit. Umara was too mature to be jealous of me and Yaksha."

"It was never a question of jealousy. Her view was practical. She knew of the vow my father had made to Krishna. To destroy all the vampires before he left this world. She knew who the last vampire was, and why my father hesitated to kill you." Matt pauses. "For many years, for more than you can imagine, my mother wanted to ease his torment by getting rid of you."

I tremble. He's telling the truth. "And you? Did you feel the same way?"

"Yes."

"Then why didn't either of you pay me a visit?"

"My father forbade it."

"Good for Yaksha," I say.

Matt's expression darkens. "Don't taunt me, Sita. Not now, not when it comes to my father. It's because of you we never saw him again. When he went to kill you, he didn't go to die."

"You're wrong. I spoke to him. He was tired of life. He

wanted it to be over. He told me. Those were his words."

Matt throws his feet over the side of the bed and stands. His old habit returns; he begins to pace. "He wanted to die *after* he said good-bye to us. *After* we got a chance to say good-bye to him. You made that impossible."

"I protected myself. I had a right."

"Yeah, you had a right. Just like a black widow has a right to kill its mate after luring it into its web."

"That's not fair. I tried to kill him, yes, he was trying to kill me. But I never tried to seduce him."

"You didn't have to!" Matt yells. "Just being who you are . . . he just had to see you and he was doomed."

"I don't understand. Before he came after me, he hadn't seen you or Umara for a long time. You told me that yourself. He must have already said good-bye."

"He did that to prepare us. To spare us."

"I didn't know. I didn't even know you two existed."

"You knew he loved you. He never stopped loving you. My mother knew it, and it was a burden she had to live with for five thousand years. You have no idea what you did to her."

I nod sadly. "You're right, I had no idea how much I hurt Umara."

"And me."

"And you. But Matt, is it fair to blame me? I loved Yaksha as much as he loved me. And I stayed away from him, and not just out of fear. I kept a distance because I wanted him to have a life free of the burden of the vow he had made to Krishna."

"Your distance didn't make that burden any less."

"It gave him a life. So your father loved me, he loved your mother as well. She was greater than I ever could be, which means my decision was the right one. He got to share his life with someone he cared for. He got to have a child. He had a family." I stop. "Something I never had."

It was Yaksha who stole away my family when he made me a vampire. Five thousand years have passed since that night, yet the wound has never healed.

In fact, right now, this instant, I feel I have never missed Rama and Lalita more. I have spent so long training myself not to think of them. But it's as if my confrontation with Matt has burst a dam inside. I don't just miss my husband, I long for him: his touch, his kind words, his loving eyes. And Lalita— my daughter used to have to smile at me to make my day complete.

All these feelings—I don't know what to do with them. Yet Matt is so close, and I wish I could just hand them to him. . . .

"I know."

"I know." Matt stops pacing and approaches me, touching the side of my face. "I apologize. You're right. When I swung my fist at you, I meant to hurt you."

"Thank God you have such amazing reflexes."

He continues to stare at me. "You know, we're alone in this world. There's no one else like us. You have Seymour and he's a good friend but . . . when you think about it, he'll be dead before we know it. Then we'll only have each other."

"Are you trying to say you love me?"

His eyes are so powerful, so vulnerable. "Yes," he says.

"But Teri . . . I can never be Teri."

He touches my chin. "Let's not talk about Teri."

"What do you want to talk about?"

"Nothing," he says, and kisses me.

I remember his lips, I remember everything about him. But the last time I was naked in bed with him, I was inside Teri's body, and the shadow of her memories made it impossible for me to surrender to his embrace.

Tonight I feel no such inhibition. We remove each other's clothes at hyper speed, before everything merges into dreamlike slow motion where every move transpires between two ticks of the clock. He kisses my neck for hours. I brush his hair for days. And as his tongue slides over my breasts and beneath my abdomen, I feel a year go by. But in all that time I don't blink, I don't take my eyes off him. Matt, he is so beautiful; the only man who ever reminded me of Yaksha. Which means I must love him, too.

We make love for two hours, according to the clock.

But I never tell him how I feel.

Why? I don't know.

He has opened his heart to me.

But I'm afraid to do the same.

A part of me waits and watches.

I fear the night has not yet reached its climax.

Matt and I lie naked in bed together, my head resting on his chest, listening to his heart pound. It could move mountains, the power of his beat. It's no wonder the Telar feared him so. He is unquestionably the strongest creature on earth.

"Seymour is waiting for us," Matt says.

"I know."

"Did he tell you how he plans to unlock your memory?"

"I was afraid to ask."

"His idea is clever. He wants to use the telepathic bond you two share—in a hypnotic session. You must have heard of mutual hypnosis?"

"It's where two people hypnotize each other. The theory is their shared trance allows them to reach deeper levels of the subconscious." I pause. "Does Seymour hope, with us, that it will work a hundred times better than normal?"

"Yes. It probably will."

I sit up suddenly. "I don't know. It could harm him. We're too close. The stuff I went through at Auschwitz, he won't be able to bear it."

"Are you worried about that or are you more afraid he's going to read your mind and know that we just had sex?"

"That is something to worry about. Maybe I should tell him before we start. We should clear the air."

Matt smiles. "Relax. Seymour's no dummy. He had Brutran give him the room between ours. By now he can probably mimic the sounds you make when you have an orgasm."

"I don't make any sounds. It's you who bellows like a bull."

"Sita, has anyone ever told you how romantic you are?"

"Not in a while."

"I'm not surprised." Matt climbs out of bed and puts on his sweats. "Did Mr. Grey say anything to you about our ultimate destination before they wheeled him into surgery?"

"He made one strange remark. He said we won't be going to Nellis Air Force Base."

Matt nodded. "That's true."

I reach for my own clothes and begin to dress. "How do you know?"

"I beat the game."

"What does that mean? Did you win a prize?"

"I reached the goal of the game."

"Please don't keep me in suspense," I say when he doesn't continue.

"I'm sorry, that's exactly what I'm going to do. The reason is because I think the game has something to do with what happened to you in the past. And I don't want to spoil your innocence just before you link minds with Seymour."

"You actually think you might influence my memory?"

"Yes," Matt replies. "On several crucial points."

"You act like I'm blocking everything that happened at

Auschwitz. That's silly. There are a few points I can't remember, probably because I was so near death. But it's not like the Nazis cast a spell over me."

"You thought the same about Landulf of Capua and his alter ego, Dante. You thought you got away clean. But we all know how that turned out."

"Fine," I mutter. In reality, I still have trouble recalling the days I spent in Sicily a thousand years ago—Seymour's record of the events notwithstanding. It's still hard for me to believe a bunch of Middle Ages barbarians were able to outfox me.

Matt and I have a final awkward moment before we leave to meet with Seymour. We are fully dressed and talking about how we should conduct the hypnotic regression when Matt suddenly steps in front of me and puts a finger to my lips, momentarily silencing me.

"What's wrong?" I ask softly. I can see he's troubled, and just minutes ago he was cracking jokes. Lowering his head, he removes his finger from my lips.

"I was just wondering how you felt about what I said."

He is referring to when he told me he loved me.

"I felt wonderful," I say.

He nods but he is not looking at me. "Good."

"You caught me by surprise. Like I said, I thought you were still upset about Teri."

"It's a deep scar. It will take time to go away. It might never go away."

I put a hand on his shoulder. "I can say it back to you. I want to say it. I just worry, you know, that now is not the right time."

Matt raises his head and shrugs. "Don't worry about it. It's not important."

"Are you sure?"

"Yes," he says.

It's after eleven when I knock on Seymour's door. Chances are I won't get back to the hospital until after one. That's fine, I think. It will give Mr. Grey more time to recover. I have no plan to break him out of the hospital. No matter how successful the surgery, he's going to need to rest a few days if he is to recover. I wish I knew why he is so adamant about staying close to me.

I expect to have a painful scene with Seymour. I know how attached he is to me. His love for me is unconditional, it's true, but he's never hidden his attraction to me. I assume hearing Matt and me screwing in the adjoining room must have hurt.

But Seymour surprises me. When I try to bring up the subject, he waves his hand and tells me not to worry about it.

"It was bound to happen," he says.

"You're not jealous."

"Of course I'm jealous. But I'm a realist. Matt's the closest thing this planet has got to a god. I'm a burned-out writer who smokes two packs a day and never exercises. How can I compete?"

I reach out and brush his hair from his eyes. "You're amazing."

"I know."

"I love you."

"Of course you do. I love you." He takes my hand and kisses it. "Now get Matt in here. We should get started."

I do as ordered. Matt enters the room a minute later.

"Where do you want to start?" I ask.

"Where you left off on the plane," Seymour says, before giving Matt a quick rundown of the points he missed, finishing with how Major Klein put a bag over my head and dragged me beneath the ground to his dungeon. Seymour adds, "Once we're in a deep trance, we'll start there."

"I can tell a lot of what happened during my interrogation without resorting to hypnosis," I say.

Neither Seymour nor Matt looks impressed.

"No offense," Seymour says. "But it's hard to rely on your memory after Major Klein got his hooks into you."

"Why do you say that?" I ask.

"Because what you told us doesn't sound real," Matt explains. "A metal box that emits a high-pitched sound—which only you could hear—that tortured you and then knocked you out? Never mind the weird cuffs that you couldn't break. No one had stuff like that during the war."

"All right," I say, in no mood to argue. "I'll tell the last part of my story in a trance."

Seymour and I sit in two chairs facing each other, our knees almost touching. Matt turns the light down low and sits on the corner of the bed, where he can keep an eye on both our faces.

Seymour is a student of hypnosis and I, of course, have my own way of inducing a trance. We stare into each other's eyes and give a minimum of relaxing suggestions. Soon our eyes are closed and I feel as if we are both enclosed in a bubble that is slowly rising high into the sky. I see stars and intuitively know Seymour sees them as well. But it is not simple intuition—it is our old telepathic bond. To this day I don't understand why it is so strong, why our minds automatically connect—they just do. The link feels as real as an extra sense.

As if from far off, I hear Seymour speak, in a whisper, and I find his choice of pronouns appropriate—we are locked so tightly together. The only reason we speak at all is for Matt's benefit.

"We're surrounded by white light. Like a radiant waterfall, it pours into the tops of our heads, filling all parts of our bodies, before flowing out our feet. The white light continues to flow, in a steady stream, from our feet back to the tops of our heads, forming an impenetrable cocoon that shields us from all negativity. Nothing we see or feel can harm us. It's as if we are watching a television screen. The controller is in our hands—we are in complete control. Now let our minds journey into the past . . ."

FIFTEEN

*T*he room is a perfect cube, twenty feet on all sides; even the distance to the cement ceiling is the same. A single bright recessed light shines from its center. The walls and the floor are solid concrete. The lone door appears to be made of the same incredibly hard alloy as my wrist and ankle cuffs—both of which have me pinned to a central pole.

Except for the dry odor of concrete, I smell nothing— no blood, no tears, not even a trace of perspiration. I suspect the room has not been used before, that it was probably constructed specifically to hold me.

I have been standing in the center of the room for two weeks.

Without food, water, or blood to drink.

No one has stopped by to visit.

And I hear nothing. Except my heart, my breathing.

I'm in terrible pain. The constant standing has worn out my leg muscles. The cramps in my arms are worse. My wrists are pinned far above my head. I'm stretched so long my toes barely touch the floor. The angle is reminiscent of a crucifixion; my suffering parallels those who have been put to death in that manner. Due to the way gravity drains the blood and lymph fluids downward in the body during crucifixion, a person usually suffocates to death.

But slowly, very slowly.

Every breath is agony.

Every minute feels like an eternity.

I know why they leave me to suffer. They want to break me, and because they know what I am, they figure it will take a great deal of pain to do it. Obviously they want something from me. But what it is I have no idea.

At the end of the fortieth day Major Klein stops by.

He brings with him a woman. Someone I have seen before, long ago, in different clothes and with different hair. Her features were dark before; now she is a blonde. It's odd but I can't recall where I met her.

"Hello, Sita. How are we feeling today?" Klein asks cheerfully.

"Wonderful."

"Good, very good." He has brought with him a small folding table, which he sets up not far from my pole. He has also brought a black bag, the contents of which he places on top of the table: his metal box with the three dials; a jagged-edged knife; a plastic spray bottle filled with a sickly yellow fluid; another spray bottle filled with water; a box of wooden matches; and a hammer.

He smiles when he sees me studying the items.

"I hope these tools don't frighten you," he says, gesturing to his toys.

"As you've probably guessed, Herr Klein, I don't frighten easily."

He nods. "Of course, it says so in your file. But still, you are not so different as you think. You are very old, strong, you need blood to survive. But none of that makes you a monster, at least not to us. You are human, too. Look at you. You are pretty, you have a sharp mind, an alluring figure. Why, I bet you are closer to being a person than those filthy Jews we're exterminating two hundred feet above your head."

It's true I haven't been able to hear their screams, but I have sensed them: the pain of thousands dying. That's why the room feels like hell, and why Major Klein looks like a devil.

I sense no exaggeration in his words. Two hundred feet is a great distance to tunnel into the earth. Have they done all this for me? They must want something very important.

"Most of the Jews I know are wonderful people," I reply. "While most of the Nazis I know are scum."

He smiles again, quickly, but this time it's forced.

"Fräulein Sita insults us again. I'm surprised. I thought my little demonstration in the Levines' flat would have taught you better."

I shrug as best I can for a person who can hardly move. "You're going to torture me no matter what I say. I may as well speak the truth."

He nods and moves closer, while his partner stays at a distance. Major Klein may act like a robot but she's in a class by herself. The way she stares, her dark eyes so vacant, I'd swear there is no one at home.

"That's where you're wrong," Klein says. "There's no reason for you to suffer anymore. All we require is for you to talk. And when you're done talking, you'll be set free. Does that sound fair?"

"What do you want me to talk about?"

"A few things from your past."

"Go on."

Klein nods pleasantly and turns away, strolling around the room. "Before we get into specifics, it's important you know how detailed our file on you is. We know you were born around 3000 B.C., and that at the age of twenty you were transformed into a vampire. Yaksha, the greatest of all vampires, created you."

"Where did you get this information?" I ask, stunned.

"Later, all that can be explained. Particularly if you choose to join us, which I think you will. For now let me present you with a few more facts. At the age of a hundred you met a teacher by the name of Krishna. He lived in the forest of Vrindavana with the five Pandava brothers: Arjuna, Bhima, Yudhisthira, Nakula, and Sahadeva—all of who were married to the same woman, Draupadi. True?"

"I see you've been reading the Mahabharata," I reply.

"I'm asking if it's true that you met these people?"

"Maybe."

Klein stops and stares. His face goes blank and he says two words. "Frau Cia."

Picking up the hammer, the woman walks toward me. I fight against the cuffs to no avail. Without blinking, she raises the hammer and strikes my left kneecap. The pain is incredible; it rockets up my leg into my brain. She raises the hammer again and breaks my right kneecap.

"All right, damn you, I met them all!" I cry.

"Thank you, Sita," Klein says as he resumes his stroll around the room. "See how easy it is to make us happy? All you have to do is talk. Just tell the truth. Now, the reason I bring up the Pandavas is because of the important role they play in the Mahabharata. And you are right, I have read the book, many times, in its original Sanskrit. The Führer has as well—he has made a life study of the book."

"I know he has read the Vedas," I whisper, my body slowly trying to absorb the shock of the two blows. In my mind, the mystery surrounding the woman keeps growing. She has phenomenal strength. If I didn't know better, I'd swear she was a vampire. But she can't be—I can tell by the sound of her heartbeat. The beat is strong but not as rhythmic as mine. I add, "That's where he got the swastika."

"True. It's a sacred symbol in India."

"Not the way your Führer uses it."

Klein halts. "I don't understand?"

"He inverted it and tilted it on its side. It's like what the satanists do when they hang the cross upside down."

Klein smiles broadly. "Are you implying that we're satanists?"

"I'm just making an observation."

"An interesting one at that." Klein resumes his stroll. "Where were we? Oh, yes, the Pandava brothers, the heroes of the Battle of Kurukshetra. When you get down to it, that's what the Mahabharata is all about. 'The war to end all wars.' Did they really use that phrase in those days?"

"Yes," I say.

"Ironic, don't you think? Of course you know who the Pandavas fought?"

"Their cousins, the Kauravas."

"Very good. Did you have any personal contact with the Kauravas?"

"Very little."

"Please, Sita, be precise."

"I stood with the Kauravas on the first day of the battle."

"Why didn't you stand with the Pandavas?"

"I was afraid I might run into Yaksha."

"You were avoiding him?"

"Yes."

"Why?"

"It's a long story."

"We have time. Nothing but time."

"Yaksha had promised Krishna he would destroy all the vampires. I knew he had been hunting them."

"You were afraid for your life, then?"

"Yes."

"Then why did you go to the battle in the first place?"

I hesitate. "To see Krishna."

"No other reason?"

"No."

"Did you get to see him? Talk to him?"

"I saw him that day, from a distance. He played the role of Arjuna's charioteer and rode out into the center of the field before the battle."

"Why did Krishna do this?"

"You've studied the Mahabharata. You must know why. Arjuna was upset on the eve of battle. He didn't want to fight and kill so many of his friends and relatives."

"The Kauravas were his friends?"

"They were related but they were enemies. The point is that Krishna took time with Arjuna to explain that the war was just and that he should fight. Their dialogue formed the core of the Bhagavad Gita, India's most sacred book."

"Were you able to hear Krishna and Arjuna speak from where you were standing?"

"No."

"Why not? With your vampire ears, you should have heard everything they said."

"I thought so too. Krishna—he must have done something to shield their dialogue."

Klein comes near, and I fear he is going to call on Frau Cia again. He speaks in my ear. "Did he talk about exotic weapons?"

"I told you, I couldn't hear them."

Klein backs off a step, standing behind me. "Did you fight with the Kauravas that day?"

"No."

"What did you do?"

"When the fighting started, I left the field and hid in the trees."

"That doesn't sound like you, Sita, to run from a fight."

"It wasn't my fight. The Pandavas and Kauravas were fighting over land. Who would control the country. I had no interest in who won. I knew I would be leaving India soon."

"Why?"

"I told you, to get away from Yaksha."

"Because you were afraid of him?"

"Yes."

Klein moves in front. "How many days did the Battle of Kurukshetra last?"

"Four days."

"In the Mahabharata it says it lasted longer. Two weeks."

"Distortions crept into the book over time. It lasted four days."

"What did you do during the battle?"

"I just told you."

"No. After Krishna spoke to Arjuna you said you retired to the woods. What did you do there?"

"Nothing."

"You hid in the woods for four days and did nothing?"

"I stayed in the area on the off chance I might see Krishna again."

Klein comes close and speaks in a sympathetic tone. "He must have meant a great deal to you. To go to all that trouble just to glimpse him in the distance. To risk running into Yaksha."

I shrug. "Like I said, I was leaving India. I thought it would be my last chance to see him."

"Not what one would expect from a monster."

He hasn't asked a question so I choose not to answer.

Klein points a finger at me. "Let's be honest with each other, Sita. You have a big heart. You love deeply. How else could you be so devoted to Krishna?"

"That was a long time ago."

"It doesn't matter, you haven't changed. You're a fool in love. Look at the way you watched over the Levines the past two years. Two filthy Jews and you felt obligated to protect them. What devotion!"

He stops, waiting. But he hasn't asked a question. I wait.

"Have you nothing to say?" he demands.

He knows I want to ask if they are still alive.

"What is your question?" I say.

"I'm trying to get you to admit something. Why is it so painful for you? I said it at the start. You may be a vampire but you are still human. Indeed, you are more human than most of humanity."

"Why is that trait so important to you?" I ask.

"It means you can join us! You can be one of us. You can help us win this war and reclaim the world."

He shakes with the energy of his pronouncement, his marble eyes bulging from his waxen face. Blood fills his cheeks but it's strange how lifeless it makes him appear. His thick lips twitch.

"You're insane," I say, even though I know what it will get me.

This time he doesn't say her name, merely gestures with his hand. Frau Cia picks up the bottle of light yellow liquid and the box of matches and walks toward me. At the last instant, just before she sprays it on my hands, I smell the fluid and know what it is.

Gasoline.

Frau Cia sprays so much that it drips down my bare arms

and stains my rolled-up sleeves. She lights a match and I blow it out. She doesn't mind. Taking a step behind me, she lights another one and touches it to my fingers.

My arms transform into torches.

Burn, burn forever, that is what the Christians say happens to all those who reject Jesus Christ. The threat is powerful; it has steered western civilization for two thousand years. It is also clever. Who could imagine a hell worse than eternal flames?

I can't imagine it. Nor can I stand it.

But I do not beg for mercy. Not from him. Never.

Still, the pain defeats me. It causes me to black out.

I regain consciousness a minute or two later. I am still on fire but Frau Cia is spraying water on my hands. It takes many squirts to put out the flames and by then my skin has blackened and begun to peel. The lumps of flesh drip in my hair, in my face, in my eyes. I hang my head and close my eyes and try not to feel the pain.

Klein steps beside me. "I have to go now, Sita. But when I return you will tell me everything you did during the four days of the battle. You will remember everything you saw. Everyone you spoke to. Understand?"

"I suppose," I whisper.

I tell myself it is not the same as saying yes.

"Good girl." He pats me on the back and turns for the door. But he stops before leaving, Frau Cia by his side. He sniffs the air and frowns. "I hate to say this but you smell no different than a stinking Jew when it burns. I'm disappointed."

He leaves. Thank God he leaves.

I don't know what day it is. I don't know if I blacked out or if I was driven into unconsciousness. I only know that when I raise my head and open my eyes I'm no longer in the concrete dungeon.

The Nazis have moved me aboveground, to a low bluff at the far end of the concentration camp. I am chained to an identical pole, with cuffs that feel no different from the previous set. I believe they are the same cuffs. I can't break them. Around me, on all sides, is a dome-shaped wire cage. I stand in the center, like before, with my arms pinned above my head, the toes of my feet barely touching the muddy ground. A light rain falls. The sky is gray and dismal.

The camp looks and smells like purgatory.

On my far right, a quarter of a mile away, is a deserted railroad track. I can tell by the excellent condition of the rails that trains roll in frequently. Next to it is a row of wooden buildings that could be dormitories. Yet I doubt anyone stays there long, for beside it, almost directly in front of me, is a wide stone structure with a low ceiling and a series of vents sticking out of the roof. The vents are at least two hundred yards distant but give off a harsh disinfectant smell that burns my sensitive nose and causes my nostrils to run.

It is not disinfectant. It is gas.

I am looking at the building where the Nazis kill the Jews.

On my left are the ovens, the tall smoking towers, where thousands—if not millions—of corpses are turned to ash. Even as I watch, the towers belch thick black clouds of stinking vapor into the forlorn sky. Ash litters the landscape; it mixes with the steady drizzle and pelts my head and stings my eyes.

No, this is not purgatory. I am in hell.

Yet a peculiar silence grips this insane world. The occupants of the last train have already been murdered; their disposal is being taken care of methodically. Faintly, I hear men speaking in hushed tones, in Polish and German and Hebrew, inside the crematorium. It takes me a minute to get it. The SS, who guard the camp, are using Jewish men to shove the bodies into the flames.

"Oh, God," I whisper.

A bald woman, wearing a drab gray prison suit, shuffles toward my wire cage. Her head is down and she moves with great weariness, but there is no question I'm her goal. It takes me a minute to realize I am looking at Harrah. My shock is overwhelming. How long was I out? How long have I been at the camp? Harrah is thirty pounds lighter than the last time I saw her, and she was thin then. Her skin has lost all luster; it resembles the ash that covers the camp.

Somehow, though, Harrah summons a smile to greet me.

"I heard they had taken you captive," she says. "I feared you were dead. It's good to see you, Sita."

"I'm sorry, Harrah, it's not good to see you. Not here."

She nods. "You warned us. We should have listened."

I shake my head. "I might be the reason you're here."

"Don't say that. The day you vanished, they picked up all the Jews left in Paris. They were watching us the whole time, waiting until the invasion."

"Did the Allies take the beaches at Normandy?"

"We've only heard rumors but we're almost certain they succeeded. The guards here are scared. They know the Russians are closing in."

"The Russians?"

"They counterattacked the Germans after the Americans and the British established a base on the continent. They'll get here first."

"How soon?" I have to struggle to hide the pain in my voice. My burns have healed but the muscle spasms in my arms, legs, and chest are unbearable. It's like my crucifixion will never end. If I were human I would have smothered to death a long time ago. My lungs are on fire from the slow drain of blood from my abdomen, and from breathing the stench of the gas.

Harrah hesitates. "It's probably best not to get our hopes up."

Now she's the realist. The Germans might be surrounded but their soldiers are highly disciplined. They won't give up without a fight. Their leader won't let them. Germany's defeat means Hitler's head. And his inner circle must know they'll be executed once the truth of the camps is made public. They'll destroy their precious fatherland before surrendering.

And they'll kill everyone in the camp before the Russians arrive.

"How's Ralph?" I ask.

"He's sick but alive. They have us working on the north side of the camp making uniforms. Sixteen hours a day and a miserable bowl of soup." Harrah shrugs. "It could be worse."

"Are there many like you? With jobs?"

"There aren't many Jews. The Poles get most of the jobs."

I have to ask. "So what makes you two special?"

Harrah stares at me. "The guards told me to go talk to you. They didn't do it out of the goodness of their hearts."

Clever. Make sure our relationship is as strong as ever, then exploit it. "They want to use you as leverage against me," I say.

For the first time Harrah shows a flash of her old spark. "Don't give in to them, Sita. They can only kill us once. Whatever they want you for, it can't be good."

I want to warn Harrah that the SS can make a single death feel like a thousand. But she knows; she just has to look around her.

"I'm not sure what they want," I say.

"They haven't told you?"

"Not directly."

"Maybe it's your blood."

"I assumed that was it. But as far as I can tell, they've taken none, and they've had me helpless a number of times. It has to be something else. Something in my past."

Harrah glances over her shoulder and moves closer to my cage. "There's talk the Beast is coming here," she says.

"Himmler?"

"He's supposed to fly in tomorrow from Berlin."

"Who's your source?"

"A Catholic priest in the kitchen. We call him Father Bob. He cooks for the guards. He's a good man. He says the Germans talk about you and nothing else." She pauses. "They act like you can win the war for them."

"Gimme a break."

"Himmler wouldn't come here unless it was important."

"The Nazis have a peculiar sense of what's important."

"Be careful around him. They say he knows black magic."

"Speaking of magic, were you able to hide the veil?"

"Yes."

"Where?"

"Here. I'm wearing it under my coat."

"Jesus, Harrah. Is that wise?"

"They came in the middle of the night. I didn't know what else to do. I had to make a decision. I couldn't leave it behind."

"Have they given any sign that they know about it?"

Harrah frowns. "I've been asked strange questions—mostly

about my family. I get the impression they've heard rumors about the tradition of Veronica but nothing substantial."

"I wish I could wear it for a while," I say.

Harrah's eyes moisten with compassion. "You're in pain."

I struggle with the cuffs, for all the good it does me. The flesh around my wrists and ankles has worn away. It's bloody, and the constant pressure on the joints keeps it from healing.

"It's this damn metal. I've never seen anything like it. One of their brilliant scientists must have come up with it." I bang the cuffs together in frustration. "Get me the key to these damn things and I'll get us all out of here."

"Ralph says he's seen the key."

"What? Where? How would he know?"

"He's seen the strange woman who tortures you. He says she keeps the key on a chain around her neck."

Now that Harrah mentions it, I remember Frau Cia wearing a gold necklace. "Tell Ralph if he can get it without getting himself killed, you'll live to see your grandchildren."

She puts a hand to her mouth. "He talks about nothing else."

"Harrah, I was joking."

"No, you weren't. And what you say makes sense. It's too late to play it safe. You're our only hope. If we can get you free, you could destroy the whole camp."

"I could destroy it at full strength. But now . . ." I don't finish.

"You're thirsty. You need blood."

"I'm all right."

"Sita, we're depending on you! If you need blood then we'll get it for you."

"From your body? If I drained every drop in your veins, Harrah, I doubt it would touch my thirst. No offense, but your neck looks like it belongs on a chicken and your head looks like a coconut."

She scratches her head. "A coconut has more hair."

"What happened to it? Did they shave it off?"

"I did. Lice. We've all got them. It's the only way to keep from scratching yourself to death."

"Lovely," I mutter. Fortunately, my powerful immune system has spared me her affliction.

Harrah looks toward the north end of the camp. "I better get back to the factory. The size of this place is obscene. It took me twenty minutes to walk here." She pauses. "I'm not sure when I'll be able to come back."

"Don't worry about me. Concentrate on staying alive."

"If Ralph can get ahold of the key, he'll visit you tonight."

"No! They'll post guards at night."

"A beautiful vampire like you can't handle a few guards?"

I see she's serious. She knows about my hypnotic ability.

"Tell Ralph not to take any crazy chances. Stay alive! Both of you! The Nazis are bound to slip up. Then I'll pounce and I'll have all the blood I need."

"What if we all pitched in? What if Ralph brought you two pints?"

"Good-bye, Harrah," I say, nevertheless wondering what she would say to the others while she was collecting the blood. *You see, I have this wonderful friend. She's not a Jew, she's a vampire, but she hates the Nazis as much as we do.* Good old Harrah, it's hard to watch her leave. I wish I had told her more how much it meant to me to see her alive.

And the veil. I'm relieved the Nazis don't have it.

Trouble is, if Harrah goes to the ovens, chances are the veil will go up in smoke. I have to get free! The ancient fire inside overrides my weakened state and I strain with all that's left inside me to pull the pole free of the ground. Unfortunately, I can generate scant pressure on the tips of my toes, and I finally realize that the pole is attached to a massive block of concrete.

Damn. Have the Nazis designed the whole place for vampires?

The day stretches on forever. My breathing goes from bad to worse. I can inhale, but when I try to relax my diaphragm and let the air out, I feel a sharp stab just below my sternum. It feels like I'm being poked by a knife and makes me want to stop breathing altogether.

I think about dying. For the first time, really.

After so many years, I assumed I would live forever.

But to die, to accept my death, to imagine my body still and lifeless, is difficult to contemplate. It seems impossible but ever since I met Krishna and he told me I had his grace, I assumed nothing could destroy me. My faith went beyond blind—it was insane. Even in the worst of situations, I have always felt I would survive. Tomorrow would come and I would be there to see the sun rise.

Now, I feel so weary, so hurt, I don't pray for death but for once it feels inevitable. My haughty words to Harrah aside, I doubt the Nazis are going to make a mistake. It's not in the German's nature to err. Just look at them, one small country on the verge of taking over the world.

Until the Americans entered the war.

I wish Patton could break through the German lines. I wish he could save us all. But even if Eisenhower has turned over command to him, which I feel is likely, Patton must still be battling the Nazis and their fearsome tanks in the French countryside. Harrah is probably right—if help does come, it will be from the east, from Russia.

Yet it won't come in time.

Night falls and the drizzle changes to a freezing downpour. I'm starved of blood, so my ability to resist the cold is poor. I picked the absolute worst time to get caught. So busy trying to help the Resistance, and prepare for the invasion, I kept postponing finding a victim to drink from. When I returned to France from London, I should have jumped the first Gestapo I saw. Now I have no reserve to fall back on. I start to shiver and find I can't stop. The icy water, as it drips over my frigid flesh, makes me feel as if my own blood is leaking away.

It is true, it is a fact. I am dying.

But as dawn breaks, the clouds disperse and the sun shines warm and soothing over my trembling body. I drink up its rays like they are nectar from heaven, and I'm reminded of the days right after Yaksha came for me, when I was first made a vampire, how the sun stung my eyes whenever I turned in its direction. My long life has granted me at least one great favor—it has taught me to love the dawn.

The respite is brief. Horror follows the new sun.

A train arrives, almost a hundred railroad cars long. It comes from the west and its cargo is the most precious—and sadly, the most wretched—imaginable. It's stuffed with Jews, and as the doors of the cars open, I'm stunned at how many people stumble out. It's as if the Germans have literally piled them on top of each other.

The men and women have already been separated, but the children are still with their mothers. But then I see a sight that goes beyond any act of cruelty I have ever witnessed. The children are torn away from their moms. Only infants, who can't walk, are left alone. But kids as young as two years old are forced into a line that leads into the first of the three gates of hell. Their cries, their pleas, their screams—I can't bear it.

I have lived too long, I realize.

It takes two hours but the train platform is eventually

cleared. The men are the last to enter the wooden structure. I doubt any of them are given a chance to see their families. On the far side of the entrance, I'm forced to watch as a steady line of naked children is marched into the second gate of hell—the stone structure with the vile-smelling vents. They are followed by an endless stream of nude, sobbing women. A few find their children; they lift them up, but there is nowhere to go. The SS guards yell out their lies.

"Enjoy your warm shower!"

"Wash your hair carefully!"

"Use plenty of soap!"

"Fresh clothes await you on the other side!"

I can't help myself. Knowing it is useless, I scream anyway.

"They are taking you to die! Fight! Fight back! They are going to gas you!"

My voice can be loud, when I put my power into it, and a few appear to hear me. They cast a dark look in my direction. But none of them listen. I can't blame them, most can hardly walk. God knows how long they've been imprisoned on the train.

The line to the stone building stops. The thick steel doors are shut tight. The SS guards back off. Even a whiff of the gas hurts the lungs and they know the routine—how many thousands of gallons of poison are about to be poured into the bodies of the women and children.

Filthy gray fumes begin to spew out of the vents. Inside,

the screams begin. They start and don't stop. I don't understand why. The gas should kill them within minutes. But a half hour after the doors are locked shut, I swear I still hear women crying in agony.

Finally, though, there is silence.

The doors to the stone building remain shut.

A third line—this one of naked men—begins to trek from the first building to a smaller stone structure behind the one where the women and children were killed. The SS guards no longer shout their lies. There would be no point. The men have heard the death screams of their wives, children, sisters, and mothers. Their faces are stamped with the black mark of total despair. All hope has been lost. They are the walking dead. At this moment, from their point of view, the death of their bodies is a mere formality.

They enter the smaller of the stone buildings.

The gas is turned on. They know what is coming but gassing is a terrible way to die. Basically the tubes in their lungs are scorched to the point where they rupture and bleed out.

I can't listen. I am forced to listen.

But I close my eyes and hang my head—an hour later, after all the gas had been pumped from the buildings—when they haul the bodies into the third gate of hell, the ovens. I can't watch, because my earlier guess was accurate. The guards refuse to dirty their hands. They use Jews to dispose of the Jews. I don't know why, but I feel this is the Nazis' greatest sin of all.

The black smoke of the burning thousands chokes the entire camp. The stink makes me vomit, although there is nothing in my stomach. The rain of ash is like a snowfall in Hades. How I swore at the freezing rain during the night, and how I pray for it now. If only to be rid of this foul coat of sin. To be so close to such an atrocity, to witness it and to do nothing—even though I can't—makes me feel I am no better than the Nazis. Now it is I who feels cursed, and I curse the mind behind this camp for making me a part of this nightmare.

Suddenly, I feel I can't die. Not until I avenge this crime.

It takes hours to cremate so many bodies. While the stacks continue to spew out a steady stream of black smoke, I have visitors. Major Klein has returned with Frau Cia, and they have brought a guest. The second most powerful man in the Third Reich. The head of the SS, chief of the Gestapo, and the one person, besides Hitler, most responsible for the creation of the concentration camps.

Reichsführer Heinrich Himmler.

His uniform is tidy, it is dry, although his boots are muddied from the hike to my cage. He is heavier than his pictures, the war has been good to him, and his brown mustache is something of an afterthought—it hardly reaches to the edge of his lips. He is not an ugly man, but he feels foul. It's his eyes, of course, and I thought Major Klein had sick eyes. Himmler's are not mere windows into a dark soul, they are holes into the abyss.

This man is not a man.

I feel it the moment we meet. There's something inside him, some kind of creature that has come from the outside, using him.

But outside where? I don't know. I feel the evil inside him more as an absence of human qualities rather than as a tangible thing. He feels like a walking pit. I hate his companions and yet a part of me wants to shout out to them, to warn them to stay away. I fear if any of us get too close to this creature we will disappear. He has only to look at me, to stand near, to make me feel weak.

While an SS guard sets up Major Klein's favorite fold-out table—he has brought the same tools as before—Klein completes the introductions. The falling ash seems to have improved his mood. He sounds positively jovial.

"Reichsführer, I'm proud to introduce our guest. The woman we have been seeking all these years. Sita." Klein pauses. "Sita, in case you don't recognize our esteemed visitor, permit me to introduce Reichsführer Heinrich Himmler."

Himmler bows in my direction. "It's an honor, Fraülein."

I almost spit in his face. There is time. I smile instead.

"Herr Himmler," I say. "Your reputation precedes you. A friend of mine, General Hans Straffer, often spoke of you."

"I'm sure in glowing terms," Major Klein interrupts hastily, looking a little worried. Naturally, I'd like to tell Himmler that when Straffer did talk about him he referred to him as "the Führer's asshole."

"He said you have tremendous organizational skills," I say, which is true.

Himmler nods. "I remember Straffer. A good man. I'll send for him the next time he's in Berlin."

"I'm afraid that won't be possible. Our dear Major Klein had him executed."

Himmler slowly turns toward Klein. "True?"

Klein stammers. "He was feeding her secret information that she was passing on to the Resistance."

"Not true. General Straffer was loyal. He would have never betrayed Germany." I say this with the hope Straffer's family will not be punished for Klein's lies.

Himmler shrugs. "It matters not. It's not why we are here."

Major Klein stands near his master. He smiles in my direction. "Sita doesn't understand why she is here," he says.

Himmler is surprised. "You don't know?"

"No," I say.

Himmler comes close. If there were the least bit of play in my chains, I would strike him dead and to hell with the consequences. But I am a bug pinned to a pole. Himmler studies me with eyes that remind me of an insect. I sense the many facets of the mind behind his gaze. It is as if the strange being inside him inhabits others as well. All thinking as one, all plotting to ruin mankind, and yet, paradoxically, all empty as well. This man's cruelty does not arise out of anger or bitterness. It comes from nothing.

He is like . . . nothing. An empty vehicle.

"I have been told you refuse to explain what you did during the Battle of Kurukshetra," he says.

"Not so. I explained to Major Klein that on the opening day of the battle I stood on the side of the Kauravas so I could catch a glimpse of Krishna. Then, after seeing him, I retreated to the surrounding woods while the battle raged on for four days."

"You did not leave until the battle ended?" Himmler asks.

"That is correct."

"Did you fight in the battle?"

"No."

"But a devotee such as yourself, who loved Krishna so much, you must have been tempted to help the Pandavas—Arjuna and his brothers. Why didn't you help them?"

"My creator, Yaksha, fought on their side. With his help, I knew they couldn't lose."

"Did Krishna take part in the battle?"

"Not directly. He played the role of Arjuna's charioteer."

"Why do you speak this way? Why do you say he played a role?"

I shrug. "The whole world was nothing but a playground to Krishna. Even a major battle did not disturb him."

Himmler nods. "Understandable."

Major Klein interrupts. "You are still avoiding the question. What did you do during the four days of the battle?"

"I have answered that question several times. I did nothing."

Klein snorts. "But watched and waited for another chance to see Krishna?"

"Yes."

"Tell us about the Kauravas," Himmler says.

"They had the larger army. The Pandavas had been in exile a long time. The people had grown used to Duryodhana and his hundred brothers, the Kauravas, ruling the country. They may have been an evil family but the average person did not see that evil. Duryodhana brought stability. When the Pandavas showed up, everything was thrown into disorder. For that reason, the Kauravas had at least twice the men."

"Would you say that war was similar to this war?" Himmler asks.

"No."

"Why not?"

I nod in the direction of the smokestacks. "Soldiers died in those four days. Not innocents."

"Do you consider Jews innocent?"

"They are like everyone else. No better, no worse."

Himmler brushes my hair from my eyes. "I'm disappointed to hear you say that. Your features are perfect—your blond hair, your blue eyes. Clearly you are one of the original Aryans. You may have been born in India but it was your ancestors who conquered it. They were great. Even your precious Krishna spoke of their greatness when he warned of the need of the caste system. Certain people are born to be slaves, others to be merchants, still others to be warriors. Only a few can lead." He pauses and gestures to the smoking stacks. "Then there are the untouchables. They should never have been born at all."

"Krishna never taught a caste system. That was a lie the Brahmins added to the Vedas three hundred years after Krishna left the world. They did so for one reason—so they could rule the land. If you're basing your persecution of the Jews on the theory that you are purifying the major bloodlines of mankind, then you are deluded. Krishna spoke of the oneness of mankind. And like Christ, he said there was no greater power than love." I pause. "A pity your Führer got it wrong at the start. Had he just talked to me, he could have saved us all a lot of grief."

Himmler smiles, or, I should say, he tries. His expression looks more like a snake before it swallows the mouse. "You sound sure of yourself. So arrogant."

"Just telling you the way it is," I reply.

He tugs at my hair, lightly at first, then harder. His smile fades and he speaks in a sudden harsh tone. "How did the Battle of Kurukshetra end?"

There's a power in his voice that makes me jump. "In fire," I say, the words leaping out of my mouth before I realize it.

"What brought the fire?" he asks.

I hesitate. "I don't know."

"Is it that you don't know? Or is it that you don't remember?"

I briefly close my eyes, trying to escape, for a moment, from his eyes. I feel as if they have begun to work inside me, although I have yet to see anyone, even Frau Cia, reach for the metal box.

The thing inside Himmler has power. It's not a human or vampiric power. It feels more primal. It comes from the earth, not the sky, from the ground far below us: the dirt the giant reptiles used to walk upon.

Whatever has ahold of Himmler is ancient.

"I don't know," I say.

"But you did see a ball of fire on the final day of battle?"

"Yes."

"How big was it?"

"Huge."

"Large enough to destroy an army?"

"Yes."

"A town? A city?"

"Yes. Yes."

"Where did it come from?"

"I told you, I don't know."

"Which side did it strike? The Kauravas? Or the Pandavas?"

I shake my head. His quick questions hit like blows to my brain. I find it hard to think. "I don't know."

He practically pulls my hair out by its roots. "Which side did it strike?" he demands.

"It hit the Pandavas."

"Then it destroyed them. They lost the war."

"They won the war."

"How?"

"It's there in the Mahabharata. Arjuna defeated Duryodhana."

"But how? You just said the ball of fire struck the Pandavas."

"It was aimed at the Pandavas. But it struck . . . in between the two armies."

"You saw this with your own eyes?"

"Yes."

"Where did the ball of fire come from?"

I turn my face away, not caring that he pulls out a lump of my hair in the process. "I'm not sure. I think it came . . . it came from the sky."

There is a sudden silence. Himmler lets go of me and steps back beside his partners, Major Klein and Frau Cia. I notice then that the three are connected. Himmler is their leader, that's clear, but they all share a puppetlike quality. Something distant pulls their strings. They nod in unison.

"You are doing well, Sita. We are making progress," Himmler says. "Tomorrow we will have a breakthrough."

With that the three of them leave.

Ralph Levine comes to me in the middle of the night. He surprises me; I am trying to sleep. But my sleep is nothing more than a continuous nightmare. It's a relief to see his kind face, although he has lost all his hair and dropped so much weight his head looks like a medical lab's skull. I loved Ralph the instant we met. He is one of those people, before I even spoke to Patton, who gave me faith in reincarnation. My feelings for him make no sense unless I've been with him in another time, another body. He feels like an older brother, just as Harrah feels like a younger sister.

Ralph glances around in the dark, holding a brown paper bag in his hand. "Do guards patrol this spot?" he asks.

"You're lucky your wife warned me you might show up. The Nazis assigned four guards to me this evening, two in front of me, two behind me. I called over a couple at a time and flirted with them. You know I know plenty of dirty German words. After a few minutes of flirting I caught their eyes and suggested they take a nap." I nod over my right shoulder. "The four of them are snoring in that shed over there. They're not going to wake up anytime soon."

Ralph nods as he studies the area. "It's odd how they've caged you out here in the open."

"It's part of their psychological attack. They want me tied to this spot so I can see how easily they destroy thousands of lives. Everything they do is geared toward impressing upon me how powerful they are, and how helpless I am."

"I've brought something that might change the equation. Major Klein's girlfriend, Frau Cia, eats with the officers. Harrah told you about our friend Father Bob. He works in the kitchen that feeds the officers. Well, tonight he gave her a hearty bowl of beef stew, her favorite. Only he laced it with liquid morphine. She barely made it back to her room."

"The key! You've got her key!"

Ralph shakes his head. "Father Bob snuck into her room an hour after dinner. By then most of the morphine would have hit her bloodstream. She was out cold. Only he couldn't slip her necklace over her head. The necklace was too short, or her head too big."

"How the hell do they use the key, then?" I ask.

"Who knows? Maybe she only rips it off in an emergency. We're lucky Father Bob doesn't panic easily. He returned to the kitchen and quickly threw together some type of dough concoction, harder than normal, and snuck back into her room. She was still fast asleep. He was able to make an impression of the key."

"Was he able to make a copy of the key from the impression?"

"A crude copy. Before he could pour boiling metal on the dough, he had to bake it first to make it hard enough to withstand the heat. He used yeast-free dough but it still expanded. Just as bad, the baked dough was still porous." Ralph reached in the bag and withdrew a black key. He held it up for me to see. "He filed it down as best he could but it's still got plenty of rough edges."

"How are you going to get it to me?" I ask. A practical

question—the edge of my wire cage is over fifteen feet away.

"With this." Ralph pulls a garden hose from his bag. "Father Bob also takes care of a flower garden on the west side of the camp."

"Flowers grow in this hellhole?"

"Sita. They have a school over there for the officers' kids."

"Tell me about it another time. You got tape?"

Ralph pulls out a roll of black tape. "I'll tape it to the tip of the hose and feed it to you. But we should go slow. If we drop the key we're doomed."

"Wait. Ralph, I know this is a lot to ask but . . . can you climb on top of the cage?"

"I was thinking the same thing. The hose isn't as stiff as I'd like. It's better if I come at you from above." Ralph kicks off his muddy shoes. "I'm glad they didn't use barbed wire when they built this thing."

"Hurry. Climb," I say.

Ralph is more nimble than I would have expected, but he's hampered by the bag he carries. I tell him to leave it on the ground, to just carry the hose and key, but he ignores me. Twice he slips and almost falls, but after a tense two minutes he's hanging like a bat over my head. Resting his body atop the wire mesh, he carefully tapes the key to the end of the hose.

"Ready?" he asks.

"Yeah. But I can hardly move my hands. You're going to have to guide the key directly to my fingers."

"I can't see your fingers. I can't see your face."

"Oh." I often forget that normal people cannot see in the dark. I lean my head back as far as the pole will allow. "I'll guide you. You're already off to a bad start. Feed the hose through a hole in the wire a foot higher. Then try to go straight down."

"The hose has a major kink in it."

"I have taken that into account. Trust me, do what I say."

The distance from the roof of my cage to my pinned hands is only six feet. Ralph bangs the pole a few more times than I would have liked but it is not long before I have the key in my hands.

Shit! He wasn't exaggerating when he used the word "crude." The two sides are relatively smooth but the most important parts, the edges, are rough. Plus the key is made of iron, not steel. I understand why. Iron melts at a much lower temperature than steel. The priest could never have mixed boiling steel with baked dough. Frankly, I'm amazed he was able to get any kind of key out of such a miserable mold.

Still, the iron content worries me. It would worry me if I were trying to break out of an ordinary stainless-steel lock. But with this alloy, if there is any resistance the key will not be able to withstand the pressure. It will bend.

All those problems, though, don't mean a thing if I can't fit the key into the handcuff lock. I know exactly where it is. The tips of my fingers have sweated over it for weeks.

Unfortunately, my hands have been so deprived of a normal

supply of blood for so long my fingers barely work. Several times I come close to dropping the key. Just as bad, I can't stretch my cramped fingers far enough—and hold on to the wide end of the key—to straighten the key so that it slips directly into the lock. I keep trying to slip it in at an angle. It is all I can manage.

"Does it fit?" Ralph asks. He is staring right down at me but to him I'm a disembodied voice.

"So far it's me that's the problem," I whisper.

"Can I help you?"

"You can help by being quiet."

"Sorry."

"Shh. Let me concentrate." Finally, I feel the key catch hold and slowly shove it into the hole. Immediately I run into a bump, but I can't tell if it's a normal obstacle or if the key is seriously deformed. The only way to be sure is to apply greater pressure to the top of the key. Even though my hands are cramped, I'm still strong. Strong enough to easily warp a two-inch-long piece of iron.

I push gently. Nothing happens.

I push a little harder. Nothing.

I push hard. The key slips past the first obstacle.

It goes halfway in. Then it hits another bump.

"Damn," I whisper.

"It doesn't fit?"

"Shut up, Ralph. Please."

I press hard enough to where I can feel the key beginning to bend. It's then I realize the truth. The problem is not because the key is made of iron. It's the wrong shape. On the positive side, by feeling the edge of the key before I slipped it in the hole, and feeling the resistance I'm now running into, I can envision what has to be done to the key to fix it. I pull it out and tell Ralph I'm taping it back onto the hose.

"We let you down," he says, sounding crushed.

"No. We're close. The second protrusion from the tip has to be filed down six millimeters. No more, no less. Also, the tip of that spot must be made rounder, less sharp-edged. Give these instructions to Father Bob, and thank him for me for risking his life to save us."

"The way the guards talk about you, he thinks you're an avenging angel."

"After today I wouldn't mind playing that role." I have secured the key to the hose. "Get ready to pull it up."

"Not yet. I have to give you something else."

"What?"

"Put the end of the hose in your mouth."

"Ralph! I told Harrah not to donate any blood!"

"I didn't let her give any. But I gave what I could and so did five other men where I sleep. I have a quart here and it's still warm."

"What the hell did you tell them?"

"I told them that you were an alien from another planet and you needed blood to survive."

"Bullshit. Tell me the truth."

"That's what I said. They believed it, or they wanted to believe it. What matters is I got the blood. Now open your mouth and let me recharge your batteries."

"I won't forget this, Ralph," I say before slipping the tip of the hose in my mouth, my lips barely avoiding the taped key. A moment later a gush of pure ecstasy fills my mouth. The blood is warm, fresh, human. It fills every cell in my body like grace-charged ambrosia. I gulp it down, yet I don't drink so fast that I miss why the blood feels almost sacred. It was given in love, in faith and hope. Another reason why I must do everything I can to save the people trapped in this camp.

I feel a huge ache when the flow suddenly stops.

"Had enough?" Ralph asks hopefully.

"Plenty!" I lie. I'm so depleted, I could have drunk a gallon. Yet within seconds of consuming the blood, my pain begins to diminish. The first to go is the cramping in my diaphragm. I can breathe again! For the night, at least, my slow crucifixion has halted. My frame of mind takes a big jump in the positive direction and I'm able to think clearer. As Ralph carefully pulls the key back up, I come up with an idea.

"Ralph, I told you, they've brought me topside to see you and Harrah, and to experience firsthand the horror of this place. But that underground room where I first woke up was built for me. It's the one cage they know I can't break out of. I bet they put me back there tomorrow. For that reason, after

Father Bob modifies the key, I need you or him to place it on top of the pole down there. There's a flat spot at the top that I can just reach."

"Will the guards see it?"

"I doubt it. The top of the post is taller than any guard. And they won't be looking for it because it's not missing. People generally don't see what they don't expect to find. The key must be left on the top side near the door. They usually have me pointed in that direction. Now, repeat what I told you about the outline of the key."

Ralph repeats my instructions word for word.

"Perfect," I say. "Now get out of here before anyone sees you."

"God must be on our side to get this far," he says as he climbs down. As he turns to leave, I almost tell him that five thousand years of experience has taught me that God doesn't work that way.

But I like to think that if Auschwitz has no other purpose, then at least it exists to test the faithful. It's a childish thought to have while covered in the ash of a thousand ghosts. I feel shame that I even try to frame such pain in my mind. Still, a part of me struggles to make sense of what I have seen.

It's as if the agony of those on the train cries for answers.

Or for a reason.

I can't block out the memory of the screams I heard today when the gas poured down on the women and children. I can't imagine what they felt in those last minutes. I can only hope in the midst of such unfathomable cruelty that a spark of something decent—call it God's grace or simply a quick blackout—came to them. More, much more, I pray that their final prayers have been answered and they have been lifted up to a paradise where there's no suffering, not even the memory of this . . . their last day on earth.

"Krishna," I cry in the dark, saying his name over and over again. As is often the case, between cursing and pleading I try my best to envision his dark blue eyes. But sadly, in such a place they elude me, and I'm left with the empty feeling that he is far, far away.

I fear the Nazis are going to beat me.

The next day I'm still locked in the wire cage when Major Klein, Frau Cia, and Himmler come to question me. Again they bring the table and their torturous tools. They place the table four feet in front of me and set down a bulky tape recorder between the knife and the bottle of gasoline. It must run on batteries. Himmler does not turn it on before facing me.

"Time to tell us what we want to know," he says.

"I have told you everything I know," I reply.

"Everything you remember?" he says.

I hesitate. "Yes."

"Your first answer was a lie. Your second, the truth." He nods to himself as he circles the pole. "You know it is possible for a human being to know something and not remember. It is common when there is a major trauma associated with the memory. For example, I have no memory of how my mother died, although I was ten at the time. I had just come from school and found my parents arguing. It seems my father had caught my mother in bed with another man. He was furious, of course, and I was worried he was going to hurt my mother. But I was also angry with her, very angry." Himmler stops. "The next thing I knew I was at my mother's funeral. Three days had passed."

"That must have been quite a shock," I say.

"It was, yes, a terrible shock. Especially when I heard my father and other relatives whispering to each other as we walked back to the car. Do you know what they were saying?"

"No."

"They were discussing how I was the one who killed my mother."

His answer stuns me. He's telling me the truth, and yet I know from reading about his life that he was close to his parents, and that both were supposed to have survived until he was an adult.

Of course, it is the Nazis who have written the story of his life.

Lies. It is all lies, and now he's telling me the truth.

Himmler stops and picks up a knife from the table before continuing. "To this day I don't recall where I got the knife I used to stab my mother in the back. I must have secreted it away at some point. The facts speak for themselves. She was dead, we had just buried her."

"I'm sorry."

"Why are you sorry?" Himmler sounds genuinely puzzled.

"You were a child. You couldn't have known what you were doing."

He smiles faintly and I feel a disturbing chill. "On the contrary, later I was to realize I experienced a moment of brilliant clarity when I pulled out the knife and stuck it in that bitch's spine." He pauses. "But it took years for the memory to come back to me."

How can I respond to such insanity? I remain silent.

"I think your situation is similar. You know what happened at the end of the Battle of Kurukshetra but it traumatized you and you have blocked it out. I also think that another trauma, equally devastating, will bring the memory back." Himmler approaches with his knife and gently scratches the tip of my nose with the blade. "What do you think, Sita?"

"I think you hated your mother long before you put that knife in her back."

Himmler is pleased. "You're right. Almost as much as I hated my father. He died when I was sixteen. Bled to death in his sleep. Someone cut his throat."

Another blip in his traditional life story.

"Lovely," I say.

He brushes the knife over my eyelashes. "But if I were to do that to you, it would not do us much good. So I'll have to be more careful. Move slowly, let you enjoy every sensation." He stops. "Or."

"Or what?"

"You can start talking now."

I consider his proposition. I could lie, I could make up almost any kind of story, but there is something about this man—he can smell a lie.

"I can't," I say.

He nods as if he expected no other answer and hands the knife to Major Klein. Himmler steps back, perhaps to spare his clothes, while Klein approaches with enthusiasm. The man is a sadist—he obviously gets pleasure from causing others pain.

"Ready, Sita?" he asks.

Like his question deserves an answer.

He stabs me two inches to the right of my left shoulder. The blade sinks in perhaps three inches and shreds the nerve bundle there. The pain is instant and total. Honestly, it is hard to imagine it could get any worse.

Until he stabs me two inches to the left of my right shoulder.

Blood leaks over my filthy shirt but it does not gush. Klein has been careful not to sever a major artery or vein. They need me alive. They need to know what happened to me five thousand years ago. But despite the trauma of the present, I cannot recall what I saw or did back then.

"Let her recover!" Himmler snaps as Klein prepares to slice into the side of my left rib cage. The major takes a step back and waits beside his boss while Frau Cia stands like a statue in the rain. The drizzle from the gray sky starts again, and the cold water, as it trickles over my front, causes a shallow pool at my feet to turn red.

Slowly, my wounds begin to heal; it is slow for me. Because of my awkward position, because I cannot breathe properly, the pain is magnified. I try not to let it show but am unsuccessful. Himmler looks on as if he is watching how an animal reacts to having its tail chopped off. The man appears devoid of even the slightest trace of empathy, and it is that lack, spread throughout the rank and file of the men and women of the SS who herd the Jews to their deaths, that is the engine that drives this camp.

How strange to think of a lack of a quality as a driving force.

Himmler is a complex mass of emptiness.

"Again," he says to Major Klein when I have stopped bleeding. This time Klein stoops low and rolls up my trousers past my knees. There is no question he has studied anatomy. He knows where the nerve bundles are. Taking the tip of the knife, placing it not far below my knee, he slowly slips the tip between my shin bone and calf muscle, before suddenly yanking down.

I let out a piercing cry. I can't help myself.

He does my other leg. Oh, God, he's never going to stop.

But he does stop, each time he cuts, just long enough for me to stop bleeding. Himmler insists on the recovery periods. Nevertheless, the red in the pool at my feet grows darker. There is only so much blood in my veins. Whatever strength Ralph's transfusion gave me last night is long gone.

My sight begins to dim as my thoughts dull. It's possible I pass out, I'm not sure, but I notice that a long period of time goes by without a fresh burst of agony. When I finally do open my eyes, I see a fourth person has entered the wire cage. A man in the same prison garb that Harrah and Ralph were wearing.

Anton. They have captured Anton.

I stare at him in utter despair.

"Why?" I cry. "Why did you come?"

He shrugs. "You came for me."

I shake my head. "Oh, darling. Do you never think?"

Himmler moves to my side and speaks so softly only I can hear. "I'm not surprised at your ability to resist pain. You are ancient, you have been through so much, suffered so many traumas. It's obvious you cannot be broken with physical torture. But your emotions, the silly things you still feel—those surprise me. I assumed you would have outgrown such nonsense. Clearly I was wrong. Still, I'm glad you possess this weakness, you should be as well. Together we can use it to restore what you have lost, and once we have the truth of those days, nothing can stop us." He pauses. "I hope you appreciate what I am offering you, Sita."

"Heinrich," I say, calling him by the name his parents gave him. "Go to hell. I will tell you nothing."

Himmler nods seriously. "We shall see. We shall see."

Guards are called for. They bring another pole, one made of wood, that they pound into the mud in front of me. Anton is strapped to it and the guards leave. All the while Major Klein paces, excited. He can hardly wait for Himmler to give him the word.

When all is set, Himmler approaches again and speaks quietly. "We are going to repeat the experiment, only this time on him. It will be much harder. He will not heal, his blood will not stop pouring out on the ground. Even though we will try to draw it out as long as possible, he won't last forever. You have to accept the cost of your refusal to cooperate."

"How can I tell you what I can't remember?" I plead.

He nods sympathetically. "How indeed?"

Himmler nods to Klein, who picks up the knife.

The major does not repeat the "experiment" exactly. No, Anton would die too quickly from the wounds Klein has given me. Instead the major chooses to slowly skin Anton alive.

He starts with the back of his hands and works upward.

Anton screams and screams. He can't stop, and the sound, the pain, it seems to resonate in every lump of mud, every brick in every building in the whole camp. Anton is my friend, my lover. Yesterday, I did not know the people the train brought to die. Yet I hear their screams in his. They are sewn into the fabric of this hellish place that no sane God should ever have allowed to be created.

I curse God then. I curse Krishna.

With all my heart, I hate the one I love most.

Until I remember something he said long ago.

Himmler sees that I remember and turns on his recorder.

He orders Klein to stop cutting and me to talk.

We both obey.

The battle is three days old and the Pandavas are close to defeat. The Pandavas have Arjuna's fearsome bow on their side, Bhima's great strength, Yudhisthira's strategic mind. They even have Krishna with them, acting as Arjuna's charioteer. But it is not enough. The Kauravas outnumber them two to one. In the end, the enemy will outlast them.

Working as a nurse to the injured Kauravas, I watch the battle from the surrounding woods and see that even with Yaksha fighting on the side of the Pandavas, they are being driven back. It's amazes me that anyone can resist him but studying the battle, I notice that three men on the Kauravas' side are able to thwart Yaksha: Duryodhana, king of the Kauravas; Bhishma, who taught the Pandavas and Duryodhana and his brothers how to fight; and Karna, the half brother of the Pandavas.

Legend has it that Duryodhana is really a demon, although he has ruled India fairly. I know for a fact that Yaksha was born of a yakshini, a type of demon. Perhaps I should not be surprised that Duryodhana is able to stand up to my creator.

Besides Krishna, Bhishma is the most beloved soul on the battlefield. He is a master to the Pandavas. They can't kill him because they don't want to kill him. Yet Bhishma fights, he's not afraid to slay those who stand before him, and so the Pandavas are losing.

And Karna: Krishna himself has said he is the first and greatest of the Pandavas, although his brothers have forsaken him because he was born of a different mother. It doesn't seem to matter how many arrows Arjuna lets fly in his direction, Karna dodges them.

All but one.

On the third day Karna takes an arrow in the leg.

His guards bring him to the doctors' tent and the surgeon in charge is able to remove the shaft, but Karna is in tremendous pain. At heart, because Krishna supports the Pandavas, so do I. The only reason I'm acting as a nurse is so I can stay near the battle and possibly see Krishna. Something about Karna draws me, however. I sneak up on him while he dozes after drinking an opiate concoction. He is barely conscious and yet I feel his kindness. On impulse, I open a vein and let several drops of my blood splash over his wound. He heals in minutes and opens his eyes.

"Who are you?" he asks.

"My name is Kunti."

"You took away my pain."

"The doctor did. He removed the arrow."

Karna is not fooled. "It was you," he mumbles as he falls back asleep.

I leave the tent in a hurry. Touching Karna has only intensified my longing for Krishna, and I run to the edge of the woods. But it is hard to get a glimpse of him in the chaos. The dusty battlefield is vast. I stand five miles from the front lines, a long way for even me to spot Krishna's eyes.

Yet I feel him, out there in the midst of the bloody mayhem, silently calling to me, and on the night before the fourth day of battle, I put aside my fear of Yaksha and steal across the lines and enter the Pandavas' camp. The moon is full, it stands almost straight overhead, and a thousand fires burn beside a hundred thousand weary soldiers. So many men, so many tents, where am I to find Krishna?

Then I spot a strange woman. Her skin is bronze, her eyes black as her long hair, and she is dressed in clothes I have never seen before. Her gown looks as if it has been woven of gold and silk.

Yet none of that matters. It's the way she moves that catches my eye. An ordinary human would not notice, but I can tell she can move from one place to another in the blink of an eye. At first I assume she's a vampire and wonder why Yaksha has not destroyed her, especially with Krishna nearby. Then I hear the beat of her heart. It is powerful, but human, too.

She is something new. I ask a soldier, a captain of men, if he knows her name. He hesitates and then whispers in my ear. "Umara. Some say she is a witch. She comes from across the sea."

The instant he says her name, I notice the woman watching me. Then, beckoning for me to follow, she leaps into the woods. I chase after her, fast as I can, and yet I'm unable to catch her. She doesn't halt until she reaches a campfire deep in the forest. There she sits on the ground beside Yaksha, across from Krishna.

Seeing my Lord, I sink to the ground where I remain hiding in the woods. The small group around Krishna is full of questions.

"Maharaj," a man says to Krishna. "Last night, while I was resting, I saw lights in the sky. Like stars, only brighter and larger. They moved very fast."

"I saw them as well," another man says.

Krishna picks up a stick and pokes at the fire, shaking the embers on the burning logs. A metal spit hangs over the flames but whatever they were cooking earlier has already been eaten. I have not eaten and ordinarily the smell of food would make me hungry. Yet it is enough, for me, to be near Krishna.

"This is the battle of this age," he says. "Many have gathered to fight. But this battle is being fought on many worlds—

realms that can't be seen with the eye. It is because of the time. This age is drawing to a close. It will end when my life ends. Then a new age will dawn, the age of Kali Yuga."

"What will Kali Yuga be like?" someone asks.

Krishna reaches down and lifts up a handful of dirt. "Kali Yuga is the dark age. It is a time when men's senses and minds will tell them but one truth—if it is true at all—that this earth is all that they are. Consider this point deeply. You are born of the earth, and when you die your body goes back to the earth. In Kali Yuga people will believe this is the ultimate truth. They will lose all touch with their spirit."

"Will they no longer believe in God?" a man asks.

"Many will continue to believe in God. But belief is of no value if one loses the joy of the soul. In the years to come saints and seers will be replaced by priests and preachers. They will talk about nothing but God. But their God will always be outside them, far off in a distant heaven, and they will curse those who refuse to worship their form of God." Krishna drops the dirt on the ground. "Fools. They would be better off believing in the earth."

"So these priests and preachers will curse God?"

Krishna shakes his head. "They will praise him. They will grow hoarse praising him."

"But isn't that good? Doesn't God value worship?"

Krishna looks at the man who questions him. "Your name is Arun, is it not?"

"Yes, Maharaj. Arun of the Maravar family."

"Are you married, Arun? Do you have children?"

"Yes, Maharaj. Two boys and two girls."

"Do you need their praise?"

"No, but I enjoy their love. I love them. They are the reason I am here fighting."

"That's a fine reason to do anything. But just as you don't need your children's praise, God does not care for or need praise. He wants only that his children should grow to know him. In the same way you want your children to grow up and be kind and thoughtful like you, Arun."

The man blushes. "I hope they turn out better than me, Maharaj."

"I am confused," another man says. "You say the best way for us to discover the soul is to repeat your holy name aloud and then in silence. Are you not asking to be worshipped?"

"Krishna is not my name," Krishna says. "Krishna is a sound that resonates with the inner body, which helps lead you to your spirit. Take the 'Kri' syllable. Repeat it attentively and you will notice it can be felt in your forehead. The last syllable, 'Na,'—repeat it long enough and you will begin to feel a warmth in your heart. The sound 'Shh' connects the two. So 'Krishna' is a practical sound that connects our head and heart. And when the two come together, when your mind ceases to fight what you're feeling, peace blossoms inside." Krishna stops. "That's why you repeat that word."

"But, Maharaj, everyone calls you Krishna."

Krishna chuckles. "Because I give the same sound to everyone."

The man who spoke first interrupts. "I still don't understand what the lights in the sky are."

Krishna is reluctant to respond. "They are *vimanas*."

"What are *vimanas*?"

Krishna points his stick at the sky. "I have explained how the stars are like our sun and have worlds circling them like this world. But what you don't know is that most of the people on other worlds are older than you. Before the first plant poked its way out of this ground, there were wise people in the star worlds. I say 'wise' because they were old even then. Over time they have learned much, and they continue to learn, which brings them closer and closer to the one who makes the stars shine."

"Are you speaking of God, Maharaj?"

Krishna shrugs. "The word 'God' means too many things to too many different people. Let's call it the Essence—the source of all things. Then let us imagine a race of people a million years old or even a hundred million years old. Think how close they would have grown to this Essence."

Arun speaks shyly. "Maharaj, are you one of these people? Do you know the Essence?"

"I am the Essence," Krishna says softly.

Arun gasps. "Is that why the *vimanas* move in our skies? Do they come to worship you?"

Krishna smiles at the man's choice of words. It's as though the man has not heard a word Krishna has said. "I just told you, even as we struggle on the field of battle, a greater battle is being fought above. Some *vimanas* fight for light, others for darkness. Both sides know Kali Yuga will come when I leave this world."

Arun sighs. "Leave, Maharaj? Where will you go?"

"When this body dies I will return to the stars."

Krishna's words move me. My eyes burn. The group falls silent.

Yet the man who first asked about the lights in the sky is dissatisfied. "Maharaj, if you know the people who command the *vimanas*, could you not order them to help us fight?" he asks.

Krishna shakes his head. "No."

"Why not?" the man demands.

"The future should never mingle with the past. The old cannot be allowed to harm the young."

"But our enemies are killing us," the man protests. "We need help."

"The *vimanas* are to play no part in your fight."

It's obvious the man is not happy with Krishna's answer. "They must be here for a reason," he grumbles.

"I have given you a reason," Krishna says.

The meeting is over. Krishna gestures that he wants to be left alone. Quickly, I run back the way I have come, not stopping until I have reached the woods where the Kauravas are camped. A few of the men know me and are happy to see me. Calling me Kunti, they offer me a place to rest by one of their fires. The spot is isolated, which suits me fine. I curl up near the dying embers and wonder if that is the last time I will see Krishna in my life. It was hard to hear him talk about his own death.

I'm dozing when suddenly I realize two people stand nearby. In a single movement I'm on my feet, ready to kill if necessary. Before I strike, though, I see one is the man who kept pestering Krishna about the *vimanas*. The other is Duryodhana, king of the Kauravas. The first man holds a metal box. Duryodhana holds a sword pointed at my chest.

"Are you sure it's her?" Duryodhana asks the man.

"She's the one. She's not human. She can do it."

"What do you want?" I demand of Duryodhana.

"I have a task for you," he says.

"Why should I help you?" I snap.

Duryodhana nods to the man, who turns a round knob on top of his box. I hear a sound. At first it's faint, but unpleasant, almost like a silent screech. It quickly grows in volume and power, piercing my ears, sending waves of pain through my head. Yet it doesn't appear to affect the men. I feel the noise in the nerves of my teeth. The pain is overwhelming.

"Stop!" I cry.

Duryodhana nods to the man, who turns the knob on the

metal box in the opposite direction. The noise ceases, the pain stops. Duryodhana takes a step toward me.

"I have no desire to harm you, but you must obey me," he says.

"What do you want me to do?"

"Follow me and you will see," Duryodhana says. He turns and walks into the woods, not waiting for my agreement. I walk behind him, the man with the box not far from my back. I consider bolting but I am curious what they are up to. I don't understand how a simple metal box can generate such a strange sound. I have never been harmed by something that did not touch me. I wonder if I can upset their plans and thereby help the Pandavas win the war.

We walk a long way, far from the battlefield. Duryodhana appears tireless but the man behind me breathes heavily. I don't understand how he could have tricked Krishna into thinking he was an ally. Yet I recall the peculiar look Krishna gave him beside the campfire and wonder if he was fooled at all.

Eventually we come to a lake where a dozen soldiers are gathered. The full moon shines bright on the water and the men's faces are clearly visible. I recognize Karna, half brother of the Pandavas. He welcomes Duryodhana but it is clear there is tension between the two. I have noticed it even in battle. Duryodhana is king but Karna is the greater warrior and does not like to be ordered around. Duryodhana points to me as he speaks to Karna.

"This is the one," Duryodhana says. "If what you say is true, she should be able to repair the damage."

Karna studies me in the glow of the moon. He is tall, like Arjuna, and their strong faces are much alike. Karna wears his hair short, however, and his dress is plain—leather shorts and boots, a metal breastplate, a sheathed sword that rides his hip. His gaze is serious but not unkind.

"It's you," Karna says. "The one who healed me."

I remain silent. Karna turns to Duryodhana.

"We can't risk her," Karna says. "She's little more than a girl."

"She is a monster. She is stronger than a dozen men."

Karna is doubtful. "But she is a nurse . . ."

Duryodhana interrupts in a haughty voice. "What's the matter? Are you afraid to put your past-life memories to the test?"

Karna turns back to him. "I know what I know. I have ridden in this type of ship before. In the blink of an eye it can cross the sky. It will take only one to drive Arjuna and his brothers back to Vrindavana."

Duryodhana speaks harshly. "I don't want them driven off. I want them destroyed."

"Their deaths are not necessary for you to remain king," Karna says.

Duryodhana shakes his head. "Arjuna is proud. Defeat him today but let him live, and he will be back next year, and the year after that. He will never bow to my rule."

"He is my half brother."

"He treats you like a bastard! Are you with me or not?"

Karna ignores him and turns to the man with the metal box. "Are you sure you can control her?" he asks.

The man gloats as he holds up the box for the others to see. "She is strong and fast but she has her weaknesses."

"Walk behind us," Karna tells him. To me he says, "Come, Kunti. You will find this interesting."

We take a path that runs along the edge of the lake. Karna walks alone by my side, although soldiers accompany the man with the box. Karna glances over at me from time to time.

"Relax. I don't bite," I say.

"So the stories that you live on the blood of the living are lies?"

"Who told you that?"

"Does it matter? Is it true?"

"You shouldn't believe everything you hear." I add, "Why do you give your allegiance to a tyrant like Duryodhana?"

"I am my own man. For now, Duryodhana uses me. But I use him as well."

"Krishna has spoken highly of you."

Karna suddenly stops. "You know Krishna?"

"We have spoken. Why?"

Karna resumes walking. "It was Krishna who gave me the memories of my past lives. He touched my forehead, between my eyebrows, and I saw a wickless flame burning deep inside. It was a joy to behold and as I stared at it I came to know that I had lived many lives before this one. I saw each life in incredible detail. At times I was a man, other times a woman. I was a father and a mother. I lived in India and occasionally I took birth on other worlds, where every chore is accomplished by machines."

"What are machines?" I ask.

"A bullock cart is a simple machine. The machines on the star worlds are so complex they can do anything. I only had to tell them what to do and they would do it."

"The ship you mentioned to Duryodhana. Is it a machine from these star worlds?"

"Yes."

"Krishna spoke of them. He called them *vimanas*."

Karna grows excited. "That's what we called them in other lives!" He pauses. "You are fortunate that Krishna confides in you. You can't be the monster that has been described to me."

"Duryodhana gave me the impression that I'm to enter this *vimana*."

Karna nods. "It's near here but its occupants are all dead." He pauses. "It fell from the sky."

"How could it fall if it was built by such a wonderful people?"

Karna is thoughtful. "I am not sure all the *vimanas* are controlled by saints. Devils fill the sky as well. I believe this *vimana* was shot down by another *vimana*."

"With what kind of weapon?" I ask.

"That's why you're here. To put away the weapons aboard this ship. It is the reason we can't enter it. The weapons must have broken loose when the ship crashed. They give off a strange kind of light. The eye can hardly see it but it's deadly." He pauses. "But I have been told it will not be deadly to you."

"Who told you all these stories about me?" I ask again.

Karna hesitates. "It's better if I don't speak of this person. But if you're afraid to enter the ship, I won't force you. I know you were brought here against your will. That was not my desire. If you want to leave now I won't stop you."

I gesture behind us to the man with the box. "What about him?"

"I've been told the sound has to be close to hurt you."

"Where did the box come from?"

"The *vimana*." Karna stops and puts his hands on my shoulders. His touch is warm and affectionate. "I understand if you want to go. But if you can repair the ship, it would mean a great deal to me."

"Because you're tired of this world and want to fly back to the star worlds?"

He gazes at me in amazement. "Can you read minds, Kunti?"

"Sita. My real name is Sita. And no, I can't read your thoughts. But if I had your memories I'd probably have the same wish as you. Alas, all I know is this world. I fear I will be trapped here forever."

He lets go of me and we resume walking. "Forever, Sita? Perhaps a few things I have heard about you are true. I was told you're immortal. Or that you can only be killed with great force."

"I admit I am not easy to kill. But tell me more about the interior of the *vimana*. Besides the spilled weapons, does the ship have other damage?"

Karna tells me that it does, and he explains what I will have to do to fix it. His instructions are long and detailed and I'm not sure I follow all his words. To me, it seems he sometimes uses phrases that come from the star worlds. They pop out of his mouth when he's distracted.

He gets distracted whenever he looks at me.

Finally we reach the *vimana*. It is like a large domed structure built half on the shore, half in the water. At first it appears to be made of metal, but as we draw near it glows with a dull orange light and I imagine it is a huge ball of glass half buried in the ground. I don't know how much of it sank into the earth when it fell from the sky. There is no door I can see but Karna assures me one will appear when I approach it.

"Do you remember everything I have told you?" he asks as the others halt far back on the path. I imagine the strange metal box cannot harm me at such a distance but I'm loath to flee from such an exciting mystery. It's hard to look at the ship without also turning my eyes toward the stars. Did it really come from another world? Karna remembers a tremendous amount from his past lives and yet there are many holes in his knowledge.

"I'll do my best to fix it," I say.

Karna is uneasy. "I have warned you about the damaged weapons, the dangerous light they give off. It won't look as threatening as fire but it's already killed several of Duryodhana's men who have tried to fix the ship."

"They died from a light you can hardly see?" I ask, puzzled.

"Yes. When you find a metal container that glows, put it away fast in one of the vaults I have described to you. Whatever you do, don't hold on to the weapons long."

"You're worried. You must have been in this ship yourself."

Karna turns away and stares at the lake. "For a short time. Then I remembered these dangers from a past life and fled." He pauses. "I'm a coward."

"Being cautious doesn't make you a coward."

Karna sighs. "But I allowed other men to be sent in after me."

I snort. "You mean Duryodhana sent them after you. That's not your fault."

Karna shakes his head. "A dozen went inside the ship. Six are still inside, dead. The others died after staggering outside." He turns and grips my shoulders. "I feel as if I have come to know you, Sita. Please tell me that the stories about you are true and the *vimana* won't harm you."

Such a dear man; I touch his face. "I don't know if it will harm me or not. But I must go inside. Remember, you're not forcing me. Whatever happens will be my own doing. If I fail to return, don't blame yourself."

Karna takes my hand and kisses it. "No, Sita, if you don't come back, I'll never forgive myself." He looks in my eyes. "I wish you would run."

I smile as I take back my hand and kiss his cheek. "I would rather fly, Karna. Fly to your star worlds."

With that I turn and walk toward the *vimana*.

SIXTEEN

When I open my eyes, Seymour and Matt are sitting in chairs on the other side of the hotel room. "What happened?" I asked.

"You stopped talking fifteen minutes ago," Matt says.

"I lost contact with your mind then," Seymour says. "It's like a wall came up between us."

"What's the last thing you heard?" I ask.

"You were walking toward the *vimana*," Matt says.

I hang my head. "That's all I remember."

Matt stands and stretches. "We're still missing the most important part. What went on inside the *vimana*. How does it connect to the Nazis and the veil?"

"But we learned a great deal," Seymour says. "The metal box Major Klein used to knock Sita out sounds exactly like the box that came from the *vimana* that crash-landed during the Battle of Kurukshetra."

"I wonder how the Nazis got ahold of it," I say.

"Didn't you see the original *Indiana Jones*?" Seymour says. "The Nazis were obsessed with finding spiritual artifacts even before the war began. Hitler was more interested in Eastern religions than Christianity. It's well documented that he sent teams of archaeologists into Tibet, China, and India. One of them must have come across the box."

"Or else he had it from the beginning," Matt says. "The box might have been passed down in a secret tradition we know little about. Recall how most of the inner Nazis belonged to the Thule Society—an esoteric satanic cult."

"That's a possibility," Seymour says. "Hell, for all we know Hitler might have used the box to help with his rise to power. But let's focus on the *vimanas* for a moment. When my mind was linked with yours, Sita, I saw the lights in the sky the people at Krishna's campfire were talking about. And while you were still coming out of our hypnotic trance, I looked up *vimanas* on the Internet and found out there are several major scriptures that talk about them—and not all of them are from India. One is called the Samarangana Sutradhara. Let me quote this one part. 'Strong and durable must the body of the *vimana* be made, like a great flying bird of light material. Inside one must put the mercury engine with its iron heating apparatus underneath. By means of the power latent in the mercury which sets the driving whirlwind in motion, a man sitting inside may travel a great distance in the sky. The movements of the *vimana* are such that it can fly vertically or horizontally or fly in circles. With help of the machines human beings can fly in the air and heavenly beings can come down to earth.'" Seymour stops and shakes his head. "We're not deluding ourselves. These things existed."

"But do they exist now?" I say. "On earth?"

Seymour shrugs. "Mr. Grey says the government is building them."

Matt paces. "He says the government is *trying* to build them. From what I heard, it sounded like the Nazis were trying to build them too. But these Fastwalkers that have been developed, they're poor imitations of the real *vimanas*."

"Because they can't travel to the stars?" Seymour says. "Or because heavenly beings are not flying around in them?"

Matt hesitates. "Maybe both."

Seymour nods. "That's an interesting idea. But let's stay with what we learned from Sita's trance. The Nazis didn't just expect her to confirm that the *vimanas* were real, they were confident she could give them hard data on how to build one. Where did that confidence come from?"

"Karna described the interior of the *vimana* to Sita in detail," Matt says.

"But I didn't hear Sita giving that detail to Himmler," Seymour says. "At least not in that meeting they had. Also, even before Sita told Himmler about Karna and saw the *vimana*, Himmler knew she knew about them. It was like he read about her in a book."

"A book Hitler's scavengers found in India?" Matt asks.

"That's the impression I got," I say, breaking in. I feel I should at least comment on my own memories. "It's obvious Klein and Himmler knew about me from an ancient source. That's how I ended up in their damn file. They had read about me. It's the only explanation."

"I agree," Seymour says.

Matt stares at me. "Why did you stop when you did?"

"I don't know." I stand and walk to the sink, picking up a glass. I'm dying for a drink of water. Blood would be even better. "There's still some kind of block."

Matt turns to Seymour. "What's the block?" he asks.

Seymour is uncomfortable. "Whatever happens next is pretty bad."

"Are you saying she's afraid to face it?" Matt asks.

"Hello," I say. "I'm right here. You can ask me."

"But you just said you don't know what is causing the block," Matt says.

"Look, let's work with what we've got," Seymour interrupts, trying to protect me, or my memory. "It's clear the Nazis believed they could win the war if they could tap into *vimana* technology. That doesn't surprise me. With a handful of ships that could move that fast, they could have destroyed the Allies' entire air force."

"They were not trying to win the war with fast-flying ships," I say.

Seymour goes to speak and stops. "How, then?"

I point at Matt. "Ask this guy."

"Why me?" Matt says.

"You said you beat the game," I say.

"So?" Matt says.

"Seymour, what is the goal of the game?" I ask. "The one the Cradle posted on the Internet?"

Seymour's eyes dart back and forth between the two of us. "To find a spaceship and fly it back to the center of the galaxy." He stops and speaks to Matt. "You really beat it?"

"Yes," Matt says.

"So you know where it is," I say to Matt.

"Where what is?" Seymour asks.

I raise my voice. "The *vimana*. The real *vimana*. The one from five thousand years ago. The one that crash-landed in the lake."

Seymour lifts his hand. "Wait a second? Are you saying that all this time the Cradle knew where a real *vimana* was?"

"Maybe they knew, maybe they didn't know," I say. "But the power they were channeling definitely knows."

"Tarana?" Seymour says.

I nod. "Does he know, Matt?"

Matt hesitates. "Yes and no."

"That's a safe answer," I snap.

"Don't get angry, I'm trying to help you remember," Matt says. "The goal of the game was not the *vimana* that Karna led you to in the lake."

"How do you know?" Seymour asks. "You weren't there."

"No. But my father was," Matt says.

"Yaksha," I gasp. "I don't remember seeing him that night."

"He was there, he told me what happened. He knew you were near the campfire when Krishna was speaking. He was worried about you, so he followed you back to the Kauravas' camp. He followed you and the man with the box and Duryodhana and Karna to the crashed ship."

"I don't remember any of this!" I gasp.

"I know," Matt says.

"Wait a second," Seymour interrupts. "I just thought of something. Sita saw Umara that night five thousand years ago. Yet Sita didn't know Umara when she met her two months ago. How is that possible?"

"Because Sita remembered nothing that happened that night," Matt says.

"How did she lose so many crucial memories?" Seymour asks.

"How indeed?" Matt says.

"You still haven't answered our question about the ultimate goal of the game," I say to Matt. "If it wasn't to find the crashed *vimana*, then what was it?"

"To find the same thing the Nazis were seeking," Matt says.

"They were trying to win a war," Seymour says. "The purpose of the game is to find a spaceship. They wanted to find the ship so they could build them and win the war. That's got to be the answer."

"That's not the answer," Matt says.

"Did Yaksha tell you the answer?" I ask.

"Yes," Matt says.

"Tell us what it is!" I say, exasperated.

"I will. Soon," Matt says.

"Now!" I order.

Matt shakes his head but doesn't answer.

"Tarana created that game," I warn Matt. "He didn't create it for your own good. The game is evil—John has told us as much. Why do you act like it contains the secret of secrets?"

"The game is important," Matt says. "But I think Mr. Grey is right. I think you are the secret of secrets. Or the key, as he said."

"Spying on me again?" I say.

Matt shrugs. "I can't help but hear what people say around me."

Seymour shakes his head. "Just when I think I have everything figured out, you bring up all this shit. What are we supposed to do now?"

"Get Mr. Grey and go to Joshua Tree National Park," Matt says.

"What's in Joshua Tree?" I ask, although I should know.

That was where John was conceived, and that was where he was taken when he was kidnapped by a monster before he was rescued by me. I have a history with the place. So, apparently, does Matt.

"The end of the game," Matt says.

Dr. Tower is still at the hospital when I arrive with Matt and Seymour. The doctor assures us the operation went fine.

"We were able to relieve the pressure and stop the bleeding in Joel's temporal lobe," Dr. Tower explains, his focus on me. "If there are no further complications, your brother should make a full recovery."

"Wonderful," I say with feeling. "Can we see him?"

"He's in recovery right now. He's heavily sedated. You can see him but don't expect him to respond." Dr. Tower looks at my two companions. "Only immediate family is allowed in."

"These are his brothers," I say with a straight face. Of course, neither Seymour nor Matt looks the least bit like Mr. Grey. Dr. Tower reacts like he's heard the line a thousand times before and doesn't care that it's a lie.

"Please keep your visit short," he says and walks away.

"How are we going to break him out?" Seymour asks.

"All we need is a gurney," Matt says.

"I don't understand why he needs to come with us," Seymour says.

"He wouldn't be here unless it was important," Matt says.

Talk about an odd remark. I fix my eyes on Matt. "Explain," I say.

Matt shakes his head. "It's complicated."

"You're acting like you know who he is," I say. "Who he *really* is."

"Because I have a pretty good idea who he is," Matt says.

"Tell us," Seymour demands.

"Patience," Matt says.

I snort. "You accuse me of keeping secrets. Breaking him out of here could be dangerous. The move might kill him." I add, "You know he has a family."

"He's the one who made you promise not to leave him behind," Matt says. "It's his choice, not yours."

I groan inwardly. "All right. But let's try to keep whatever drug-laced IVs are flowing into his veins intact. He just had his head sawed open. We have to be careful he doesn't get a seizure or a blood clot."

"We should borrow one of the hospital's ambulances," Matt says.

"'Borrow'?" Seymour says. "Will they see it again?"

"Doubtful," Matt says, and smiles. He has not smiled in a long time, not even while making love to me. Something is about to happen that he's looked forward to for a long time. I see it in his face without having any idea what it is.

Naturally, the medical staff on duty are no match for me and Matt. At most the doctors and nurses see a few weird blurs and suddenly one of their patients is missing. The only bump in our great escape is that Brutran is waiting for us beside the ambulances.

"Did you think I would stay at the hotel and watch HBO?" she says.

"Who's watching Jolie?" Seymour asks.

"The hotel has an excellent babysitting program. Anyway, Jolie's asleep. I'm hoping we get back before dawn." She says the last with a glance at Matt.

"There's an excellent chance we'll all be dead by dawn," Matt says.

Brutran is not intimidated. "I've been living on the edge so long I feel lost without it." She goes to climb in the ambulance. I'm surprised when Matt blocks her way.

"I'm serious," he says. "What we're about to do . . . it's extremely dangerous. Jolie needs her mother."

Brutran can't believe the guy she's been kissing up to is betraying her at such a critical moment. "None of you would have gotten this far without me," she snaps.

"We're grateful," Matt says. "But that changes nothing. You're staying."

Brutran looks to me for help—without much hope— before her eyes switch to Seymour. He just hangs his head but I detect a faint smile. Finally she turns back to Matt.

"What am I supposed to do if none of you return?" she asks.

"Try your best to live a decent life," I say.

Matt puts a hand on her shoulder. "I do this for your daughter. That's the only reason. Go, one of us will call you tomorrow. I promise."

Brutran is sharp enough to know Matt is immune to her persuasive powers. "Best of luck," she says before she walks away. When she is out of earshot Seymour pokes the side of Matt's arm.

"How come you're not worried about me getting killed?" he asks.

Matt just smiles. But it is not a reassuring smile.

We load Mr. Grey—and an assortment of tubes, needles, and bags of fluids—into the ambulance and hit the road. Matt drives while Seymour and I sit in the back. The rear seats are uncomfortable but I want to keep an eye on Mr. Grey.

Joshua Tree is 250 miles southwest of Las Vegas, a four-hour drive. I figure we'll reach it before sunrise. If perchance we get lost, I remember the towering Joshua trees that mark the historic spot.

Which makes for a curious coincidence.

Matt has already made it clear that the *vimana*—it's hard to imagine that we're actually going in search of a spaceship—is guarded by two magnificent Joshua trees. As we drive toward the national park, I feel a sense of having come full circle.

While we drive, I let Seymour study *The Story of Veronica*. He devours it in one greedy read. He's always been a fast reader.

"I want the last chapter," he complains when he finishes.

"Mr. Grey told me he hasn't translated it yet," I say.

"There's only one page left," Seymour says.

"I know, he's lying," I reply.

"Why?"

I frown. "That I don't know."

"It's interesting how the Master and Krishna sound so similar."

"The same but different," I say. "Like General Grant and General Patton."

"It's hard to imagine they were the same person."

"The same soul. That's the whole point. The personality changes as the body changes." I add, "That might even be the same with Krishna and Christ."

"Do you think the Master that Veronica spoke to was Christ?"

"What do you think?" I ask.

"Nothing he said sounded like the Bible."

"True. But he was talking to a young woman about her life. She never heard him address the public."

"And time has a way of distorting even the wisest words. Who knows what Christ even taught?" Seymour stops. "But whoever Veronica's Master was, I would have loved to have met him."

"And her," I say. "She was a gutsy little thing."

Halfway to Joshua Tree, Mr. Grey wakes up. He opens his eyes and carefully scans the compartment. He smiles when he sees me.

"Thank you, Sita," he says.

"You're welcome, I hope. You know this trip could kill you."

"This is where I belong. Do you know where you're going?"

"Matt's the one who's driving. He's taking us to Joshua Tree National Park." I pause. "What would your superiors say to that?"

"They would be pleased." He pauses. "It's time I checked in with them. Do you have a cell I can borrow?"

I hand him mine. "You're going to talk to them in front of us?"

"Not exactly." At first I think Mr. Grey is sending a text message but he only hits eleven keys—like a phone number. I hear it ring on the other end. Someone picks up. Mr. Grey hits another button before hanging up. Obviously he's sending someone a prearranged message. He keeps the phone and I don't ask for it back.

But I'm not happy with what he's done.

"I thought you might call your family," I say.

"Not yet," he says.

A few minutes go by. Outside, beneath the glow of the moon, the dark desert rolls along. Matt is driving at eighty miles an hour. I don't worry about getting stopped by the police. Matt will know when one is in the area. No, my concerns are much more serious.

"Did you translate the end of Veronica's story?" Seymour asks.

"Not yet," Mr. Grey repeats. He is definitely lying, and I have never heard him lie before.

I still care for him but I suddenly don't trust him. The opposing emotions are hard to bottle up inside. I should, though, it would be the wiser move. But I seldom do the wise thing when I'm pissed off.

"How do you feel?" I ask.

"Weak. Sore. Do you have any water?"

"Seymour, open one of those Evian bottles. Be sure to put a straw in it. Thank you." Seymour hands me the water and I hold the straw to Mr. Grey's mouth. He drinks hungrily and then coughs. I quickly pull away the bottle, saying, "Small sips. You don't want to choke."

He gestures to the IVs in his arms. "Are these necessary?"

"Dr. Tower says you need your medicine," I say.

"I'm pretty sure Dr. Tower is wondering where I am about now," Mr. Grey replies with a grin.

"How about Sarah Goodwin?" I ask.

Mr. Grey blinks. "Pardon?"

"Is she wondering where you are? Where we are?"

"I don't know." Mr. Grey looks suddenly pale in the moonlight that peeks through the ambulance window. Or else he's frightened by my grim expression. "What's the matter, Sita?" he asks.

"Who did you call just now?"

"It's not important."

"But it is. Tell me."

Mr. Grey lies back and closes his eyes and mutters, "Damn."

"What's going on?" Seymour asks, confused.

"Do you know what's going on?" I call to Matt.

"Mr. Grey sent someone a signal," Matt calls back.

"Who did he call?" Seymour asks.

"He dialed the number Shanti scribbled on the back of the lawyer's business card. That mysterious number none of us dared to call." My eyes narrow on Mr. Grey. "Are your superiors and Tarana one and the same?"

Mr. Grey opens his eyes. "No. They have nothing in common."

I go to yell at him but catch myself. I hear truth in his words. But then I begin to doubt the accuracy of my own abilities. I fell for Shanti's lies. Perhaps Mr. Grey is deceiving me just as easily.

"Why?" I ask.

"You can't save Sarah Goodwin unless someone brings her to us."

"How do you know they'll bring her?" I ask.

"They used her grandmother last time and it worked. They'll use Sarah this time." Mr. Grey glances at Seymour. "They'll use whatever it takes."

"Damn you, I saved her grandmother from the camp. I saved her grandfather. It didn't work last time. How dare you . . ." I don't finish, I can't. I'm so angry I can't find the words.

"Are you saying the people who have been trying to kill us are going to be at the spaceship?" Seymour asks.

"In a manner of speaking," Mr. Grey replies.

Seymour is obviously shaken by the possibility—he is not the only one. However, at the same time, I can tell he is thinking deeply, and that he is aware that I feel betrayed. He reaches over and takes my hand.

"Sita. Think," he says. "Whoever posted the game on the Internet knew the solution to the game. So whoever they are, they're not using us to find the *vimana*. They already know where it is. They want something else from us."

"Logical," I say, appreciating his insight. "Are you suggesting they want to bargain with us?"

"I suspect it will be more of a duel than a negotiation," Seymour says.

"Like Auschwitz," I say.

"Possibly," Seymour says.

"But I won at Auschwitz," I say.

"If you'd won, you wouldn't be fighting the same battle all over," Mr. Grey says. "At best you reached a stalemate with the enemy during your stay at the concentration camp, and that's being kind."

"Tell me straight," I say. "Are you working for Tarana or us?"

Mr. Grey stares at me with his warm brown eyes. "I'm loyal to you. Only to you."

Damn, I could swear he's being sincere. For the life of me I don't know what the hell is going on.

We reach Joshua Tree an hour before dawn and park well off the road. Matt appears confident that we're close to our goal, but suddenly I'm not so sure. The area looks different from the last time I was here, when John was just an infant. I don't see as many Joshua trees, and the ones near the road are not very impressive.

Yet Matt radiates certainty. Climbing out of the ambulance, he points to a distant hill. In the glow of the full moon it looks like a levitating lake—possibly because its soil is a lighter shade than the surrounding terrain.

"We're almost there," Matt says. "That's where the game ended."

Seymour groans. "That hill's a four-mile walk."

"More like three miles," Matt says, searching the area. "I think we got here first. I don't hear anyone."

"We're alone," I say.

"What do you want to do with Mr. Grey?" Matt asks.

"Shoot him," I say.

Matt is amused. "He finally pissed you off."

"Duh. He called Tarana. Or whatever human being Tarana happens to be inhabiting."

Matt nods. "All right, I'll carry him then. But I'll have to remove his IVs."

Matt turns to the back of the ambulance while Seymour

and I collect a handful of water bottles and stuff them into a pack. The air is cool but bone-dry. We won't have to walk far to get thirsty. Tossing the pack over my back, I start toward the hill.

"What are we looking for exactly?" Seymour says. "The *vimana* that crashed during the Mahabharata war?"

"I'm not sure. A lot more happened that night I spent with Karna and Duryodhana. I wish I could get over this memory block. You can't imagine how frustrating it is. Hell, I remember everything I did for the last five thousand years."

"Every person you killed?"

"Sure."

"Every guy you slept with?"

I look at him. "And every woman. But seriously, Seymour, trauma alone can't explain why I can't recall what went on at the end of that war."

"Let's try another regression. It would probably work better out here than in a Las Vegas hotel room. Assuming we have the time."

"Are you talking about the local vibe? That's awfully New Age for a cynic like you."

Seymour shrugs. "Hey, whatever works."

"I'm willing to give it a try. I'm pretty sure where we stopped is where I stopped with Himmler, too. The next thing I remember is being back in that underground cell. That was where the shit really hit the fan."

"Did Ralph manage to get you the key?"

I hesitate. "We'll see. I don't want to say anything off the top of my head and be wrong."

Seymour points to the hill. "If there's a ship out here, we have to assume it's buried. We should have brought a shovel."

"If it's buried, it's going to take more than a shovel to dig it up."

Seymour glances over his shoulder. Matt is still at the ambulance, trying to figure out the best way to carry Mr. Grey. The man is so weak it's doubtful he'll be able to hang on to Matt's neck. Matt's probably going to have to cradle him in front like an infant.

I still feel annoyed at the stunt Mr. Grey pulled on the road. I have known him a lot less time than I did Shanti and yet his betrayal—if that's what it was—has a much sharper sting to it. The only thing that reassures me is that he made the call in front of me. It was like he wanted to get caught.

"Matt seems to know something we don't," Seymour says.

I nod. "Yeah. And his mood improved the instant he beat the game. It was like something clicked inside and he was suddenly more sure of himself."

"Maybe the game finally managed to reprogram his brain. John told us it was bad news."

"What if John was using reverse psychology?" I say.

"Are you serious?"

"Consider. Matt's a control freak. He's the strongest man

on the planet. But suddenly this kid comes along and tells him he can't do something. That it might harm him. To someone like Matt, that's worse than a slap in the face. Especially since he knows John's not afraid of the game."

"Are you saying Matt kept playing it to spite John?"

"I think it challenged Matt to examine the game. But eventually he must have seen something in it that was important to him."

"He realized it was a means to find a *vimana*," Seymour says.

"Exactly. Those ships the government's building, those Fastwalkers, they're not the real thing. But that's not to say the Pentagon's not trying to create the real thing."

"By the real thing you mean a ship that can travel faster than light."

"That's only part of it," I say. "Remember that talk Krishna gave at the campfire that night. He asked those listening to imagine a race of beings a million years older than mankind. He spoke about how advanced they would be. How attuned they would be to the Essence. That night, while he was speaking, I actually saw such a race in my mind's eye. It was so evolved that we'd consider them gods. Just as so many of us looked up to Krishna as a god."

"Not as a god but as *the* God," Seymour says.

"Good point. In the past, when these great beings visited our world, we automatically saw them as incarnations of God.

To the early Christians, it wasn't enough that Christ was a great master. He had to be the son of God. The same with Krishna, to the Hindus he had to be Lord Vishnu. Yet, ironically, since Christ and Krishna were so attuned to this Essence, they *were* one with God. Except from their perspective they saw everyone as evolving toward their state. Neither of them saw himself as unique."

"Do you think such an ancient race would have the power of life over death?" Seymour asks.

"It would have to have that power if it was one with the Essence."

Seymour suddenly chuckles. "Now who is getting all New Age?"

"There's a practical side to this discussion. The *vimana* we're searching for might be more than a ship that can travel faster than light. It might be capable of taking people to higher realms of existence." I add, "It might even be capable of time travel."

Seymour's face brightens. "Like that ship that picked you up in the desert and sent you back to the Middle Ages to defeat Landulf?"

"Yes, that definitely happened. I suspect that's why the Nazis were so anxious for me to help them build a *vimana*, or else find one. Hitler didn't want the ship to shoot down the Allies' planes. He wanted to go back in time and fix the mistakes he'd made during the war."

"Sita, that's it, that's the answer. You're a genius."

I shake my head. "It can't be the final answer. Mr. Grey says I'm the answer. I'm the key."

"The key to what?"

"The future."

Seymour can't resist the taunt. "Is it wise to put so much faith in a guy who has brain damage?"

"Don't worry. I lost my faith in Mr. Grey when he made that call."

There's a faint glow in the east when we reach the foot of the hill. My concern about the lack of tall Joshua trees has vanished. Atop the summit are two strong-armed trees that stand over eighty feet high. It's impossible to stare up at them and not feel that they're protecting the spot. They look like ancient sentinels.

And they feel alive.

Alive in the sense that they know we're here.

Matt lays Mr. Grey on the sandy dirt and tucks a folded sweatshirt beneath his delicate head. "He passed out not long after we left the road," Matt says.

"Thanks for being careful with him," I say.

Matt raises an eyebrow. "You still care for him."

"I wish I didn't."

Matt gestures to the hill. "What do you feel?"

"Something. A magnetism across my forehead."

"You used to get the same sensation around Krishna."

"This place definitely has a high vibration."

"Then maybe Seymour's suggestion is a good one. You two should try another regression. This spot might help you punch through whatever is blocking you."

"I thought you had everything figured out."

"Come on, Sita, I haven't been that bad."

"You've been a total asshole."

Matt reaches over and pulls me close. He speaks softly. "The last few days I've had a lot cooking inside. Stuff I haven't been able to talk about."

"Stuff you've refused to talk about. What did your father tell you?"

He lets go and takes a step back. "It's better if you remember it for yourself."

"What's wrong with giving a girl a little help?"

Matt ignores me and stares in the direction of the road. "They'll be here soon. If we're going to do it, we better start now."

"Fine. Where do you want to do it?"

Matt points to the top of the hill. "Up there."

We climb the hill, the three of us. It's not steep. The sand that makes up the summit is definitely different from the local terrain. Besides being a light yellow, it has a moist, chalky feel to it. I can't get rid of the feeling the hill is artificial. That someone piled up the sand long ago.

The two Joshua trees, separated by fifty yards, tower over

the summit. They are not as tall as redwoods but they look even more powerful. Their arms continue to haunt me. I keep expecting them to move. . . .

Seymour and I sit cross-legged across from each other, our knees touching. Our eyes meet and he begins the suggestions. I don't recall closing my eyes but suddenly I feel myself falling. The past images come faster this time, more like explosions of sight and sensation. I worry that Seymour will feel everything I begin to feel. I fear it will kill him.

I stand in the center of the concrete room, chained to my original pole. My leg and arm muscles got a brief respite when they marched me underground from the wire cage in ankle and wrist chains—a dozen SS guards pointing their rifles at my head. But now I'm back to being a pinned bug. The bonds are tighter than before.

So tight I can't reach the flat area at the top of the pole.

Ralph's key could be an inch away and I can't tell.

My cramped muscles and burning lungs are in agony. There's nothing I can do to relieve the suffering. I can't even kill myself.

Himmler enters with Major Klein and Frau Cia. They have brought their usual tools of torture. Plus a surprise—five men in suits. Curiously, three appear to be Jewish. Himmler introduces the men as scientists but doesn't give out names.

"They're here to learn about the *vimanas*," he says.

"I told you all I remember. It crash-landed on the shore of a lake. I walked toward it and went inside. But the interior—I couldn't tell you if it was shiny silver or pretty pink. Your scientists are going to have to figure out how to build their own flying saucer."

Himmler comes close enough to whisper in my ear. "Anton is three stories up. Locked in a room with twenty other dying men. His hands and arms, where he was skinned, are infected. He's delirious with pain. He needs penicillin, morphine. I'll give him whatever he needs if you help us."

"I wish I could," I say.

He nods. "You're telling the truth. That's something. Perhaps your memory needs another jolt."

"No!" I say quickly.

"It worked last time. Why shouldn't it work again?"

"Anton can't take any more. Torture him again and he'll die."

"I'm not talking about Anton."

There is no sense in pleading with Himmler. One does not beg for a glass of water from the devil. He snaps a finger and Harrah is brought in.

She stands before me in gray prison garb. But I see a cloth wrapped around her top beneath her standard Auschwitz issue. It's the veil; she has turned the face of Christ toward her skin so the Nazis can't see it. She looks at me with pleading eyes, her gaze moving repeatedly to the top of the post.

So it is true. Ralph did manage to put the key there.

And I can't reach it.

"Roll up her sleeves, use the gasoline," Himmler says. "Sita enjoyed it so much last time, her friend should be treated no worse."

I'm a coward, I close my eyes. I don't understand why God made sight the only sense that can be blocked off. Especially when Harrah's screams start. It doesn't seem right that the machinery of the human body can't be shut down during a major crisis. The mind, too; I wish more than anything in that instant that I could turn it off.

Himmler knows that, of course. That's his secret.

In trying to turn off my mind, I turn it on.

I remember . . .

The outside of the craft is a dull orange, the inside is as red as the evening sky after a bloody day of battle. I have seen such sunsets recently.

The interior is circular. I count three levels, each connected by a winding black staircase. I enter at the mid-level, see an assortment of chairs, couches. I assume this is where the occupants relax and sleep.

On the top level are panels with colored lights and bright rectangles that glow with symbols that I assume are part of a language. I suspect this is the ship's control center.

A hum comes from the bottom floor. Here is the heart of the ship. Here are the dead men. They lie in a tangled heap beside the staircase, as if they were trying to climb out when death stole their last breath. Karna gave me the impression the men have not been dead long, but that does not seem possible. What skin they have left has turned to ash; it clings to their bones like a fungus growing on an animal that died in a swamp.

Still, I know this is the center of power for the ship because of the glass pipes that encircle the walls. A silver fluid—I suspect it's mercury—flows through the tubes, pulsating like blood in a vein. The rhythm of the movement seems to generate a power my whole body feels. It's hot, hotter than fire—I can only get so near. Yet I'm confused that the rest of the lower deck is not boiling. The heat pours from the pipes, only to vanish into the air.

I see two of the cracked-open metal cylinders that Karna told me to beware of. They lie against the wall, beside an iron pit whose top has been lifted. A black-blue glow comes from a lump of stone at the center of each cylinder. It's clearly the material that killed the men. To their eyes the glow must have been faint, perhaps invisible, but to mine it looks like a light that has no place in our world. The glow is not conscious, no evil mind lurks behind it; nevertheless I feel if ever I were to meet a demon from the dark realms, its eyes would give off such a light.

Moving as rapidly as possible, I shove the lumps of stone back into their cylinders and twist the sides shut. My task is only partially successful—the weapons still have cracks in them. I put them back in the metal hole from where they spilled and close the top, locking it with a bar.

As I do so the mercury in the glass pipes accelerates.

A wave of dizziness steals over me and I reach for the stairway. I manage to climb back to the second level but have to stop and rest. My arms and legs feel disconnected from my brain. I know I should get outside, at least close the portal that leads to the lower level, but lack the strength. My vision blurs. I can see the door that leads to the outside but it looks a mile away. If I close my eyes and rest for a minute, I think, I should be strong enough to escape.

That's all I remember until I awaken to find Yaksha kneeling beside me. His expression is puzzling. Clearly he has come to kill me. Krishna made him swear to destroy all the vampires. But his face is grim.

"Sita," he says. "What have they done to you?"

"Are you here to kill me?" I mumble.

"I'm here to rescue you. How do you feel?"

"I'll be all right." I try to stand, with his help, but suddenly bend over and vomit. The urge to vomit is strange—it won't stop, not even when the last scrap of food has been expelled from my body.

Then I see my hands, my arms. My skin has turned black and begun to peel off. "Yaksha," I gasp.

"We're leaving," Yaksha says as he suddenly sweeps me off

my feet. He turns toward the door and it opens, but Duryodhana and the man with the metal box block our way. In the woods behind them I see Karna.

"You will stay aboard," Duryodhana commands, brandishing his sword in Yaksha's direction.

"Sita is sick," Yaksha says. "I have to get her out of here."

"We'll need one of them if we're to use the weapons," the man with the box says to his king. Duryodhana nods and speaks to Yaksha.

"I'll release both of you when we're finished with this ship."

"I don't take orders from you!" Yaksha swears. Setting me down, he rushes the king. A sudden piercing sound fills the ship, the same sound I heard when they came for me earlier. Only this time it's louder and I black out.

When I awaken Yaksha and I are chained to the central staircase. The metal is strong—I can't bend it. However, I'm relieved to see my hands and arms have healed. I know why I have recovered.

"You gave me your blood," I say.

"You were dying."

"Isn't that your goal now? To destroy the last of the vampires?"

Yaksha shakes his head, annoyed. "Not now, Sita."

I hear steps overhead, count three people. "Has Karna come aboard?"

"Yes. He has taken control of the *vimana*. We're high above the battlefield. They're preparing to drop a weapon of some kind."

"We have to stop them. The way Duryodhana described it—the weapon can destroy all the Pandavas and their army at once."

"We can do nothing as long as that man can create that sound."

Above us, through the opening in the ceiling that leads to the control room, I see glimpses of blue sky and green forest. We must be miles above the ground. I can see the two armies moving into position to fight. This will be the fourth and probably the last day of battle. I struggle with the chains to no avail.

"Can you break us free?" I ask.

"Yes. But I told you, the man with the box . . ."

"He can't deal with the two of us at once. Break us free and rush the man with the box and Duryodhana. Spare Karna, he's a good man. While you're busy with them, I'll destroy the weapons."

"It was the weapons that almost killed you."

"Better I die than the Pandavas and Krishna. Come, we have to hurry."

Yaksha has to focus all his strength to break our chains. He's close to exhaustion by the time we're free. But there's no time to recover. He runs up the stairs while I head back down.

A light flashes green beside the pit where I stored the

weapons. But it turns red as I approach. I hear the weapons shift beneath the floor and know they are seconds away from being released. I don't know what to do. I fear I'm too late to save Krishna.

I lash out at the glass pipes with my hands and feet. Boiling mercury pours over the floor. Overhead, the awful screech sound from the metal box begins and then suddenly cuts off. Before the mercury can touch me, I leap onto the stairs and rush back to the second level. I slam the portal shut behind me.

A blinding ball of fire explodes over the battlefield. It swells in size until it appears to cover both armies. But as the light begins to dim I see the weapon has burned more Kauravas than Pandavas.

I hear a loud popping sound and an invisible fist smashes me to the floor. Suddenly I weigh a hundred times my weight. Above me the blue sky turns black.

Once more, for the third time, I lose consciousness.

When I awaken I'm sitting near Yaksha on the upper level. Countless stars drift by. In the distance I see an extremely bright star. Yaksha tells me it is the sun.

"It can't be the sun. It's too small," I say.

"Its size has not changed. It is farther away."

"How did we get here? Who is flying the ship?"

"No one. Karna is dead. Duryodhana is dead. So is the man with the box. I put their bodies below. They died when the ship flew above the sky."

"Why?" I ask, sad to hear Karna is gone and with him his dream of visiting the stars.

"You must have felt the pressure. It was too much for the others. Every bone in their bodies snapped. They died instantly."

I stare out at the black sky and the bright stars.

"How are we to get home?" I ask.

"I have no idea," Yaksha says.

"That's it?" Himmler yells at me as Harrah sobs in the corner. They put out the flames when I began to talk but they have done nothing to soothe her burns. Himmler continues to rant, "All you recall is you and your lover floating away to the stars?"

"I never said we reached the stars," I say. "I told you what happened. What else can I do? You should be satisfied."

Himmler slaps me with the back of his hand. "Don't tell me what is satisfactory! How did you get back to earth?"

"I don't know."

"Where did you land the *vimana*?"

"I don't know."

"How did the rotating mercury create the force that lifted the ship?"

"I don't know."

"Were the glass pipes surrounded with magnets?"

"I don't remember any magnets."

"How hot was the mercury?"

"Boiling."

"Boiling!" Himmler cries at me, hysterical. "Do you want to see what that word means? Tell me what I want to know or I put your friend's hands back in the flames."

"I hate you!" I swear, putting so much hate in my voice I'm surprised the walls don't crack. Yet Himmler drinks up my bitterness as if it were a caress. He enjoys it! He brings his face close to mine. His eyes are nothing but swollen pupils. They are holes; there is no bottom to his madness.

"At last you understand," he says softly.

I spit in his face, the saliva hitting his lips. He wipes away most of it with his tongue. "Burn the Jew," he orders Major Klein.

"No!" I yell. Arching my back, I strain with every fiber of my being to reach the top of the pole. The handcuffs refuse to break but this time the metal stretches slightly. Just enough to let me touch the key.

I knock it into my palm and clasp it tightly.

Himmler takes a step back, his expression puzzled.

I move too fast for a human to follow. Inserting the key in the lock, I twist it clockwise and the lock snaps open. Kneeling, I slip it into the ankle cuffs and twist the key again. I hear a second snap and step away from the pole.

Himmler turns for the door. I grab his arm and pull him back. But before I can reach up and snap his neck, the soul-piercing noise of the box fills the room. Major Klein holds it at eye level and twists the black knob all the way around. A wave of agony strikes from every angle. Knowing I'm close to blacking out, I drop to my knees. But I realize if I allow myself to lose consciousness, the nightmare will never end, for me or my friends.

Himmler runs out the room. The scientists chase after him. I crawl toward Major Klein, and he makes my task easier by taking a step toward me. He wants to shove the box down my throat. I see his wolfish grin.

I refuse to scream. Reaching up, through a shower of agony, I grab his arm and snap the bone in two. He drops the box, and with my free hand I slap it out the door, where it strikes a wall and falls silent. Standing, I grab ahold of his other arm and snap that bone. I smile as he begs for mercy.

"Like you know what the word means," I say just before I break his neck. How satisfying it is to kill him.

But how foolish it is to take my eyes off Frau Cia.

Besides myself and Harrah, she's the only one left in the room. The Puppet Lady, I have called her in my thoughts. Yet it's clear I've underestimated the woman. For she is the only one who stays behind to fight me. At first I think her a fool, a brave woman but an idiot nevertheless. Then I realize she's holding the bottle of gasoline, the one from the table, and the box of matches. It's no reason to panic. I'm a vampire, I think, I can easily disarm her. . . .

In a blinding move she throws the entire bottle of gasoline over me, taking me totally off guard, soaking me from head to toe. Before I can respond she lights a match. Such a small flame, it shouldn't threaten me. Even if she tries to throw it at me, I can easily knock it away. . . .

Holding the match out as if it were a steel blade, Cia dives straight toward me. I'm not only soaked in gasoline, I'm surrounded by a cloud of fumes. It's the fumes that ignite first—they require only a spark. She is three feet away and still coming when my combustible aura meets her flame and I'm transformed into a human torch.

I've been burned before, of course; even in this very room. But to be engulfed in flames is not the same thing. No, to become one with the fire is like embracing an eternity of punishment—all condensed in a few seconds of infinite horror.

I dance around the room like a wounded animal. I try to scream but the flames burn away my voice. Laughing, Frau Cia runs from the room—I see her leave through a blistering red haze—and slams the door shut. I don't care. All I know is pain.

I feel I've become one with the fire. I feel damned.

Harrah throws a cloth over me and somehow wrestles me to the floor. I hear her whispering, I hear her prayers. I even hear steam rising from my blackened skin. The fire is out. How can the fire be out? It doesn't matter, I'm in too much pain for it to matter.

For a long time, forever it seems, I pray to die.

But then slowly, I return to life, to the world.

I open my eyes and see Harrah smiling at me.

"You're going to be all right," she says.

"How?" I ask, my voice shaky.

"You have on the veil. It healed me, now it's healing you."

"No. You mustn't let it get dirty."

Harrah chuckles. "You're not dirty, child."

Slowly, the pain begins to recede and I'm able to stand. I hug the veil tightly, afraid to let it go, afraid I'll catch fire again. I have been to hell and back, and I pray to Christ I never return. At this moment, I believe in him. I believe he is every bit as great as Krishna.

When I can think, I step to the door. It's locked.

"Shit," I whisper. "We're trapped."

"Are we?"

I point to the special alloy. "This metal, I can't break it."

"Try."

"What? I have done nothing but try."

"Try now," Harrah says.

She's telling me that because I wear the veil, nothing can stop me.

I leap in the air and lash at the door with both feet.

It convulses. It breaks. The door falls to the ground.

"Where is Ralph?" I ask.

"In the factory, making uniforms. I'll lead you to him."

We find Ralph and I take him and his wife and rush the SS soldiers who guard the camp's north corner. I kill a dozen in seconds before I rip apart the wire fence and lead my friends outside. I hide them in a cluster of bushes.

"Stay here. I have to find Anton," I say, giving Harrah the veil. She pushes it back.

"Keep it," she says.

"I'm healed now, I'll be all right."

I return to the camp. I feel strong. I'm surprised how good I feel. The fire . . . well, I don't want to think about the fire. But I feel confident I can rescue Anton and get the four of us out of Poland alive.

I remember Himmler's words.

"Anton is three stories up. Locked in a room with twenty other dying men. . . ."

I'm grateful the fool gave me such precise directions. All I have to do is return to the building where I was being held and find the floor he spoke of and break down the right door. No problem.

Yet as I enter the building I fled moments before, I see Frau Cia. She stands outside the door of a cell, and even from this distance I can hear my lover's moans mingling with the cries of the other prisoners. He's in pain, and every now and then he whispers my name, praying that I'll save him a second time.

Frau Cia does not hold the box, nor a bottle of gasoline, or even a box of matches. But the way she stares at me is unnerving. Everything I despise about Himmler is suddenly magnified in her. Her eyes, they are black, they have no whites. Her expression is blank, it has no life, no anger, no hatred, nothing. Yet it's her nothingness that causes me to pause. The presence I felt working through Himmler, I feel it now inside of her.

Only more focused, more dangerous.

I don't know why but I suddenly feel afraid.

Worse, I *know* if I try to save Anton I'll be caught. I'll be tortured. They'll burn me again. They'll keep burning me. It will never stop.

Frau Cia holds open her arms. "Sita, come. Join us. You are so close to us now."

"No!" I cry, spinning on my heels and fleeing. I run all the way back to where Harrah and Ralph huddle in the bushes. They try to calm me. For a long time I can't speak, I can't stop shaking.

"Did you find Anton?" Harrah asks finally.

I hesitate. "He's dead. We have to save ourselves now."

SEVENTEEN

I exit the session in an instant. One moment I'm crouched in the bushes outside Auschwitz, the next I'm sitting across from Seymour on top of the hill in Joshua Tree National Park. Matt stands over us.

"That was gruesome," Matt says.

"You heard what I did at the end?" I ask.

Matt nods. Seymour speaks quickly. "It's nothing to be ashamed of. You did everything you could to save Harrah and Ralph. Anton . . . he was severely injured. He would never have made it out of Poland."

My guilt is unbearable. I wonder if it's the reason I blocked out the memory. It's hard for me to tell the others how I feel but the compulsion to confess is strong.

"He risked his life to save me and I left him to die. I left him to be tortured to death," I say.

"You once told me that Krishna said guilt was the most useless of all emotions," Seymour says.

"It is useless. That doesn't make it any less real," I say.

Seymour stands and offers me a hand, pulling me to my feet. "Let's focus on what we learned. You really did go aboard a *vimana*. A nuclear bomb was detonated at the Battle of Kurukshetra, like the legends say."

"The Mahabharata called it *Pashupata*," Matt says.

I shake my head. "How were Yaksha and I rescued from the *vimana*? The last thing I remember was staring out at the stars." I look to Matt for answers. "Did your father talk to you about what happened?"

Matt nods. "That's why I'm here. You might even say that's why I spent so much time playing the game."

"I don't understand," I say.

Matt points down the hill. "I'll have to explain later. They're coming."

Three figures approach from the direction of the road. The light in the east has grown but sunrise is still thirty minutes away. I don't need the sun, however, to recognize Sarah Goodwin and Frau Cia. The man—I have never seen him before—looks like a younger version of Himmler.

It makes no sense but Frau Cia has not aged.

The young man kicks Mr. Grey's leg, forcing him awake. He orders him to stand. Mr. Grey, his head heavily bandaged, appears resigned to the task. He and Sarah Goodwin trudge up the hill behind the other two. Sarah herself looks in poor shape—it's obvious she has been tortured. Her blue sweats are streaked with blood and both her eyes are blackened.

Still, although she is hurting, she makes an effort to help Mr. Grey climb the hill. She must have a piece of Harrah in her, I think.

"Did anyone think to bring a gun?" Seymour asks anxiously.

"I've got one," Matt says.

"It won't help. The guy has the box," I say.

"I thought you broke it," Seymour says.

"It looks like it's been fixed," I say. We're assuming there is only one box—the one taken from the *vimana* that crashed five thousand years ago.

Soon they stand before us, although Sarah and Mr. Grey quickly move to our side. Their act does not bother Frau Cia and . . . Himmler's child? It must be his child, or his grandchild—the man has characteristics of Cia and Himmler. I see both parents in the lines of his face and the darkness in his eyes. He holds the box and keeps his fingers close to the black dial.

Cia radiates the inhuman horror I felt from her at Auschwitz. She and her child are like twin objects that float in a vast black sea—an impersonal ocean that controls what they do. The fact that they're here is enough to stain the hill.

I lean over and whisper in Sarah's ear. "Are you all right?"

She sighs. "I've been better. Have you been searching for me?"

"Frantically."

"Is Roger . . ."

"He's dead. I'm sorry."

Her head drops. "I knew, he was so hurt."

I speak softly in her ear. "Do you have the veil?"

Sarah nods.

"Sita," Cia interrupts in a German accent. "It's been a long time."

"Frau Cia. You haven't aged. Yet you're not vampire or Telar."

Cia nods. "We met during the war, and close to a thousand years ago, in Landulf's castle. I can see you're puzzled."

"The woman who posed as Landulf of Capua's consort died in the Middle Ages," Seymour says. "Her heart was cut from her body."

Cia smiles faintly. "That must mean I have no heart."

She taunts him. She's saying Seymour wrote her as having no heart because a part of him sensed—through my mind—that she was devoid of all human feeling.

She has a heart, though, it pumps with unusual vigor. Either she stole my blood long ago or else the creature that chose her as a vehicle keeps her from aging. It's possible both are true. I only know she's strong and very fast, and that Tarana lives inside her. The same for the man.

"What do you want?" I ask.

Cia shrugs. "What you want. We have come for Vishnu's *Vimana*."

Vishnu's Vimana. Vishnu is a name for God in India. Specifically, the word refers to that aspect of God that maintains the creation. In Vedic texts, Brahma creates the universe and Shiva destroys it at the end of time. Shiva, Brahma, and Vishnu make up the holy trinity of the Vedas. Many scholars feel they parallel the Christian concept of the Father, Son, and Holy Spirit. However the name is viewed, it's odd to hear a monster like Frau Cia speak of seeking a holy vessel.

"You believe it's here?" Matt says.

"We know it's here. Can't you see it?" Cia gestures to one of the tall Joshua trees on the hilltop, the one on our right.

"Very funny," I reply. "Are you saying it's cloaked as a tree?"

"Yes," Cia says.

Matt appears to accept her answer. Perhaps something in the game pointed to the Joshua trees, I don't know. I watch as he nods to the Joshua tree on the left. "What type of *vimana* is that?" he asks.

Cia laughs softly. "*Our* kind. The kind that strikes fear into every living creature."

"We're not afraid of you," I say firmly.

"No? The last time we met you looked frightened. When you ran from the camp and left Anton behind. By the way, he died cursing your name. I thought you should know."

"For such a powerful woman, you're remarkably boring." I yawn. "But I suppose you're a big hit with all the Pentagon generals."

Cia snickers. "You think I still work with those fools? I gave them sixty years to figure out how to speed up their damn ships. And they're still stuck circling the planets."

Seymour is puzzled. "So you don't work on the fast walkers anymore?"

"Nope," Cia says.

Matt intrudes. "You've known where Vishnu's *Vimana* is. Yet you have waited until now to come for it. Why? Is there something that keeps you from boarding it?"

Cia looks at him with approval. "A thinking man. I like that. Yes, the *vimana* is difficult to enter. It only responds to someone it recognizes."

Cia and Matt look at me; they all do.

"I've never seen this Joshua tree before. Or Vishnu's *Vimana*," I say.

"You have," Cia says. "But like everything that has to do with this topic, you don't remember. In Auschwitz we did our best to help you with this block. But it's time you got over it for yourself." She adds, "You don't want us to help you again."

"You and your tedious threats," I mutter.

Cia turns to her companion. "Give them level three."

The man turns a dial on the box. The faint screeching sound starts, low at first, then louder, bringing with it brain-bursting pain. Matt and I double up; it's impossible to block it out. The pain vibrates every nerve in our skulls. I have never seen Matt cry out before.

Then I notice we're not alone. Seymour is also suffering from the sound. I don't understand why. Is our telepathic link still intact? Is the tiny amount of blood I put in his veins to cure his HIV infection resonating with the noise? He drops to his knees and blood runs from his nose. The sound is killing him.

"You've made your point!" I gasp.

Cia signals to the man, who twists the dial back to zero. The pain recedes immediately. Matt kneels to attend to Seymour, but my attention is diverted. For a few seconds, as my jangled nerves were calming down, I saw the faint outline of a red *vimana* where the Joshua tree on our left is standing. It was not a mirage, it was real.

Indeed, I suspect it's the trees that are not real.

"You learn faster these days," Cia says. "Or is it that you value your companions so highly?"

"I have no memory of Vishnu's *Vimana*," I reply.

For the first time Cia steps close. She stops within striking distance, and I have no doubt she's taunting me. A leap into the air, a kick with my right foot—I could decapitate her in an instant. But what would the man with the box do? Turn the dial up to ten? Seymour's head would explode. Certainly Matt and I would be knocked out, leaving the others helpless.

Our foes have planned this encounter carefully.

"By now you must recognize the pattern," Cia says. "All memories relating to the *vimanas* are blocked inside you. Until we stimulated you at Auschwitz, you had no memories at all of what went on during the Battle of Kurukshetra. You didn't even recall listening to your blessed Krishna's talk about the *vimanas*."

"Go on," I say.

"Shortly after you left Auschwitz, you blocked the memories again. To put it bluntly, Sita, something inside you is forcing you to play the fool. Knowing your fiery temperament, that must annoy you. Personally, it would enrage me. I wouldn't stand for it—no, I'd fight against the block with everything inside me."

"Unless the block was put there for a reason," Matt says.

Cia's face registers a flash of anger before she hides it with a fake smile. "Can you suggest a reason for the block?" she asks.

Matt considers. "Not long before he died, my father told me about the *vimana* you seek. Hearing about it affected me deeply. Suddenly the world was no longer enough. Simply knowing the *vimana* exists here on earth has driven me to find it. I'd go so far as to say it has come close to driving me nuts."

"It affected you that much?" I say.

Cia snorts. "You would have reacted worse. You would have spent your entire life trying to locate the *vimana* so you could fly off into the stars and find the magical world where your blessed Krishna lives."

I go to snap at her but realize she's right.

"It's the time for all the old secrets to be revealed," Cia says. "Tell Sita everything Yaksha told you, Matt. She deserves to know the truth."

"Matt," I say when he doesn't respond.

"I hate talking about it in front of them," he says.

"But they already know. They have always known," I reply.

Matt hesitates. "The two of you didn't drift forever in the damaged ship. You were rescued by celestial beings my father had no words for. They brought you home, and yet it was so painful for you to leave them after what they had shown you, you asked that all your memories be erased." Matt pauses. "You're the cause of the block. You're the one who asked for it."

His words almost knock me over. "Did Yaksha?"

"No."

"He knew the truth all these years?"

"Yes."

"Then how come he didn't leave?"

"He had made a vow."

To destroy all the vampires, I think. *To kill me.*

"I understand," I say.

Cia continues. "Now that you know the truth, you can finally be of some use to us. The situation is simple. The Vishnu *Vimana* will only open for a person who has entered it before. Sita, you're the only living person who's been inside it. You might say you're the key that can unlock its door." She points to the Joshua tree on our right. "Enter it now or we'll kill your companions. Starting with your beloved Seymour."

"Don't listen to them," Seymour says, the front of his shirt stained with blood. His nose has barely begun to stop leaking.

"Quiet. Let me think," I say, studying the ground around the Joshua tree and the tree itself. Besides being extremely tall, it has four arms, not two like its companion. It reminds me of how devotees in India often paint Krishna with four arms. It's said that when Krishna showed his divine form to Arjuna on the battlefield of Kurukshetra, he revealed himself in his four-armed form, among others.

"If I enter it, what's to stop me from flying away?" I ask.

"Your friends," Cia says.

I shrug. "You're going to kill them anyway."

"We wouldn't kill them, at least not for a while. We would make them pay for your lack of cooperation. In the same way we made Anton pay." Cia pauses. "You still hear his cries in the night, don't you, dear?"

"Bitch," I mutter.

Cia smiles. "Are you going to help us or not?"

"What are you going to do with the ship once you have it?"

"That's no concern of yours."

I turn to Mr. Grey. "You say you're loyal to me. Show me. Show me now."

"What do you want?" he asks.

"Advice."

Mr. Grey studies our assailants. "Go along with them."

Cia appears to take notice of Mr. Grey for the first time. "You called us here at the right time and I'm grateful. But now I want you to leave."

"He stays," I say. "He's resourceful. Who knows? I might need his help finding the doorway."

Cia takes her time answering. "Very well, proceed."

I turn and walk toward the Joshua tree. It seems to grow in height as I approach. Over a hundred feet tall, it's equal to a dozen of the mightiest specimens in the national park. Reaching out to touch it, I feel it has skin rather than bark. In reality the tree is wrapped in countless tiny fibers. Wound together they have a rubberlike consistency.

Joshua trees have no growth rings; it's impossible to determine their age. Experts believe they can live as long as the redwoods. Thousands of years, like me. Perhaps the greatest miracle is how they're able to thrive in such a hostile climate. Their root system is vast, they can survive for years without a drop of rain.

"Do you know I'm here?" I ask as I circle the tree, staring up at its branches. It's late summer; its flowers have already bloomed and died. I can understand why the early Mormons crossing the desert were so taken by the trees that they named them after a biblical hero. My tree's bare arms are so thick they look like they're made of solid muscle.

My tree. It feels familiar.

Yet touching it, talking to it, chanting mantras to it, fails to elicit a response. I return to the others. Cia stares at me, her face difficult to read.

"Can you give me a hint of what I'm supposed to do?" I ask.

"It should recognize you," Cia says.

"It doesn't."

"Then you're of no use to us." Cia glances at her partner.

I hold up a hand. "Stop with the threats, would ya? They're not going to help you get what you want."

Cia gestures to the eastern horizon. "Time is short."

"What's the matter?" Seymour snickers. "Are you vampires? Do you turn to dust in the sunlight?"

Cia waves a finger at him. "I don't like you. You . . ."

"Give Sita something to work with," Matt interrupts.

"Either the *vimana* welcomes her or not. There's no trick." Cia pauses. "Except perhaps the purity of her heart."

"What would you know about a pure heart?" I say.

Cia shrugs. "It's something the ancient scriptures mention. It has nothing to do with us."

"Sita," Sarah whispers. I turn toward her, step near.

"Yes?"

Sarah whispers in my ear. "The veil's in my coat pocket."

"Why did they let you keep it?"

"They beat me until I told them where it was. But they let me hold on to it. They seem allergic to it." I feel coarse silk brush my hand. Sarah is trying to give it to me without Cia seeing. *Good luck*, I think. "Take it," she says.

"All right." I stuff the veil in my pocket and walk back toward the tree. Once behind it, hidden from view, I cover my head with the veil. It brings a familiar comfort.

But it does nothing to change the tree into a spaceship.

I drop to my knees and plead with it. "If you really are there, we need your help," I pray.

The tree does not hear me. The tree remains a tree.

Yet I feel something different in that moment. The certainty that it *is* a *vimana* solidifies inside me. And I know it's the *vimana* that rescued me and Yaksha when we were drifting in space. The certainty raises serious questions. Why did the celestial beings who built the ship, who roamed the galaxy in it, leave it here to be found?

Why did they leave it for me?

It's obviously a powerful vessel. If I turn it over to Cia and her partner, what will they do with it? For all I know they could use it to destroy the world. It becomes clear to me right then that I can't let them have it, no matter what.

Putting the veil in my pocket, I walk back to the group.

"Are you sure we have the right tree?" I ask.

Cia is not amused. "You test my patience. You have been in this ship before. It should respond to you."

"I don't know what to tell you," I say.

"Perhaps you're not sufficiently motivated," Cia says.

She turns to her companion, who hands her the box. The man pulls out a revolver—a Colt Python, which carries .357 magnum rounds. There's plenty of stopping power in those bullets. He points the weapon at Seymour, and I immediately leap in front of my friend.

"Kill him and I'll never help you," I warn.

"You're not helping us as it is." Cia nods to the man. "Kill him."

"Wait!" I cry, pulling Seymour near my back. "Let's talk about this. You want something only I can give you. Kill Seymour and you lose all leverage with me. You know I'm serious. You'll both be rotting in hell before I try to open that *vimana* for you."

Cia steps toward me and locks her eyes on mine. Never in my life have I felt so sickened by a pair of eyes. Holes, pits, emptiness—the words fail to convey the icy void behind her gaze.

Yet buried in the abyss is a dark being. A creature that was once so bright, so radiant, that it was named the Light Bearer—Lucifer. Or the name it has now chosen—Tarana.

Frau Cia, the woman who stands before me, is long gone, consumed by this thing that crept out of black space and entered our world. Because she looks human, because she talks like a human, it's easy to forget what she really is. But I remember Auschwitz, the millions who died there, and I know I will never forget.

There's no bargain I can make with Frau Cia that she'll keep.

She nods as if reading my mind. "We already made our deal, Sita. Don't you remember? But you tried to cheat your way out of it."

Her words cast a spell over me, transport me.

"I remember," I say.

I step up to the front and nod to the Scale and the Caretakers.

"I am Sita. I am five thousand one hundred and fifty-two years old."

A stir goes through the room. Voices murmur all around.

A tall red-hooded Caretaker orders everyone to hush.

Something about his voice sounds familiar.

Keeping my eyes open, I stretch out my arms. As I place my hands above the plates, palms upward, I feel as if something reaches out and locks them in place. The invisible grip is strong enough to hold a normal human in place. Of course, I'm not human, yet I suspect that even I could not break free.

Diamonds begin to collect on the right side, small ones. This goes on for a while and I feel encouraged but then black pearls start to pour onto the left plate. I realize this must be a result of when Yaksha changed me into a vampire. Back in the days when we killed whoever crossed our path.

Then something miraculous happens.

A single giant diamond appears above the right plate. It

drops onto it from a height of several inches and heavily weighs it down. In an instant I know the precious jewel is from the day I met Krishna and took a vow not to make any more vampires.

Then fate intervenes.

Pearls and diamonds begin to pour out of the thin air at an incredible speed. There are so many on each side, they begin to fall off the plates onto the table. I have to ask myself how I managed to commit so many good and bad deeds. The Scale acts like I never stopped killing or saving people.

Near the end, the flow begins to slow.

Especially on the diamond side. The pearls take over.

The left side looks like it's going to win.

Then a handful of extra-large diamonds appears.

The Scale wobbles back and forth, up and down. More than half the pearls and diamonds, half my life, lie spread over the black table. It's not fair but I realize this isn't a place where you get to argue your case.

At some point the invisible grip releases my hands, and my arms fall to my sides. I close my eyes. My fingers feel stuck in the black pearls and diamonds. I feel my life inside them. My heartbeat has returned. I feel it breaking.

The room falls silent.

A screeching sound suddenly fills the room.

I open my eyes and see the left plate is lower.

The black pearls have won.

The tall red-hooded Caretaker grabs my left arm.

I try to shake him off and fail. He is very strong.

"I know what bloody door I have to take," I snap.

He doesn't raise his hood and I cannot see his face.

Yet he speaks in a voice I know.

"You have been judged and there is no escape from that judgment. You are damned. A word from me and you will be taken through the red door, where there is only fire and pain. There you will burn. But not like you burned on earth. In the world of the living you were a vampire. There you would heal quickly. But in the world of fire, there is no relief. There is only agony."

I cower. I want to tell him to forget his speech and get on with it but I feel as long as he's talking, I'm not suffering. In that moment, even an instant without pain feels like a blessing.

I bow my head. "I am listening," I say.

He comes near. "I have the power to give you a respite from your judgment," he says.

"How long a respite?"

"Does it matter? Say no to me now and you will burn."

I can't allow this monster to put me in the fire.

After suffering such agony, I'd never be myself again.

From the shadow of his hood, his eyes bear down on me. Once more, my spirit cowers. My fear is too great. I choose without really choosing.

"What do you want?" I ask.

He tells me what to do and I agree to do it.

He offers me his hand and I shake it.

Deal.

Frau Cia's mouth smiles, even if her eyes don't. "You *do* remember."

"That deal was made void," I say. "You tried to trick me. It was my own guilt that caused me to place my thumb on the black-pearl side of the Scale. I damned myself, but before I passed into your accursed realm, I realized what I was doing and freed myself."

Cia throws her head back as if to laugh. But no sound comes out of her mouth. Her eyes suddenly lock on the stars as they fade with the rising light in the east. She stands staring into space as if remembering her own ancient past. The surrounding air suddenly darkens and I feel an invisible black hand brush near my heart. Long ago, the same hand came for her and she invited it in. I would pity her if I didn't hate her so much.

Finally she looks at me. "You made the deal. It doesn't matter that afterward you forgave yourself. You shook on it. A deal is a deal."

I begin to tremble. I don't want to, not in front of my friends, and definitely not in front of her, but I cannot help myself. She's talking about returning to the fire Tarana threatened me with in front of the Scale. The eternal flames that never stop burning . . .

"I was free of this world," I say. "Krishna invited me into his realm. I only came back to help. I cannot be damned because of that choice."

"To help?" Cia sneers. "The first thing you did when you returned to this world was break Umara's neck! And she was your friend!"

"You told me to do that!"

"Yes! It was part of our deal. Then you blew up a building filled with children. Seymour begged you to stop but nothing was going to stop proud Sita. You pushed the button."

"I killed them because I had to. They were part of the Cradle. They were evil." I hesitate. "They were working for you."

Cia finds my excuse a joke. "Ask yourself, Sita, how many black pearls did that explosion cost you? Enough to tilt the Scale against you?"

I shake my head. "No. It's not possible."

"I'm afraid the answer is yes," Cia says.

"Sita, don't listen to her!" Seymour says, jumping out from behind me. "It's all lies. You know what she is."

Cia nods to her man. "Shoot him."

The man turns the gun on Seymour and pulls the trigger.

I rocket into hyper mode. I see the flash explode out the tip of the barrel. I see the bullet fly out from the center of the orange and red fire. The round is a hollow point, made of copper, which means it will crumple on impact, flatten out, cause tremendous internal damage. The bullet flies a foot from the gun, two feet, three feet—already I can compute its trajectory. It will strike Seymour in the center of his chest. If it doesn't hit his heart it will at the very least tear open a major artery. Either way the shot will kill him.

Matt stands to Seymour's right, I'm on his left. Matt is faster than me; he also sees the bullet coming. He moves to intercept. But whereas Matt is six feet from Seymour, I'm only two. I stand a better chance of stopping the bullet. But in the time it takes me to halve the distance to Seymour, the bullet covers more than half the distance to his chest.

The only way to save him is to leap in front of the bullet. Swatting it away will not be possible. A feeling of déjà vu sweeps over me. I have done this before for Seymour, when Matt tried to shoot him.

I leap. I wait. The bullet screams toward me.

It should enter my chest any moment. . . .

Matt strikes my side. He feels like a freight train. His momentum is overwhelming. I fly back the way I came. Yet out of the corner of my eye I catch a glimpse of him knocking the bullet out of the air. Man, is he fast. I have never seen anyone, not even Yaksha, move like that.

Cia claps in approval. "I'm impressed. For a moment there I wasn't sure which one of you was going to be the hero."

Seymour looks down at the bullet on the ground and then at his chest. "Whoa," he whispers.

"You were saying," I say to Cia.

She loses her smile and the demon eyes return.

"I was saying that this little charade proves nothing. We know you're not afraid to offer your life to save another. Your failure at Auschwitz was of a deeper nature. Sure, you should have saved Anton, we were surprised when you ran. But that was only a blip on the screen of your life. What really frightens you is what you so richly deserve—eternal damnation."

"The deal is void," I repeat weakly.

Cia turns to her partner. He takes the box back and gives her the gun. Aiming it at Seymour, she approaches to within five feet. A bullet fired from that range, especially one fired by her, will kill my friend.

Matt and I exchange a look. We would strike Cia if the man did not hold the box. He can knock us out before we can reach her.

"A deal is a deal," Cia repeats. "If you can't open the Vishnu *Vimana* for us, then you're to come with us, in our *vimana*."

"Where are we going?" I ask, trying not to let her hear my fear.

"Oh, I think you know."

"Sita, let them kill me," Seymour pleads. "You said it yourself, with me dead they'll have no leverage over you."

"No," I say.

Seymour is suddenly emotional. "You can't go with them. You were free. You only came back for us."

Cia enjoys his outburst. "See what that got you," she snickers.

"Sita, put it on," Sarah whispers.

"No way," Cia says, shaking the gun, making it clear she intends to shoot someone. "Sita, give the veil back to Sarah. That's a good girl."

I hand the veil to Sarah, who shakes her head violently and pushes it toward me. But I'm stronger than her; I force her to take it.

"It's all right, Sarah," I tell her. "It won't help me where I'm going."

"That it won't," Cia says, offering her hand. "Do we have a deal?"

I stare down at her hand and see Tarana's hand. I see the Scale and hear the screams of torment of those who failed its final judgment. Those who were taken along the dark path, through the red door, into the inferno. Cia is only offering her hand but if I agree to shake it I know I'll burn. I'll never stop burning. Nothing could be worse.

Except giving in to these creatures.

The hidden *vimana* has told me that much.

I cannot give in to my fear. The price will be too great.

And the only way to not give in is to shake her hand.

Drawing a deep breath, fighting to steady my trembling, I stretch out my arm. Cia quickly clasps my hand and I realize a part of her wants me, my soul, almost as much as the *vimana*. Her fingers close on mine like a steel clamp.

"Deal?" she repeats.

I nod. I refuse to say the damn word.

Cia releases my hand and chuckles. "Take your time, Sita. Say good-bye to your friends. Take a minute, take two. There's no hurry now."

"No!" Seymour cries, tears bursting from his eyes. He grabs my arm. "You can't go with them just to save me."

How much I love him right then. My love is so great I feel it can touch the sky. I touch the side of his face. I take him into my arms. I hug him as close to my heart as possible. There are no words I can say to him, nor is there any need. In that instant we're closer than we have ever been. I hear his every thought, and he hears mine.

"It's all right, Seymour. This was meant to be."

"No, Sita. No!"

"I have to do it. To save you, to save everyone. I was born for this."

"But I love you."

"I know, I know. You are my love. But now you must leave this place. You must live your life. You're my muse. You still have so many stories left to tell."

All these words we exchange in silence.

In the end I kiss Seymour's cheek and let him go.

He can't look at me, and I understand.

Matt embraces me next. He seems confused, in shock. In his own way he pleads with me to stop.

"It can't be over, Sita. Not like this. Not this way."

I hug him in return and think of how he held me in bed at the hotel. How he finally opened his heart to me after hating me for so many years. I press my lips close to his ear so only he can hear.

"I love you more than you know," I say.

"Then stay," he begs in a whisper that only I can hear. "I'm stronger than you know. I can fight them. I can stop them."

I pull back from Matt and sadly shake my head. "They cannot be stopped by fighting. They can only be stopped with a sacrifice."

He tries to argue but I put a finger to his lips and shake my head. He must see the determination in my eyes for he lowers his head and steps back.

Sarah comes next. Her words gush out. "My grandmother told me about you when I was a little girl. I used to listen to her stories and wonder if such a creature like you really existed. Now I know she wasn't exaggerating." She presses her head to mine. "Thank you for saving me, for saving us all."

I pat Sarah on the back. "You have your grandmother's heart."

Mr. Grey is the last to say good-bye. He embraces me tightly and quietly repeats my name. "Sita. Sita. Sita."

I hug him close and whisper in his ear. "I've figured out who you are. You're a time traveler," I say.

He stiffens in my hands. "An interesting idea. How did I get here?"

"I don't know and I don't care. I only want to know how *The Story of Veronica* ends."

He glances at Cia before turning back to me. "I'm glad. Veronica didn't write the last page of the book. Her brother, Thomas, did. Veronica wasn't present when the Master died. She was in Rome."

I'm confused. "But the veil has Christ's face on it." I stop. "You're not saying it's a fake?"

"No," Mr. Grey says. "The Veil of Veronica is the most precious of all Christian artifacts. You see, when Veronica traveled to Rome with her brother, she made a living painting the walls he built. But eventually her reputation grew and she was invited into the homes of wealthy citizens and senators. They hired her to paint their portraits or landscapes—all kinds of beautiful paintings. Before long she was the best-known artist in Rome. It was then she began to talk about the Master's teachings."

"Oh," I groan, knowing what's coming next.

Mr. Grey nods grimly. "She loved the Master so much, his words burst out of her. She even taught people to meditate, telling them that the kingdom of heaven was within. That angered certain people in power and she was arrested and condemned to die." He stops. "She was crucified."

"Tragic," I say. "But the veil . . ."

"She wasn't dead when she was taken down from the cross, but she was near death. Thomas laid the veil over her so the people gawking at her could not see how they had torn her face. But as she died a light shone in her eyes. Everyone there saw it but only a few understood that the light came because her every thought was focused on her Master." Mr. Grey pauses. "It was that light that created his image in her veil."

"In the end, she was one with her Master," I say.

"That's why the veil is so precious. It proves they were the same."

A wave of incredible freedom suddenly washes over me.

My love *does* reach to the sky. My whole being does.

No story ever told to me has meant more. Again and again Krishna says in the Gita that the Essence resides inside every man. And I have read the Gita countless times. But to hear of this young woman with so much love for her Master that she was able to find him inside her heart—it means more to me than any scripture.

Especially since I'm about to go to hell.

Suddenly, it no longer scares me.

My whole life I have longed to be with Krishna again.

Meeting him was the greatest event in my life.

It was also a curse.

A curse because it kept me looking for him outside myself.

Now, in this instant, I know he's inside me.

It no longer matters where they take me, or how they torture me.

I will be with Krishna. I will be happy.

"Time to fulfill your bargain," Cia interrupts.

"Just so we're clear," I say. "You let my friends go and never trouble them again. That's the price you pay for me going with you."

Cia nods. "That's the deal."

I turn toward the Joshua tree on the left. "Let's get this over with."

Cia gestures to the man who turns the red dial on the box. In an instant the tree transforms into a pulsating red *vimana*. I can feel the heat of it from a distance and know that the instant I step inside it I'll begin to burn.

I remain fearless. I'm utterly content. I feel Veronica near me, and know if she can die under such extreme circumstances and still hold on to her Master, then there's no reason I can't do likewise. Of all the teachers I've met in my five thousand years, she has turned out to be the greatest.

I walk calmly toward the red *vimana*. Indeed, I lead the way and almost stop and encourage Cia and her partner to quit lagging behind. I have already entered my own inner kingdom, the same kingdom Veronica's Master spoke of. The outer form of the Lord is unimportant. The Master meant what he told Veronica—he is always with us.

The door of the red *vimana* opens. I pause at the threshold, and Cia and her son draw even with me. But as we stop to look at the others, I see Cia's face drop. My attention is drawn to a flicker of light out of the corner of my eye.

Looking over, I see that the four-armed Joshua tree has suddenly been replaced by a golden *vimana*. It floats two feet off the ground, and although it doesn't resemble a gold crown, it reminds me of one. Kingly, reverential, enchanting, powerful. It looks like a ride Walt Disney might have imagined in a dream but never found a way to construct on earth. The ship is round with no sharp edges but it's not saucer-shaped. The Vedas would have called it a celestial chariot. I like to think of it that way.

"Change of plans?" I ask as we stand on the threshold. The interior of the red *vimana* is clouded with stinking smoke. The odor reminds me of the smokestacks of Auschwitz. The rot of burning flesh. I don't think it's a coincidence.

Hitler and his inner circle created the concentration camps to have a place where they felt at home. Let's call a spade a spade. The Third Reich was a demonic organization.

To my surprise Cia appears undecided. Perhaps fearful.

"I never thought it'd come for you," she mutters.

"It must be because of the purity of my heart," I mock. Suddenly I realize the *vimana* has not come for her. It has come for me, and there is no way she will be able to enter it. I am certain that this is true.

Cia turns to her partner. "I'll investigate. Keep the box handy. Kill them all if Sita steps out of line."

"Hey, I've done what you ordered," I protest.

"Now I'm ordering you to follow me," Cia says.

Leaving the red *vimana* behind, we trek back across the top of the hill. The golden apparition doesn't waver and I have to remind myself it was the tree that was the illusion. Matt and Mr. Grey are excited. Seymour and Sarah look confused. I motion for them to remain where they are.

The sun begins to rise at our backs as we near Vishnu's *Vimana*. The ship greets the dawn by sending forth a radiance of its own. A shower of golden light begins to rain down ten yards beyond the perimeter of the ship. A circular door opens and I hasten toward it, passing beneath the delicious shower. Every pleasure center in my body awakens. I want to run toward the door. It's so wonderful. Nothing can stop me. . . .

"Stop!" Cia snaps at my back. I turn to find her standing outside the shower of light, although from the prints at her feet it looks as if she stepped over the boundary before hastily retreating. Cocking her pistol, she speaks in a deadly tone. "You tricked me."

"Gimme a break. You wanted the door to the *vimana* open, now it's open. You're never satisfied."

"I can't enter through this door," Cia says.

"Well, I don't think there's another one."

Cia looks past me to the ship. "You won't take this ship to hyper-speed velocities. I won't allow it. You won't stop us from re-creating the future."

"Whatever. I'd be happy to just visit the moon and bring home some cheese."

Cia raises her gun. "A pity it has to end like this. So sudden, so painless. It's not what I had planned for you at all." She stops. "Look at me, Sita."

I don't want to but I look. I have to.

Her eyes invade my own. Even beneath the canopy of golden light, when she focuses her gaze on me, I feel my control over my body shudder.

"Be still. Be very still," she says.

Her words, her will—she's trying to make me an easy target.

"Good-bye, Sita," she says, and pulls the trigger.

I see the bullet approach. I want to move, I try to move, it's heading straight for my chest. But her witch's spell is potent. All I manage to do is bounce on my toes, which does nothing to stop the bullet. It strikes an inch beneath my sternum and I feel a large vein shred inside.

I fall to my knees, trying to breathe, not having much luck. I know how rapidly I can heal, and at the same time I know this wound is fatal. It is all right, I tell myself. Everything will be fine.

Cia rushes back to the red *vimana* with her partner and they disappear inside. Actually, the *vimana* itself vanishes and the two-armed Joshua tree returns. As I topple to the ground, my friends run to me. Mr. Grey is above my head, Matt on my left, Seymour on my right. Sarah drapes the veil over me; she has absolute faith in it. I hate that my blood might ruin the image of Christ. On the other hand, I like the idea that the blood on the veil actually belongs to Veronica and that mine is mingling with hers.

I choke on a thick clump of blood.

"You're going to be all right," Seymour says. "I just called for an emergency medical helicopter. They'll be here in thirty minutes."

I have to spit out my blood to speak. "I'll be dead before it's fueled."

"I'll open a vein," Matt says. "I'll pour my blood over your—"

Sarah interrupts. "No. The veil will heal Sita. It healed her before."

"All of you, shut up and listen," Mr. Grey says. "Sita's only hope is to enter the *vimana* and exit this timeline. Then she'll have an eternity to heal."

"How do we do that exactly?" Seymour asks.

Mr. Grey takes charge. "Matt, lift her up and carry her inside. The rest of you, keep a hand on her. It's the only way we'll be able to enter with her. Hurry."

Matt swoops me off the ground and carries me inside. The others touch me in various places. I feel Matt could be more gentle considering the fact that I'm bleeding to death. Not that I haven't been in this situation before. Once I caught a stake in the heart immediately after I blew up a house with Yaksha in it, but that didn't count because . . . well, I lived to tell the tale, and I'm pretty sure I'm going to die now.

Inside the *vimana*, Matt lays me down beside a trickling pool. The floor is soft and comforting. Golden light surrounds me on all sides. So many pleasing odors fill the air: camphor, sandalwood, roses, coconuts—I smell coconut milk. There's also music; I hear it more with my head than my ears, and the sound invokes so many wonderful feelings.

None of this matters, though. I'm still dying.

Mr. Grey's "eternity to heal" has yet to arrive.

I'm rapidly bleeding out.

Matt and Seymour kneel beside me. The other two have gone off to try to fire up the warp engines. The interior of the *vimana* is warm but I shiver. Excess blood loss—it can bring a deathly chill. Seymour's eyes burn with tears.

"You have to hang on," he pleads.

"Why won't you accept my blood?" Matt asks.

I find it too much of a strain to keep my eyes open; I close them.

"This is Mr. Grey's moment," I say. "It's why he came to us."

"How do you know?" Seymour asks.

"I was terrified to enter their ship. I knew where it would take me. I could never have actually done it without him. And all he did was tell me the end of Veronica's story, and my fear left." I pause. "Seymour, Cia would have shot you if I'd hesitated for a second."

"What miracle are you expecting from him next?" Matt asks.

"What miracle are you expecting?" I whisper.

Matt puts his head next to mine. "Have you guessed?"

"You want to say good-bye to your father," I say.

I can feel Seymour shift in confusion. "What does Yaksha have to do with right now?" he demands.

"Tell . . . ," I mumble, losing the ability to talk.

Matt speaks to Seymour. "If Mr. Grey can get this ship afloat, it can transcend relative velocities. Which will allow it to step outside time. Five thousand years ago my father was aboard this ship. But once we pass light speed, there will be no was. There will only be the eternal now."

"And you expect to meet your father here?" Seymour asks.

"I hope. It's something I've hoped for a long time."

The floor of the ship shakes. I feel as if I am rising. It could be the ship shooting into space or else my soul leaving my body. It may be the two events are related. Matt and Seymour fall silent as a gentle but powerful hum vibrates the vessel.

"Sita! There are stars outside!" Seymour exclaims suddenly.

That's nice, I think. I want to say it but the words feel like such an effort. I can't complain, though. I feel little pain. After all the crap I've been through, I couldn't have hoped for a better death.

"We are leaving earth orbit," I hear Matt say from far away.

"Hell, we're leaving the solar system," Seymour says.

Sarah and Mr. Grey reappear. I don't see them but I hear them.

"How is she?" Mr. Grey asks.

"She's out cold," Seymour says.

Yeah, right, I think. I feel someone touch my wrist.

"Her pulse is getting stronger," Mr. Grey says.

I don't know about that. I still feel as if I'm dying.

"Will she live? Don't bullshit me," Seymour says.

"She can heal herself. She just needs time," Mr. Grey says.

"Has time stopped yet?" Matt asks.

Mr. Grey speaks. "Yet? That word has no meaning aboard this ship. Time has begun to turn back on itself. On earth you experience time as linear, as a sequence of moments, one second followed by the next second, all in a straight line. But time is much more dynamic than you realize. In a sense it's alive. If life is a play that takes place on a stage, then time is the director. He—or it—says when the curtains are to be raised and when they are to fall. There can be no life without time, and life itself creates time. Do you understand?"

"Gimme a break," Seymour says. "Of course we don't understand."

Matt speaks up. "I heard what you and Sita said. Are you really from another time?"

"Yes and no. The Mr. Grey you see before you was born in your time and hopefully will die there. But the mind that currently occupies this body is a projection from the future."

"From how far in the future?" Matt asks.

"Ten thousand years," Mr. Grey says.

"How did you come back? Why?" Seymour asks.

Mr. Grey answers. "In our time we're capable of building ships that can travel faster than light. And we discovered, as you'll soon discover, that once we transcended that barrier, time no longer held us bound. I am a distant descendant of the Mr. Grey you see standing before you. Ten thousand years from now, I entered a ship such as this and sent my mind back through my genetic line to his body. I took over his body."

"Why?" Seymour repeats.

"To fix what was broken. In our time—in our history books—the Nazis won World War Two. All the mistakes that you saw Hitler make were negated by a powerful force working through the Third Reich. That force did so to create the template of a purely materialistic society. A society where science is the only God. Where even the idea of something beyond the physical creation is seldom contemplated."

"It sounds like a pretty sterile world," Seymour says.

Mr. Grey sighs, a heavy sigh that holds much grief. "You have no idea. In my time there is no magic. There is no mythology. Our scientific achievements are beyond your wildest dreams, but our culture is stagnant, without purpose. We know there's no God, no angels, no demons. We have proven it scientifically. It doesn't matter where we travel in the galaxy, what other cultures we discover. They all see the universe as we do. You might say we have discovered the ultimate truth, and found that God doesn't exist."

"How can earth's history affect other worlds?" Seymour asks.

"You can't uncover what you know doesn't exist. I come

from a reality that is black and white, colorless. Nobody experiences a flash of intuition or a sense of déjà vu. None of our children grow up believing in Santa Claus or the Easter Bunny. On our birthdays we don't even blow out candles and make a wish. No one even bothers to write fantasy stories. Why should they? No one would read them. The word 'mystical' cannot be found in our dictionary. I have never met a person who has ever stopped to pray to God. The Third Reich did not form the seed of a cruel and barbaric world. It did something much worse. It formed a society that has forgotten the meaning of the word 'hope.'"

"Where do you fit into this black-and-white picture?" Matt asks.

"I'm a historian. In the midst of our search to absolutely prove there was nothing left for us to uncover, I was given permission to use a technique our scientists have discovered that allows us to view the past. How the technique works is beyond your understanding, but suffice to say it can only be used aboard a ship that is traveling faster than light. While scanning our past I came across a remarkable fork in the road of our evolution. It was as if someone had seen it before me and had already adjusted it—without our knowledge. I studied this fork for years, trying to understand what caused it, why it was created, who was behind it. After decades of research it finally became clear to me that Sita stood at the center of the fork in the road."

"Are you saying she caused it?" Seymour demands.

"No. I was never able to define who caused it. But I saw that Sita could fix it. Fix our past."

"Why Sita?" Matt asked.

"Stop and imagine what it was like for me to stumble onto her. Here was a young woman who was five thousand years old. She wasn't even human, she was a vampire, and everyone in my world knew there was no such thing as vampires. Not only that, she had met gods and fought with demons—beings that didn't exist in our universe."

"You must have thought you were hallucinating when you found her," Matt says.

"That's not far from the truth. I spent years just trying to confirm that she really existed. Then I discovered something equally strange. I saw that Sita herself—like our entire society—had been manipulated several times in her life. In the Middle Ages, when she fought Landulf of Capua and Dante. In World War Two, when she was taken captive by the Nazis. Worst of all were the events of this morning, when she allowed Frau Cia and her partner to take control of the red *vimana* and fly unchallenged into the sky."

"But they took off unchallenged this morning," Seymour says.

"Not true. Even as we speak, this ship is hot on their tail."

"I don't understand," Seymour says.

"You intend to destroy them," Matt says suddenly.

"Yes," Mr. Grey says. "With this ship we can easily destroy them."

"I still don't understand why you had to enter our time," Seymour says.

"When I originally viewed Sita's past, I saw her panic on top of the hill and refuse to go with Frau Cia into her *vimana*. The prospect of eternal damnation was too much for her, even if facing it meant she could save your life. In a sense she failed a major moral challenge."

"A challenge any sane person would have failed," Seymour says in my defense.

"True. But Sita is unique to your world. Besides living an endless life, she has come in contact with a being that many in your past considered a god. I'm speaking of Krishna. Her relationship with him linked her to the supernatural, to both angels and demons. In a sense it has been Krishna's grace that has made her life so magical. But it has exacted a terrible toll on her as well. Sita has faced and passed an incredible number of painful moral tests."

"But why does she keep getting tested?" Matt asks. "And what is this force that distorted your time in the first place?"

"I'm glad you asked the two questions together," Mr. Grey says. "The answers are linked, I believe, although I have to admit I'm still not sure what exactly this force is that altered mankind's timeline. For lack of a better word I would have to call it evil. I say that because in order to defeat it Sita had to choose what was right or good." Mr. Grey pauses. "Forgive me for being so vague. Remember, I come from a world where the concepts of good and evil don't exist."

"I understand," Matt says thoughtfully.

"I don't," Seymour nearly explodes. "Are you saying that because Sita was willing to sacrifice her soul to save me that mankind's future has been fixed?"

"It has been corrected," Mr. Grey says. "It will now be the way it was supposed to be. In a practical sense—if I can use such a word while discussing such matters—it was Sita's sacrifice that caused the Vishnu *vimana* to manifest on top of the hill this morning. And with this *vimana* we'll be able to catch and destroy Frau Cia's *vimana*. Once she and her partner have been removed from this present time, the connection this unseen force has to earth will be greatly weakened."

"Why didn't you just return to our time in one of your fancy spaceships and destroy them?" Seymour asks. "Why all the song and dance?"

"We can send our minds back in time. We cannot send physical objects back."

Matt interrupts and there is pain in his voice. "So even aboard a ship such as this it's not possible to go back in time and visit with, say, a deceased parent?"

"Yes and no. You can send your mind back to when you were an earlier age. You can send your mind back to the body of your father at an earlier age. But you cannot send your present-day body back in time."

"Let's stay on point," Seymour insists. "You still haven't explained why you returned to help Sita."

Mr. Grey replies. "My purpose in returning was to give Sita the moral courage to face down Frau Cia's challenge."

"But *how* did you do that?" Seymour demands.

"By translating *The Story of Veronica* for her," Mr. Grey says.

"I don't understand," Seymour says.

I hear Mr. Grey kneel by my side. I feel him; he touches my hand.

"Sita understands," he says, shaking my hand gently. "You have stopped bleeding. You're almost healed. Time to open your eyes."

I do as he commands, but as I stare up at him I'm forced to blink. Mr. Grey leans over me, I see him, and yet I see another figure as well, a ghost of a man, overlaying his face. This man is hairless, the dome of his skull is larger than normal, and his eyes are emerald green, so bright they would make him stand out in any crowded room. I realize I'm seeing him as he looks in the future, the real Mr. Grey who came back in time to save us and the rest of mankind.

"Thank you," I say.

The ghost image smiles. So does his human body.

"I should thank you," he says. "I expect my home will be a lot different when I return."

"Will they believe in fairies and unicorns?" I tease.

"Anything is possible."

I suddenly realize the full implications of what we're doing.

"Wait a second," I say. "Will you even exist in your future?"

"I honestly don't know."

He is trying to let me down gently. With a change in the timeline as big as this, the chances of him being born a hundred centuries in the future must be incredibly small.

"Do you have to leave so soon?" I ask, feeling crushed that he probably only has minutes of life left. I loved him from the instant I met him, and never understood why until now. If ever there were guardian angels, Mr. Grey was mine. He did not just save me from death, he saved my soul.

He nods. "It's time."

"But the other *vimana* . . ."

"It was destroyed while I was speaking. And I've programmed the ship to take you and your friends home." Mr. Grey pauses. "That is, if you want to go home."

I close my eyes and let my mind wander through the past. Of course, right now, aboard this ship, traveling faster than light, I can do far more than wander. . . .

"You know me too well," I say.

EPILOGUE

Stand near my hut in India. Inside, my daughter, Lalita, and my husband, Rama, sleep peacefully. Although it is late at night and the forest is silent, a faint noise has awoken me and brought me outside to investigate.

It is Yaksha who made the noise.

He has come for me. Holding me in his powerful hands, he makes a terrible offer. I can come with him and become like him. A monster who feeds on the blood of the living. A creature as strong as him, one who even time cannot destroy. All I have to do is leave my family and promise to stay with him.

If I refuse, Yaksha will kill Lalita and Rama.

I have no choice.

Or I should say I *had* no choice.

Unknown to Yaksha I hold a sharp wooden stake in my right hand. I wear a loose-fitting white sari and keep the dagger hidden behind the folds of silk. Even with his great strength and reflexes, he can still be killed. He is not expecting an attack. And he stands so near. . . .

If I thrust upward beneath the tip of his sternum, drive the stake into his heart, he will die and my life will go on as it should.

The stake—I picked it up before leaving my home.

I knew he was coming for me . . . this time.

Yaksha stares at me in the dark, waiting for my answer. I don't know why I delay. I won't have a better chance. Perhaps I'm afraid. If my aim is off by a fraction of an inch, or if I hesitate as I stab, he'll snap my neck. It doesn't matter that he loves me and feels he needs me. He's a yakshini, a demon by birth, and, at this point in his life, he's cruel. If I allow him to change me, I'll be no different from him.

Yet there's something in his eyes I've never seen before. He appears uncertain, and he's giving me more time than he should to decide. I don't understand why he's the one who is hesitating.

"You can do it, you know. I won't stop you," he says.

Damn, I think. He must have seen the stake.

Yet I'm missing something. This isn't the Yaksha I used to know.

"I don't know what you're talking about," I say.

He brings his head close to my ear. His warm breath brushes my skin, and I'm puzzled because he's always felt so cold before. Plus there is an inexplicable sorrow in his voice.

"I suspected you would try this. Even though it means I'll never be born, that I'll never exist."

I realize in an instant what is happening.

I'm not talking to Yaksha!

"How did you know?" I blurt out, accidentally exposing the stake in the process. He stares down at it with disappointment in his eyes.

"Sita," he says, and I've never heard so much pain in my own name.

"I'm sorry," I whisper.

"Can you tell me why? Just that—why?"

"I'm so tired. I feel I can't live all those years over again."

"But you've already lived them. Return to the present with me and your whole life will be just like a memory."

"You don't understand. I want to remain in this time. I want my husband back. I want to hold my daughter again. I *need* my family." I pause. "I tried to tell you that night in the hotel when I told you that Yaksha was given a chance to have a family."

"Ah." He nods in understanding. "And you'll lose your family if we leave tonight alone."

"Yes."

He hesitates. "You love Rama that much?"

He is really asking why I don't love him as much.

"Yes," I say.

The word seems to strike him like a stake. Yet he drops his hands and spreads his arms, leaving his chest vulnerable. "Then do it," he says.

I nervously fiddle with the stake, touching the sharp tip, drawing a drop of blood. My eyes burn. "No, it's not fair."

"Life is not fair." He chuckles at the irony in his remark. "Of course I won't have to worry about my life if you do it." He pauses. "Go ahead, Sita. Be honest with yourself. This is what you have always wanted."

A terrible fear grips me. If I kill him while he's in his father's body, I'll still be killing his father. And without Yaksha, I'll never live to touch all the people I have. Matt will never be born. Seymour and I will never meet, even though I'm stealing a page from one of his stories by returning to this time. All of history will be altered.

"The legend is vague on this point. I don't know what it means. But the legend does say that the Abomination will destroy our history for the love of a witch."

I can't worry about the Telar's legend of the Abomination. It was a bunch of nonsense, it has to be. In their story Matt had to meet a witch to destroy history and I'm not that witch.

I'm just a young woman who wants a normal life.

I raise the stake but have to stop to wipe away a tear. "You can stop me. It's up to you. It's your choice," I say.

"I'm not going to stop you."

He waits, as does the night, and the future.

It's tragic but I have dreamed of this moment all my life.

I honestly don't know what I'm going to do next.

TURN THE PAGE FOR
A PEEK AT
CHRISTOPHER PIKE'S
NEWEST NOVEL:

CHAPTER ONE

ONCE I BELIEVED THAT I WANTED NOTHING MORE THAN love. Someone who would care for me more than he cared for himself. A guy who would never betray me, never lie to me, and most of all never leave me. Yeah, that was what I desired most, what people usually call true love.

I don't know if that has really changed.

Yet I have to wonder now if I want something else just as badly.

What is it? You must wonder . . .

Magic. I want my life filled with the mystery of magic.

Silly, huh? Most people would say there's no such thing.

Then again, most people are not witches.

Not like me.

I discovered what I was when I was eighteen years old, two days after I graduated high school. Before then I was your typical teenager. I got up in the morning, went to school, stared at my ex-boyfriend across the campus courtyard and imagined what it would be like to have him back in my life, went to the local library and sorted books for four hours, went home, watched TV, read a little, lay in bed and thought some more about Jimmy Kelter, then fell asleep and dreamed.

But I feel, somewhere in my dreams, I sensed I was different from other girls my age. Often it seemed, as I wandered the twilight realms of my unconscious, that I existed in another world, a world like our own and yet different, too. A place where I had powers my normal, everyday self could hardly imagine.

I believe it was these dreams that made me crave that elusive thing that is as great as true love. It's hard to be sure, I only know that I seldom awakened without feeling a terrible sense of loss. As though my very soul had been chopped into pieces and tossed back into the world. The sensation of being on the "outside" is difficult to describe. All I can say is that, deep inside, a part of me always hurt.

I used to tell myself it was because of Jimmy. He had dumped me, all of a sudden, for no reason. He had broken my heart, dug it out of my chest, and squashed it when he said I really like you, Jessie, we can still be friends, but I've got to go now. I blamed him for the pain. Yet it had been there before I had fallen in love with him, so there had to be another reason why it existed.

Now I know Jimmy was only a part of the equation.

But I get ahead of myself. Let me begin, somewhere near the beginning.

Like I said, I first became aware I was a witch the same weekend I graduated high school. At the time I lived in Apple Valley, which is off Interstate 15 between Los Angeles and Las Vegas. How that hick town got that name was beyond me. Apple Valley was smack in the middle of the desert. I wouldn't be exaggerating if I said it's easier to believe in witches than in apple trees growing in that godforsaken place.

Still, it was home, the only home I had known since I was six. That was when my father the doctor had decided that Nurse Betty—that was what my mom called her—was more sympathetic to his needs than my mother. From birth to six I lived in a mansion overlooking the Pacific, in a Malibu enclave loaded with movie stars and the studio executives who had made them famous. My mom, she must have had a lousy divorce lawyer, because even though she had worked her butt off to put my father through medical school and a six-year residency that trained him to be one of the finest heart surgeons on the West Coast, she was kicked out of the marriage with barely enough money to buy a two-bedroom home in Apple Valley. And with summer temperatures averaging above a hundred, real estate was never a hot item in our town.

I was lucky I had skin that gladly suffered the sun. It was soft, and I tanned deeply without peeling. My coloring probably helped. My family tree is mostly European, but there was an American Indian in the mix back before the Civil War.

Chief Proud Feather. You might wonder how I know his name, and that's good—wonder away, you'll find out, it's part of my story. He was 100 percent Hopi, but since he was sort of a distant relative, he gave me only a small portion of my features. My hair is brown with a hint of red. At dawn and sunset it is more maroon than anything else. I have freckles and green eyes, but not the green of a true redhead. My freckles are few, often lost in my tan, and my eyes are so dark the green seems to come and go, depending on my mood.

There wasn't much green where I grew up. The starved branches on the trees on our campus looked as if they were always reaching for the sky, praying for rain.

I was pretty; for that matter, I still am pretty. Understand, I turned eighteen a long time ago. Yet I still look much the same. I'm not immortal, I'm just very hard to kill. Of course, I could die tonight, who's to say.

It was odd, as a bright and attractive senior in high school, I wasn't especially popular. Apple Valley High was small—our graduating class barely topped two hundred. I knew all the seniors. I had memorized the first and last name of every cute boy in my class, but I was seldom asked out. I used to puzzle over that fact. I especially wondered why James Kelter had dumped me after only ten weeks of what, to me, had felt like the greatest relationship in the world. I was to find out when our class took that ill-fated trip to Las Vegas.

Our weekend in Sin City was supposed to be the equivalent of our Senior All-Night Party. I know, on the surface that sounds silly. A party usually lasts one night, and our parents believed we were spending the night at the local Hilton. However, the plan was for all two hundred of us to privately call our parents in the morning and say we had just been invited by friends to go camping in the mountains that separated our desert from the LA Basin.

The scheme was pitifully weak. Before the weekend was over, most of our parents would know we'd been nowhere near the mountains. That didn't matter. In fact, that was the whole point of the trip. We had decided, as a class, to throw all caution to the wind and break all the rules.

The reason such a large group was able to come to such a wild decision was easy to understand if you considered our unusual location. Apple Valley was nothing more than a road stop stuck between the second largest city in the nation—LA—and its most fun city—Las Vegas. For most of our lives, especially on Friday and Saturday evenings, we watched as thousands of cars flew northeast along Interstate 15 toward good times, while we remained trapped in a fruit town that didn't even have fruit trees.

So when the question arose of where we wanted to celebrate

our graduation, all our years of frustration exploded. No one cared that you had to be twenty-one to gamble in the casinos. Not all of us were into gambling and those who were simply paid Ted Pollack to make them fake IDs.

Ted made my ID for free. He was an old friend. He lived a block over from my house. He had a terrible crush on me, one I wasn't supposed to know about. Poor Ted, he confided everything in his heart to his sister, Pam, who kept secrets about as well as the fifty-year-old gray parrot that lived in their kitchen. It was dangerous to talk in front of that bird, just as it was the height of foolishness to confide in Pam.

I wasn't sure why Ted cared so deeply about me. Of course, I didn't understand why I cared so much about Jimmy. At eighteen I understood very little about love, and it's a shame I wasn't given a chance to know more about it before I was changed. That's something I'll always regret.

That particular Friday ended up being a wasteland of regrets. After a two-hour graduation ceremony that set a dismal record for scorching heat and crippling boredom, I learned from my best friend, Alex Simms, that both Ted and Jimmy would be driving with us to Las Vegas. Alex told me precisely ten seconds after I collected my blue-and-gold cap off the football field—after our class collectively threw them in the air—and exactly one minute after our school principal had pronounced us full-fledged graduates.

"You're joking, right?" I said.

Alex brushed her short blond hair from her bright blues. She wasn't as pretty as me but that didn't stop her from acting like she was. The weird thing is, it worked for her. Even though she didn't have a steady boyfriend, she dated plenty, and there wasn't a guy in school who would have said no to her if she'd so much as said hi. A natural flirt, she could touch a guy's hand and make him feel like his fingers were caressing her breasts.

Alex was a rare specimen, a compulsive talker who knew when to shut up and listen. She had a quick wit—some would say it was biting—and her self-confidence was legendary. She had applied to UCLA with a B-plus average and a slightly above-average SAT score and they had accepted her—supposedly—on the strength of her interview. While Debbie Pernal, a close friend of ours, had been turned down by the same school despite a straight-A average and a very high SAT score.

It was Debbie's belief that Alex had seduced one of the interviewing deans. In Debbie's mind, there was no other explanation for how Alex had gotten accepted. Debbie said as much to anyone who would listen, which just happened to be the entire student body. Her remarks started a tidal wave of a rumor: "ALEX IS A TOTAL SLUT!" Of course, the fact that Alex never bothered to deny the slur didn't help matters. If anything, she took great delight in it.

And these two were friends.

Debbie was also driving with us to Las Vegas.

"There was a mix-up," Alex said without much conviction,

trying to explain why Jimmy was going to ride in the car with us. "We didn't plan for both of them to come."

"Why would anyone in their right mind put Jimmy and me together in the same car?" I demanded.

Alex dropped all pretense. "Could it be that I'm sick and tired of you whining about how he dumped you when everything was going so perfect between you two?"

I glared at her. "We're best friends! You're required to listen to my whining. It doesn't give you the right to invite the one person in the whole world who ripped my heart out to go on a road trip with us."

"What road trip? We're just giving him a three-hour ride. You don't have to talk to him if you don't want to."

"Right. The five of us are going to be crammed into your car half the afternoon and it will be perfectly normal if I don't say a word to the first and last guy I ever had sex with."

Alex was suddenly interested. "I didn't know Jimmy was your first. You always acted like you slept with Clyde Barker."

Clyde Barker was our football quarterback and so good-looking that none of the girls who went to the games—myself included—cared that he couldn't throw a pass to save his ass. He had the IQ of a cracked helmet. "It was just an act," I said with a sigh.

"Look, it might work out better than you think. My sources tell me Jimmy has hardly been seeing Kari at all. They may even be broken up."

Kari Rider had been Jimmy's girlfriend before me, and after me, which gave me plenty of reason to hate the bitch.

"Why don't we be absolutely sure and invite Kari as well," I said. "She can sit on my lap."

Alex laughed. "Admit it, you're a tiny bit happy I did all this behind your back."

"I'm a tiny bit considering not going at all."

"Don't you dare. Ted would be devastated."

"Ted's going to be devastated when he sees Jimmy get in your car!"

Alex frowned. "You have a point. Debbie invited him, not me."

On top of everything else, Debbie had a crush on Ted, the same Ted who had a crush on me. It was going to be a long three hours to Las Vegas.

"Did Debbie think it was a good idea for Jimmy to ride with us?" I asked.

"Sure."

I was aghast. "I can't believe it. That bitch."

"Well, actually, she didn't think there was a chance in hell he'd come."

That hurt. "Love the vote of confidence. What you mean is Debbie didn't think there was a chance in hell Jimmy was still interested in me."

"I didn't say that."

"No. But you both thought it."

"Come on, Jessie. It's obvious Jimmy's coming with us so he can spend time with you." Alex patted me on the back. "Be happy."

"Why did you wait until now to tell me this?"

"Because now it's too late to change my devious plan."

I dusted off my blue-and-gold cap and put it back on. "I suppose this is your graduation present to me?" I asked.

"Sure. Where's mine?"

"You'll get it when we get to Las Vegas."

"Really?"

"Yeah. You'll see." I already had a feeling I was going to pay her back, I just didn't know how.

CHAPTER TWO

I WAS AN IDIOT TO GET IN ALEX'S CAR. BUT I WAS NOT fool enough to sit in the backseat between Ted and Jimmy. Debbie ended up sandwiched between the boys, where she looked quite content.

It was two in the afternoon by the time we hit the road. Our parents had insisted on taking us three girls to lunch, but it was only fun as long as our appetites lasted. We were anxious to get to Vegas. Also, there was tension between Alex's and Debbie's parents.

It was rooted in the UCLA fiasco and the ugly talk surrounding it. The truth was Debbie had only been accepted by the University of Santa Barbara—an incredibly beautiful campus, in my humble opinion—and she had graduated second in our class, while Alex had finished thirty-eighth. Alex made no effort to soften the tension, wearing a UCLA T-shirt to lunch.

Out of the five parents present, my mom was the only one who did much talking.

No one was jealous of me. I had finished tenth in our class and my SAT scores equaled Debbie's, but I hadn't bothered to apply to college. It was a money thing, I didn't have any. And I couldn't apply for financial aid because my father was rich.

Silly me, I kept hoping my father would suddenly remember he had a daughter who had just graduated high school and who needed six figures just to get an undergraduate degree. But so far he had not called, or written, or e-mailed me.

My mom didn't appreciate his silent rejection. She bitched about it whenever she had a chance. But I took the rejection in stride. I only cried about it when I was alone in my bed at night.

I hardly knew my dad but it was weird—I missed him.

"I enjoyed your speech," Jimmy said to Debbie as he and Ted climbed aboard in a deserted parking lot far away from any stray parental eyes.

"Thank you," Debbie said. "I was afraid it was too long. The last thing I wanted to do was bore people."

Christ, I thought. Her thirty-minute speech had been twenty minutes too long. I knew because neither Alex nor I could remember the last twenty minutes.

Debbie had spoken on the environment, of all things. What did she know about that? She had grown up in a goddamn desert.

We didn't have an environment, not really, just a bunch of sand and dirt.

"Your point on the impact of methane versus carbon-dioxide gases on global warming was important," Ted said. "It's a pity the tundra's melting so fast. I wouldn't be surprised if the world's temperature increases by ten degrees in our lifetimes."

"Won't happen," Alex said, swinging onto the interstate and jacking our speed up to an even ninety. She always sped and often got stopped by the cops. But so far she had yet to get a ticket. Go figure.

"Why do you say that?" Ted asked.

"We'll never live that long. We'll die of something else," Alex said.

"Like what?" Jimmy asked.

Alex shrugged. "That's my point. Here we're worrying about carbon dioxide raising the temperature and now it turns out methane is the real culprit. That's the way of the world, and the future. You can't predict nothing."

"Anything," Debbie muttered.

"Whatever," Alex said.

"What are you majoring in at UCLA?" Jimmy asked Alex.

"Psychology. I figure there's going to be a lot of depressed people pretty soon."

"You plan to cash in on their sorrows?" Debbie asked.

"Why not?" Alex replied.

"You're so altruistic," Debbie said sarcastically.

Alex laughed. That was one of her great qualities—she was almost impossible to insult. "I'm a realist, that's all." She added, "Jessie thinks the same way I do."

"Not true," I said. "No one thinks the same way you do."

Alex glanced over. "You have the same attitude. Don't deny it."

"My attitude changes from day to day." Ever so slightly I shifted my head to the left, to where I could see Jimmy. I added, "Today I feel totally optimistic."

Jimmy was dressed simply, in jeans and a red short-sleeved shirt. His brown hair was a little long, a little messy, but to me it had been a source of endless thrills. It might have been because it was thick and fine at the same time, but when I used to run my fingers through it, I always got a rush. Especially when he would groan with pleasure. One night, I swear, I did nothing but play with his hair.

His eyes matched his hair color, yet there was a softness to them, a kindness. People might think "kind" an odd word to apply to a guy but with Jimmy it fit. He was careful to make the people around him feel comfortable, and he didn't have to say much to put others at ease.

When we had dated, the one thing I had loved most about him was how he could sit across from me and stare into my eyes as I rambled on about my day. It didn't matter what I said, he always made me feel like the most important person in the world.

It had been early October when he asked me out. He came into the city library where I worked and we struck up a conversation in the back aisles. I knew he was dating Kari so I kept up a wall of sorts. I did it automatically, perhaps because I had liked him since our freshman year.

He must have sensed it but he didn't say anything about being broken up with Kari. It was possible they were not formally divorced at that exact moment. He kept the banter light. He wanted to know what I was going to do after graduation. He was in the same boat as me. Good grades, no money.

He left the library without hitting on me for my number. But a week later he magically called and asked if I'd like to go to a movie. I said sure, even before he explained that he was free and single. He picked me up early on a Friday and asked if I felt like going to Hollywood. Great, I said, anything to get out of Apple Valley. We ended up having dinner and watching three movies at the Universal CityWalk. We didn't get home until near dawn and when he kissed me good night, I was a total goner.

First love—I still feel it's the one that matters the most.

We spent the next ten weeks together and it was perfect. I was in a constant state of joy. It didn't matter if I ate or drank or slept. I just had to see him, think of him, and I'd feel happy.

We made love after a month, or I should say after thirty dates. He swung by on a Saturday after work. He was a mechanic at the local Sears. My mother was at work at the nearby Denny's, where she was the manager, and I was in the shower. I didn't know he was coming. Later, he said he'd tried knocking but got no answer. That was his excuse for peeking inside my bedroom. But my excuse, for inviting him into my shower, I can't remember what it was. I don't think I had one.

It didn't matter—once again, it was perfect.

I felt something profound lying in his arms that I had never imagined a human being could feel. I was absolutely, totally complete, as if I had spent my entire life fragmented. Just a collection of cracked pieces that his touch, his love, was able to thrust together and make whole. I knew I was with the one person in the world who could allow me to experience peace.

Later, when I tried to explain my feelings to Alex, she looked at me like I was crazy, but I sensed she was jealous. Despite her many lovers, I knew that she had never felt anything close to what I had with Jimmy.

Six weeks after our shower, he was gone.

No, that would have been easier, had he just vanished. Had he died, I think it would have been simpler to bear. But no, I had to see him every day at school, Monday through Friday, with Kari—until she graduated early, at the end of January. He told me he had to go back to her. He didn't say why. But watching them holding hands across the courtyard, I couldn't help but feel the smiles and laughter he shared with her were all fake.

But Alex said they looked real to her.

And she was my best friend. I had to believe her.

"Jessie," Jimmy said, startling me. It was possible my discreet peek out of the corner of my eye had accidentally lengthened into a long, lost stare. Had he caught me looking at him? He was too polite to say. He quickly added, "Do you guys know where you're staying?"

"At the MGM. Aren't you? That's where our class got the group rate." I paused. "Don't tell me you don't have a reservation."

He hesitated. "I wasn't sure I could get off work this weekend. By the time my boss finally said okay, I tried calling every hotel on the Strip but they were booked. I thought when we got there I'd see if there were any cancellations."

"That will be tricky on the weekend," Debbie warned.

"No biggie—you can always stay with us," Alex said.

A tense silence ensued. Ted must have immediately shorted out at the thought of Jimmy sleeping in the same suite as me. The idea drove me nuts as well, but for radically different reasons. Debbie was annoyed that a guy might be staying with us period. Despite her lust for Ted, she was a prude. She glared at Alex and spoke in a deadly tone.

"Nice of you to volunteer our accommodations."

Alex ignored the sarcasm. "Hey, the more the merrier." I knew what was coming next. Alex was never going to let me get away without putting me on the spot. She glanced my way and smiled wickedly. "Let's vote on it. Jessie, you okay with Jimmy sleeping in our suite?"

I had to act cool, I thought, it was my only escape.

"As long as we get to use his body in whatever way we see fit."

Alex offered me five. "Amen to that, sister!"

I gave her five while the three in the backseat squirmed. Ted turned to Jimmy. "If you get stuck, stay with me and Neil. We can always call down for a cot."

"You're rooming with Neil Sedak?" Alex asked, stunned. "That guy's never stepped out of Apple Valley in his life. Plus he was our class valedictorian, which means he's got to be a nerd."

"You have something against nerds?" I asked.

"I love nerds!" Alex said. "You know me, I'm never ashamed to admit my best friend works at the library. But I'm talking about Ted's rep here. Ted, if you spend a night with Neil, everyone will assume you're unfuckable."

"Hardly," I said. "I know two girls who've slept with Neil."

"Who?" Alex demanded, getting out the first half of the word before suddenly grinding to a halt. I smiled at her knowingly.

"Is someone forgetting a certain confession?" I asked.

Alex acted cool. "Confession is private."

"Oh, my God, Alex. You didn't," Debbie squealed with pleasure. Screwing Neil the Nerd went above and beyond the UCLA admission-man rumor. This one would be all over Las Vegas before the weekend was done. Alex cast me a dirty look.

"Tell her it ain't so," she ordered.

"It's possible it ain't so," I said. There was more truth to

Alex's remark than I let on. I *was* a bit of a nerd. The reason I worked at the library was because I loved to read. I was addicted. I read everything: fiction, nonfiction, mysteries, sci-fi, horror, thrillers, biographies, romance novels, all the genres, even magazines and newspapers. It was probably why my brain was stuffed with so much arcane information.

"Explain that I was only joking about Neil," Alex insisted.

The sex secrets of Alex and Neil could have gone on another hour if Jimmy hadn't interrupted. He was not a big one for gossip.

"I don't give a damn about Neil's sex life," Jimmy said. "But I do appreciate your offer, Ted. If I get stuck for a place to stay, I'll give you a call."

"No problem," Ted said, a note of relief in his voice. He reached in his pocket and pulled out a card. "Here's a fake ID if you plan to gamble."

"Great." Jimmy studied it. "This license looks real."

"It's not," Ted warned. "Don't use it at the MGM's front desk to check in. It'll fail if it's scanned. But don't worry about gambling at the other hotels. I haven't seen them scan IDs on the casino floors."

"How do you know?" Jimmy asked.

"He's been to Vegas tons," Alex said. "He's a master card counter."

"Wow." Jimmy was impressed. "Is it hard to learn?"

Ted shrugged, although it was obvious he enjoyed the

attention. "It takes a good memory and hard work. But you don't have to be a genius to do it."

"You should teach us all this weekend," Debbie said, a bold comment coming from her. Ted shrugged.

"I can teach you the basics. But it takes hours of practice to make money at it. And the casinos keep changing the rules, making it harder to get an edge."

"The bastards," Alex muttered.

We reached Las Vegas before sunset so we weren't treated to the famous colorful glow suddenly rising out of the desert night. It was a curious phenomenon, I thought, but during the day Las Vegas looked far from imposing. Just a bunch of gaudy buildings sticking out of the sand. But I knew when night fell, the magic would emerge, and the town would transform itself into one gigantic adult ride.

Alex drove straight to the MGM, where we checked in to our room, a decent-sized suite with a view of the Strip and three separate bedrooms—plus a central living area that came equipped not only with a sofa but a love seat. The price wasn't bad, one hundred and fifty bucks: fifty bucks when split three ways. Still, the weekend was ruining my savings. The library was not exactly a high-paying place to work.

With the sofa and love seat, we had room for another two people. But Jimmy, damn him, was too much of a gentleman to impose. He also seemed reluctant to take Ted up on his offer. He tried his best to find his own room, using our hotel-room phone to call several hotlines that supposedly could find you a suite on New Year's Eve. But it was all hype; it was Friday evening at the start of summer and Las Vegas was bursting at the seams. Jimmy struck out.

"This couch is softer than my bed," Alex said, sitting not far from where Jimmy had just finished dialing. I was glad we had temporarily left Ted—who had gone off to find his own room. Alex, it seemed, was determined that Jimmy stay with us.

"We settled the sleeping arrangements in the car," Debbie said, studying the minibar. Because it was filled with tiny bottles of liquor, and we had checked in to the room using our real IDs, the bar should have been off-limits. But Ted had managed to bypass the locking mechanism before departing for his quarters. I was glad, I loved minibars. The snacks tasted ten times better to me, probably because they cost ten times as much as they were supposed to.

"When we talked about it in the car, we didn't know this suite would be so large," Alex said.

"We only have one bathroom," Debbie growled.

"Do you plan on spending the weekend throwing up?" Alex asked.

Jimmy interrupted. "Hey, it's okay—remember, I've got Ted's room as a backup. Don't worry about me."

Alex went to reply, but then her eyes slipped from Jimmy to me. Her unspoken message couldn't have been clearer. She wasn't worried about Jimmy, she was worried about me. Or else she was trying to force the two of us back together, which, in her bizarre mind, was the same thing.

It didn't matter. The elephant standing in the room had just quietly roared. It could no longer be ignored. Jimmy and I had to talk—soon, and alone. But I felt too nervous to say it aloud. I stood and caught his eye, and headed toward my room. Jimmy understood, he followed me and shut the door behind him.

Before I could figure out where to sit, or what I should say, he hugged me. The gesture caught me by surprise. I didn't hug him back, not at first, but when he didn't let go, I found my arms creep up and around his broad shoulders. It felt so perfect to stand there and listen to his heartbeat. Yes, that word again, I could not be free of it when I was around Jimmy.

The hug was warm but chaste; he didn't try to kiss me. He didn't even move his arms once he had ahold of me. Although we were standing up, we could have been lying down together, asleep in each other's arms. I don't know how long the hug lasted but it felt like forever . . . compressed into a moment.

Finally, we sat on the bed together. He was holding my hands, or trying to, but I had to keep taking them back to wipe away the silly tears that kept running over my cheeks. He didn't rush me to speak. But he never took his eyes off me, and I felt he was searching my face for the answer to a question he had carried with him a long time.

Of course, I had my own question.

"Why?" I said. The word startled me more than him. It felt so blunt after our tender moment. The question didn't offend him, but he let go of me and sat back on the bed, propping himself up with a pillow.

"Do you remember the day we drove to Newport Beach?" he asked.

"Yes." It had been during Christmas break, a few days before the holiday. I wasn't likely to forget because it was to turn out to be the worst Christmas of my life. He dumped me December 22. Then I hadn't known what to do with the presents I had bought, or the ones I had made for him. In the end, I hadn't done anything. I still had them in my bedroom closet. They were still wrapped.

"When we got back to Apple Valley, Kari was waiting at my house." Jimmy paused. "She said she was ten weeks pregnant."

I froze. "We were together ten weeks."

Jimmy held up a hand. "I never slept with her once I was with you. I never even kissed her."

"I believe you." And I did—he didn't have to swear. Jimmy was incredibly rare; he didn't lie. I added, "Did you believe her?"

"She had an ultrasound with her."

"That doesn't mean it was yours."

"Jessie . . ."

"Saying, 'I'm pregnant, Jimmy, you have to come back to me.' That's like the oldest trick in the book."

"I know that. I know Kari's not always a hundred percent

straight. But I just had to look in her eyes. She was telling the truth."

I crossed my arms over my chest. "I don't know."

"And she was showing a little bit."

"At ten weeks?" I asked.

"It might have been twelve."

"And it might have been a folded-up pillowcase."

He hesitated. "No. She lifted her shirt. It was for real."

"And she wanted to keep it."

"Yes. That wasn't an issue."

"She wanted you back. That was *the* issue."

He lowered his head. "I don't know. Maybe."

It was a lot to digest. It was a minute before I could speak.

"You should have told me," I said.

"I'm sorry. I wanted to, but I felt it would hurt you more to know she was having my baby."

I shook my head. "You've been good so far, real good, but that, what you just said, is nuts. Nothing could hurt worse than that call I got. Do you remember it? 'Hello, Jessie, how are you doing? Good? That's good. Hey, I've got some bad news. I don't know exactly how to tell you this. But Kari and I are getting back together. I know this is sort of sudden, and the last thing I want to do is hurt you, but Kari and I . . . we're not done yet. We have stuff we have to work out. Are you there, Jessie?'"

He stared at me. "God."

"What?"

"You remember it word for word."

"I'll remember it till the day I die."

"I'm sorry."

"Don't say that word again. Tell me why."

"I just told you why. She was pregnant. I felt I had to do the right thing and go back to her."

"Why didn't you tell me the truth?"

"I was ashamed, it's true, but I honestly thought the truth would hurt you more."

"That's so lame. Didn't you stop to imagine how I felt? You left me hanging. Hanging above nothing 'cause I knew nothing. One moment I'm the love of your life and the next a cheerleader has taken my place."

He nodded. "It was dumb, I made a mistake. I should have explained everything to you. Please forgive me."

"No."

"Jessie?"

"I don't forgive you. I can't. I suffered too much. You say you felt you had to do the right thing so you went back to her. Let me ask you this—were you still in love with her?"

"I was never in love with Kari."

"Were you in love with me?"

"Yes."

"Then what you did was wrong. So she was pregnant. So she wept and begged you to come back for the sake of your child. That doesn't matter. I was more important to you, I should have been more important. You should have said no to her."

"I couldn't."

"Why not?" I demanded.

"Because when she rolled up her shirt and I saw that growing bump, and realized that it was true, that it was mine, my flesh and blood, I knew I had to take care of that baby."

"Bullshit."

"You're wrong, Jessie. At that moment, nothing mattered more to me than that child. And yes, forgive me, but it mattered even more than us."

I stood. "Get out."

He stood. "We should talk more."

"No, leave. This was all a . . . mistake. Go stay with Ted."

Jimmy stepped toward the door, put his hand on the knob. He was going to leave, he wasn't going to fight me. That's what I liked about him, how reasonable he could be. And that's what I hated about him, that he hadn't fought for me. I was the one who had to stop him.

"Where's the baby now?" I asked. Kari had graduated at the end of January and left campus early. I assumed she'd had the child.

But Jimmy lowered his head. He staggered.

"We lost him," he said.

"She had a miscarriage?"

"No." The word came out so small. I put my hand to my mouth.

"Don't tell me she had the baby and it died?" I gasped.

He turned and looked at me, pale as plaster. So frail, so hollow. I felt if I said the wrong word, he'd shatter.

"His name was Huck. He lived for three days."

"Why did he die?" I asked.

The wrong words. Jimmy turned, opened the door, spoke over his shoulder. "You're right, I should go. We can talk later."

He left; it was amazing how much it hurt. It was like he was breaking up with me all over again. It was then I wished I hadn't said the "why" word. We should have left it at the hug.

CHAPTER THREE

I DID NOT LEAVE MY ROOM FOR SOME TIME, AND WHEN I did, I found a note from Debbie and Alex. They had left to find the kids from our class and plan the night's festivities. That's the word Alex chose—"festivities." I doubted she had seen Jimmy's face when he had left our suite.

I was tired and knew we'd be up late. I tried napping but had trouble falling asleep. Huck haunted me, perhaps the way he haunted Jimmy. I didn't fool myself. Jimmy had won our fight—if it could be called that. And here I had been positive I would humiliate him when we finally spoke. I was sure I owned the moral high ground. But Jimmy was right, the child was his own flesh and blood; it transcended infatuation, even our love, never mind that the infant had died.

I kept wondering what had killed Huck.

A part of me sensed Jimmy did not know the whole story.

At some point I must have blacked out. The next thing I knew, Alex was sitting beside me on my bed. "You all right, Jessie?" she asked softly.

She had seen Jimmy's face after all. She was concerned about me.

I sat up quickly. "I'm fine. What time is it?"

"Five."

"Five! Why did you let me sleep so long?"

"You looked exhausted. Besides, the gang's not getting together until six."

"Who exactly is the gang?"

Alex continued to study me. "Not sure, whoever comes. But I've got some good news. You know how you said you wanted to see *O*?"

"Don't tell me you got tickets?"

"Six seats. Ted got them from a scalper. He says he doesn't care who comes with us. He's even volunteered not to go, in case you want to bring a date."

"Bullshit. He never said that."

Alex shrugged. "All right, I made that up. But he's not stupid. He saw the way you and Jimmy were looking at each other." She paused. "Can you tell me what happened?"

"Later," I said.

I took a quick shower and put on the only dress I had brought—something short, black and sexy that Debbie had sewn for me for my birthday. She had designed it after a dress we had seen on *Project Runway*—we were all addicted to the show. Debbie's dress was even more inspired than the one on TV. She was a woman of many talents. A pity she kept most of them hidden.

Our class was staying at the MGM, but our celebratory dinner was to take place at the Bellagio. It was supposed to have the best restaurants. Our reservations were for a high-priced Italian bistro but our class was no sooner gathered in the Bellagio lobby than an argument broke out. Half our gang didn't like Italian—they wanted to eat elsewhere. On the surface that didn't seem like a major problem. Unfortunately, as Debbie shouted over the bedlam, we had already promised the hotel a minimum of two hundred guests.

"If we don't all eat here, we lose our discount," Debbie said.

"How much is that?" someone demanded.

"Forty percent," Debbie replied.

About fifty percent of our class didn't give a damn. They split for other hotels. When we finally made it to the restaurant, the manager looked like he'd have a nervous breakdown when we told him we were missing half our entourage. He screamed at us in Italian, but since none of us spoke the language, it didn't do much good.

He had no choice, he had to seat us immediately. We were taking up the entire waiting area. Jimmy didn't show, which hurt. I had told him where we were eating. Of course I had also told him to get out of my room.

Ted sat beside me. He said he had not seen or heard from Jimmy. "He didn't stop at your room?" I asked.

"No," Ted said.

"Did you try calling his cell?"

Ted looked annoyed. "I'm not his babysitter. I offered him a place to crash. If he doesn't want it, that's his business."

I touched Ted's arm. "You're right. Sorry."

Ted tried to act casual, and would have succeeded if he didn't sound like he was choking on his next question. "You two back together?"

"Absolutely not," I said.

The food was excellent. I had a pasta dish with shrimp. The cook had seasoned it with a fantastic mix of herbs. The incredible taste quickly improved my mood. By the end of the meal I was laughing with the rest of my class. It might have been the alcohol. Alex had flashed her fake ID and convinced our waiter we were teachers from Apple Valley High. He brought us two bottles of chilled wine that the outside heat caused us to polish off way too quickly.

I cannot hold my liquor. Two glasses of anything above ten proof and I fall in love with the universe. Worse, the love created by my inebriated state usually wants to flow in a direction. And since kindhearted Ted was sitting beside me, I couldn't stop thinking how he had gotten us O tickets and fake IDs, offered Jimmy a room, and broken into our minibar. . . . Why, I felt I just had to express my undying gratitude to him.

I suddenly leaned over and kissed him on the lips.

It took me maybe two seconds to realize what I had done. *Shit! Oh, shit!*

Talk about sending wrong signals. His face broke into an expression of pure delight. But Debbie—who sat to his right— cast me a look so dirty I felt like our friendship wouldn't survive the blow. Plus Ted grabbed me after the kiss, probably hoping our brief oral contact was the beginning of something extraordinary.

"Have I ever told you how wonderful you are?" he said with feeling.

"Maybe once or twice," I muttered, trying to extricate myself from his arms without being too obvious.

Alex was as drunk as I was. She studied her empty wine glass and waxed philosophical. "Why is it we always say such emotional crap at times like this? The truth is the feelings you two share are as obvious as a one-way street."

"Huh?" Ted said, blinking. He'd had some of our wine.

"Don't be so cold," I said quickly, diplomatically, still trying to slip from his bear hug. "Ted is a dear old friend."

"Friends," Alex said, practically spitting the word. "What good are friends? You can't f—"

"Why did you just kiss me?" Ted interrupted, his joy slowly fading.

"Because I care," I said.

"And she's drunk," Alex added.

"Is that true?" Ted asked, his expression darkening.

"Well," I said.

"Ignore her," Debbie said, reaching over and taking one of his hands, which gave me one less hand to escape from. "When Jessie gets drunk, she always acts like a whore. We were at this party once where she downed a six-pack and got up and started dancing on the tabletop. She stripped down to her panties."

Ted released me all of a sudden. He practically shoved me away. He looked upset, confused. "What's going on here?" he mumbled.

"Knock it off, Debbie, would ya? You know damn well that was me," Alex said. "And the panties didn't stay on."

"I really am grateful for all you've done for us," I told Ted.

"For us?" he snapped, beginning to sober up.

I searched inside for the perfect remark that would completely repair the damage I had caused. The only problem was I was working with an IQ of around fifty.

"For all of us," I told Ted. "For me, for Alex, and especially for Debbie. You may not know this but Debbie has a major crush on you. She's had it for years but she's too much of a coward to tell you. So I'm telling you now."

My words didn't go over as well as I hoped. Debbie threw down her napkin and got up and ran from the restaurant. Ted watched her go, then turned to me, probably hoping I would clarify my remark. The best I could do was belch, which sent Alex into an uncontrollable fit of laughter. Ted had finally had enough. He shook his head and stood and handed me two tickets.

"I got you great seats," he said in a bitter voice. "Enjoy the show."

He left, chasing after Debbie, or so we assumed. The rest of our long table fell silent and stared at me, making me feel like a total ass. But Alex was quick to reassure me.

"Although your drunken stupor is obvious to all," she told me, "your words were positively brilliant. Your remarks may even change the course of those two mediocre lives."

"Don't call them mediocre," I said.

"Their lives will be if they get married two years from now. All because of what you said here tonight."

I sighed, and studied the tickets in my hand. "I just hope we're not sitting beside them during the show."

"When does it start?" Alex asked.

My eyes slowly focused on the tiny print on the tickets.

I gasped. "In ten minutes!"

We paid our share of the bill, in theory, although we probably cheated our classmates since we were the only ones who had ordered wine. But we didn't have time to hang around and haggle over an exact figure.

We were lucky *O* took place in the Bellagio. A hotel employee was kind enough to lead us to the appropriate hall. He could tell we were stinking drunk. We kept giggling and bumping into each other.

I had read so much about the show, I worried my high expectations could never be met. But the truth was, it blew me away. The stage was supposed to have cost fifty million to build. The money had not been wasted. It kept changing shape. One minute it was filled with water, like a small lake, and the next it had shallow streams running down the center. Then all the water would disappear and it would be covered with gravel.

The performers were close to superhuman. They could bend and twist their bodies into positions that would have challenged Gumby. Several times Alex and I gasped and grabbed hands. One of the leads did high-wire stunts a hundred feet above the stage and then dived into a square pond less than three feet across. What nerve! The exotic colors, the brilliant lighting, the hypnotic music, the songs, the dancing—I felt like I'd been transported into another dimension.

For a time I forgot about Jimmy and the others. It was a relief, in a way, we didn't see another person from our school.

Alex and I were sober by the time the show finished, but neither of us had any desire to return to our suite. Alex wanted to gamble. She was keen to play twenty-one, blackjack. But I was worried we'd lose too much money and suffer for it the rest of the weekend. I pointed to the small signs on the sides of the tables.

"Look, the minimum bet's twenty bucks! We can't afford that!"

"The Bellagio's for high rollers," Alex said. "Come on, we'll find a place with a five-buck minimum."

"Where?"

Alex nodded toward the hotel exit. "Let's hit the Strip, there's a hundred hotels out there. We'll find what we're looking for."

Alex strode toward the door. I had to struggle to keep up. "Why blackjack? We'll get creamed without Ted's help. Why don't we play the slots?"

"Blackjack's the best game to meet guys," Alex said, pulling a small plastic card from her purse. "You get to sit at a table and talk to the other players. It's the only game where you really get to know them. Plus I got this cheat card—it tells you exactly when to hit and when to stand. It was designed by a computer, it gives you the best possible odds. We won't lose too much."

"I don't want to lose anything. I want to win. We need Ted."

Alex put an arm around me. "Sorry, sister, but that kiss you planted on his lips has made him radioactive for the rest of the summer. At least when it comes to you."

"I was drunk. He'll forgive me."

"The only way he'll forgive you is if he ends up having sex with Debbie, and I don't think they've made a cheat card that could compute such lousy odds."

"I don't know. He ran after her pretty fast."

"Whatever. The point is, we don't need Ted. There will be plenty of cute guys at the tables to help us play."

I studied Alex. "Are you planning on having a one-night stand?"

"You say that like I'm some kind of slut."

"Well, it would be a pretty slutty thing to do."

"This is Vegas! People come here for three reasons: to drink, to gamble, and to get laid. Those are the only reasons this place exists."

I sighed. "All right. But if I give him a thumbs-down, you can't bring him back to our room."

Alex took my hand and pulled me out the door. "Jessie, you can be sure whoever has the good luck to end up with me is going to have his own luxurious suite."

"You'd sleep with a guy just because he has money?"

"Money and a dick."

"Whore."

"There are no whores in this town. Only givers and takers."

Outside was the real Las Vegas. The sun had set and the town glowed with a million electric rainbows. Not to mention the fantastic fountains in front of the Bellagio. We stared at them, mesmerized, as we crossed the long entrance. The entire Strip looked surreal. Paris was across the street, New York was to our right. There was a pyramid and a castle down the road. I loved how so many of the hotels had adopted exotic themes. The sidewalks were jammed, with most of the people laughing and carrying on. The smell of booze was all-pervasive.

The night air was hotter than at home, in the high nineties.

I knew it would take all night for the temperature to drop another ten degrees. Then the sun would rise and another scorcher would begin. As we walked, our thirst quickly returned. We had barely reached the Tropicana when Alex pulled me inside.

"This is an old hotel but it has class," she said. "Plus they have low minimums. We should be able to find a five-buck table."

"How about a dollar table?"

"Sure. Hop on down to Mississippi and catch a steamboat on the river."

It being a Friday night, the place was jammed. We didn't have our choice of blackjack tables. Indeed, it took a long wait before we found a table that could seat us both. Fortunately, they barely looked at out IDs.

We ordered drinks before trading our cash for chips: four large Cuba libres—the name translates as "free Cuba," in English—Coke, rum, and lime. The table drinks were supposed to be watered down but these babies packed a punch. I had barely finished my first when I began having trouble counting to twenty-one.

The minimum was five bucks, the maximum ten thousand. Alex and I each bought a hundred bucks' worth of five-dollar chips and prayed we didn't lose it all in the first twenty minutes, which I had done before. I was not a total novice—I had played the game before in Las Vegas with my mom and knew the basic rules. Of course, when I had played with her, I'd had to dress up and wear plenty of makeup so I looked older.

To start, we relied on Alex's card. The hardest thing for me was when to split and when to double down. The card made it simple. It had three color-coded columns. If the dealer is showing this, and you have that, then do this . . .

We were at the table maybe half an hour, and I was down fifty bucks and Alex was ahead a hundred, when a guy showed up. He caught my eye instantly. It wasn't just because he was handsome. Las Vegas had no shortage of beautiful men.

Nor was it the fact that he set down a fat roll of hundreds and asked for thirty thousand in chips. Again, the town was loaded with high rollers. It was more his calm expression, his quiet confidence, that drew me in. As he casually stacked his chips and lit a cigarette, he looked neither happy nor sad. He was just there to win.

A man a few seats over—he was a truck driver out of Chicago, and he had hit on me and Alex the second we had sat down—called to the new guy. "Hey, dude, can't you read? This is a no-smoking table."

The guy stared at him with large, steady eyes. They were blue, but so close to black they looked as if they had never seen the sun. "No," he said, and blew smoke in the man's face.

Trucky got annoyed. "No what?"

"I can't read."

"Listen, put out the cigarette or find another table."

"Go find your own table."

Trucky stood. "Looking for a fight, bud?"

The guy smiled easily, still calm and cool. He was six-two, muscular, probably in his mid-twenties. He could have been a cop, someone who worked in a dangerous field. He had that kind of vibe. Although he looked at ease, I had the feeling Las Vegas was not home. He had closely cropped blond hair and a slight accent I couldn't place.

Facing the dealer, I was on the far left. Alex was to my right and the new guy was next, followed by Trucky and a young Japanese couple who could not stop staring at the newcomer's mountain of chips.

I hoped the threat didn't scare him off. I doubted it would. From the moment I saw him, I felt I knew him, like he was a piece of my past I could no longer remember clearly. I wanted him to stay.

"Not afraid of one," he told Trucky.

Trucky went to snap at him, then suddenly seemed allergic to our newcomer's stare. He lowered his head and spoke in a meek tone. "I don't smoke. I shouldn't have to inhale your crap."

Alex spoke. "You heard the guy, he can't read. It's not his fault."

The guy turned and smiled at her. "Thank you." He offered his hand. "I'm Russ."

"Alex." She shook his hand and added hastily, "This is my friend Jessie."

"Jessica." His eyes lingered on my face, long enough to where I ended up blushing. There was power in his gaze. "Love that name."

"Bets down," the dealer snapped. He was frail, three times our age, and already showing signs of the disease that would probably kill him. His face was not merely pale but pasty. He could have washed it with bacteria-friendly soap. The few gray hairs he had left looked like they were glued on. I had tried joking with him earlier but he only responded to tips. He was a smoker, though; it was obvious he liked when Russ exhaled in his direction.

We laid down our bets. Twenty bucks for the truck driver. Five for me. Twenty for Alex, who was feeling bold with her extra hundred in her pocket. Russ put down a grand, which caused the Japanese couple to gasp. They talked excitedly in their native tongue before they each put down twenty. The dealer dealt us our cards.

"Damn," I swore when I saw mine. A powerful ten, followed by a feeble six. Sixteen, worst hand in the book, especially against a dealer who was showing a ten. The computer card said I had to hit, but it also said I was probably already going to lose. Trucky was in the same boat as me. I could tell from his disgusted expression he was going to stand.

The Japanese couple each had nineteen, which meant, of course, they were going to hold tight. Alex had eleven— the perfect hand to double down on. Russ also had eleven. I assumed he would play the odds and double his bet.

Nevertheless, I watched him closely. There were two reasons why he might choose to ignore the odds: the size of his bet and the dealer's powerful ten. Myself, I would have simply hit. But I suspected Russ had more guts than I did. And money.

Alex turned to Russ and acted like she knew nothing about the game. It was Alex's firm belief that there had never been a male born who did not enjoy telling a female what to do. "Should I double?" she asked.

He shrugged. "The book says you should."

"You're going to double, right?"

"Nope."

Alex was surprised. So was I. Russ looked like an experienced player but his choice indicated he was not—at least, according to our card.

Alex doubled, shoving out four more chips. Russ left his grand alone.

Russ hit and got three. Now he was looking at fourteen—a shit hand. He hit again, which he couldn't have done if he had doubled down. He got a seven, twenty-one, sweet.

Alex had forty bucks riding on one hand. The dealer hit her and she got two, the worst possible card on a double down. She cursed her cards and the dealer. The latter didn't blink. Against my better judgment I took one and got an eight and bust. Alex lost as well.

Russ was the only one who won.

Then, the nerve of the guy, he let his two grand ride. It was such a ridiculous amount to bet on one hand, the rest of us didn't pay attention to our own hands. Except for Alex.

She was pissed she had lost the forty and was trying to make it back in a hurry. She put down a stack of eight five-dollar chips.

"You're throwing away your winnings," I warned her.

"Hush!" she snapped.

I stayed at five bucks. Trucky and the Japanese couple played twenty. Our dealer hit me with another sixteen, which made me feel cursed. Trucky got twelve. The Japanese couple got nineteen again. Russ got ten. Unfortunately, the dealer also showed ten.

Alex got a miserable fifteen.

"Do I hit?" Trucky asked Russ. A few minutes ago the man had wanted to punch Russ. Only in Vegas.

"Don't ask me for advice," Russ said.

"Come on," Trucky insisted.

"Well, you can't sit at twelve."

"Maybe the dealer will bust," Trucky said.

Russ shrugged. "You decide."

Alex appealed to Russ. "How do I get out of this mess?"

Russ didn't hesitate. "Hit."

It was decision time. The Japanese couple stood. Trucky hit and got nine—twenty-one. He patted Russ on the back, called him a good man. Russ drew another ten for an even twenty. Alex also drew ten, which caused her to bust. She slammed her fist down in disgust.

"You told me to hit!" she complained to Russ.

"I also said not to ask me for advice," he said.

I hit and got six and bust again. I was down to forty in chips and only had another hundred in my purse to last me all weekend. The dealer turned his hole card over. He had only seventeen. The Japanese couple had won, as well as Russ, who was already three grand ahead. Wow.

The smart thing for me to do was leave. Alex was already packing up to go. She was annoyed at Russ, at his attitude, although she should have accepted it had been her decision to bet so much at once.

"Come on, Jessie," she grumbled.

I hesitated. "I want to keep playing."

"You're getting shit hands every time. Let's try somewhere else."

I glanced at Russ—who lit another cigarette—and turned back to Alex. "Go ahead, I'll catch up with you later."

"Right."

I nodded toward Russ. "I promise. I'll call you on my cell."

Alex got the message. "Remember, most cells don't work inside these places. Go outside if you can't reach me." She leaned over and whispered in my ear. "Watch out for this guy, he looks like trouble."

I just nodded. Hadn't we come to Vegas for trouble?

We played another hour, together, and no one left the table except the dealer. The breaks he took were short. With our original dealer back at the helm, my meager bankroll began to dwindle again. Actually, the situation got serious. I dipped into my purse and took out the hundred I'd sworn I was going to save for the next two days. I was playing with money I couldn't afford to lose. True, my room was paid for but I needed the cash to buy food and drinks.

Why was I being so reckless?

It made no sense but I felt my luck had to change. Plus I wanted to stay near Russ. I had moved closer to him, taking Alex's vacant chair. For the first time in a long time, Russ looked over at me.

"How much are you in the hole?" he asked.

"Close to two hundred."

"Can you afford that?"

"Hell, no." I had been watching him play. He was easily a hundred grand ahead. I thought maybe he was going to offer me a loan, not that I would have taken it. I had too much pride. He surprised me when he told me to bet everything I had left on my next hand.

I shook my head. "Are you nuts?"

He stared at me. "I'm serious, Jessica."

"It's Jessie."

"Bet it all, Jessie."

I gestured to his stacks of chips. "That's easy for you to say, you're winning like a fiend. How much are you ahead?"

"I don't know, I can't count."

"You can't count and you can't read. What a winning combination."

"It hasn't hurt me tonight."

"Should I bet everything I've got?" Trucky interrupted.

Russ ignored him. He was focused on me. The dealer was demanding we place our bets. "Decision time," Russ said.

There was something in his confidence that made me reach into my pocket and pull out my final forty. There was no point in asking him again how he knew it was time to go all out. He had said what he had to say and that was that. I could trust him or forget it. Taking a deep breath, I shoved the red chips into the white circle painted on the green velvet.

"No guts, no glory," I said.

Russ smiled and put down ten grand. "True."

I shook my head at the size of his bet. "You're crazy."

"Gambling's crazy."

"True. But you're ahead. You should quit while you're ahead."

"Why?"

"Duh. You're playing against the odds. In the long run, you can't win."

"I'm not playing against the odds."

"Really?"

"I'm playing against myself."

His remark should have been sufficiently cryptic to ignore. Except for the fact that I had watched him for more than an hour and he had won over eighty percent of his bets. A person who could play at such a high level and consistently win either knew something the rest of the world didn't or was one lucky bastard. Hell, look at me, I was trusting him with my last few chips.

The dealer dealt once more. My first card was an ace. God in heaven, I prayed. If only my next card were a ten . . .

I got a queen of diamonds. Blackjack, which paid one and a half times my original bet. Suddenly I was sixty bucks richer and back up to a hundred. I should walk, I thought. Walk away with enough cash to maybe rent a boat on Lake Mead and go waterskiing with Jimmy, or else return to that Italian restaurant at the Bellagio with him. Jimmy loved pasta; he loved food.

But Russ was watching me with his navy blues. The sea behind them was too deep, too calm, to say no to. He wanted me to let it ride.

I left the hundred bucks on the table.

The dealer made up a new shoe and dealt. I got seventeen, an awful hand, especially when the dealer was showing a ten. I could only wait and see if he bust. I wasn't Alex, I didn't snap at Russ. I had made my own decision and I'd have to live with it.

"Hit," Russ said when the dealer got to me. He had won his last hand and with another twenty sitting in front of him it looked like he was going to win again. His ten-grand maximum bets kept piling up.

I snickered at his suggestion. "Right. And pray for a four, a three, or a two. Those are the only cards that can help me."

"You need a four," he said.

None of the original players had left. For the first time, they were focused on me. They knew the hundred was all I had left.

"But the odds . . . ," I began.

"Screw the odds," Russ said.

"That's not what you told Alex."

"That's because I wanted you all to myself," he replied.

He was saying he had given her bad advice on purpose. To piss her off so she would leave. Who was this guy?

"Hit me," I told the dealer.

I got a four—twenty-one. The table cheered loudly. Trucky wanted to hug me. The dealer turned over his card. Russ had been right, I had needed the four. The dealer had twenty.

I had won my money back. I shoved my loot toward the dealer so he could give me two black hundred-dollar chips to take to the cashier's window. But Russ stopped me.

"Change them into greens and play some more," he said.

Greens were twenty-five-dollar chips. A person could win or lose awfully fast at that rate.

"I need to find my friend. I think she's mad at me," I said.

"This is Vegas. No one stays mad for long here," Russ said.

I tried arguing with him but my heart was not in it. Especially when he offered to tell me when to bet heavily. I was no fool, I could see what he was capable of. If I could make money and flirt with a cute guy at the same time, then to hell with Alex.

I asked for another Cuba libre and gulped it down. Russ ordered us both more drinks and we lined up our chips and prepared to do some serious gambling. He had finally stopped to count his chips. He was up a hundred and fifty thousand. He told me with a straight face he wanted to win half a million. He tipped our dealer ten grand—the guy finally smiled—and then he appeared to change our strategy and instructed me to bet low for a few bets. That meant I had to cash in two greens for ten five-dollar chips.

I lost the next five bets. Naturally, I was relieved I was playing at the casino minimum. But as soon as the dealer whipped up a fresh shoe—there were actually six decks of cards in the shoe, all mixed together—Russ told me to bet a hundred. That was more than half what I had left, but there was no saying no to him. Especially with Trucky begging for help on the far side.

"Why are you helping her and not me?" he demanded when I won the next hand.

Russ turned to him. "You want some advice? Leave the casino now and don't come back."

Poor Trucky, Russ had hurt his feelings. "What did I do to you? I stopped complaining about your smoking."

Russ ignored him and focused on the game. The dealer tossed out the cards with practiced ease. I bet another hundred and got a twenty, which made my heart skip. Especially when the dealer ended up with nineteen.

Suddenly I was up two hundred. Ten minutes later I was

a thousand ahead. It was just the start. Russ varied his bets between one thousand and ten thousand, nothing in between. After I had won more than three thousand, he told me to vary my bets—either five hundred or fifty.

Of course, Russ told me when to place the big bet. But that didn't stop my hands from shaking every time I pushed it out.

I assumed he was counting the cards, but based on what Ted had told us, he was winning far too often for an ordinary counter. No, I thought, he must be using another kind of system. But what?

I wasn't the only one who was stumped. His winning streak naturally attracted the pit bosses. We had at least two standing over us from the time Russ passed a hundred grand in winnings. Eventually the floor manager appeared, a big burly guy with a neck as thick as his thighs. He had "mob" written all over him.

The manager occasionally glanced up and signaled with his hands. I realized he was communicating with the "eye in the sky" that Ted had told me about. All the casinos had people watching the tables from above with special cameras, searching for cheaters, for counters in particular. Yet none of them seemed to feel Russ was counting. They let him play, even though he kept winning. I assumed they hoped his luck would change and he'd lose it all back, and then some.

I leaned over and whispered in Russ's ear.

"Does it bother you, all this attention?" I asked.

"Nah. They're like everyone else. They hate parting with their money."

"What if they ask us to leave?" I asked.

"These are private clubs. We'd have to leave."

The alcohol went to my brain and danced. I suspected the bar had upped the juice in our drinks so Russ would play recklessly, although to be honest, I was drinking more than he was. I was playing like a robot that had an internal happy switch broken in the on position. The money we were making made me want to sing. It felt unreal. I stared at the stacks of chips piling up in front of me and I told myself that they had not given me real chips. That I was playing with Monopoly money. The idea did not disturb me because, well, in real life no broke eighteen-year-old chick from Apple Valley ever went to Las Vegas and won huge sums of money.

Our dealer went for a break and never returned. It seemed we had a new dealer—a hard-looking fifty-year-old female who wore her makeup so thick it looked like it held her nose on her face. Russ instructed me to keep my bets low. Ten minutes later he leaned over and spoke in my ear.

"We're leaving. This woman is what's called a mechanic. Her hand and eye coordination are extraordinary. She's the best I've ever seen. She's hitting us with cards that are two, three, or four deep in the deck. Trust me, if we stay, we'll keep getting losing hands."

I nodded. "Okay."

The woman, along with the floor manager and pit bosses, waited for us to make our next bet. Russ pushed all our stacks of chips forward and told the dealer to count us out.

"Excuse me, sir?" the woman said, clearly unhappy.

Russ stayed cool. "Do you want to count us out here, or should we do it at the cashier's window?"

The floor manager stepped forward. He offered his hand to Russ and they exchanged names and other pleasantries. He ignored me completely. He seemed concerned that Russ didn't want to leave his winnings in the hotel vault, so he could play again at a later date. From my side, I would have brought up the fact that they were trying to cheat us with a mechanic. But Russ apparently knew better.

He told them we wanted checks for the amounts we had won, and insisted the chips be counted in front of us so that they never left our sight.

Our chips were loaded into two glass racks: one for Russ, one for me. We followed the loot and the floor manager to a cashier's window. The manager wanted to take us in the back but Russ insisted he count the chips right there on the counter. He seemed reluctant to pass through any door that could be locked behind us.

The manager agreed to Russ's terms. He called for two women who grouped the chips in stacks of twenties, after first separating them by color. Russ had won so many gold chips— worth a thousand dollars a pop—it made my head swim. Yet

Russ seemed to take it all in stride. It was just another night at the casinos to him.

The women completed my count first. $57,800.

"You've got to be shitting me," I gasped.

"Would you like a check or cash?" the manager asked me.

"A check," Russ replied. "Jessie, is your legal name Jessica?"

"Yeah. Jessica Ralle. Do you need my middle name?"

"It's not necessary unless your bank prefers it," the manager said.

"Hell. My bank has probably never seen a check that large."

The women finished with Russ's count. $642,450.

"My full name is Russell Devon," Russ said.

"We need to see both your IDs," the manager said. "And as I'm sure you're aware, we'll automatically be withdrawing the sum you'll owe the IRS for these winnings."

I suddenly felt faint. Of course, I had been playing with a fake ID. I had never planned on winning an amount where they would need to see my ID, never mind withdraw money for the IRS. I leaned against Russ and buried the side of my face in his ear.

"I need to talk to you alone," I said.

Russ asked if we could be excused for a few minutes and the manager was agreeable. We went around the corner, out of earshot, and even before I could explain what the problem was, I burst out crying.

"Shit, shit, shit," I kept saying through my tears. Luck like this really didn't happen in the real world. I wasn't going to get the money.

Russ stared at me with a faint smile on his lips.

"Let me guess," he said. "You're not twenty-one."

"I'm so sorry, Russ."

"Relax. Did they ask for ID when you two first sat down?"

"We showed them something our friend whipped up on his computer. These guys will know it's fake."

"I'm sure they will, since they'll want your Social Security number as well. But it's not as big a problem as you think. You're going to leave here, now, and walk across the street to the Mandalay Bay. It's only two hundred yards up the Strip. That's where I'm staying and that's where I planned to take you for coffee when we were done here. Go through the front door and take a sharp right. You'll find a coffee shop that's always open." He checked his watch. "I'll meet you there in fifteen minutes."

"What are you going to do?"

He shrugged. "Tell them that you were obviously playing with my money and under my direction and that we changed our minds and want it all under my name. But I'll take out sixty grand in cash so you get your share tonight."

"Will they give you that much cash?"

"They won't want to. But I'll tell them if they can handle this whole matter quietly, I'll promise to return tomorrow night to gamble. They'll go for it. At this point, all they care about is getting a chance to win their money back."

I wiped at my teary eyes. "I feel like such an idiot."

He leaned over and kissed me on the forehead.

"Not at all. Anyone else would have gotten hysterical if they thought they had lost so much money." He paused and glanced around. A pit boss watched us from a distance. "It's important you leave before they stop and check your ID. If they see it's fake, they'll deny your winnings."

Just then a faint doubt stirred deep inside me.

What if I went to the coffee shop and sat there for thirty minutes and I started to get nervous with him taking so long? And what if another half hour went by and he still didn't show up? Then, finally, what if I went to the front desk and asked them to ring Russell Devon's room and, lo and behold, he wasn't registered at the Mandalay Bay?

What would happen?

I'd realize I was the biggest fool on the whole damn Strip.

"Shouldn't we meet in your room?" I asked casually.

He didn't hesitate. He pulled a room card from his pocket. "First tower. Room four-three-one-four. Be careful, that's the only key I have on me. I'll knock four times."

I suddenly felt much better. "Great." I went to leave.

"Jessie?" he called.

I paused. "What?"

"What's my room number?"

"Four-three . . . Ahh . . . damn, I'm drunk."

"Four-three-one-four. Say it aloud three times."

"Four-three-one-four. Four-three-one-four. Four-three-one-four."

"Once you're in the room, call down for coffee and dessert."

"What kind of dessert do you want?"

"I'll have what you're having. Now get out of here."

The moment I stepped out of the casino and onto the busy Strip, I felt a wave of relief wash over me. The night was still warm but I felt embraced by a delicious joy that cooled my brain. I had just won an impossible sum of money, I realized, but it seemed as if my happiness came from another source. Russ was not an ordinary guy, he was a magic man. I had a strange feeling that if I stayed close to him, really got to know him, I'd discover the source of his magic.

ABOUT THE AUTHOR

CHRISTOPHER PIKE is a bestselling author of young adult novels. The Thirst series, *Witch World*, and the Remember Me and Alosha trilogies are some of his favorite titles. He is also the author of several adult novels, including *Sati* and *The Season of Passage*. Thirst and Alosha are slated to be released as feature films. Pike currently lives in Santa Barbara, where it is rumored he never leaves his house. But he can be found online at christopherpikebooks.com.

SECRETS. REVENGE.
BUT BEST OF ALL, BLOOD.

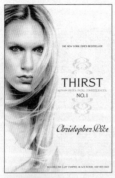

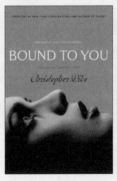

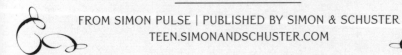

simonTEEN

Simon & Schuster's **Simon Teen**
e-newsletter delivers current updates on
the hottest titles, exciting sweepstakes, and
exclusive content from your favorite authors.

Visit **TEEN.SimonandSchuster.com** to
sign up, post your thoughts, and find out what
every avid reader is talking about!

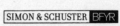